PAWLEYS ISLAND

**Center Point
Large Print**

**This Large Print Book carries the
Seal of Approval of N.A.V.H.**

PAWLEYS ISLAND

Dorothea Benton Frank

CENTER POINT PUBLISHING
THORNDIKE, MAINE

This Center Point Large Print edition
is published in the year 2005 by arrangement with
The Berkley Publishing Group, a division of
Penguin Group (USA) Inc.

The text of this Large Print edition is unabridged. In other
aspects, this book may vary from the original edition. Printed in
Thailand. Set in 16-point Times New Roman type.

ISBN 1-58547-654-4

Library of Congress Cataloging-in-Publication Data

Frank, Dorothea Benton.
    Pawleys Island / Dorothea Benton Frank.--Center Point large print ed.
        p. cm.
    ISBN 1-58547-654-4 (lib. bdg. : alk. paper)
    1. Pawleys Island (S.C.)--Fiction. 2. Seaside resorts--Fiction. 3. Plantation life--Fiction.
4. Women artists--Fiction. 5. Women lawyers--Fiction. 6. Art dealers--Fiction. 7. Friendship--
Fiction. 8. Secrecy--Fiction. 9. Large type books. 10. Psychological fiction. I. Title.

PS3556.R3338P39 2005b
813'.6--dc22

                                                                                2005007641

*This book is for the beautiful woman
who redefined the term sister.
Lynn Benton Bagnal*

TANGLED

We return to hear the waves
rolling onto the beach
one after the other
connecting us like blood.

We were listening long
before we came here,
remembering wind
spinning salt
through interrupted sunlight.

This is a place
where dreams return
as fish bones
tangled in seaweed.

Whatever sorrows come
are folded into the sea,
rinsed clean and kept—
unbearable secrets.

—MARJORY HEATH WENTWORTH
South Carolina Poet Laureate

ACKNOWLEDGMENTS

There are so many people to thank whose patience, good ideas and expert advice made this novel possible. First and foremost, I'd like to extend my gratitude and love to all the wonderful people of Pawleys Island and the surrounding area. You live in one of the most charming and magical spots the Lowcountry has to offer, and I thank you for allowing, encouraging and helping me to place this story in your backyard. I have tried to include some local folklore here for the amusement and edification of my readers, and if those details are incorrect or fall short of expectation, it is entirely at my feet.

I owe the largest debt to Tom Warner and Vicki Crafton of Litchfield Books. They loaned me volumes of historical reference material, took me all over Pawleys Island to feel its unique character, squired me around plantations, answered my questions with patience and grace and tried to give me local color not found in other printed material. Most important, they honored me with their friendship and fed me some extremely fabulous meals. I adore you both. But you know that. Thank you, Tom and Vicki, from the bottom of my pea-picking heart.

Special thanks to Lee Brockington and the late Eugene B. Chase Jr. for their excellent edition of *Stories from the Porch*, and for his fine book *Pawleys Island Historically Speaking* and to the Pawleys Island Civic

Association. They were very useful and inspiring and contain wonderful information and stories for anyone interested in the true history of the area.

To Frances Graham MacIlwinen, whose generosity and graciousness know no peer, please accept my warmest thanks.

Marjory Heath Wentworth, South Carolina's Poet Laureate, has done it again! Everyone should know that Marjory wrote her fabulous poem "Tangled" just for this book, and here's the kicker: She did it without ever having read a manuscript of *Pawleys Island*. If you have the patience to slug your way through my story, go back and read her poem again if you want a crisp example of Jung's whole concept of collective unconscious. Or maybe it's just that old spooky Lowcountry magic raising her mysterious head, grinning at us. Whatever the case may be, Marjory's poetry is the perfect reflection of my storytelling, and Marge? Girl? You blow me away! I thank you for your friendship and the tremendous generosity of your beautiful, creative mind. And folks, she makes a wicked good (Marjory is originally from Maine, after all) chocolate pecan pie! I think that recipe came from one of Nathalie Dupree's amazing cookbooks, and if you don't own Nathalie's *Comfortable Entertaining: At Home with Ease & Grace*, you should go buy it right now. Hey, Nathalie! Anyway, Marjory and Nathalie are two of the greatest women I know, and I am forever grateful for being allowed into their lives.

And speaking of gratitude for being in someone's life

even in the slightest way, I thank the following: Roger Pinckney for his fabulous spirit, Antoinette Kuritz and John Hamilton Lewis, Ann Ipock, Bill Doar and most especially the wonderful Nancy Rhyne, whose stories about Alice Flagg and the Gray Man fascinate and inform.

Always and forever Pat Conroy, Cassandra King and Anne Rivers Siddons. Special hugs to Ronda Rich, Josephine Humphrey, and my hurricane girlfriend, Mary Kay Andrews.

Love to my wonderful writer friends of Montclair, New Jersey, Pam Satran, Debbie Galant, Deborah Davis and Benilde Little. I owe y'all the fine southern delicacy of ice-cold Cokes in bottles with a little bag of Planters peanuts thrown in—better than a MoonPie and an RC Cola any day! I'm just so glad I know you.

Next there are the legal minds. Robert and Susan Rosen, Claudia Kelly, Sabrina Grogan, Larry Dodds and the great Judge Bobbie Mallard—I owe the Judge a Coke with a scoop of ice cream! Thank you all for your wisdom and advice and for trying to make this knucklehead understand what life is like in a court of law. Okay, folks, I didn't go to law school like Grisham. And divorce laws are different in almost every state by one little detail or another. In writing class, the first thing they tell you is to write what you know. I have butchered that rule in this novel, and I apologize to the entire legal profession of the world for any glaring mistakes. I'm sure there are more than a few. To them I offer this small consolation: in this story the attorneys wear white hats.

How can I ever thank Ted and Alice Harrelson? All the stories you told me soak these pages with visions of life on the Waccamaw River. And the beautiful afternoons we spent together, walking the breathtaking grounds of Arcadia are emblazoned in my heart. The egrets! Great heavens, the egrets! Thank you so much.

I owe huge thanks and cold Coca-Colas to many others such as Betsy Altman of Pawleys Island Real Estate for her guidance and advice. Betsy, you cannot imagine what a difference our brief meeting made to this story. And also to my cousin Charles "Comar" Blanchard Jr., who did twenty-eight million favors for me and my family all year so I could make this deadline and still have a normal life—well, *normal* such as it is defined by the Franks. But, hey, Comar? You are the best thing that ever swam our gene pool, bubba, and all the Franks love you, especially this one.

Thanks to Richard H. Moore of Coastal Carolina University for his help in identifying the double-breasted cormorant. Thanks to Chris Skodras from Sam's Corner at Pawleys Island for continuing to sell Cokes in little bottles and sausage biscuits. And huge thanks to Louis Osteen, the gracious and esteemed proprietor of Louis's Fish Camp for sharing your fine taste and your tasty finery with all of us—I wish you all good things. Don't even think about a visit to Pawleys Island without a reservation for lunch or dinner there.

To my great friends, who appear as characters in this story, please tell everyone that this is pure fiction and the use of your name is intended merely to tickle your funny bone: Adrian Shelby, Mary Ann O'Brien, Everett Presson, Anice Geddis Carr, Frank Del Mastro, Karen Tedesco and Frances DuBose. Thanks and I love y'all!

To Amy Berkower and my first mentor, even though he never knew it at the time, Al Zuckerman, what can I say? I love y'all to death! And Sandi Mendelson? Isn't it time to go to the Lowcountry so I can show it to you? Thanks y'all for everything!

To the team at Berkley Publishing, starting with Leslie Gelbman, the epitome of what a publisher should be. Leslie? I am so grateful to you and always will be. Here's our fifth Lowcountry Tale (which, by the way, is borderline Lowcountry territory, depending on who you ask!) and I still can't believe how many wonderful things have happened to me since you came into my life! Kissing your footprints, still! And I always will! Seriously.

And then there's Gail. That's Ms. Fortune, my editor extraordinaire, with the eye of a wizard and the heart of a saint. There's nothing I can say to express my appreciation and gratitude to you. Five books! Five! Here's to five more! We rise together, honeychile!

And always to Norman Lidofsky, Ernie Petrillo, Sharon Gamboa, Don Rieck, Patrick Nolan, Trish Weyenberg, Don Redpath, Rich Adamonis, Joe Crockford and Ken Kaye—y'all could teach the world of sales a thing or two! Always, thanks to Joni Friedman and Rich Hasselberger for the fantastic cover for this book! And of course, a most dramatic curtsy to my dear and precious friend of extraordinary talent, Jack Alterman, the artistic jewel of Charleston, who, with the soul of a true southern gentleman, arrested the quintessential photograph for this cover—wow! I want to crawl in that hammock and read! Man, I love you! But extremely! (In the most correct way, of course.) And Liz Perl and Heather Connor! My knees are calloused from praying for your good health and everything else! Love you, love you!

Oh, gosh, golly, gee whiz! I love this part of my life when a book is finished and I get to thank people! (Even though no one probably reads this except . . . I don't know. Oprah? Yeah, sure.)

Okay, still carrying on here. Can we talk about the booksellers for a moment? Last summer, when I was on tour in August for *Shem Creek* we had five hurricanes. Not one, not three—five. They were horrible. I wasn't worried about my book sales as much as I was about book readers and those *soldiers in the army of the written word* who braved the elements to open their stores so the customers could swim in. It was intense. I just want to say thank you in the most serious way to all of you. You know why, and I regret all the many inconveniences caused by the weather and my inability to whip it into submission. Talk about a rough tour? Thank God, I'm a May book this time! And believe me, I will come to every store I can and sign books for you until I can't sign any more. More than anyone, I owe you all the most, and I know I can never repay you for your support except with my respect and admiration. And you have that for sure. Hugely.

Especially Patti and Avery and all the team at Barnes & Noble in Towne Centre in Mount Pleasant, South Carolina. I still miss Buzzy, but he's alive and well in Queens! Hooray! And the amazing team at the Waldenbooks in Charleston. And all the grand folks at Bay Street Traders in Beaufort and I could go on and on to the High Point Literary League and the Hilton Head Women's Club, and SEBA, and all the Friends of the Library organizations who asked me to come and run my mouth. Are you kidding me? These people are better than family when it comes to support!

Speaking of family, I've got a big and gorgeous one to thank. First the obvious cast—my sister and brothers. Huge thanks to Ted and Joanne Benton of Winchester, Massachusetts, Mike and Jennifer Benton of Irving, Texas, Bill and Pat Benton of Mount Pleasant, South Carolina—thank you for loving me and asking your friends to read my work. To my only sister, the unbelievable Lynn, and her truly incredible husband, Scott Bagnal, of Edisto Beach, South Carolina, you know how I feel about you and how deep this river runs. But most of all to Peter, Victoria and William, who truly are the lights of my days and nights—never doubt that I love you with my whole heart.

Victoria? She's away at college. Honey? Are you wearing a sweater? Let me tell the world this: there's no one like Victoria Frank. She is beautiful, passionate, brilliant, talented and fall-down funny. And she supports me like crazy when the going gets tough.

William? He's finally a little taller than his father, smarter than anyone in the house and the kind of superbly intelligent young man who can become anything he wants. I don't know a teenage boy with a bigger or more beautiful and loyal heart.

And before closing, another word on loyalty. Debbie Zammit, who came blasting from my past to help me write a book each year, is the best kind of friend a girl could have. Some know that Debbie and I once thought we ruled the world of acrylic sweaters in the garment business in New York. Without nitpicking, talk about lofty aspirations? Um, that's a yarn joke. Ah, well, point is, this book never would have made it to print this year without her. So, Debbie? I owe you and I thank you profusely for everything.

So shoot me. I'm sentimental and don't care who knows it.

CONTENTS

PROLOGUE

People have secrets. Everyone does. And, at one point or another, many people say they would like to run away and start life over in a place where no one knows their business. I know that I have felt that way. More than once. And I am no stranger to disaster, and most certainly no one would ever call me a coward. Coward or not, sometimes you just want to slip away into the night.

What drives us to that point? Did you do something horrible? Or, did something horrible happen to you?

Maybe you just feel like you need some anonymity. You have endured all the questioning, opinion-giving and gossiping humanity you can bear. It's time to strip away everything, all the clutter and noise, and look at your life, how it got to that point and figure out what you intend to do about it. At least, that's how it was for me.

When my tragedies occurred and getting through the days felt like pulling a wagon of bricks that was missing a back wheel, the only choice was to move back to Pawleys Island and attempt to put everything in perspective. I should have packed a seat belt. First, I met Huey Valentine. Huey, one of the most wonderful men who ever lived, befriended me and eventually gave me the swift kick I needed to put down my golf clubs for a while. That kick came when Rebecca showed up and Armageddoned the pattern of self-indulgent com-

17

placency that ordered my shallow and insignificant life, which in all my precious stupidity, I thought I was enjoying. Yeah, I thought it was fabulous—okay, it wasn't fabulous and I knew it. But it was usually better than bearable, and to be frank, until she appeared, I couldn't think of any better way to occupy my time. Golf and tennis. Tennis and golf. A party here, an opening there. Pretty shallow and useless.

I didn't think I had much in common with Rebecca until the divorce was all over, only to discover we had everything in common; we were simply at different stages in our lives. If her parachute hadn't landed on Huey's doorstep, I'd still be treadmilling in my sandy island rut. And if we all weren't there to engage Huey's mind, his life would have been one narrow garden path slowly tiptoeing back to the eighteenth century.

Here's the other lesson I've learned. You only see what you want to see and believe what you want to believe. I'm not talking about the Gray Man or Alice Flagg, Pawleys Island's most famous walking dead residents. No, no. This goes back to my eyes and those of my Pawleys friends. I thought we were all lonely and making the best of it, and we were to some degree. But my vision was warped. I was everyone's mother; Huey was my chaste and antiseptic spouse; Rebecca was our daughter. Huey belonged to me, and Rebecca did too. Wrong!

What we all taught each other was stunning and, honest to God, life altering. But here's the thing. I will never accept that these changes could have come about any place but Pawleys Island. Sure, you've heard about the handmade hammocks and the pristine beaches. You've seen gorgeous pictures of the sunsets and the marsh teeming with wildlife. But you don't know Pawleys until you've been there and experienced its tremendous power. It is only a tiny sandbar south of Myrtle Beach and north of Georgetown. But be warned. It is there that the Almighty Himself would like to engage you in conversation and redirect your soul. Listen to me: for all the jokes I make, this time I'm not kidding.

If you're happy in your misery and determined to remain so, don't ever go to Pawleys. If you do make the trip, be on guard. Truth is coming to get you, and peace isn't far behind. But it all comes at a price. You'll have to be the judge of whether it's worth all the hullabaloo.

This is how it happened to me.

ONE

WELCOME TO GALLERY VALENTINE

I looked out across the dunes and up and down the beach. Another gorgeous day. Blue skies, billowing clouds and the sun rising with the mercury. Eastern breezes rustled the palmettos and sea oats. Sun worshippers by the score had accepted early invitations to assume the lizard position. They were scattered and prone, armed with coolers, beach chairs, novels, visors and canvas bags of towels, toys and lotions, littered all along the edges of the Atlantic in both directions. They looked like clusters of human solar batteries recharging themselves in drowsy warmth. The waves rolled in low murmurs of hypnotic suggestion, washed the shore and pulled away.

The weather that day seemed without guile, but I knew better. As soon as the hands of time crossed noon, Mother Nature would bellow the flames of hell's furnace, blowing unspeakable heat all over the Lowcountry, and the sensible lizards would retreat to shade and hammocks until later in the day. The others would fry, fooled by the breeze and lulled into a comfortable stupor by the ocean's song.

Let me tell you something, honey. You'd never catch me in a swimsuit smelling like cocoa butter and fruit, sticky with salt and sand, half catatonic and dehydrated from exposure. No. I had better things to do with my time, like feeding Huey. Or playing golf in that same sun. It was the lying around part that was a problem for me. Besides, who needed to see me in a bathing suit? I assure you, no one.

But back to my current priority . . . feeding Huey.

After his call, I picked up sandwiches from The Pita Rolz and drove over to his gallery in the Oak Lea Shops. He had been practically breathless on the phone, but private-audience breathless drama was pretty much Huey's modus operandi.

"Abigail! Darling! Drop everything and come! You must meet Rebecca!"

"Who's Rebecca?"

20

"Our savior! You'll see!"

"Well, we *could* use a savior . . ."

"And, would you be a dear and bring us some lunch? Just tuna for me, on rye, but only if it looks fresh, and turkey on white bread with mayonnaise for our darling girl, and of course get something for yourself. My treat."

Huey Valentine had not missed a meal in all his fifty-five years. I had to laugh. When Huey got excited, he thought about food. When he was depressed, he thought about food. What can I say except that Huey was well fed. I imagine the least insulting but most accurate term one might use to describe Huey's appearance would be *portly,* but in a way *portly* suited his entire demeanor, which, when in the company of close friends, grew a shade larger than life itself.

Huey was the consummate southern gentleman, an aristocratic Nathan Lane, never rude to anyone's face but felt no remorse about a wicked comment to me about others, especially tourists.

You could set your wristwatch by Huey. He was never late for an appointment or a dinner party. He wrote thank-you notes on his Dempsey & Carroll ecru hand-engraved stationery that was so stiff, folding it cracked it like an egg. And he always used an ornate fountain pen, signing with the flourish of John Hancock. Speaking of John Hancock, Huey Flagg Valentine could probably trace his ancestry back to Charlemagne's grandparents. Evergreen, the plantation where he lived with his mother and houseman, had been in his family's name since fifteen minutes after the land was claimed for King Charles II.

I had never seen him dressed in anything but all white, summer and winter, and yes, he wore a hat. But not to affect a grand attitude so much as to save his balding head from the terrors of melanoma. Everything about him was stylish and elegant. He couldn't help it. All those generations of social grace and good taste were imbedded in his DNA.

I just adored him. Everyone did.

It was on Huey's arm that I had gladly attended every party, concert, dinner or gallery opening for the past three years, since my return to Pawleys Island.

Life was so strange. I thought I was going to move into my family's house and write my memoirs, but I was slightly embarrassed to admit that all I had done was exercise and slide in and out of social commitments with Huey. It wasn't the worst thing, really. I mean, heaven forbid that I had a little fun. Besides, the thought of reliving my past through writing it all down? Well, let's just say that I had yet to arrive at the moment where I felt comfortable enough to play with my inner gorillas. They could wait. In any case, I questioned the real value of an autobiography because it seemed like vanity in the extreme. It wasn't like I abandoned a career as a backup singer for the Rolling Stones and that my writings would become the latest zeitgeist on sex, drugs and rock and roll. Frankly, my therapist recommended that I give writing a whirl, saying it might be good for an exercise in closure. Instead, I had closure with everything else—my frantic law practice, my marginal personal life and my nice expensive therapist. I simply closed up my house in Columbia and came back to Pawleys just to think about things.

I imagine you could say I'm a lucky woman, at least in terms of inheritance and assets. My mother died when I was very young, and then Daddy finally gave up the ghost after a short bout with leukemia six years ago. Since I am an only child, the house on Pawleys came right into my hands. The old rockers, the creaking floorboards, the tongue-and-groove walls, the ancient kitchen and the claw-footed bathtubs were all mine. The only changes I made were to add a furnace, a fresh coat of paint, window boxes of flowers and new screens. Oh, and I did update the bathroom and kitchen fixtures but that had to be done—you know how salt corrodes everything in its path.

If you looked twice at my house you would scratch your head wondering why I loved it so much. Anyone with a developer's eye would want to knock it down and replace it with a home with central air-conditioning and heat and, probably, God forbid, wall-to-wall carpet, an in-wall vacuum system, doorbells and every other invention of the twentieth century. No thanks. I still preferred floors I could sweep, friends calling out to announce their arrival over the roar of the ocean, and I could not have cared less what mysterious wonders the damp air performed on my hair. Once I crossed over that causeway, leaving the mainland, the plantations and the Waccamaw River, the world ceased to exist.

On very hot nights I used the ceiling fan in my bedroom because I loved to hear the waves at night and the birds in the morning. And I loved the memories. If I closed my eyes, I could hear my mother's gentle voice, negotiating with Philemon, the creek man and an island institution during my childhood. He had a bucket of fresh flounder and another one of shrimp, and from them Momma would buy our dinner.

I could see us at the table, Daddy telling Momma how delicious the meal was. Later I would squeeze in between them on the porch swing, while Momma sang sweetly and I drifted off to my dreams. When you lose a parent at a young age, those few memories you have are more precious than any single ring or necklace left to you. Whenever I was here, even alone as I am now, I could stand where they once stood and somehow in the magical workings of the Pawleys Island salt air, I could bring them back to me. For that and for a thousand other reasons too, I would never sell this house or leave it for too long.

Daddy inherited our home on Myrtle Avenue from his father, and his father inherited it from his mother. Our family's Pawleys Island history went back almost as far as Huey's plantation origins. Somewhere around the time Mr. Lincoln freed the slaves, Daddy's father's mother's husband hauled it in sections (we think) to this parcel of land from Butler Island and put it all back together. If you were inclined to inspect the underside of this great relic, you would still find the mortise-and-tenon joints with pegs.

When I was a girl, Daddy and his friends would fix cocktails and go under the house to have a look, reappearing later, amazed by nineteenth-century building skills. It was no doubt that her meticulous construction kept Miss Salt Air from flying to Kingdom Come during Hurricane Hugo, our most foul visitor of 1989. Oh, she got her bonnet blown off (lost the roof) and there was water damage to be sure, but Daddy brought a team of men up from Charleston and raised her from the dunes to new and dignified heights on sturdy pilings of brick.

Anyway, it's the island, really, that spins the spell. The house helped, but the most compelling reason for my return here was to languish in great peace as opposed to despair. For all of my life, any time spent here made everything right.

I could stand on the porch and breathe in with all of my lungs, exhale my troubles in a whoosh, and the breezes carried them away. My shoulders dropped back to their natural position. I moved differently, slowly but with deliberateness. I slept soundly remembering all my dreams.

That seemed to be the general consensus of everyone on Pawleys Island. It's a simple retreat for some and a spa for the soul to others. One thing is certain: it's unlike any other place in God's entire creation.

Even Huey agreed with that. As much as the Waccamaw waters flowed through his veins, on many evenings I had seen the look on his face when we shared the end of day, watching the moonrise over the

Atlantic. *You can't paint this,* he would say. And he, who possessed the heart and soul of the artist, was right.

With that statement, Huey claimed a corner in my heart, which until then had been under lockdown. So, if Huey said, *Drop everything and come meet our new savior,* I dropped everything and did as he asked. I bought lunch and drove my old Jaguar sedan right over to him, cursing the entire United Kingdom over their wimpy air-conditioning.

I pushed open the door and spotted him right away by the framing table in the rear of the gallery. Huey was the Rosetta stone for body language. His hands were in midair, whirling with excitement, and he shifted from one foot to the other. He turned at the unobtrusive musical sound of the automatic doorbell, saw me and rushed to my side.

"There you are! Come! Say hello! Let me help you with that!" He took the bag and cardboard tray of iced tea from me, delivered two air kisses to my cheeks, stood back and smiled. "Did they have decent tuna?"

"Huey, baby? The tuna is life altering. I watched them make it, which is what took me so long." The tiny brunette was waiting patiently with her portfolio opened, and what I guessed to be her work was spread all over the counter. "You must be Rebecca."

She extended her hand to shake mine. "And you must be Abigail. But please call me Becca. My friends call me Becca."

"No! No! No!" Huey said, researching the contents of the sack of food. "You must be *Re*-becca! We cannot

26

defile the great name of Rebecca. I'll get plates."

"Didn't anyone ever call you Abby?" she said to me, looking for some support.

"Over their dead body," I said. "My parents named me for Abigail Adams."

Huey placed three plates on the counter and began unpacking lunch. "Abigail Adams was one of America's first feminists, you know. She was always giving John the business about the inequality of education between men and women."

"Oh," Rebecca said.

"Well, it makes sense today too," I said. "People used to think that education was wasted on women because they wound up staying home with children. Of course, I'm not sure how an education could ever be *wasted*." What an inane thing for me to say, I thought.

"You can say that again," Rebecca said.

"Anyway, this generation of women *works*. And not necessarily because they want to." Another pearl of genius from me, but people said vapid things to each other just to put the other at ease.

"You can say that again too!" Rebecca said.

I took the plate from Huey and eyeballed this diminutive Rebecca, thinking that if she agreed to agree with every word I spoke, then surely there was an exalted position available for her in our little tribe.

If that sounds egotistical, let's get something straight right now. The last thing I needed in my life or even in the periphery of my life was someone telling me I was wrong, what was wrong with my politics, what was wrong with the world. I knew what was wrong with the world. Everything. I had seen enough of what people did to each other and I just didn't want to deal with it for the foreseeable future.

"So where are you from?" I said.

"Charleston," she said. "I came up here to see if I could sell some of my work."

"Abigail. Look at this."

Huey had closed her portfolio so that a flying crumb of tuna or a splotch of mayonnaise wouldn't ruin anything, but he reached down and pulled up one of her paintings. He flipped back the parchment paper cover and there it was: the classic watercolor of two children, a boy and a girl, playing by the edge of the shore on a beach. I had seen hundreds of them, and all of them were cures for insomnia.

But this one was profoundly different. The sky and the water looked as radiantly alive as the sandpipers pecking the wet sand and then running from the waves. But the children, their backs to the viewer, seemed to be a thousand miles away. And you got the sense that while they were probably siblings, that they didn't want to play together or that they were tremendously unhappy for some inexplicable reason and preferred to live in their misery alone. The scene was haunting and bothersome, but I couldn't stop looking at them. I wanted to rush inside the painting and save them. I turned and looked at Rebecca.

"It's very powerful," I said.

"Children aren't always happy, are they?" she said.

28

"No, they are not."

"Rebecca, darling? We have a show opening tomorrow and I was just thinking . . ."

"Huey!" I said. "Her work isn't framed, and besides . . ."

"Oh! Gosh!" Rebecca said. "I can make frames if you have the material . . ."

"Rebecca? Sweetheart? You make frames?"

"Yes, in fact, I am told that, well, I'm rather good at it. I mean, well, I don't mean to brag . . ."

"Stop! Humility is unflattering, especially for an artist of your talent! You need some *attitude,* girl! Seriously!"

We all had a giggle at that, but Huey was right. This mouse had to stop squeaking.

"Huey, I . . ."

I was trying to speak, but when Huey got his engine in gear, there was no stopping him.

"Sweetheart. You finish up your sandwich, and then I want you to have a look around in the storage room. There's enough material back there to hang a frame around Georgetown County, including the new waterslide at Myrtle Beach."

Huey sniffed and I knew it was because of the waterslides, putt-putt courses and all manner of NASCAR contraptions that had been erected under the guise of entertainment but reeked of crass commercialism. And that, my friends, was the scathing difference between genteel plantation living, the arrogant shabby of Pawleys Island and the wild consumerism of Myrtle Beach. All that said for the antielitist dart throwers in the crowd, Huey the King Snob liked nothing better than a round of putt-putt followed by a snow cone dripping in tutti-frutti syrup.

"The former framer was recently relieved of his duties," I said, thinking I would speak to him when Rebecca was out of earshot.

"I fired the nitwit," Huey said. "What a pathetic simpleton! He drove me crazy. Didn't he ever hear of *measure twice, cut once*?"

"Apparently not," I said.

Inside of a minute, Rebecca, who was slightly confused as to why she should inspect the inventory of framing materials when she had come to Huey's gallery to sell her work, balled up the remains of her turkey sandwich and went to the storage room to sniff around like a good dog.

"So what do you think?" Huey said in a conspiratorial whisper.

"Huey Flagg Valentine! I think that Sallie Anne Wood will definitely scratch your eyes out! I know I would! You can't promise someone a one-woman show and then just sort of casually have another show going on at the same time! It's unethical!"

The opening, which was the following evening, was a one-woman show for Sallie Anne Wood, an established egomaniacal diva artist from Charleston.

"Listen to me, Abigail Thurmond. Sallie Anne Wood has had a thousand shows. She'll sell *enough* to make her happy tomorrow night. Right? Look. I cannot resist Rebecca's work! I don't know why, but I sense an

30

urgency in Rebecca and I think she needs us. I mean, you must agree, Rebecca's work is rather astounding."

"It *is* that."

"God! I wonder what she could do in oil! She'd be biblical! Rebecca at the Well! Great thundering Zeus! I remember that from the show at the Chagall Museum in Nice. *Women of the Old Testament*! *Matriarchs in Search of Motherhood*! I wish you had been with me then . . ."

"Me too. Huey? This is still a problem, you know. You cannot possibly expect Sallie Anne to walk in here and be happy to see Rebecca's work hanging in the same gallery on the same night as her opening! And, Huey, I know you would not enjoy the cognizi of Litchfield and Pawleys calling you an opportunist, now would you?"

"I can sell everything Rebecca can paint. Every blessed last piece. And you know it."

"Framed or unframed. But, Huey? Darlin', we hardly know this child! Are you hiring her to be our new framer? She's an artist, for heaven's sake! Don't you think she will be insulted?"

"I'm going to ask her if she'll be the assistant manager of my gallery."

"And who is the manager? *You?*"

"Okay! I'll make her the *manager!* Happy?"

"Oh, Huey, Huey, Huey. If you really want this puppy, then I know you'll have this puppy one way or another. Lord help Rebecca! She's falling down the rabbit hole and doesn't even know it."

Two

Meet Miss Olivia

My darling son, Huey, bought me a corsage to wear to his opening tonight. I don't have the heart to tell him that it's old hat to wear a corsage these days, so I made him a boutonniere. I picked one perfect gardenia from my own garden, added a sprig of rosemary and wound them together with florist's tape. When I pinned it to his lapel I confess that I became a little weepy, remembering all the times I had pinned them to my late husband Chalmers's lapel, and, oh well, he's been dead for a thousand years and who cares about that anymore? Life goes on whether you like it or not.

The reason I chose a gardenia was because Huey is so sweet, but the rosemary is to remind him to never forget to love his mother. You know, in Victorian times, brides would give rosemary sprigs to all their family and friends. Even though she was leaving to start a new life, a sprig of rosemary let them know she would never forget them. Don't ask me who started that bit of foolishness. I simply couldn't tell you. There are so many traditions to honor that it just wears me out.

The reason I was looking forward to this opening was that I was to meet the young woman Huey has been raving about, this girl Rebecca, an artist from Charleston. Huey hired her just like that! Doesn't even know who her people are! It just seems to me that when you have someone handling your money, you should know all about them. But that's my boy. He's gets an idea that he wants thus and so to be thus and so and the next thing you know, it's thus and so. In all my eighty-four years, I have never met another man so determined to have his own way. All right, eighty-six years, and it's no one's business.

My job tonight is to get the poop on Rebecca because my Huey can't stop flitting around long enough to do it himself. He's just like a bumblebee in a garden of blooms, darting from one budding beauty to the next. Ah well, that little weakness in his deportment is also why he's so good at selling paintings. Huey just loves people and artists most especially. Probably because, and I mean this in the most charitable way, it's all my Huey can do to draw his breath! Oh, Lordy! That's a little art joke, you know.

After I looked at all the paintings, I had to agree with Huey's enthusiasm for Rebecca's work. Poor Sallie Anne Wood was sure to have a pebble in her shoe when she arrived and saw Rebecca's paintings all hung in the framing area. Huey was clever to install them in the rear of his gallery, well distanced from the show he had put up for Miss Wood. But even though he had repainted the front walls in Ralph Lauren's new ivory metallic paint and had special lighting adjusted for each of Miss Wood's canvases, it just didn't help one fig. Miss Wood was a fine painter, a competent artist to be sure, but Lord have mercy, did the world need another painting of a beach path with palmettos?

Rebecca's watercolors grabbed you and held you. Period. End of story. And Sallie Anne Wood's work was lovely but it would never keep you up at night. Well, I hoped there wouldn't be a catfight between the two of them. You know how artists can be. I would simply flatter Miss Wood to pieces when she arrived and hope for the best.

So after I had my little tour, Huey and Byron, his houseman, propped me up here in this chair like the reigning queen. I don't like to get knocked around, and heaven knows, there must be two hundred people expected here tonight. Why in the world I would want to meet all these people eludes me, but Huey insists that I am his good luck charm, so I haven't missed an opening since he started up this business. I try to be gracious, but so many people! It is a little annoying, and besides, these days I feel a little more tired. I keep telling him that my get up and go got up and went. He just smiles and asks me what color my dress is going to be so he can go waste his money on another corsage.

It certainly would be nice to have a little something to drink.

I turned to see Huey approaching with a young woman on his arm. It had to be Rebecca, so I sat up straight and smiled to meet her while giving her the once-over in a way that could not be detected as a once-over.

"Mother?"

"Yes, dear?"

"This is Rebecca Simms. Rebecca, this is my mother, Miss Olivia."

"Well! I am so pleased to know you," I said. "Huey has told me all about you."

"And he's told me all about you! I am so happy to meet you too."

I took her hand and held it for a few moments. She did seem like a very nice person, so tiny, like a Dresden figurine. She had a nice watch and no manicure.

"Huey? Be a dear and bring your mother a little glass of sherry, won't you? Then I can have a few minutes with Rebecca. Come sit by me!"

Rebecca smiled, sat down, and Huey winked at me as he walked away.

"Now, then. Tell me all about yourself! Where are your parents from?"

"My parents? Oh! Um, Manning. My family is from Manning. My father was a farmer—cotton and soy-beans—and my mother, well, I didn't know my mother very well."

"Oh! I am so sorry. Was she ill? Did she pass away at a young age?" I took the glass from Huey, thanked him and fastened my attention on Rebecca's face. She had very pretty blue eyes, and if she tweezed her eyebrows, one might even notice them.

"So that's pretty much the story about my mother," she said.

"Oh! I'm sorry, dear. You'll have to pardon me. I was just thinking you had the prettiest blue eyes I've seen in many a day. Yes, you do. Now please indulge me and

35

tell me again about your mother."

Well, don't you know she told me that her mother had stayed on her father's farm just long enough to get her out of diapers? She left town with a cigarette salesman and ran off to Spartanburg and then Santa Fe, New Mexico. It broke her father's heart but at least the hussy had the consideration to leave a pantry filled with hundreds of mason jars of bottled string beans, corn, tomatoes, chow chow, bread-and-butter pickles and two kinds of jam—peach and strawberry. Her mother died of a lady cancer before Rebecca was twelve, not that she ever did the poor child a lick of good as a role model, and her death? Well, it served her right. Jezebel.

"My! Goodness! Gracious sakes alive! Some people in this world . . ." I just shook my head and she nodded in agreement.

"It's the truth. I don't know how some people live with themselves."

"So then your daddy raised you?"

"Well, I guess, but my grandparents moved in and helped. They were wonderful people. My daddy worked by his father's side every day, and then there was a drought that lasted for four or five years. Daddy saw that he couldn't support us with what the farm was bringing in, so he quit farming and rented the land to somebody else. Finally, my granddaddy retired and my daddy opened up a Tastee-Freez and ran it for years. He would laugh and say there was more money in corn dogs and push-ups than there was in a zillion acres of cotton."

"And he never married again?"

"No. No, he didn't. I think he was so embarrassed by what Momma did that he swore off women forever. Manning is a pretty small town, you know."

"Yes, but it's so lovely. I can remember trips with Chalmers, going up Highway 301 when all the wisteria was in bloom . . . It was just breathtaking."

"Yes. It still is, I imagine."

"Rebecca?"

"Yes, ma'am?"

"You are a very talented painter. I'd wager a bet that every single one of your paintings walks right out the door tonight. When Sallie Anne Wood gets here and sees them she's going to, well, the poor dear. Let's just be very nice to her."

"Don't worry, Miss Olivia, I'll just reach down in my psychoanalytic bag of tricks and fix her right up!"

"What? Psychoanalytic bag of tricks? Whatever do you mean, child?"

"Oh, a thousand years ago, I got my Ph.D. in psychology from Carolina. I worked in HR for Wal-Mart for a year, but then I married Nat and the babies started to come and that all went out the window . . . You know what I mean?"

"Rebecca? Would you mind refilling my glass? I am so parched tonight!"

"Oh! I'm sorry! I should've noticed!"

She hopped up and left me in a dither. HR? Who was Nat? What babies? Huey told me she was living in a condo at Litchfield Beach! He didn't say a word about her having a husband and family. Had she run off and left them like her mother did? I reached in my purse for a mint and tried to compose myself. I knew I was getting worked up and even though that fool doctor at the Medical University in Charleston said I was fit as a fiddle, I knew that getting riled wasn't good for my heart. Mercy! A husband and children! Do you see what I mean about my Huey? She might be a good painter, but she also might go crazy and shoot the place up! *Oh! My stars, Olivia! The girl's not a crazy person!* Yes, I had developed the unattractive habit of talking to myself out loud, but you can tell me about it when you've reached my age and not before. Now, where was I? Well, here she comes with my drink and it was time for me to gather myself together and get to the bottom of it.

"Oh, thank you, Rebecca!" It looked like she was going to leave again so I said, "Now sit here with me for few minutes."

"Actually, Byron wanted me to help him."

I patted the seat and she sat.

"Let him open all the wine bottles himself! That's what he gets paid for! I want to hear about your husband and children. Are they here with you at Litchfield?"

"No. Oh, Miss Olivia, it's a long and complicated story and I don't think you would really want to hear it. Honestly."

"Rebecca? I am so glad I still have my hearing that I'd listen to a politician! And let me tell you this. At my age, I have heard just about every story there is to tell. You cannot shock me." I put my drink down on the table and folded my hands in my lap, indicating that I expected to hear her full story.

"I feel awful that I might burden you with my mess on a night like this."

"Come on now, I'm not getting any younger."

"Well, all right then." She took a deep breath and blurted it all out at once. "Just ten days ago, the day after my children left for their summer camps, I was served with a summons for divorce and a complaint alleging that I was an unfit mother. The next week I found myself in court and the judge granted full custody of the children and the house to Nat. So I packed up my watercolors, which Nat and the children made fun of all the time, and came to Litchfield to stay in my friend's condo until I could get my brains together. That's the story. The kids are in camp, Nat's in the house and I'm here."

She shrugged her shoulders, her chin began to quiver and her eyes became bloodshot and watery. She didn't make a single sound, but the tears spilled over her eyelids in a flood, washing right down her face and neck. My heart just sank. I felt like crying too. It was inconceivable that this talented, soft-spoken, genteel woman before me was an unfit mother. She was a precious girl and that man of hers had done her dirty. And why had I made her reveal herself? Oh! Sometimes I was so nosy. There I had been thinking that she was going to swindle my Huey and the fact was that *she* had been swindled out of her own home and children. I reached in my purse and handed her my handkerchief.

"Thank you. I'm so sorry. I just don't know why or how it even happened. I never saw it coming. One day I was sewing name tags in my children's socks and the next day I was . . . my whole life was gone."

She took a long breath and I wondered what in the world I could say to her. There had to be more to the story. I knew that much. I felt perfectly wretched.

"Rebecca. *Dear* child. You *must* say that you will forgive me. I am *so* deeply sorry that I pried into your personal life. I had *no* right to do it. And I had no idea you had suffered *such* a tragedy. I just wanted to know who you *were*. Now, you go wash your face and let's just forget about our discussion for the rest of the night."

The gallery was beginning to fill with guests. That considered, it seemed to me that the best solution was to sweep the whole business under the rug for the night and deal with it in the light of day. She went to the powder room and to help that bossy boots, Byron, and I went to find my Huey. He was easy to spot. After all, he had been shopping in the husky boys department at Belk's since he was twelve years old, bless his heart.

"Mother! Come say hello to Sallie Anne Wood!"

It was small comfort that her mother had not named her Sandy. Or Sandal. Or Cherry.

"Hello, my dear," I said and extended my hand to her, which was a peculiar habit of the younger generation. In my day, a lady never shook hands. To begin with, we

40

wore gloves, thank you. "Congratulations on your beautiful show!"

"Oh, thank you, Miss Olivia, and it's lovely to see you again."

"And to see you also . . ." No sooner did the words tumble from my lips than she began to scout the room, her eyes drawn to Rebecca's paintings in the very rear of the gallery. There was going to be the devil to pay, I thought, and then decided to keep an eye on her. She released Huey's arm and began to work her way toward Rebecca's work. I took my boy's arm and pulled him down so I could whisper in his ear.

"I have to . . . I have to speak with you, son," I said. Well, he could tell that I was upset, and so we slipped into his office for a moment, closing the door behind us.

"Mother? What ever is the matter? The gallery is filled with . . ."

"Huey? Don't reprimand me! I know exactly what is and what is not occurring on the other side of that door! This is of the utmost importance or else I would never have asked you . . ."

"Oh, I'm sorry, Mother! Of course! Tell me what it is. Please."

He took a deep breath and I looked up at him and thought here is my unmarried son, who, for his own reasons we do not discuss, will never give me grandchildren. Would he possibly be sympathetic to Rebecca's woes? But when I told him the story as I knew it, he reacted as I hoped he would.

"Miss Olivia?"

I loved it when he called me that because it meant we were in it together, whatever the *it* happened to be at the moment.

"Yes?"

"Here is what I think. I think we don't have all the facts. And most importantly, I refuse to allow you to become all upset over this until we know what has happened to her. But I agree with you. It doesn't sound right or seem right. Rebecca? Unfit? No, no. Can't be. When this evening is over, we will have Rebecca out to the house for dinner. Maybe tomorrow night. And then we will speak to her without all these distractions. If what you say is true, it is time for our Miss Abigail to come out of retirement. It's that simple."

I was so relieved, just so relieved. I just nodded my head and thought that one more sherry would be very nice. Huey opened the door and led me back to my chair. Sallie Anne Wood was working her way through the crowd, took Huey's arm and led him away to Rebecca's paintings. Her hair was in flames—well, not literally, of course. I strained to make out her words by lip reading from across the room, which was a difficult task as there were people in the way.

Byron brought me a tiny glass and put it by my side.

"What's happening, Byron?"

"Miss Wood's a little bit furious, I think. But don't you worry yourself, Miss Olivia. Huey can handle her." Byron was a nice man, really. Well, at least he was solicitous. I drained the miserable little thimble of a drink in one sip and looked over at Huey and Sallie

Anne. She was waving her arms and carrying on like a banshee and my poor Huey was staring at his shoes, just letting the prima donna rant and rave like she was Monet's little sister. People nearby were watching them from the corner of their eyes and smiling at her public display of displeasure. She was well within her rights to be provoked with Huey, I will admit that much, but Huey's lapse in judgment did not excuse her own bad manners. No one, but *no one,* was going to dress down my boy in public.

"Give me your arm, Byron, and help me up this instant!"

"Yes, ma'am!"

I went right up and stood in between them, putting my hand on Huey's arm in a show of support.

"Now, see here!" I said and looked her square in the face. "What's all this fuss about?"

"Ooh!" the diva said and started to turn on her heel and flounce away, but I stopped her.

"I don't think I can quite believe my eyes," I said.

"What?" she said, spinning back to face me.

"Mother!" Huey said. "I can handle . . ."

"Hush! Now, Miss Wood, were you about to turn your back on *me* and walk away? Is that *possible?*"

"Well, I . . ."

She became very flustered, little bits of her spearmint LifeSavers–scented spittle flying in every direction. I imagine little old ladies didn't take Sallie Anne Wood to the woodshed very often. Wood to the woodshed? Perfect!

"Sallie Anne's upset with me, Mother, and I don't . . ."

"Huey! Hush, son!" I took a deep breath and looked back to her face for an explanation. "Well, Miss Wood?"

"I'm sorry. This is supposed to be a one-woman show and it's not," she said. "I have never been so humiliated in all my . . ."

"Oh, psssh! Settle yourself down and stop huffing and puffing! What is there to be humiliated about? Huey, how many of Sallie Anne's paintings have you sold?"

"Eleven! And six more are on hold! I mean, Sallie Anne, don't you think that's incredible?"

"Son, that *is* incredible! Aren't you pleased, Miss Wood?"

"I want another ten percent for this outrage and a feature article in *Myrtle Beach Magazine*."

"Done!" Huey said.

"Christmas issue!"

"I'll try," Huey said.

Sallie Anne took a deep breath and smiled as wide as she could, revealing some rather dilapidated dental work. "It's a pleasure doing business with you, Mr. Valentine!" She walked away, her sense of self-importance fully restored.

"Ridiculous woman," I said for Huey's ears alone.

"You were wonderful, Mother."

"Anytime, son." Let's face it, Sallie Anne Wood wasn't the first bully I'd dealt with on my son's behalf.

"Come, let me get you a victory drink."

"Well, all right."

Huey poured me a healthy portion from his private stash and helped me take my seat again. I drank it all up like a good girl, and I declare, the gallery had become so warm and comfortable that I drifted off to sleep and unfortunately into a terrible dream that a soldier from the north was trying to kidnap me and take me away. He said he wanted to marry me. I was too young! He said it didn't matter to him. I was terrified.

I cannot leave my family! I do not want to go to Connecticut! My daddy would die if I left the plantation! What? Unhand me! You brute! If this is what Yankees are like . . . I will throw myself in the river! I swear it!

I felt someone shaking my arm and looked up into Rebecca's face.

"Miss Olivia? Are you all right?"

The gallery was nearly empty. I had slept through the entire party.

"Of course! Of course!" I straightened myself and smoothed my hair, which had become a little tangled and was no doubt in disarray. "It's time for me to go home."

"Huey is very happy," she said.

"And why is that?"

"Well, he sold several of my paintings and almost all of Sallie Anne's."

She helped me to my feet and I ran my hands over the skirt of my dress, thinking I must have been some sight. Suddenly, I remembered what Rebecca had told me earlier. Then along came Abigail and Huey. Abigail so sophisticated in all black and Huey so angelic in all white. It made me choke up a little to think they would probably never marry. They were a study in opposites, which is probably why they so enjoyed each other's company. People were always drawn to that which they did not possess.

"Miss Olivia? Let me take you to the car," Abigail said. "We are closing up now."

All at once I became quite provoked with my son.

"Huey! Huey! How could you let me sleep like that? In front of all those people?"

"Mother? You were so comfortable and even smiling in your sleep! And besides, I didn't know you *didn't* want to rest!"

Sometimes Huey tried my patience, I can tell you that.

I took Abigail's arm and turned back to Rebecca.

"Rebecca? I like you, sweetheart, and I think your husband has done a *terrible* thing. A heinous thing! We simply cannot let him get away with this! I think I might have to cut a switch and go down to Charleston and tan his hide!"

Abigail, who didn't know a thing but soon would, looked at Rebecca and said, "Honey? You don't know Miss Olivia and I have no idea what she's talking about, but when she starts talking about cutting a switch, you may as well head for high ground! Looks like we're in for the storm of the century."

THREE

REBECCA IN THE MORNING

Nat was gone long before we separated. The happiness in his eyes flickered, faded and went blank. It just went blank. My perfect family began to fall apart.

Do you know how there are conversations, disagreements and even verbal slights that wound you so badly you remember everything about them? The mere thought of them evokes a sweat. You recall the heaviness of the blue denim shirt you were wearing, or you can still smell the chicken you were roasting. You can envision the dirty dishes in the sink and feel what the temperature was. You relive those kinds of memories in a physical power surge, and all the knots you felt when they happened are suddenly alive and in your present.

In the days Nat loved me, he would glide through the door in the evenings, happy to be home. *How was your day? Where are the kids? What's for dinner? Oh! Wait till I tell you what happened! No! I'll save that for later! Anything in the mail? How are you? Let me give my wife a kiss . . .*

For years, we spoke the same words, asked the same questions that filled the air of a thousand homes in Charleston. Dusk would settle in, covering us in its delicious glow of contentment. Another day of work was ending and we were all safe and with each other.

We would have supper, clean the kitchen together as a family. Then Nat and I would put the children to bed. Most nights we would watch a movie or read together, turning in before midnight, sleeping like spoons.

One day, without warning, the pot-stirring hag slipped through the walls and began to skulk in our shadows. Nat began to miss dinner all the time, claiming business reasons. He went to every Clemson football and basketball game and took the children, not me, saying he needed some time with them alone to make up for all the weeknights he was out. I hated football anyway, so at first I didn't mind. But over time, they returned from Birmingham or wherever the Clemson team played and communicated with references and inside jokes that didn't include me. Sami covered her walls in Clemson sports memorabilia— pennants, programs, posters—and she announced that her life's ambition was to be a Clemson cheerleader. Evan was going to be a quarterback.

I became the target of constant criticism. My small flaws became large issues. The issues became *irreconcilable*. The air turned rancid and its stench blew and hissed in my direction on the breath of Nat and the children.

Like any mother, I urged Samantha and Evan to do their homework, pick up their clothes and put them in the hamper, put their glasses in the dishwasher and turn out lights when they left a room. Nat used to say, *Do as your mother says.* Somewhere along the line he began to ask me why I nagged them so much. Eventually he said these things knowing the children heard him. *Wipe up the counter, Sami* became *You'd better wipe up the counter, Sami, or* SHE *will go completely crazy.*

The children started calling me a nag, and Nat would say nothing. Later I watched his lips curl into a smile as they hurled words and insults at me I never would have spoken to anyone.

They say that domestic abuse starts with sarcasm, then yelling. Next the shoving begins and then one day it's a slap, then a punch. Women are murdered all the time because rage goes out of control. Nat raged over nothing. He began to say things like, *This is my house and I can act any way I want.* I would reply, *There's no place in a civilized world where you or I can act any way we want.* His grumbling increased in exponential leaps with each rebuttal. Soon we were barely speaking. Then the pivotal event occurred.

One day this past spring I put together a barbecue for the kids and their friends. School was almost out for the year. I was grilling what seemed like hundreds of hamburgers, slipping them in buns and arranging them on trays. The yard was crawling with youth, calling out to each other as they jumped in and crawled out of the pool. Sami was wearing a bathing suit that I thought was too skimpy. I just didn't think that a fifteen-year-old girl needed to wear an underwire padded bra top with a teensy bottom that barely stayed tied on the sides.

Every time I would ask her to tighten her bottom, Nat would snicker at me. It was very hot and humid and the

49

heat from the grill made the outdoor cooking almost unbearable. I became fed up with him and his snickering and lost my temper.

"What's so funny?" I said.

"You. You're funny. Don't you realize she doesn't give a shit what you think?" He moved his face very close to mine and said in a low voice, "No one does, Becca. No one."

"Know what, Nat?" I whispered back to him. "*You're a shit.*"

I could see that little vein in his forehead start to twitch, the one that twitched when he got angry. I didn't think he would do anything crazy because we were surrounded by teenagers. I was wrong. He picked up a hamburger, still hot from the grill, and pressed it into my face with a shove.

"Nat!"

"You repulse me," he said and walked away.

You repulse me.

Those words would bang around the inside of my head forever.

From that moment on, we were finished. Our intimate life ceased to exist. But I wouldn't give up. I begged Nat to make love to me, and when he gave in, he treated me like a whore. I had hoped that kind of closeness would bring some apology or some words of regret from him. But he never said a thing. When I finally said, *Why?* he looked at me with a blank face and said, *You're pathetic.* The sadistic pleasure he took in insulting me in the most vulnerable moment was stark and plain. Still, I didn't understand why it was all happening. What had I done? I would lie there in a pool of my own tears, and he would leave the bed in a silence of inexplicable disgust to sleep in the guest room.

I would have done anything to hold my family together. I made their favorite meals. They said dinner sucked. I asked them if they'd like to watch a movie, that they could use pay-per-view and choose anything they would like to see. They said no way, they had other plans. No matter what I did or what I offered, it was refused and refused callously with everything from eye rolling to snide remarks. By the time Sami and Evan left for their summer camps in Maine, I just held my breath waiting for Nat to deliver the hand grenade. He did not disappoint.

I came to Pawleys Island as soon as I could and not just to escape the gossip. Like any small city, Charleston's drums would beat with a jungle-like fervor when there was news of a domestic blowup. I could only guess what people were saying about me. After all, what kind of a mother loses her children? Her home?

A bad one. An unfit one.

That's what kept me up at night. Had I become like my *own* mother? I would call you a liar if you repeated this, but the truth, the deep ugly truth, is that in some secret part of my heart, I was relieved to be out of there. I felt so weary and bruised from playing all the mind games with Nat. My children had broken my heart into thousands of pieces. They said they hated me. My own children hate me. Can you imagine such a horrible thing? All I had ever done was to love them and try to be a good parent and they hated me for it.

I had never slapped them or abused them in any physical way. Their clothes fit and were clean, pressed and neatly put away. Every afternoon I greeted them with snacks—some cookies or brownies—when they came home from school. I never made personal plans for anything until I knew that their needs were met. I had been den mother to Evan's Cub Scout troop and class mother for Sami at least three times, and I had taken them to Sunday school without fail to be sure they received a religious education. I made beautiful birthday parties for all of them and holidays were out of a magazine.

I volunteered for everything to try to distinguish our family's reputation. I had been an officer in the Junior League and chaired committees for the symphony and the museum. I had done everything I could to make them happy and to set a good example. They hated me.

Anyone would have wanted to run away—at least, that's what I told myself. Litchfield Beach was the perfect escape for me.

My old roommate from Carolina, Claudia Kelly, was the closet thing I had to a best friend. My friends in Charleston were carpool friends, soccer game parents—but that's what happens when you're raising children. Claudia was the only friend who had survived all the changes in my life. Even though she lived in Atlanta and had a very busy practice in plastic surgery, we still managed to stay in touch and to see each other at least once a year. The condo I was staying in at the Crescent was hers. She had always said, *Use it! Use it!* So, with the subpoena still in my hands, I had called her from outside the courtroom. She was as completely surprised by Nat's shock-and-awe campaign as I was.

"Becca! That's outrageous! How can he get away with this?"

"I don't know," I said.

She said, "You'll go to the condo at Litchfield and stay there. Don't tell the son of a bitch where you're going either. Let *him* explain to everyone where you are. I'll come down as soon as I can and we'll figure this out."

I knew that there was nothing anyone could do. It seemed to me that Nat had somehow sewn up the whole deal before I even knew what was afoot. The only people he would have to explain my whereabouts to were the parents of our children's friends. Most kids were away at camp, so I wouldn't be talking to their parents until school started again. And, of course, there was his dad, Tisdale, but I was guessing that he already knew. Funny. I hadn't heard from Tisdale in weeks. Yes, he probably knew.

I was pretty damned depressed but hiding it quite well, or at least I thought I was. In the tradition of sailors surviving stormy seas, I seized Claudia's port. I knew that the sight and sounds of the ocean would make me feel better. I didn't know a soul at Litchfield. I would not be bumping into people day and night who would say, *Oh, Becca! I heard! We are so sorry! Is there anything we can do?* You knew in the pit of your guts that all they wanted was a tidbit of juice they could rehash over a gin and tonic with their spouse that night. It may be human nature to behave so disingenuously, but I wasn't ready to face them.

My plan, as I was driving from Charleston to Claudia's condo, crying so hard I could hardly see, was to dive into painting. Hopefully I would find some kind of a job to keep myself alive and fed until I could sort out my life. And there it was: Huey Valentine's gallery, right on Highway 17, sitting there like Christmas morning. I had seen the sign that said Oak Lea and Gallery Valentine listed among the tenants and pulled over.

Did I have an inkling that they didn't sell little statues of shrimp boats made from shells with little peg-legged captains on the bow? No. Did I know that it was a legitimate art gallery? No. Did I know he needed a framer? No. Luck! What a wild card. I had often thought about luck. Pretty arbitrary. It was better not to depend on it.

I was still adjusting to the idea of selling my work and Huey's excitement over it. And Abigail's. Last night's opening had been your basic baptism by fire, but I somehow had managed to survive the craziness. I was bone tired, I'll admit that much. The muscles in my arms ached from making so many frames.

I was late getting dressed and gathering up other watercolors I hadn't taken to show Huey the first day. It must have been ninety-five degrees and it was just early morning. The air was oppressive and the sun was a burning laser. Just a glance into its face made my eyes stream water.

I decided to turn on the car and let the air conditioner run for a few minutes to cool it down, and then I would drive to work. The worst part of the car was that it had dark charcoal leather seats—a gift of torture from Nat. You don't know what *hot* is until your bare legs have been stuck to dark leather seats in a car that's been baking in the Carolina July sun.

My steering wheel, not my seats, had been special ordered in beige leather because the standard one was black. Forget black steering wheels, unless you're a criminal and want to have your fingerprints removed. Just like folks in Minneapolis preheated their cars in February, we precooled our cars in July.

When the cars cooperate and start, that is. My car was as dead as Kelsey's cow, whoever Kelsey is or was. Not a sound came from the dashboard area when the key was turned. I must have tried it ten times, and nothing. When I started to perspire and could feel that the hair on the back of my neck was already sopping wet, I gave up and ran back inside to make an air-conditioned call to the gallery.

"Huey?"

"Rebecca? Sweet angel? Are you on the way?"

"Yeah, well, I was, but my car won't start. I don't know what's wrong. It was fine yesterday."

"Listen to Uncle Huey. Don't fret. Abigail is coming here in thirty minutes. I'll call her to pick you up. And I'll get Byron to see about your car."

"Oh! Thanks! Huey, seriously, thank you so much!"

I hung up realizing I was on the verge of tears. It had been so long since anyone besides Claudia had offered to do anything for me that I choked up and wanted to cry. What did that say about my mental state? Pathetic.

My cell rang moments later and it was Abigail, saying it was no big deal and she was on her way.

"Precious place!" she said, when I opened the door.

Precious? Where did she live? The Taj Mahal?

Crisp described her manner and her dress. She was wearing black Bermudas, a starched white sleeveless shirt, a black alligator belt and a black-and-white visor in the tiniest check print. Although she had on black sandals, I suspected that somewhere in her car there were a pair of black-and-white golf shoes. I watched as she glanced at the row of photographs of my children.

"Thanks. It belongs to a friend of mine from Atlanta."

"Three bedrooms?"

"Yeah, and a great view of the ocean," I said. "Come see."

I put my portfolio against the back of the sofa and opened the curtain over the sliding glass door that led to the balcony. We stepped outside into the breeze, and Abigail leaned over the rail.

"Too bad we can't bottle the air," she said. "We could all retire tomorrow."

"Isn't that the truth? This apartment is pretty far from the beach, but the view still takes my breath away. Especially at night."

"I'm sure. Well, we'd better get going. Huey My

Love is waiting for his Coke."

"Coke?"

I slid the door back and locked it, not that anyone was going to scale the building and burglarize the place.

"Don't you drink Coke for breakfast?" Abigail said with a laugh.

"Uh, no. When I was a kid I did, if I could get away with it."

"Well, our Huey has a Coke for breakfast every day. Sometimes two. Only in little glass bottles."

I grabbed my portfolio and closed the door behind her. "Well, in this sweltering heat . . ."

"Sometimes he puts peanuts in them and calls them lunch!" As we stepped into the sun, the heat hit us full force. "Whoo! Gonna be a thousand degrees today! And genius that I am, I'm playing golf!"

"I never understood golf," I said. "Especially in the summer . . . unless you're in Scotland or something . . ."

"You don't play golf?"

"Uh, no. A little tennis but that's about it."

She just looked at me, shook her head and added my lack of appreciation of golf to the list of many things that I thought she and Huey intended to change about me.

Sure enough, I spotted an expensive pair of black-and-white spectator, flapped and tasseled golf shoes in the backseat. Obviously, Abigail had money. Besides her Jaguar and no visible means of support, on the three occasions that I had seen her she had been dressed and accessorized to the hilt. I wondered for a moment why someone as together as Abigail was happy to trot around with Huey. Why wasn't she married? Where did her money come from, and what was *her* house like?

She blasted the air-conditioning, turned down the radio and backed out of her parking space.

"I really appreciate this," I said. "My car was fine last night."

"Glad to help! I'm stopping at Sam's Corner. Want something? I'm dying for a sausage biscuit."

"Sure. Do you mind if I just wait in the car?"

"No problem. Want a Coke?"

"Diet?"

"Sure."

I reached in my handbag to get a dollar and she stopped me.

"Don't worry about it. I'll start a tab."

She smiled at me and disappeared inside the restaurant. Sam's Corner. The parking lot was always crowded. I guessed all the locals got their breakfast there, The Eggs Up Grill or the Litchfield Restaurant. Unless you did fast-food drive-through, which was totally disgusting to me. I mean, there wasn't anything in the world like McDonald's french fries when they were right out of the hot oil. But breakfast? I'd rather go without than eat plastic cheese, rubber eggs and greasy sausage on a gummy biscuit.

Abigail returned in minutes, and we made polite conversation all the way to the gallery. When we arrived, Huey was in a bit of a dither, arranging the sold paintings in stacks along the wall, taking notes in his book.

"Good morning!" he said. "Did you bring your car keys?"

Abigail kissed him on the cheek, and I handed him his Cokes and my keys. "Abigail bought you several since it's so hot," I said.

"Bless you, angel!"

He took the bag, disappeared into his office, where he kept a small refrigerator. I went to the framing area, where I thought I would be spending most of my day, unwrapped my sausage biscuit and took a bite. It seemed like a normal moment until I looked up. Abigail and Huey were staring at me.

"What?" I said. "Is something wrong?"

They looked at each other, unsure of where to start.

"Spit it out, Huey," Abigail said.

"Okay, okay." He took a drink, draining his first Coke of the morning.

"Want another one? I'll get it for you . . ."

He shook his head. "Listen, Rebecca, sweetheart. My mother told me that you have a Ph.D. in psychology and that you have a husband and children in Charleston. And that your husband was given custody and the house. Are you in some kind of trouble? I mean, is there something we can do?"

I was stunned. But Pawleys Island was no different than Charleston. People talked. I couldn't even respond to him. I didn't want to talk about it.

"Listen to me, Rebecca. Byron is coming to pick up your car and take it to the garage where I get mine fixed. They're very fair and do excellent work. I want you to come for dinner tonight. Come out, spend the evening with us and we will try to help you straighten this mess all out."

I was furious. My disaster was my disaster, no one else's.

"Rebecca?" Abigail said.

"What?" My face was red hot.

"You aren't the first woman who ever had this happen to her. I'll make you a bet."

"What?" I said again.

"I'll bet you my Rolex that your husband has a girlfriend and that's why he wanted you out—so he could move her in. I'll bet you my diamond studs that he did this to avoid paying alimony and child support. And I have never met your husband, but I'll guarantee you that he's more arrogant than Donald Trump."

A girlfriend? Avoid alimony and child support at the expense of my relationship with my children? Would Nat do that? Would he? I had never thought of Nat as scheming or diabolical until that moment. Since I'd left, I had driven myself nearly insane trying to figure out why he didn't love me anymore. But then maybe he did love someone else and I'd been too blind to see it.

"What time is dinner?" I said.

"Always at eight," Huey said.

"I'll pick you up," Abigail said.

"Fine," I said and I felt all the blood drain out of my face. "Thank you."

All kinds of things were spinning around in my head. I had come here to avoid gossip and now my problems

60

were scheduled as the main topic of conversation for the night. Part of me was very angry—I didn't want to relive the battles simply because they felt a need to know about them. I thought introspection was futile.

They were meddling. I didn't want to be the cause célèbre for a little group of people who had too much time on their hands. I just wanted to work, support myself and be left alone to paint. Was that too much to ask? Did a paycheck entitle Huey and then Abigail to the lurid details of my marriage? I never should have opened my big mouth.

FOUR

ABIGAIL SAYS, NOTHING COULD BE FINER

Why I consented to play nine holes when the heat index was somewhere in the stratosphere was anybody's guess. Maybe some optimistic sliver of my postmenopausal brain still thought I was a young girl and that a good sweaty round of golf in the blazing sun would be rejuvenating. But to tell the truth, the heat left me dizzy and slightly nauseous. The day had been hot and sticky like you cannot believe.

Rebecca was on my mind as the hours ticked by. I knew she was smoldering from our prodding and I understood why. She thought her personal business was hers alone, and technically she was right. However, and this is the big however, she didn't know *us*.

There is so much to be said about power and its correct usage that it's all but impossible to choose a beginning point for the discussion. But let's just say this. I was not the kind of woman who could stand by with my mouth closed and watch a bloody crime unfold. And Huey was not that kind of man. We didn't bring home kitties from the rain, but whenever we could stomp out a wrongful fire, we did. We dispensed plenty of unsolicited advice for the good citizens of our community who, believe it or not, actually thanked us. On occasion. Well, not often.

There are all levels of transgressions that people commit against each other. In Rebecca's case, it was one of two things. Either Rebecca had been so thoroughly demoralized by her husband that she had somehow been fooled into believing the courts had done the right thing. Or Rebecca *was* an unfit mother, a concept that we absolutely could not swallow. I was coming in on the side of bamboozle. The courts had made a terrible mistake, probably based on trumped-up evidence or hearsay or some campaign gone awry. Huey had taken the first step in helping her by giving her a job.

We had liked her right away. Her talent was rather astounding. She fit a need in the gallery for a framer, and I would have advised Huey to give her a try, which he did before I could even articulate an opinion. As her employer, there was no reason why we—that is,

Huey—shouldn't know a little more about her. Despite its global fame, Pawleys Island was a small town. It would be better for her when the inquiring minds asked questions, and we knew they would, if we knew what to say. If someone new moved to Pawleys and Fate plopped them in the spotlight, as it had Rebecca, then the residents of Pawleys and Litchfield were going to want to know every detail about them.

We were a little worried. For all we knew her ex-husband might be a lunatic. Pawleys Island was just a short drive from Charleston, and who could say what form his anger might take? People committed crimes of passion every day, and far-fetched as it may sound, Huey and I didn't want to be caught in the middle of some risk to our personal safety—that is, if there *was* risk. Who knew? So the pragmatic side of us wanted to know and the humane side just wanted to be helpful.

I thought about all this as Rebecca and I drove in near silence to Huey's. She was on her guard, and so was I. I had a CD playing of Ella Fitzgerald singing great crooner music to try and put both of us in a social state of mind.

"I think I would have enjoyed living in the forties," I said, trying to lighten the air. "Life was so much more civilized."

"What do you mean?"

"Well, men were gentlemen and women were ladies. People were modest about themselves. I mean, they knew what they were supposed to do and how they were supposed to act. Life now is so, I don't know, loose."

A pithy pause ensued.

She finally said, "That's true, but I don't know if it was really any better then. There was polio and TB."

"Polio and TB? Heavens to Betsy, girl! What a thing to think of! What about the good things? Like the fashion? All those padded shoulders and platforms? And women worked in real jobs . . ."

"And got pushed out of the workforce after the war. It just seems like we're smarter today. But they did have great shoes. And cars."

I smiled and glanced over to her. She was smiling then. I said, "Love the cars, the clothes and the music. But I'm not sure we're any smarter."

I could see her head swinging in my peripheral vision, weighing the question of our collective national intelligence.

"Well, we've got technology. Yeah, boy. We've got technology in spades. But you're right. We're probably not any smarter. We're just flooded with information that nobody knows how to use. God knows, we still have war. So how far have we really come?"

"I always say that women should run the planet. Don't get me started on the politics of war. It would be even more interesting if our *elected* officials actually had a voice. Instead we've got this cockamamy cabinet of old zealot farts running the bloodletting, but we could talk about them all night, couldn't we? And here's our turn."

I turned on to Huey's road, opposite the entrance to DeBordieu. If I hadn't known where the plantation was,

I would surely have missed it.

"Anyway, screw politics. I think about this stuff, probably more than you would guess. Our government is such a disappointment. All of them . . . this entire out-of-control testosterone thing . . . Let me tell you about Huey's house."

"Holy hell!"

The big house had just come into view. And it was a spectacle to behold, with its spreading wings and grand front stairs fit for the arrival of Queen Elizabeth herself.

"Yeah, isn't that something? That was Miss Olivia's family home, but they don't live in it anymore. The taxes were ridiculous, so they made it into a museum. See? There's the parking lot for the tour buses. Huey and Miss Olivia have houses down the road by the river."

We continued to drive, my car crunching along the gravel road, and had yet to catch sight of Huey's or Miss Olivia's.

"Good grief! How many acres do they own?"

"Honey, around here we just say *enough*. But I think it's around fifteen thousand."

"Holy hell!"

"You said it, sister."

We finally arrived at Huey's house and spotted Rebecca's car, pulling in alongside of it. We were close to the row of boxwoods that served as the wall between Huey, his mother and the rest of the world. That may sound like a bit of braggadocio, but it was true. Once you rounded the long span of English boxwood hedge, time stopped and you found yourself light-years away from the gnawing panics of twenty-first-century living. It was not surprising that Huey had created such an oasis. His eighteenth-century gentleman's spirit could never survive without a sanctuary for quiet reflection.

I opened the car door and the humidity slammed me so hard it nearly took my breath away.

"Ugh," I said.

"You would think that by eight o'clock the heat would be broken," Rebecca said.

"We'll be all right in a minute," I said.

As predicted, we rounded the hedgerow and the breeze from the Waccamaw washed us in cool waves of Japanese honeysuckle and sweet olive. It was going to be a beautiful night.

I loved coming here and had always thought that Huey's gardens were one of the best-kept secrets in the world. The terrace floor of ancient rose-colored hand-made bricks was laid out in a basket-weave design, held together with a cracking mortar that allowed baby moss to creep through here and there. Around the edges at perfect intervals of twenty feet stood great lead urns planted with decorative grass climbing for heaven and asparagus ferns that dusted the earth. All of it waved in unison to the rhythm of the river's breeze.

Huey was standing by Miss Olivia, who was seated in one of eight wrought-iron chairs that surrounded the heavy glass-top dining table. The relentless sun had faded the magenta-striped cushions in the seats and backs of the chairs, but they were still cool and inviting.

There was a centerpiece of pink hydrangea blossoms stuffed in a large cut-glass bowl. On either side of it stood oversized hurricanes, tall enough to ensure the glow of its columned candles.

Off to the side, closer to the house, was another seating area with chairs and glass-topped end tables. Nearby stood the butler's field table on which was placed a silver Revere bowl of cracked ice and silver tongs. Crystal tumblers and bottles of white wine in an oversized silver ice bucket waited on a round silver tray. There was bourbon in a decanter and Perrier wrapped in a linen napkin. Byron moved in the sidelines in his starched linen mandarin-collared jacket, coming forward to offer a cheese straw or a napkin or to refresh a drink.

Whatever it was that Miss Olivia was saying, Huey's face was filled with delight. Their affection for each other was so obviously genuine that anyone would have wanted to be a part of their lives.

It was the kind of freeze-frame you found in a magazine feature article on old money and how the vastly rich really passed their time. Dressed for the evening and drinks with mother at dusk. The music of water and floral air gently moving the landscape back and forth in a dance of grace. Delicious bits served on silver trays to whet the appetite for the beautiful dinner that was sure to follow.

Rebecca was excited. Huey spotted us and waved. I couldn't wait to walk on the Valentine stage and take up my part.

"This is like a movie," Rebecca whispered to me as we walked toward them.

"Yep. It's Cary Grant and Bette Davis all over again, except that Cary's a plump old bird."

Rebecca giggled and I made a guilty face.

"Hello, Mr. Valentine! Miss Olivia!" I said. "What a perfect night!"

"Don't you look fabulous? As always . . ." Huey said to me, and then to Rebecca he said, "Miss Rebecca! You shame my rose garden! Look at you! Come join us!"

Byron had already poured a Perrier for me and offered the goblet from his small cocktail tray. Even the tray had a linen doily with lace edges, starched within an inch of its life.

"Good evening, Miss Abigail," he said and arched his eyebrow in familiarity. I was sure he plucked them. They were too perfect.

"Byron," I said, nodding my head in greeting. "Thank you."

"And what can I get for this lovely young lady?"

"A glass of white wine would be nice," Rebecca said.

"Tonight we're pouring an extraordinary ninety-six Louis Jadot, Meursault and a three-ninety-nine California char-doe-naay that I wouldn't serve trailer trash. Does the lady have a preference?" His eyebrows began to undulate as he waited for Rebecca to respond.

Rebecca didn't know whether to be horrified or entertained, so I answered for her.

"I think the Meursault will do the trick. And Byron?"

"Hmmm? Oh!" He reached in his pocket and handed Rebecca the keys to her car. "Good as new!"

"Thanks!" Rebecca said.

"Where on earth did you get the swill?"

"Miss Olivia bought a case at Sam's Club the last time she took off and drove herself to Charleston. It would destroy her not to offer it."

"Save it for the next opening—we can make sangria," Rebecca said.

Before turning, Bryon waved his hand behind his head and then pointed his finger in Rebecca's direction. "Sangria! Oh, I *love* it. It's so *eighties!* Isn't she the *clever* one?"

"He's a little—I mean don't you think he's . . ." Rebecca said.

"Over the top? Of course he is! But he's hilarious and I'm just used to him, that's all. His squeal is a little bit addictive."

"What do I do about the bill for my car?"

"Don't worry. Huey will twist it out of you."

Rebecca smiled and shook her head.

We sat with Miss Olivia. Huey finally took a chair and we began to talk about everything except Rebecca and how she lost her home and children.

"We had a tourist nearly drop dead today in the big house," Miss Olivia said. "Screamed bloody murder and passed out. Some woman from Pennsylvania. They said she looked like a giant halibut, just flopped on the floor! EMS came and everything!"

"Yet another sighting," Huey said, as droll as Oscar Wilde.

"Sighting of *who?*" Rebecca said.

"Alice," I said, "the ghost of Alice Flagg. She's always coming around, or so they say. She used to take music lessons here in the big house from Miss Olivia's great-grand-something or other. I guess she feels at home here."

"Who is Alice Flagg?" Rebecca said.

"Oh, my dear!" Miss Olivia said, as though Rebecca had spent the most of her life on the moon. "You've never heard of Alice Flagg? Why, it's the most romantic story in the world!"

"Sentimental sop, if you ask me," Huey said. "I wish she'd find that ring and get her misery moving to the light."

"What in the world are you talking about?" Rebecca was either politely stonewalling us, getting down to the dirt, or she had a fascination with the other side.

"Well," said Miss Olivia, moving closer to Rebecca, fully ready to reveal the goods on Alice, "she was a young woman in love with a fellow from the wrong side of the tracks . . ."

"He was the son of a merchant—not a rag picker, Mother."

"Don't interrupt me, son, or I'll go get a switch! Anyway, as I was saying, her family wanted her to marry the son of another plantation owner so they could join the properties."

"It's always about money," I said and gave Huey a

little jab in the ribs.

"Quite," he said.

Miss Olivia cut her eyes at us and continued. "Well, the story goes that she took this young man's ring, caught a terrible fever and had to be brought home from school to recuperate. She was very ill and her brother spotted the ring around her neck on a chain or a ribbon or some such thing that kept it near her heart. He snatched it away and threw it in the Waccamaw, and Alice has been coming back ever since, looking for her ring. Isn't that the saddest story in the world?"

Huey played four violins with his fingers and Miss Olivia reached over and slapped his hand. Huey and I smiled along with Miss Olivia, but Rebecca was somber.

"What's wrong, honey?" I said.

"It's not the saddest story in the world. Mine's worse, don't you think?"

By this time, Rebecca was working on her third glass of wine, Miss Olivia had knocked back her third sherry and Huey had drained his third bourbon. The tide turned and the elephant was on the table for inspection.

"How old are your children?" Huey asked.

"My daughter, Samantha, is almost fifteen and my son, Evan, is almost thirteen."

"And they're in camp in Maine?" I said.

"Yes. Sami's at Arcadia and Evan's at Pinehurst. The camps are very close to each other. They've been going for years."

Rebecca's voice became quiet, and she looked at the

river like she might like to be in it, drifting along with its current to a better life in a faraway place. Either I was going to speak now or let it go for another night. You know me. I spoke.

"Who was the judge?" I said.

"Campbell. Avery Campbell," Rebecca said. "Look, I really don't want to sit up here and monopolize the night talking about my problems. There's nothing to be done about it anyway."

"Dear," Miss Olivia said and reached out to Rebecca and covered her hand with her own, "I just don't understand. Why in the world would a judge allow this to happen?"

"Because it was what my children wanted," Rebecca said. "They wanted to live with their father."

"And because he's a lazy judge who prefers a clean desk over a long hearing. Let me explain it, Rebecca," I said. "Miss Olivia? I know this is going to sound crazy, but here it is. In this state of ours a child can be heard by the courts at age thirteen."

"Thirteen! That's outrageous!" Huey said. "When I was thirteen I didn't know what socks to wear!"

"Well, sometimes the law protects children and sometimes it doesn't. The closer the child is to eighteen, the more the court will listen to their preference for custodial parent. All Rebecca's husband would have had to do was to get the children to sign papers saying why they wanted to live with their father and why they didn't want to live with Rebecca. The stronger their complaint, the more the court listens. Especially if both children express a desire for one parent over the other—well, that's how it is."

"That's horrible," Miss Olivia said.

"And there was a statement from the children's guidance counselor saying that the children constantly complained to her about their home life. About me, basically."

"Oh great. The larger problem is that it should be against the law for one spouse to alienate the children from the other."

"There's a law?" Rebecca said. Her face drained of all color and I thought she might faint.

"I wish it was, Rebecca. It's called parental alienation—it's a syndrome. Didn't your attorney go over that with you?"

"No. No, he didn't."

I could see where this was headed, and I decided to just ask a few hard questions, intending then to change the subject so that Rebecca didn't feel like she was getting raked over the coals.

"Who did you use?" I asked.

"Jeff Mahoney," she said. "He lives down the street from our—I mean—where I used to live. He's extremely nice. He usually does wills and estates, but he offered to handle this for me and I trusted him, so I said yes. Nat was furious with me and said we were just wasting money. He said I didn't even need a lawyer."

"I'll bet," I said and winced. "Who did he use?" I was afraid to ask, knowing he had probably used a pit bull.

"Harry Albright," she said. "Do you know him?"

I could feel bile rising in my throat. Harry Albright should have been disbarred years ago. He was totally unethical and always in the headlines, billed more phony hours than anyone, was on his fourth wife and I had always suspected that he drank. He probably kicked his dog, if he had one.

"Yeah, I know him," I said, as nonchalantly as I could master.

"Dinner is served!" Byron announced in his theatrical voice.

Huey got up to help Miss Olivia to her feet. Rebecca and I would follow them into the dining room, but I held back for a few moments to ask Rebecca a few other questions.

"Rebecca? Wait. Listen, what did he have on you? I mean, is there any reason that the courts would have accepted you as unfit?"

"Nat said I was mentally unstable."

"Are you?"

"I was fine until I found out he wanted my house and children and then you can bet the ranch that I went crazy!"

"Of course. Who wouldn't? But did you have an affair or do drugs or drink too much?"

"Heavens no! I taught Sunday School for goodness sake!"

"Then what? What did he have on you?"

"He said I was negligent. That the children had to wait too long for me to pick them up from school. And that I was impossible to please—that I nagged the children and made them depressed."

"Is that true?"

"Sometimes. Look, I'm not perfect, but I was a good mother. A good mother."

I believed her. Somehow we got through dinner and got through it without any more conversation about Nat, the children and the divorce. But I was uneasy. I smelled a large male skunk, maybe two.

FIVE

THE SANDS OF PAWLEYS

All through the night, the air in my bedroom nearly crackled with my annoyance. It was as though my body was producing its own heat lightning, flashes of warmth and the heavy stillness that followed. The hours passed as I tangled and smoothed out my sheets. The ceiling fan clicked, feeding my mood with each rotation. The pillows radiated under my neck; the hair at the nape of my neck was damp with perspiration, and no matter how I rearranged and replumped the pillows, I couldn't get comfortable. I was having a rough night.

If Rebecca's situation was what I thought it was, my fury was going to torment me into the next century if I couldn't do something about it. And why? Why did I care? I thought about it for a while. What had I been doing with my life? Becoming more and more useless to anyone, that's what. Hedonistic. Self-serving. In perpetual denial. Cowardly. What happens to a woman with infinite blessings—good health, plenty of resources, a reasonably sharp mind, decent looks—what happens when she drops off the face of the earth to her entire past and begins again in a tiny magical kingdom like Pawleys with no demands on her time other than the ones she arranges herself? When she has no responsibilities other than to feed herself, dress herself, be witty and pleasant and pretend that her friendship with an aging gay man who owns a gallery is enough to sustain her? When she has no challenges other than improving her handicap?

I'll tell you what happens. She gets bitter. Dull. She smolders in her self-inflicted pit of insignificance. Smiles for the outside world and is miserable inside—that's what she is. A phony. And then one day, along comes another dumb-ass like herself and she sees herself in the dumb-ass's face. She's not Narcissus admiring her own reflection in the water. No, the recognition she has fills her with self-loathing, and she is compelled to save the other from drowning.

Rebecca was unaware of the nearly insurmountable despair that would follow her to the end of her days if she allowed herself to comply with her expulsion from her home and her children's lives. It was the only thing about which I was certain. Life has a way of wrenching your heart. No one escapes trials. Rebecca didn't understand the weight of accepting this wretched fate imposed on her and that it could ruin her soul beyond recognition.

Indeed, these days I hardly recognized myself.

Rebecca was a nice woman—I was pretty sure about that. Her husband was a philandering, lying, abusive, manipulative, asshole—I was pretty sure about that too. But her timidity and insecurities were going to leave her in extraordinary pain for the rest of her life because nobody, including her, had been brave enough, and certainly not noble enough, to see the truth.

A man wants a divorce? Big deal. It happened every day of the week. I say, go have your divorce, but for the love of God please try and be a gentleman about it? Please? Don't manipulate the children like a puppet master and turn them against their own mother. Don't make them sign papers and scoot them off to camp without the mother even knowing what transpired.

I called Rebecca the next morning at eight o'clock, which seemed to be the earliest you could call someone when you wanted to chat over mounting an offensive.

"Hey! You up?"

"Yeah, I was just getting ready to go walk on the beach."

"Want company?"

Rebecca paused and then said, "Sure. Why not?"

"I'll be there in ten."

I drove to Litchfield thinking about my own heavy rocks in my sack. That was the worst feature of getting involved with Rebecca's mess. Dealing with hers might force me to face mine. I wanted to avoid that in the worst possible way. Whenever I felt a little introspection coming on, I just whacked thousands of tennis balls and golf balls, trying to forget.

My cell phone rang. It was Huey.

"Morning! Where are you?"

"Actually, I'm on the way to Rebecca's to take a walk on the beach. Want to join us?"

"Me? Exercise? Do you want me to ruin my reputation? No, but thank you. Listen. Do you have a moment?"

"Just about one. I'm pulling into Litchfield right now."

"Well, Abigail. I've been up all night worrying about that child. You know we have to do something, don't you?"

"Who?"

"Well, obviously it's you."

"Huey, I was up most of the night as well. I don't want to get involved in this, this awful business. I'm retired."

"It scares you, doesn't it?"

"Hell, no. Nothing could scare me after what I've seen in this world."

"Humph. You can say whatever you want, but I think her trouble falls under the headline of *man's inhumanity to man.*"

"When a couple wants out of a marriage, they can do terrible things to each other."

"When you know someone's being hoodwinked, you are just as guilty if you don't say something about it."

"We'll see. I don't have enough information yet,

Huey. And it's not like she's asked us for help. If anything, our little questions annoy the daylights out of her."

"I suppose. You coming in this morning?"

I knew what that meant.

"Want a Coke?"

"And a sausage biscuit?"

"I'll see you around ten."

"You're an angel, Abigail. An absolute angel."

I didn't feel like an angel at all as I pulled into the parking lot of Rebecca's building and got out. She was sitting on the bottom step, tying her sneakers.

"Let's go," she said.

"Okay."

We crossed the dunes, and as always the spectacular sight of the wide and long stretch of beach made my heartbeat quicken. The blue sky was clear with the tiniest shreds of white clouds stretching out just above the horizon. Flocks of seagulls flew in formation overhead, and scattered pelicans slowly circled and then dive-bombed into the waters, catching sushi. Hundreds of little sandpipers darted to the edge of the shore, digging for periwinkles, and scurried away on the arrival of each foamy wave. The water sparkled under the rising sun and the salt-scented eastern breeze blew our hair away from our faces.

We began to walk in earnest and talked now and then about safe topics—the day, the view and so on. She told me about Claudia Kelly, her plastic surgeon friend from Atlanta. This led us to discuss the many sins of the

79

media and how it hyped public opinion that women over forty were finished unless they got a surgical overhaul.

"The number one reason men leave their wives is for a younger woman."

"How come you know so much about divorce?"

It seemed like the moment to give her some background information on myself, hoping she would feel more comfortable to talk about her disaster.

"I'm an attorney," I said. "I was a senior partner in the largest matrimonial practice in South Carolina. Until I quit."

"Oh? Why did you quit?"

I stopped, leaned to put my hands on my knees and breathed deeply. Rebecca stopped too, waiting for me to answer. If I thought I had the right to grill her about her private life, then was she not entitled to the same privilege? I considered it and then decided I would tell her.

"My son died. My husband died two years later. I needed to reorder my life. It was a lot to take. It still is."

"Oh! My god, Abigail! I am so, so sorry. Can I ask what happened?"

"Sure. My husband went into the hospital for knee replacement surgery. When he was in college, he played football for Carolina and tore up his knees so many times that he had to . . . Well, we're all familiar with the agony and the ecstasy and so forth. Anyway, he was too heavy, and while he was under the anesthesia, he had a heart attack. They couldn't revive him. He was only forty-seven."

"Good Lord! That's awful! And your son?"

"Car accident. He was twenty. That's the worst. Yeah. Ashley was just twenty. My beautiful boy. My only child."

I choked up and struggled to regain my composure. Rebecca didn't know what to say. What could she say? Only what everyone usually managed to sputter . . .

"Oh, Abigail! I am *so* sorry!"

"Yeah, well, thanks. That's the story. I can't stand around and see people I like be taken advantage of. It's my perpetual lawyer gene or something. I'd give any-thing to have my husband and son back. Anything. So I'm thinking that if I can't have mine, maybe I can at least see if it's possible to do something about what's happened to you. That's why I have been asking so many questions, I guess. Besides that, I guess Huey and I probably *are* a couple of busybodies."

I started walking again. Rebecca followed, working to keep up pace. I took a number of deep breaths. I hated to talk about Ashley. If I just kept the story to myself, if I didn't say the words, then maybe it wasn't true. Maybe it had not all really happened. Maybe Ashley was home with John, watching a ball game. Maybe I was just on vacation at Pawleys for a few weeks or months, in some kind of limbo that would keep me from the reality of my horror. Stolen lives. Death. So final and unbelievable that it was impossible to accept. If I didn't look at it, think about it, talk about it . . . I could stay sane. I worried that if I lingered around it too much, I might be in danger of something happening to me. Something just as final, to relieve my pain.

Over the last three years, there had been so many winter nights at Pawleys when, surrounded by darkened houses, I would go to the dunes in my bathrobe, stand under the milky moon, under the wild stark sky of deep night, and scream like an animal until my throat was raw. There was no one to hear me over the roar of the waves and no one to stop me. I had begged God to help me, with no response. I begged night after night until I came to understand that what had been taken from me was permanent and there was nothing to be done about it.

It was my therapy. If the remembering in the day was too hard, I could promise myself the reward of a night of releasing screams. I finally realized that it was how I spent the rest of my life that mattered now. You can't bring back the dead—unless it's Alice Flagg. The days and nights that numbered the rest of my life were laid out before me like steppingstones, a path to where? More sorrow? It didn't matter I had to just keep going. All those realizations put on a plate in front of me to inspect, and I believed they were true, I still carried unbearable sorrow. Truth did not heal, and to date, neither did time.

Rebecca had been done a bad turn but at least her family was still *alive.*

So I walked on, my pace harder and my feet sinking deeper with each step. My breathing was uneven, and I knew I was on the edge of falling apart in broad daylight, right there on the beach. If I did, there was no reason for her to have any faith in me or my ability to help. I felt her hand on my arm and I slowed down and stopped, looking down at my sneakers. One of them was untied and I knelt to retie it.

"Abigail?"

"What?"

"I don't think you're a busybody. Or Huey."

"Thanks."

The ocean was at half tide and rising. Soon there would not be enough beach for us to walk. If I didn't move, my running shoes would be soaked in salt water by the small but threatening waves that raced ahead of the tide. Warnings. I had ignored too many all my life. I stood to face Rebecca.

"Let's go get Huey his Cokes and sausage biscuits."

"Okay."

I knew she thought I was a little manic. First, I had called to see if she wanted a walking buddy, and within minutes of beginning that walk I had begun to skirt that dangerous part of my psyche. My mood changed so dramatically that I frightened myself. It was time to put my monsters back in their closet. No one wanted to see them.

I waited while she changed clothes, and then she followed me to Sam's Corner. I ordered six bottled Cokes and four sausage biscuits—one for her, two for Huey and one for myself.

I followed her to the gallery. Just the short distance

from the car to inside where Huey waited was enough to break a sweat. In the span of time it took us to drive from the beach to Huey's, the temperature and humidity climbed so much that the thick air was wet like a sauna. If I had known the name of the person who invented air-conditioning, I would have sent the genius the most outrageous and spectacular orchid in captivity.

"Huey? Breakfast is here!"

"Bless you! How are we this gloriously tropical morn?"

"Practically growing moss under my fingernails," I said. "Other than that, I'm great." I opened the bag and Huey opened the Cokes.

"Morning, Huey," Rebecca said.

"Morning, sweetheart." He handed her a Coke, and she said, "No, thanks. Refined sugar. But thanks."

Huey clutched his heart and gasped. "Mah dee-ah! Surely you are merely lacking in understanding of what *food of the Gods* truly means! Besides, you're too skinny."

"I even got one for myself," I said when I saw Rebecca's face pleading for a bailout. "Eat."

"Oh, fine," Rebecca said. "Fine."

Rebecca ate in silence, picking up errant crumbs with the tip of her unmanicured fingers and depositing them back on the waxed-paper wrappers. Huey and I chatted about the inane—how delicious dinner had been the previous night, how well Miss Olivia seemed and once again about how successful the opening had been. I watched Rebecca from the corner of my eye. She was having trouble swallowing, but then that had always been the problem with biscuits and sausage. Thick, hot, crusted dough and a greasy, tough sausage patty—delicious, but a difficult combination to work through, even when life was perfect. Poor Rebecca, I thought as Huey went on and on about the daily grind of running a chic art gallery. She took a sip of her Coke, and Huey stopped her.

"Rebecca? Co-Colas are intended to be chugged, not sipped like Madeira. Ah, Lord! When I was a young rascal, my father would pile me in the car and take me to Marlow's store. Now it's Frank's Restaurant. And in those days, it was really something. Marlow's had a great red cooler filled with freezing-cold bottles, all hung inside by their necks, like the doomed, on this little metal track. The bottom of the cooler was filled with ice water. Anyway, Mr. Marlow would say to my father, *I see you've come for your Coke!* He would push back the top, slide two bottles along the track, liberate them and pop the tops with the church key he kept attached to the cooler with a piece of string. My daddy would throw back his head and drain the Coke without a breath."

"Chugging anything is considered an art form by most Southern gentlemen," I said.

Rebecca giggled and continued picking up bits of crust and biscuit. Then she wiped her hands, picked up her bottle and took two large swigs. "Satisfied?" she said.

"It's a start," I said. "Frankly, except for these early-morning chugalug fests, I usually have mine in a glass over ice. My mother would roll over in her grave if she could see me consume anything straight from a bottle. Historically, Southern ladies don't do this kind of thing."

"Well, Miss Abigail, I'll have you know that this little bottle has more than a footnote in history. Did you know it was invented in 1915? It was made this way for several seriously artistic reasons. First, the grooves on the sides are supposed to resemble a cacao pod. And its color . . ."

"Get comfortable, honey," I said to Rebecca, well within Huey's hearing. "His sermons can go on for *days*."

"Shush!" Huey said, mildly irritated. "Its *color* was meant to enhance the brownish liquid to make it appear black like coffee, thereby broadening the market appeal to adults and children alike."

"Most days I prefer an espresso," I said, "but when it's *this* hot . . ."

"It becomes the *perfect* coffee substitute!" Huey said, beaming. "I must say, though, there is *no* substitute for how the bottle feels. I mean, seriously, ladies, would you prefer this lovely little perfectly balanced jewel against your lips, or one of those nasty ragged plastic bottles?"

"Well, that is a good poi—"

"It's rhetorical, dear," I said to Rebecca and rolled my eyes. Honestly! Sometimes she was exasperating. All

86

that naivete? "Yes, Huey darling, it's like drinking from Stueben."

"Oh, go kiss a goat's fanny," Huey said. He blushed and turned to Rebecca. "Forgive me, Rebecca, but sometimes our Miss Thurmond gets up on the wrong side of her duvet."

"Sorry."

Huey puffed himself up. "That's not the issue. The issue is chicken walking."

"What? What's that?" Rebecca was mystified once more.

One more puff and he said, "Chicken walking is what hens do in a chicken yard—they peck around and around. That's what we're doing here. I've known Abigail Thurmond long enough to know when she's upset. So, before the entire morning slips into the hands of the Lily Pulitzered decorators searching for the perfect painting to match a divine blue and yellow plaid couch, may we please—just us three—may we have a word about Rebecca's *situation?*"

"What is there to say?" Rebecca said, shifting her weight and wrapping her arms around herself.

"I could make a phone call," I said, wondering again if I really wanted to get involved, much in the same way a diver changes his mind in a midair jackknife.

"What possible good could a phone call do?" Rebecca said.

I drained my Coke and put it on the counter. "Huey? I sure could go for another one of these. Why don't you be a sweetheart and go back to Sam's. Buy every cold one they've got. Rebecca and I can watch the store and then we can chat alone—attorney/client privilege, right?"

Huey raised himself from the bar stool where we all sat in the framing area and made one of his campy departure speechettes.

"You are quite correct," Huey said. "The fine details are none of my beeswax. It's blazing hot and it's best to keep consuming liquids. I shall return in two shakes of a lamb's tail with enough hydration to fortify us for the day!"

We watched Huey leave and shook our heads, smiling at each other as the door closed behind him. Huey's dramatic craziness was crazy-like-a-fox craziness. He had seen Rebecca flinch when I offered to make the phone call. So had I. I hadn't even said who it was I intended to contact, or what they did. Still, she had gripped her hands on her bare arms so tightly that white spots immediately appeared where her fingers pressed her flesh.

But Huey and I had made careers from dealing with people. His typical client was a little insecure about the art world and just wanted to be sure they were investing their money wisely. My clients ran the entire gamut. In any case, Huey knew that if he lightened the mood, ducked out for a moment and left Rebecca in my hands, I would begin the process gently, letting Rebecca set the pace. I would not prod her any further than she wanted to go. On a curious note, this was a first for me. Usually the client sought me out. Here I was practically soliciting her business.

"So? Who are you thinking of calling?" she said. "Here, give me that."

She took the wrappers and napkins, put them all in the bag to toss away, squirted the counter with Windex and began wiping up the nonexistent remains with nervous anticipation of what I was about to suggest.

"Sherlock Holmes," I said.

"Be serious."

"I used to know a guy who's a PI—private investigator—who's a regular Sherlock Holmes. I used him all the time. He owes me one. Actually, he owes me a lot. He's fabulous."

"What would he do?"

"Follow your estranged husband around for a few days, take pictures if there's anything interesting going on, then report back to me. If there's something fishy, you'll know it. You can do what you want with the information. You can turn the tables on your rat, Nat."

"What if he gets caught? What if Nat shoots him? Nat carries a handgun."

"Nice of you to mention that." Jesus, I thought, what else has she got up her sleeve? "Look, Everett Presson can handle himself. If he gets caught, he knows what to do. But just so you know, he's never been caught."

"I don't know . . . I can't imagine Nat is up to something like another woman or something. I mean, he's just not *like* that."

"Yeah, that's what Jack Welch's wife said, and Hillary Clinton, and Ivana Trump—honey, it's a long list. You don't think men cat around?"

"No. No, I know they do, it's just that I would've known it. At least I *think* I would have." Her voice trailed off as she began searching her memory.

"Sure."

Rebecca took a deep breath. I could read her mind. She didn't want to know what was really happening and she wanted to know what was happening. In a way, I didn't blame her.

"Go ahead then. Call your friend, this Everett Presson person, this private whatever he is. Is he going to charge us a lot of money?"

"Zero. I told you. He owes me."

"Okay. Abigail? Thanks. I mean, I appreciate your advice. Maybe you're right, I don't know. It's just that—well, let's not talk about this anymore unless something turns up, okay?"

I understood. Constant facing of the demon that's eating you alive is just too much to bear. Especially when the demon might be you.

SIX

DIGGING THE DIRT

It was six in the morning, and once again I was staring at the ceiling fan. There was too much I didn't know about Rebecca's husband, and the more I thought about it, I knew I had to talk to Rebecca again before I unleashed Everett Presson to her husband's shadows. Like, for starters, I didn't even know what the lout did for a living. We'd had the chat at Huey's, and the moment he returned I'd left for a hair appointment. That just goes to show how reluctant I was to immerse myself in this.

I kicked back the bedcovers, washed my face and made coffee, taking it out to the porch to watch the ocean for a while. I settled myself in one of the Kennedy rockers and rocked. I wondered what could make a woman so passive, so meek that she wouldn't fight back when something like this happened to her. It didn't quite add up in my book, but then I wasn't Rebecca. I would have killed anyone with my bare hands who tried to touch my son, much less take him away from me. But I had never had the chance for that fight, and I had lost him anyway.

I got up to refill my cup, stopped at the porch rail and looked out at the horizon. When the world was so filled with trouble, how could the day be this magnificent, this stunningly beautiful? Everything before me was so perfect it could have been the location for an ad for the department of tourism. The soft dunes were so fragile, one after another, springing plumages of feathered sea oats from the crowns of their heads. Buttercups, black-eyed susans and clumps of yellow-green grasses crept around the bottoms of them, happy to live on droplets of water during dry spells and growing rampant after heavy rains.

Beyond them, for as far as I could see, was the

sparkling water of the Atlantic—another day dawning, birds repeating the hunt for food today as they surely would tomorrow. Everything about the birds and the plants was designed not only for their survival but for them to thrive. Maybe that was one reason I loved Pawleys Island so much. Eternity seemed to be in sight but slightly out of my grasp. Maybe it was the challenge to bring them together that convinced me Pawleys was the only place where my imagination and my soul could live in sync with nature's plan.

I wondered what Rebecca's real story was. Battered women—whether it was physical or emotional or both—sometimes they believed they deserved the punishment. But what woman could believe she deserved to lose her children?

I refilled my mug, found a little pad of paper and a pen and decided to stroll down the beach, making a list of questions for Rebecca. The first thing Everett would want to know was where to find Nat. I needed the address of his office, their home, his usual haunts and so forth. If she could give me his license plate number, that would be helpful. I could already envision her giving me the information but with reluctance. She didn't seem frightened of Nat. It wasn't that. The more I thought about it, her complacency made no sense. In fact, it seemed slightly grotesque. But I decided that my own experience was coloring my judgment and that I had to wait until the facts came in.

I decided to go by the gallery to bring them Cokes, or *Co-Colas,* as Huey said. So two sacks in hand, I pushed open the door at ten-thirty and found Huey and Rebecca actually working. Rebecca was cutting a mat and Huey was writing checks.

This Coke-slash-sausage-biscuit routine was not healthy for anyone, and I knew it. I made a mental note to make some fruit salad for tomorrow.

"Morning all!"

"The sausage angel! My love!" Huey said.

Rebecca giggled and stopped working.

"Sausage angel?" she said and laughed again. "That's some title!"

"Don't mind him, Rebecca. He's just a little cracked, that's all."

Huey took two Cokes and, after counting what was in the bag and pouting at me, only one sausage biscuit. "Are you putting me on a diet?"

"No, baby. I just need you to stay healthy for my sake." I smiled at him and he shook his head.

"Women," he said. "Forgive me if I take this to my office. I have a pile of checks I want to get out in the morning mail."

"No problem," I said. "Mind if I join you?" I said to Rebecca.

"Of course not!" she said and cleared away her work from the counter.

"So listen," I said, taking a bite of my biscuit, "I need a little bit of information and then I can unleash the hounds."

"Sure," she said.

I asked Rebecca for the information I needed, and she

very willingly supplied it. Nat was Nat Simms of Simms Autoworld. The business was started and still very tightly held by Nat's father, Tisdale, although his father had given Nat a letter on his thirtieth birthday granting him a twenty-five percent ownership. I had indeed seen their television ads all my life. *Hi! I'm Tisdale Simms! When you're in the market for a new car* . . . They were horrible. I could still see the old man in his straw hat, squinting at the camera, reciting his lines from an unseen poster and smiling from ear to ear. Navy jacket, white shirt, red tie, khaki pants—it was the Lowcountry good old boy uniform that erased the lines of class and wealth and joined men together. You'd buy a car from a guy who seemed like your best pal, wouldn't you? Apparently a lot of people thought so, because Nathaniel Tisdale Simms and his boy Nat sold more cars than anyone in the entire state of South Carolina. It also meant they had more money than the Saudis. And while money shouldn't have been an issue, it was. She explained it was her father-in-law who owned the big boat, the mountain house, the beach house, the art collection. Nat's partnership in his daddy's business was on paper only and paid no dividends. I tucked that information away in the back of my mind.

I just listened to her, nodded my head, took a few notes and a few bites of breakfast and thought, my, oh my, what an interesting can of worms am I about to open.

I couldn't wait to call Everett Presson, which I did as

soon as I got back to my house on Pawleys. Maybe I'd even take a drive to Charleston and look for a car for myself. Yes! That might be fun!

"Everett? Hi! It's Abigail Thurmond!"

"Well! As I live and breathe! How the heck are you? Where have you been?"

"Oh, Lord, Everett, it's a long and, I'm afraid, sad story that I'll tell you when I see you. Listen, I'm calling you because I need a favor."

"You just name it! After all you've done for me? Just name it."

I told him about Rebecca and her husband, Nat, and he listened carefully, stopping me now and then to take notes or to clarify things, and at the end he said exactly what I thought.

"This guy's got a girlfriend. I'd bet my Chevy on it."

I told him I agreed and then gave him a little grief about his car. "You still driving a Chevy? Same old nasty clunker? With all the checks I signed to you, you should be driving a giant Benz!"

"Hey, I gotta be low-key, you know. I looked at a Buick last year, but it had too much chrome. Anyway, just give me a few days and I'll report back."

I gave him my home number and said, "Thanks, Everett. I mean it."

"Sure thing."

For the next ten days I filled my time with a member guest tournament at a golf club in North Myrtle Beach, placing fourth. I could not have cared less, but the women I played with were all out of sorts.

"Hey! We won a little nut dish, didn't we?"

The glare of their bitterness was so intense that I slipped away as soon as I could. Honestly, some people took this golf business just way too seriously for me. I picked up my dry cleaning, the *New York Times* that was saved for me at Litchfield Books and decided to go home. At the last moment, I decided to swing into the Bi-Lo and see what I could make for dinner that wouldn't require too much effort.

I was pushing my cart by the hermetically sealed boneless, skinless chicken breasts when I felt a tap on my shoulder. It was Rebecca.

"How was your tournament?"

"We placed fourth, which I thought was pretty darn good, considering it was ninety-five in the shade," I said. "You cooking tonight?"

"Yeah, Huey decided to close early, so I thought I would just grab something easy. What are you up to?"

"The same. I'm hitting the sack early tonight. I'm exhausted. Too much sun."

"No word, huh?"

"You mean from Everett?" She nodded, and I said, "No, but as soon as I hear anything, I'll call you right away."

"Okay."

Well, at least she was curious.

Several days later I found a day-old message in my voice mail from Everett.

"Call me," he said. "I've got lots of nice pictures . . ."

It was after seven. I dialed him as fast as I could,

kicking myself that I hadn't given him my cell number (but it didn't work half the time anyway) and cursing Bell South for their lousy voice mail service.

"Everett? Everett? Hey, it's me, Abigail! Sorry to call you after five . . ."

"No problem. When are you coming to Charleston? Or Mount Pleasant?"

"I can be there tomorrow morning if you'd like me to."

"I've got something in the morning, but how about we meet at Jackson Hole for an early lunch? It's on Shem Creek. Do you know it?"

"Hole is the operative word. But they have great crab cakes. Eleven thirty?"

The hour was fine with him, and I knew that if I asked him what kind of pictures he had, he wouldn't want to tell me. Everett would rather have the pleasure of seeing the shock on my face and I could certainly give him that. He deserved it.

In general, the public didn't fully appreciate how dangerous private investigator work was. Contrary to what I'd told Rebecca, Everett had been in more than one rumble with one angry husband or another, and his nose had been broken so many times it was sort of a scrapbook of his adventures. Each bump and turn it took was a reminder of another battle weathered and won. But he was still the best in the business because he took those risks and always got results.

I crawled into my Pawleys Island hammock—what other kind would I own?—and began reading the Week in Review section of the *Times*. The only thing I could focus on was the political cartoons, which perfectly rendered the climate. It was another election year and the mudslinging was well under way.

Maybe it was just me, but the political world that had once fascinated me now just left me shaking my head wondering how America, who had fed, sheltered and defended the masses, had arrived at a place of such low esteem to the rest of the world. Clearly, part of it was fanatical religious ideology and the exported vulgarities of our culture. I mean, if I had never known an American and I watched a few episodes of *Sex and the City* or even the old reruns of *Dallas*, I would think Americans were totally immoral. Even though those shows were designed to parody our lives, if I didn't know better, I might believe what my eyes saw on the television or movie screen.

Everything was perception. Even from my hammock on Pawleys Island, this little spot in the Atlantic Ocean, I could smell a trace of disdain from across the water. But of course, I knew that was in my own head because I was only wondering about myself and how I would stand up to scrutiny. I, who had made a living of dissecting the lives of others, would wither, dry up and evaporate under public examination. Worse, I had become a *crone,* stirring the pot of Macbeth. How in the hell had I let that happen?

With the heel of my foot, I pushed back from the banister to make the hammock swing gently back and forth until I was so drowsy that I knew if I didn't get up then,

I would wake up with rope marks all over my body. I stood up from the hammock as it came to its resting position and looked out over the dunes. It was low tide and the beach was illuminated by the stars overhead. There in silhouette I saw the form of a man in a coat. He was all gray. My heart lurched as my first thought was, who in the world was on the beach alone at that hour in an overcoat in late July? When I looked back again, he had vanished. The Gray Man? Ridiculous.

In the morning I thought about the Gray Man again. He was our local insurance adjuster of sorts, except that he had been dead for over a hundred years. No matter. The story goes that he was returning on horseback from the big war (he was wearing *gray,* after all!) to his fiancée's home on Pawleys. It was raining to beat the band. The horse fell in a muddy hole, the Gray Man went flying and he died as a result of his injuries. I don't know what happened to the horse, but apparently he got up dead and went to her house and rapped on her windows. She saw him waving frantically to leave the island. She did leave with her father, and the house was spared from the storm. So if there's a storm coming and you see him, your house will survive intact.

I saw him right there that night. It wasn't my imagination. I was sure of that. But there was no hurricane in the forecast other than some piddling tropical depression off Florida's coast. The only real hurricane was the one we were about to cook up for Rebecca.

On the drive to Mount Pleasant, I thought about calling Huey and then decided against it. I would call him after I met with Everett. I listened to the weather reports and they were predicting afternoon thunderstorms. So what else was new? Every morning the temperature climbed with the humidity, and when Mother Nature couldn't stand it anymore the skies grew dark, lightning crackled and it rained like the end of the world. Around eight, the sun would appear for a few minutes until it began to slip away. I loved that hour, and nowhere was it more lovely than at Huey's. I would call him to see if he wanted to have dinner. I would tell him my alleged Gray Man story, and he could update me on the ghost of Alice Flagg. We would talk about the supernatural world that Huey believed in so strongly, and I would argue that it was all nonsense. But I really didn't want to believe that it was. If there was nothing to the Gray Man or Alice Flagg, then where were Ashley and John? No. I couldn't vouch for Alice, but I had seen the Gray Man with my own eyes.

SEVEN

GIVE ME A RING

When I walked into Jackson Hole, it took my eyes a few moments to adjust. The sun, catching the edges of the thousands of beer cans lining the ledge around the ceiling of the area, was throwing beams of corneal abrasion around like a Las Vegas light show. I had forgotten how delightfully

tacky the place was, and I took a deep breath, anticipating a relaxed lunch.

Someone named Linda, wearing a diamond as big as
a judge's gavel, greeted me and showed me to the table.
Things must be good in the cheap seafood restaurant
world, I thought.

"Here we are," she said. "I hope you enjoy your
lunch."

I could never figure out why these people who
worked in all these restaurants that littered the shores of
Shem Creek seemed so happy. If I had been forced to
spend my days in a dump like Jackson Hole, I would
have been the Zoloft queen. But what did I know?
Maybe all the tourists were serious tippers, but I
doubted that.

"Thanks," I said, and before sitting down I gave
Everett a huge hug. "How are you, Everett?"

There was Everett in khaki shorts and a knit shirt,
and I had overdressed in a black linen dress. Was it my
fault the dress codes of the world had fallen to something a notch above pajamas? But I realized I was
something of an old fart so I brightened up to match his
enthusiasm.

Everett was just bubbling over and couldn't wait to
show me what he had. "How am I? Great! You look
fabulous! So tell me what's going on with you? Where
have you been?"

"Everett? I'm gonna give you the Cliffs Notes version
of my horrendous story, and then we are going to move
on to other more pleasant topics." I took Everett

through the chain of death, and he was completely surprised and somber.

"Good Lord, Abigail, I wouldn't wish any of that on my worst enemy. I am so damn sorry."

"Thanks. I know. But I'm okay, really—I mean, as well as anyone would be in my shoes. What can you do? Life goes on, right?"

"Yeah, I guess, but man oh man, that is too much."

"It is exactly as much as I could stand without losing my mind, and believe me, there are still moments when, if I think about it all too much, I might still go insane. That's why it's good for me to get busy. So tell me what you found."

"Okay, her name is Charlene Johnson," he said, handing me a manila envelope. "And guess what? She works for Nat in his daddy's business. Isn't that a coincidence?"

"Bloody convenient too. Tsk, tsk. Why does it always happen in the workplace?" I opened the envelope and removed two folders. The first one held a stack of eight-by-ten black-and-white photographs. I began flipping through them. First there was a picture of them leaving the Bank of South Carolina on Meeting Street and another of them using an ATM machine at the Bank of America on Savannah Highway. Then there were pictures of them at Community Firstbank and Washington Mutual, and all I could think was, gee, they sure do go to the bank a lot. Not very romantic. At the bottom of the stack were a few pictures of them coming and going from the cosmetic surgery center on Calhoun Street.

What was that about? Well, it looked to me like Charlene was just a regular girl in the first photograph but in the last one she had become Jessica Rabbit. Poor thing. Who would ever take her seriously?

I opened the other folder. They were grainy and some were slightly out of focus, but one thing was obvious. Nat Simms knew Charlene Johnson in the biblical sense, and we're talking *in detail.*

"How did you get this picture of them?"

"There's a huge live oak across the street. I just shinnied up the trunk and positioned myself with my zoom lens . . ."

Before I could stop myself I said, "Looks like Nat positioned his zoom as well."

Everett burst out laughing and I turned a thousand shades of red. "Abigail!"

"Sorry! Sorry! Sorry! I just couldn't resist."

That was the kind of joke I might have made with Huey, but never with someone from my professional life. Maybe I was mellowing after all. I continued to stare at the pictures, one after another, but I kept going back to one of them in the living room of Rebecca's house. They were smoking what looked like a cigarette, but I knew it wasn't a cigarette by the way they handled it.

"Everett? Let me ask you something. In your professional opinion, does this look like they're smoking pot to you?"

"Yep. Absolutely. In fact, I could smell it across the street. I'd bet if I went back and hung around for a few days, I could figure out where he's getting it or who he's getting it from. I saw them getting high on several occasions, but this was the clearest photograph I had of them actually smoking. You say this guy got custody of their children?"

"For the moment."

"Well, I don't think family court would approve of this, do you?" Everett handed me another folder from his briefcase and grinned widely. "Take a look at this."

I opened the folder and nearly fainted from what I saw. There was Charlene Johnson spanking Nat's bare backside with a hairbrush. He was lying right across her lap. But not to worry, it wasn't like Nat was naked. He was wearing a Clemson football jersey.

"I guess his panties got lost in the shuffle some-where?" I was choking on laughter.

"He's got issues," Everett said.

"Uh, yeah!"

As the young waitress approached I closed the folder as quickly as I could.

"Hi! I'm Gracie and I'll be your server this afternoon. I'd like to just go over the specials with you . . ."

Gracie was as cute as a bug and she chattered on with so much perkiness as though she could save our eternal souls from the flames of hell by convincing us to order the seafood plat du jour. The more she described the food the wider her eyes became. This was one very dra-matic young woman.

"And if you're *really* hungry, there's the Captain's Platter. That's a *dozen* sautéed scallops, a *dozen* shrimp, two deviled crabs and a *whole* fried flounder. It comes with two sides. Personally, I'd get the red rice and the collard greens and ask for extra hush puppies, but then the fried okra is banging . . ."

"Whew! Gracie! Too many choices! I'll just have the crab cakes and a side salad. How 'bout you, Everett?"

Everett ordered a fried fish sandwich with a side of fries. We both ordered iced tea and some crab dip to pick on while we waited for our entrees. The irrepressible Gracie swept away and I pondered youth being wasted on the young for a moment and then checked my watch. How long would lunch take to get here? Knowing I had the evidence to prove Nat was a skunk had left me absolutely ravenous.

Every now and then I would pull out the folder and sneak a look at the pictures. Everett would say, *Good, huh?* And all I could think about was Nat's ass and the old saying about someone who was cheap—that they were tighter than a gnat's . . . Well, you get the drift, I'm sure. Basically, I giggled my way through lunch, pausing every thirty seconds to thank Everett and to sneak another peek.

Cruising back to Pawleys, I fretted over how best to handle the kryptonite in the envelope next to me. Those pictures were so hot I could almost feel them radiating from the passenger seat. Rebecca would probably have hysterical fits when she saw them. It was one thing to think that your husband might, just *might* be fooling around. It was quite another to hold a photograph in your hands of your husband sprawled across the lap of his mistress, wearing a football jersey and getting his fanny spanked. *Naughty dog*. And, let's be honest, Nat wasn't just fooling around. He was doing drugs and engaging in what the courts would certainly view as unhealthy behaviors.

I had to consider the location for dropping the bomb. I couldn't do it in the gallery and it didn't seem right to invite her over to my place. I decided to call Huey.

"Huey?"

"Abigail! Where are you?"

"I just passed McClellanville. I had an appointment in Charleston today. Listen, I need your advice."

"Uncle Huey is all ears."

"I've got a stack of pictures in my hot little hands that would take the wind out of Johnny Cochran."

"And I assume that these photographs are of Rebecca's Rat?"

"And his paramour. Huey, I am not kidding, they are so gross and trashy that if Rebecca sees them she is going to die." I knew I shouldn't have said that. It was unprofessional. But it was out of my mouth before I knew it.

"Good Lord." Huey was silent for a few minutes, and during that eternity I sighed for all the world. "What's in them? I mean, what are they doing?"

"Huey, you know I can't tell you that. I shouldn't have said anything to you. You have to promise me you'll keep it to yourself."

"I am a paragon of discretion, Abigail. You have my word."

"Thanks. I just want to know how you think I can handle this in the most sensitive way possible."

"Well? You could always throw them away. I mean, you could just say that your fellow in Charleston didn't turn up anything, couldn't you?"

"I can't do that. I just can't."

"Well, then, go by her apartment and just hand them to her and then leave. How's that?"

"Too cowardly. God, Huey, this whole drama keeps rolling around in my mind. I mean, I only did this because I thought she got duped, not because she came to me begging for help. I honestly think that she thinks if Nat doesn't want to love her anymore, then *fine*. And I agree with that, but I sure wouldn't give up my home and family unless I was making a fully informed decision. Sometimes being right is the worst thing in the world. She's going to hate me."

"That's ridiculous, Abigail. Rebecca thinks you're the smartest and most elegant woman she's ever met."

"Well, at least she's right about *something*."

"Abigail! Hubris!"

"Sorry. Joke, joke. But let me make a little prediction. She's going to blame me, Huey. I've seen it happen thousands of times."

"The old shoot the messenger. You know, Abigail. This *is* rather a sticky wicket, isn't it?"

"I love it when you do your Rumpole, Huey. Help me figure this out. Huey? Huey?"

The phone went dead. We had lost our connection. I tried redialing him, but I couldn't get any service.

The dead zone. Huge sixteen-wheelers zoomed by, and it was all I could do not to be consumed by the fact that I was traveling the same piece of road that had claimed the life of my son.

When other people traveled Highway 17, heading north from Mount Pleasant, they thought of Boone Hall Plantation, Brookgreen Gardens, Hobcaw Barony or all the beautiful places to visit that give the Lowcountry its unique reputation of grace and splendor. In contrast there was the rustic home cooking of Seewee Restaurant, the great charm of the shops on the waterfront at Georgetown and all the seafood restaurants at Murrell's Inlet. But I rarely thought about those places. I thought about my own agony.

I tried to move away from my dark thoughts, remembering that when I was a child my father would take me to the Hammock Shops at Pawleys just to swing and to have an ice cream cone. Even today I knew lots of people who would drive from Columbia or Greenville only to have dinner at Louis's Fish Camp, then spend the night in a hotel or a friend's condo, take an early morning walk on the beach, drinking in the salty air before leaving the fantasy. Oh, yes, Highway 17 meant something wonderful for many people, but not for me. I could feel my chest tighten with anxiety as I approached the strip of land where the accident happened.

In an act of emotional self-defense, I tried Huey's number again and this time the call went through. I cleared my throat and sighed, collecting myself so that

Huey would not detect my passing panic.

"Hi! Sorry. We got disconnected."

"Abigail, listen to me. I have been thinking about this, and there are several ways to deliver the news to Rebecca. One, you hand them to her, say you never looked at them and walk away. She'll know you're a liar, but she'll have the opportunity for a private nervous breakdown—but she might do something crazy. So I don't think that's what you should do. Two, you hand them to her and say something like, *Look, this is going to upset you. I can stay if you'd like or you can look at them in private.* I think that's the best bet. And obviously, I think the best thing is to give them to her outside of work in a relaxed environment. Why don't I invite her over for supper and you come too. Maybe the best way to do this will come about naturally. What do you think?"

"I don't know, Huey. What if she's embarrassed that we're both there? Two against one?"

"Look. I'll make myself scarce if it comes to her actually opening them. But I think she might benefit from a man's perspective, don't you?"

"I think you want to see the pictures."

"You know it, sugar. I'm already drooling."

I knew if Rebecca opened them she would show them to Huey at some point anyway. I mean, who were we kidding here?

"I just . . . I think . . . oh, fine. What time?"

The guillotine was hoisted, Nat's head was on the block and he may or may not be revealed as the venomous skank he was, depending on the depth of Rebecca's curiosity and the strength of her will that very night.

At seven-thirty, I pulled around Huey's road, passing Miss Olivia in the backseat of her Mercedes Benz, driven by Byron. They waved and I waved back. I could see Miss Olivia asking Byron to stop, and so he did. I lowered my window opposite Miss Olivia's.

"How are you this evening?" I said.

"We're just running out to get a few more string beans! We'll be right back!"

I nodded and raised my window, smiling to myself. Miss Olivia didn't trust Byron to even choose string beans. In her eighties and she still thought she had to— well . . . what could you say? She was just a pistol.

I pulled in and parked. Rebecca's car was there. Good, I thought, maybe she's had a glass of wine and loosened up. As I got out of the car I looked up. Like the old man down at Mr. Marlow's store used to say, *Low, looks like it's making up a storm!* There was a storm coming for sure, and I was glad of it. Maybe it would wash away the humidity.

I walked around the hedges, stopped for a moment and for maybe the hundredth time looked at what Huey had created for himself and his mother. By slipping away from the main house, and with the magic of landscaping, he had created a cul-de-sac that looked like it had always been there. His house sloped down toward the water, and hers appeared to adjoin his. It was only separated by the courtyard. The architecture of each

110

house was identical but the main difference was that her interior was all of Universal Design. Outside, her entrance had a gentle slope up to her front door, in case, God forbid, she ever needed a wheelchair or a walker to move around. Inside, there were no saddles in the doorways, where she might accidentally trip, fall and break her hip. The windows were all on springs so she could open them with the lightest touch. Naturally, all the sinks had swing-arm faucets, and the bathroom was outfitted as you would expect, but beautifully so.

It must have been a source of great comfort for Miss Olivia to know she was so loved. Forget my own personal life. I knew it was going to shatter Rebecca when she discovered how profoundly Nat did not love her.

EIGHT

CIRCLES

I pressed the imposing brass handle of Huey's front door and it clicked open with an ominous sound, like a handgun fired by someone playing Russian roulette, my life spared by an empty chamber. Rebecca was alone in the living room. She turned to face me and she smiled, her left lip dipped in nervous self-consciousness. For the first time I noticed that she looked smaller; thinner, really. The collar of her blouse stood away from her neck with such a gap that it could have been filled with a large scarf and still have been easily buttoned. She looked tired. Probably not sleeping very much. Or eating.

"Gosh," she said, "seems like I'm here for dinner all the time. I mean, I should have y'all over for a barbecue, don't you think? I can't cook like Byron, but I can put steaks on a grill, at least I think I can."

"Don't worry about it. Huey is mother hen to us all." I gave her a polite hug that always for some unknown reason included a pat on the back. It was a lady hug and one that indicated sorority sister affection. "You can cook for me anytime. I'm thinking of turning my kitchen into a sauna. It's the least-used room in my house."

I helped myself to a glass of mineral water while Rebecca chattered. All I could think about were the photographs (most of which I had kept aside in my car), and I didn't hear a word she was saying. When I turned to face her, she saw in my expression that I wasn't listening to her.

She stopped in midsentence and said, "Whatever it is you want to tell me, just go ahead." Her face was blotchy, probably also from nerves. "I knew something was wrong the minute I arrived. Huey said he had to return some phone calls. And Miss Olivia went to the store."

Huey had done as promised and had given Miss Olivia the cue.

Before I could say anything Rebecca said, "You found out something about Nat, didn't you."

It was a statement, not a question.

"Look, Rebecca. My PI friend in Charleston, the guy I told you about that I've known for twenty years, did a little digging around and found out some, well . . . Look, I'm just going to say it. I have this manila envelope with pictures. You can take them home and look at them in private. Or you can look at them now *or* you can throw them in the river. I mean, it's up to you."

"I knew it."

"Well, unfortunately, you were right."

I held them out to her. Rebecca trembled slightly as she took the envelope, held it to her chest and gave a long sigh of resignation. She dropped the evidence in her purse without opening it, which surprised me. I would have ripped the envelope open immediately.

"You've seen them, haven't you."

Again, a statement, not a question.

For a moment, I considered making up something but I hated liars. Besides, lying would have placed me in the realm of her foul husband.

"Yes."

"Are they horrible?"

"They're not wonderful."

"On a one to ten?"

"For me they would be about a nine and three quarters."

I could see she was bracing herself. She inhaled deeply and searched my face for answers. Was it infidelity? I could see that she suspected it. Did the pictures reveal more than infidelity? To me they did. They were about betrayal at a lethal level. I knew I was facing her down. I didn't want her to throw them away. I wanted her to see what her husband was doing and who he really was.

"Oh, hell! What should I do?"

"Well, I know what I would do . . ."

She sank to the couch and put her face in her hands, her elbows stabbing her knees. I noticed that she still wore her wedding band. Knowing what I knew, if Nat Simms had been mine, I would have bribed his dentist to grind it and fill his front tooth with it.

After a few moments she looked up, not at me but at the portrait over the fireplace mantel of Huey's very serious great-grandfather. He was dressed in the formal manner of his day, but like a spooky painting of Christ, his piercing eyes followed you.

Rebecca's facial blotches had progressed to a deep crimson blush, and her eyes were brimmed with tears. I would not have blamed her for an instant if she had cried all over Huey's silk jacquard couch. The strength of the storm whirling in her thoughts was all but impossible for me to detail. But to describe it in Lowcountry terms, although the hurricane was still off the coast of Puerto Rico, small craft warnings were in effect until further notice all the way to Maine.

She stood up, shaking and fidgeting, grabbed her purse and started for the front door.

"Rebecca! Are you leaving?"

"Leaving? Leaving? No. I'm going outside for some air. I'm going to look at this pile of bullshit your self-righteous, know-it-all conscience couldn't resist shoving in my face, and then I will decide if I am leaving. Or if I am ever speaking to you again."

She slammed the door, and the sound of it echoed like thunder all over the entire house. I stood there in the foyer, unable to move. I was completely surprised by her uncharacteristic fit of temper. I had expected it, I had predicted it, but when it burst forth from her in such an explosion, I was mortified. I had done something terrible and irreversible. Was I self-righteous or a know-it-all? It was an ugly thing for her to say. Either way, the price of my actions would perhaps prove to be more than she wanted to pay. An innocent woman would now suffer tremendous pain and humiliation because of what I had brought her. I was ashamed of myself.

Huey was standing next to me and I hadn't even yet noticed.

"Should we go after her?" he asked.

"No," I said. "Let her have some privacy."

We moved back to the living room where Huey poured himself a large glass of bourbon over ice and crushed mint. I stood by the window and watched her. She was all the way down at the dock and had yet to open the envelope, as far as I could tell. Her shoulders were heaving, her head was thrown back. I knew she was crying like a two-year-old. I felt like a scavenger, something treacherous and sneaky.

"This reminds me of the time the rattlesnake was on my porch. I called animal control and they came right away. They couldn't find it, but after they left I did. It was curled around my doorknob. Oh, Huey! What in the world have I done?"

"We. And you haven't wrapped a rattler around her doorknob. I am a partner in this, Abigail. I take at least half of the responsibility."

"Oh, Lord! Look at her! She's hysterical!"

Rebecca was walking in circles around the dock. I was afraid she would lose her footing and fall in the river. From our distance we could see that the sky and waters had grown dark and the swollen tide was swift and terrible, moving in bundles of choppy frenzy.

"I think I should go and get her. It's getting very dark, Abigail, and any minute the skies are going to open up and rain like mad."

But it wasn't raining, just distant rumbles, and Rebecca had only just removed the envelope from her handbag. We watched, voyeurs mired in a horrible intrusion, as she flipped from one photograph to another and then all over again from the start. One by one, she tore them into little pieces and threw them with all her might into the wind.

"Well, there goes the goods," Huey said with a sigh. "Abigail? Either we have saved her or we have destroyed her."

"Huey. I feel absolutely ill."

"What's that? Who's sick?"

It was Miss Olivia who must have entered the house through the kitchen door with Byron. We were so focused on the scene of Rebecca at the river that we hadn't even heard her approach. Her eyes squinted and traveled with ours in the direction of Rebecca.

"Mercy! What's happened?"

"I'm afraid that Rebecca has been the recipient of some very disappointing information about her husband, the scoundrel."

Miss Olivia elbowed her way in front of us, peering with all her power to evaluate Rebecca's state. "Get me a sherry, Huey, please, son, and don't let her see you. Goodness gracious! You two are spying on her like a couple of guard dogs! You may as well be barking your fool heads off. Now watch me! You have to stand to the side of the curtain panel like I am! See? Not just out there for the whole world to catch you!"

Huey handed her a small sherry; she swallowed it in one gulp and held the glass out for Huey to refill without so much as a *Thank you and another, please?* Huey complied and we continued to watch. Finally the rain began to fall in great pellets and within the space of seconds it was pouring. I saw Rebecca then as she sank to her knees, ran her hands through the water and wiped her face. But then she stayed on her knees, and it was plain to see that she was weeping. At first I had thought she was considering a fatal swim, and I can tell you this much. We were all becoming very frightened—for Rebecca's safety and her mental state.

"I'm going to get her," Huey said. "She's getting soaked to the skin and she'll catch her death."

Miss Olivia called out, "Byron? Byron?"

Byron appeared so quickly it was obvious he had been listening just out of our sight.

"Yes, ma'am, Miss Olivia?"

"I'm going to take my dinner in my own house." Miss Olivia held her glass out for the second time. "This is too much commotion for me."

"Yes, ma'am, Miss Olivia. I will bring it to you as soon as it's ready," Byron said and left the room.

I took Miss Olivia's glass and filled it because Huey had moved to the hall to get an umbrella from the closet.

"Here we are," I said, handing it to her.

She drained it quickly and said, "Oh!" When Huey opened the front door, the sounds of the storm rushed in on wet air. The storm was so violent we may as well have been outside.

"Take me home, son," Miss Olivia said. She took his arm, snuggled into his side and they left.

I watched them lean into the wind and cross the front terrace to Miss Olivia's door, which was actually more expedient than taking the long covered pathway from the side of the house. If we were having storms like this in July, what in the world would the hurricane season bring?

Soon Rebecca and Huey were back. They were absolutely drenched. I didn't want to talk about the pictures unless Rebecca did, and anyway the obvious first step was for them to get dry. Huey led Rebecca to the guest room, offering her a bathrobe and a hair dryer and saying that Byron would dry her clothes. She glared at me as she passed the living room, where I had curled myself up into the corner of the couch.

While they were gone, I tortured myself. *Don't*

shoot the messenger. Yeah, sure.

Byron reappeared with a tray of fruit and cheese, offering it to me.

"Some drama, hey, Miss Abigail?" he said dryly with a little smile.

"You know what, Byron? When you say these things, I am never sure how to respond."

He stood back waiting for me to continue but I was not comfortable enough with Byron to engage him in gossip. Besides, he was Huey's houseman. He put the tray on the coffee table, and sensing that there was no camaraderie forthcoming, he threw his hand back.

"That's all right! You don't have to dish it with me. I hear it all anyway."

He turned, left the room and to his back I muttered, *I am sure you do.*

"I do," he said from down the hall.

Well, that was just Byron and I was as sure of anything that Huey probably sat around with him at night and recounted every detail of his life. I don't know what I thought about while I waited there alone for Huey and Rebecca to return, but I can tell you that the time passed slowly and I was hugely relieved when Byron called us to dinner.

Huey sat at the head of the table and I sat opposite Rebecca. Byron placed a tureen at my elbow and filled my soup plate. It looked like cream of asparagus, but it could have been broccoli or artichoke, for all it mattered to me. We waited in silence as he went around the table serving the first course, pouring wine and water and offering bread. Finally he left the room and Huey attempted to break the ice.

He raised his glass and said, "Here's to friends. There is no greater love than that of a good friend and no greater loyalty than that of a good friend. Their value is inestimable!"

We clinked all around and took a sip. Hesitating, Rebecca raised her glass and said, "Here's to friends honoring each other's privacy and not discussing each other's problems when the troubled one is absent."

Huey touched the edge of his goblet to Rebecca's and then turned to me. I placed my glass back on the table. I wasn't going to quibble over this insinuation. I was going to get it straight.

"Rebecca. You have not known me long enough to know that I would never give away any single thing you ever said to me in confidence. It is human nature for friends to discuss friends. It's the tone of that discussion that counts. If it's malicious, then you would have a right to your bitterness . . ."

"I'm not bitter . . ." She shot me a death ray.

"All right then, your suspicions . . ."

"I'm not suspicious either." Another laser of destruction was lobbed my way.

I took a deep breath and dealt with her as I would have any client. "All right then, what would you call it?"

Huey was on the edge of his seat holding his breath. He hated confrontation, and especially at the dinner table. So did I. Rebecca was quiet for a few moments, and then she finally spoke in surrender. It seemed that

Rebecca didn't have the wherewithal or the desire to have a battle with us.

"I would call it disappointment," Rebecca said. "I am very deeply disappointed."

"About Nat and his behavior?" Huey said.

"Well, of course she is, Huey," I said.

"Of course I am upset about that," Rebecca said. "It's horrible. But I'm more upset about his choice of a lover. Do y'all know who the woman is?"

I kept quiet and Huey shook his head.

"I was never privileged to see what you all are discussing," Huey said with a trace of royal jealousy. "And whatever you may think, Rebecca, Abigail told me almost nothing. Except that she was concerned, deeply concerned about how best to give the information to you."

Rebecca looked up at me and this time she seemed apologetic. She was going to need a lot more spine that she apparently possessed to get any justice from her creep of a husband in a court of law.

"I just don't like y'all talking about me, that's all. You hardly know me. I came here to paint and to get away . . ."

"Yes, we know that, Rebecca. You've said it a thousand times. But while you're away and painting you are allowing Nat to rob you of everything you are entitled to . . ."

"Ostrich!" Huey offered, smiling, pleased with his cleverness.

Rebecca and I stopped and stared at him.

"Honest to God, Huey," I said.

"Thanks a lot, Huey," Rebecca said. And then she added, "You're right. He's right, you know. It's just that I don't want to fight with Nat. You don't know how he is. He's ruthless. If he wants the kids and the house, let him have it all. I quit. And he can have that lowlife Charlene too."

"Lowlife?" Huey said.

The kitchen door swung open. All conversation ceased as Byron cleared the untouched soup and replaced them with plates of tiny lamb chops propped on mounds of risotto, drizzled with a gleaming sauce. He put a bowl of watercress salad on Huey's left and excused himself.

"I'm going to see about Miss Olivia now," he said.

"Of course. Thank you, Byron," Huey said. "This looks beautiful."

"Is she not well?" Rebecca asked.

"No, she's fine. Just a little tired," Huey said. "Now, back to Charlene? Who is she?"

"She's gross! She has a flat chest, a flat butt, barely a high school education, nasty hair . . . I mean, y'all, she's a little redneck nothing! She makes minimum wage and . . ."

"Um, Rebecca, she doesn't have a flat chest. Or a flat anything," I said.

"She has ears like a mule!" Rebecca said.

"No, she doesn't," I said.

"She most certainly does!" Rebecca said with insistence.

"Not anymore, and I can prove it," I said.

"Please do!" Rebecca said.

"What in the world . . ." Huey said, thoroughly confused.

"I have other pictures in the car. Should I get them now?"

"You have other pictures *in the car?* By all means!" Rebecca blurted.

"Abigail, darling," Huey said, "let's have dinner first. We didn't touch Byron's soup and I'll hear about that for sure, and if you don't eat dinner he'll have a fit, and besides . . . it's still pouring outside."

"There's an umbrella by the door," Rebecca said. When we looked at her, incredulous that she would send me out into the proverbial dark and stormy night, she said, "What? I want to see the pictures!"

"So do I," Huey said. "Take my raincoat from the hall closet."

I ran to my car thinking, well, at one point in her life she had gumption, and although my favorite sandals were squishing from the puddles of rainwater and the great crackles of lightning terrified me, I was glad to see Rebecca speak up for herself. It was about bloody time! And who was Huey kidding to suggest that we eat before looking at the pictures? But on second thought, it would take an earthquake to get between Huey and a meal on a plate in front of him.

When I got back, Huey was gobbling up dinner and Becca was pushing hers around the plate. The pictures remained on the table, tucked inside the pages of

People magazine, where I had slipped them to keep them dry. There was a photograph of them leaving the bank and, yes, I had censored the one of them taken from the tree across the street from Rebecca's bedroom. I don't know what had made me pull that one out but I guess I couldn't bring myself to have Rebecca see her husband in such a sordid position. And the one of them leaving the bank? It was bothering me, that's all. There were a few others—less incriminating, but shots of this Charlene clear enough for Rebecca to say whether or not Charlene had altered her appearance with surgery.

Huey couldn't finish dinner fast enough. His eyes twinkled with devilment anticipating what he was about to see.

"Well?" he said, sitting back and wiping his lips with his napkin.

"All right," Rebecca said, "let's have a look."

I passed the magazine to her and she pulled them out, gasping and passing them to Huey until she came to a really graphic one.

"They were in my bedroom!" she said. "What kind of nerve!"

"Let's see, hon," Huey said.

"No, I don't think so," Rebecca said. "I'll just keep this one to myself."

Huey shot me a look, and I shook my head to say, *Let it go, Huey.*

"I'll go get the magnifying glass," Huey said and got up from the table.

We went over them again and again until Rebecca

finally said, "There's no question about it at all. She's had massive work done. Those aren't even her teeth! He wouldn't pay for marriage counseling, but he paid for this?"

"Heavens!" Huey said.

"I mean, I could understand if Nat left me for someone who was beautiful and aristocratic, but this tramp Charlene is the trashiest thing you can imagine! I mean, y'all, she's as thick as a brick! Dumb as a post! She's stupid! She has nothing, I mean *nothing,* going for her!"

"She's got something," I said. "She probably makes Nat feel like the king of the world."

"Well, next to her, he is!"

Then the funniest thing happened. Rebecca began to laugh, which of course, gave us the signal to laugh with her.

"It's just, I don't know, *absurd!*" she said.

"People can be so stupid," I said.

"Lord! She's tacky!" Huey said.

When we all finally regained our composures, I said in my theatrical attorney's voice, "Mrs. Simms? Can you say with reasonable authority that those are new breasts?"

"Absolutely! Goodness! She went from Little Orphan Annie to Dolly Parton!"

Huey suppressed another giggle attack and so did I.

"And these ears are different?"

"Honey? She had ears that stuck out so far you'd have thought she could take off in a stiff wind and fly the whole way to Florida!"

"And these buttoc—I mean her rear, um . . ."

"Her derriere?" Huey offered.

"Yes! Thank you, Huey! Her derriere?"

"Abigail? Her booty, her teeth, her ears, her bazooms—the whole woman has been rebuilt! How can she pay for this when she earns minimum wage? Well, she didn't, did she? Y'all know what? Now I am *officially* pissed off in purple. Abigail, will you help me at least recover some of my money?"

"Rebecca? This is the most egregious and appalling misuse of marital assets I have ever seen in all my years. I will represent you and with pleasure! And on the house! I'll extract my fee from your sorry excuse for a husband as I scrub and polish the courthouse floor with his arrogance and stupidity."

"But call Jeff Mahoney first, okay?"

"What would you like me to call him?"

"Abigail! I haven't ever seen you quite so animated!"

"Huey, baby? You ain't seen *nothing* yet!"

I looked at Rebecca again and my eyes went to her hands as she flipped through the pictures once more. Her wedding band was gone.

"Rebecca? Did you toss your wedding band into the Waccamaw?"

"What? No! Heavens! It *is* gone!"

"Alice Flagg, cupcake. Alice Flagg came and stole your ring. Happens all the time," Huey said.

"Well, if she wants Nat Simms, she can have him!"

"I think Alice has better taste," I said. "Even from the grave."

NINE

ABIGAIL'S GOT GAME

Rebecca reminded me to call Jeff Mahoney to advise him that I was taking over her case. In any other circumstances I would have made the call simply as a matter of course, but I was already convinced her Jeff was such a moron that I didn't feel like extending any courtesy to him. I mean, what did this guy ever do for her? Let's see . . . lost her house, her children, her life? He probably got his law degree online while watching live cams of coeds. And, what contribution could he make toward the win? Probably nothing. It didn't matter. I simply added his name to my daily agenda of things to do.

I got up with the sun and walked the beach. What in the world was making me so cranky? Well, for one thing, I had this intense reluctance to enter a courtroom. I kept seeing myself pushing through the oversized doors, walking up the center aisle, dropping my briefcase on the floor and my folder on the table, looking up, over or back into the face of Julian Prescott and then falling off the cliff of propriety into the abyss.

His face played in my head like a CD with a deep scratch. What would happen if I saw him? The one indiscretion of my entire life. In the daylight I regretted our affair with my whole heart, but there were many nights I would have given anything to have it happen all over again. But I'm not here to tell you about that chapter in my past. I only mention it so that you won't think I'm trying to paint myself as Joan of Arc, some sexless icon of the battlefield. I understand desire and lust as well as I know betrayal and the pain it brings. I've known nothing but guilt and remorse since then.

We were married to other people. Ashley had just died and John was drinking too much, which was his way of dealing with it. I was considering divorce and I wound up in bed with Julian at a conference in Chicago. I couldn't help myself. Neither could he. There was this invisible thread between our hearts, something that in another place and time would have been a beautiful thing . . . We knew it was wrong, that the stakes were high and that if we continued, we would be found out. And, to our surprise, we were.

His wife was devastated, had a complete nervous breakdown, including the nastiest case of shingles I have ever heard described, and had to be hospitalized. Julian was so stricken with guilt that he completely stopped talking to me, saying only that it had to be over. And my John? It broke whatever was left of his spirit and I know it contributed to his death.

No, I had no desire to ever hurt anyone again. My love for Julian Prescott and my ambitious law practice swallowed my life whole. I had not only allowed it, I had invited it. Now I was completely alone. In one way I believed it was a sentence I deserved, that the penance for my sins was to be paid right here by being alone.

If any one thing was to be said of Pawleys Island, it

was that it reminded you of what was true in the most basic terms. You were born, you lived and then you died. And while that was no revelation to anyone, I was always amazed at how many people just banged their way through year after year, never giving a thought about what their lives meant. Or how they intended to make them mean something.

All along the shores of Pawleys Island stood houses that had been there for a hundred years or more. The families who occupied them were the same ones whose ancestors had built them. Oh, sometimes they were sold to someone outside the family, but for the most part they stayed in the hands of the original family. If any of the houses were blown away by a hurricane, an improved duplicate replaced it.

Pawleys Island residents walked land soaked with the memories and dreams of their relatives who had gone on before them. It was an awesome reality. The tide rose and fell anyway. It didn't matter which generation occupied the house.

It was hard not to think about your allotted years with that kind of continuum staring you in the face. Of course I thought about my beautiful Ashley and how I missed him. And of course, John.

In many ways I had been a willing zombie, acting so fine, so well for my tiny audience of Huey and the others. Inside I was dead, thinking somehow that I had already lived my life and lost what happiness I would ever have. And that it served me right. I was waiting for death to find me—that is, until this whole business with

Rebecca Simms found its way to my plate. Now I could feel the strength of my heartbeat and I was somewhat glad to be useful again.

I sat on my bottom step and knocked the sand from my sneakers and went inside to begin my day with a phone call to Jeff Mahoney, Idiot Attorney.

To my utter astonishment, he was a gentleman. As soon as I explained the reason for my call, his first words conveyed certain tenderness for Rebecca and genuine despair over her unbelievable predicament.

"How is Rebecca? Mrs. Simms, I mean. Where is she? Is she well?"

"How is she? Well, I suppose she's as well as any woman could be in her situation."

"May I be candid with you, Ms. Thurmond?"

"By all means."

"In all my years, not just my professional years, but in my years on earth, I have never seen anything to match the ruthlessness of her husband or the animosity of her children. Just incredible."

"What do you mean?"

Jeff Mahoney began to gush like a bloated river, charging over its banks, swirling in every direction at once.

"It's just that I heard all these terrible stories."

"For example?"

"Nat Simms went to Clemson and played football for them, right?"

"And so?" Don't get me started on football, I thought.

"And so, his daughter, who adores him and could

never play football, only wants to be a cheerleader for Clemson."

"What's so terrible about that?"

"Well, the scuttlebutt is that Mr. Simms promised her breast implants to improve her chances of becoming one if she would sign papers stating her preference to live with him. I don't think she's even sixteen. She's in my daughter's class."

"Excuse me, Mr. Mahoney, but you *are* kidding me, aren't you?"

"I wish I were. And there's more."

"I can hardly wait to hear." I shouldn't have been surprised. After all, Nat's girlfriend was practically bionic.

He cleared his throat, sensing his own overenthusiasm and a highly probable lack of propriety.

"Look, I want you to understand something, Ms. Thurmond. My own wife of twenty years just died from breast cancer last month. She was only forty-three. She was the sweetest woman I have ever known and I don't say *sweet* to imply she wasn't a highly intelligent, extremely competent woman in any situation. She could have held her own in a senate hearing or in a bank robbery. I have the greatest respect for women."

"Bravo," I said, with a taint of sarcasm, and then realizing the man's wife had just passed away, I added, "I am very sorry about your loss. I lost my husband not long ago, so I know something about what you must be feeling."

"Thank you. Look, all I'm saying is that there's more to this than met the eyes of the court. Nat Simms had some other agenda going on. I mean, I think it's fair to say that he fell out of love with Rebecca a long time ago. Ask anyone. The stories of his public humiliation of Rebecca are legendary in our neighborhood alone. There hasn't been a dinner party in the last four years when Nat didn't do something to embarrass Rebecca and their hosts. He's sadistic, and to tell you the truth, he was a little frightening. People thought he was a loaded bomb, if you know what I mean."

"I don't mean to sound dense here, counselor, but a loaded bomb can mean a lot of things. You have to tell me exactly what you mean if I am to help her."

"I mean that, for his own reasons, and no one yet knows what they are, Nat Simms wanted Rebecca out of his life and the lives of his children. The conundrum is that I cannot imagine why anyone would want Rebecca Simms out of his life! She was faithful to her family and she never forgot anyone in need or failed to thank anyone who had shown any member of her family a kindness. And she's a good-looking woman. I mean, what *more* could a man want in a wife?"

"I don't know."

In the next few minutes, Jeff Mahoney, who I now almost liked, agreed to FedEx me all the paperwork he had on Rebecca's case. Then he gave more examples of Nat Simms's temper and recounted different scenarios of how the children rebuked Rebecca, and how Nat supported their positions. Jeff offered to answer any questions, anytime, including offering himself up as a witness for a sworn deposition. I said, *Yes, thank you,* to that.

We hung up and I went out to the porch for a few minutes to collect my thoughts. I considered myself to be a rather cool customer. I was not easily upset. My conversation with Jeff Mahoney made me very uncomfortable.

Nat Simms was dangerous. Now it was easier to understand why Jeff Mahoney had allowed Rebecca's family, home and assets to slip away. Simply put, he decided Rebecca's very life may have been at stake and that custody of her hateful children wasn't worth dying over. Possession of her house was not worth her life. And a reconciliation with Nat? Hell, to hear Jeff tell it, Rebecca was lucky to get away with her skull intact.

The more I thought about it, the more angered I became. We knew that Nat had a girlfriend—a tacky specimen to be sure, but a girlfriend all the same. We suspected he had footed the bill for her transformation. Now we had another example of Nat and his promises of plastic surgery. What had he promised their son? Who knew? A trip to the moon?

I came to several conclusions. Nat would have Charlene. No argument there. For the moment, he could have the house and custody of the children as well. Rebecca was entitled to half the assets they held, which meant a huge cash settlement for her. The children? I didn't know them but I knew I could demand a psychological evaluation and convince the court that Nat had to pay for therapy for them. He obviously and in a very methodical manner worked to undermine and eventually completely alienate the children from their mother. Rebecca had cowered. She probably thought that biding her time would pay off, that Nat would come around, that the children were going through a stage . . . she had guessed wrong and lost.

Nat Simms was a bulldog, and this whole drama he produced was still most likely about money and about lust. It was a new trend in the land of divorce and one that I despised. In the old days, a gentleman would never have sued his wife for the house, custody of the children and child support. Now it happened all the time. It was a déclassé intimidation technique.

Nat didn't love Rebecca, and he probably didn't love Charlene either. But Charlene was easy. Charlene was some poor, uneducated woman who probably struggled to keep food on her table. Was she going to give Nat a hard time about going to every football game Clemson played? No. Did Rebecca? Yes. Rebecca told me she was sick to death of football. If Nat didn't want to go to the Charleston Symphony but preferred to watch golf on television, would Charlene put up a fuss? No. She probably opened a can of chili, nuked it and served it to him. Charlene had probably never heard of the Charleston Symphony or stepped one foot inside the Dock Street Theater either. Had Rebecca? Yes. Rebecca loved the Dock Street and the Symphony and had served on tons of committees as a volunteer to organize benefits for them.

The only problem I had with what Jeff had told me was that I couldn't decide if going after Nat's wallet would jeopardize Rebecca's personal safety.

I decided I would do everything in my power to see

that it did not. There were probably more laws on the books and more legal precedent in divorce law than in any other area. I read somewhere recently that a million people get divorced every year. For whatever reason Nat Simms would claim, he couldn't just boot Rebecca out without a dime after twenty years of marriage.

My next step was to call Nat's attorney, the infamous Harry Albright, and put him on notice. I took a deep breath, went inside and dialed his number. I gave my name and the reason for my call, was put on hold, expecting to have the secretary come back and take a message. That's what I would've done. If I had been Harry Albright I would have called Nat Simms and asked him why a new attorney was calling. But his arrogance prevailed and Harry Albright picked up the phone.

"Hello?"

"Mr. Albright? This is Abigail Thurmond calling."

"What can I do for you, Ms. Thurmond?"

"I wanted to let you know that I have been retained by Rebecca Simms to represent her in her divorce from your client, Nathaniel Simms."

"Don't waste your time, Ms. Thurmond. The judge has already handed down a decision and . . ."

"We'll see about that, Mr. Albright. You might want to advise your client that I am going to begin discovery of his financial affairs . . ."

"I'm sure he will be delighted by the news," he said with a little laugh that sounded like a snort.

"Tell him to expect an interrogatory," I said.

"Sure thing," Harry Albright said. "But it's an exercise in futility."

"We'll see what's futile. And I will be investigating his personal relationships as well," I said.

"What do you mean *personal relationships?* Nat Simms is a straight arrow! A family man!"

"Yeah, sure, and my grandmother was a samurai."

Albright got quiet and the conversation took on a new tone.

"Another woman? He never told me there was another woman . . ."

"Well, Mr. Albright, you have to wonder how many other lies he told you, don't you? He sure lied to his wife plenty. But I'll get this all sorted out . . ."

By the time I said good-bye to Harry Albright, which was as soon as possible, he was seriously annoyed.

No attorney appreciated being lied to—especially the dregs like Harry Albright, whose reputation oozed the slime of a tar pit. Attorneys acted on information the client provided, and in the end, if counsel acted on lies, it reflected badly on not only the attorney but the entire firm. In Harry Albright's case, he was a dank firm of one, having squirmed down to the swamp one sleazy win at a time. I mean, his mother was his secretary, okay?

It may have been a conceit to admit, but I was itching to dismember Harry Albright almost as much as I relished the vision of Nat Simms writing checks for Rebecca. It made me feel lighthearted.

I looked around my living room, which until that

moment had seemed like a perfectly fine living room to me—two old lumpy sofas, slip-covered in charcoal ticking, two old armchairs with ottomans, upholstered in pale blue pinwale corduroy, a scuffed up walnut coffee table from the Ding Dynasty, with neat stacks of *National Geographic* magazines from the seventies and every end table sagging under the weight of family photographs that chronicled our lives. The furniture needed Botox worse than I did.

What did it mean that I had kept things as they had been for fifty years? Did I think that keeping my parent's furniture and even the layout somehow kept them alive? No, that was too weird to consider. My encounters with them were for late nights on the porch. I think the state of my décor meant I was too lazy to do anything about it.

I had a cell phone in hand, and my parent's old rotary phone from the sixties sat on the phone table—end of office equipment inventory. I had no fax, no copier, no laptop, no printer. It didn't exactly look like Churchill's war room.

I decided I would use my parent's old bedroom as an office. Why not? It had great light. I pushed open the door and looked inside for the first time in a very long while. It did not have great light. The windows hadn't been washed since I had moved in. The shades were yellowed and split. Their old creaking iron bed and nightstands were still there, made up for company that never came. Two overstuffed chairs upholstered in sun-rotted floral print chintz sat in front of the windows that faced the beach. I mean, we Pawleys Islanders prided ourselves on being "arrogantly shabby," but this was testimony to the state of denial in which I had been living. When I had moved in permanently three years ago, I hadn't noticed any of these flaws.

The bedroom needed everything. At the very least, the bedroom needed to be thoroughly dusted and cleaned. The housekeeping required was beyond my available time. I would ask Byron if he could help me find someone to pull this place together and maybe even maintain it.

I decided to begin the reluctant resurrection of my career by buying a laptop and a printer. Although I was determined that Rebecca's case would be the only one I would handle, I could use a laptop and a printer for many other purposes—shopping, general correspondence and reading about the outside world on the odd occasion when the mood struck.

I knew there was an office supply store or something like it on Highway 17 that would do the job. These were places I had diligently avoided since I retired, and now I was about to be a customer.

I pulled into the parking lot of the shopping center and sat in my car thinking about what was ahead of me. I didn't want to go back to work. I mean, I *really* did not want to print business cards and letterhead. But Nat's behavior was so well, evil. Nat Simms had all the earmarks of a narcissistic sociopath. If I had believed in demonic possession, I would have said that Nat Simms might be an example of it.

No matter how successful I had ever been, this would not be easy. I was in for a fight. Experience told me that Nat Simms and Harry Albright would do everything in their power to discredit Rebecca and see the judgment stand. I knew that the judge's decision was a terrible mistake but at the same time, it was clear that I would have to take this one careful step at a time to earn the win.

TEN

REBECCA TAKES THE CALL

I was pretty well caught up on all the framing jobs at the gallery, so I took the day off to paint. Huey was sweet about it. He knew I was a bundle of nerves. I was.

I was in the middle of setting up my easel and thinking about how screwed up I had become. With each passing day, it was increasingly hard to concentrate on anything. I was upset all the time. In fact, I think I was more upset since Abigail had taken over than I had been when Nat had me thrown out. Maybe that was because I had seen Nat's blow coming and now I didn't know what would happen. The only thing working in my favor was that I didn't have anything else to lose.

I wouldn't say I was elated to have someone like Abigail in my corner because I didn't want to rehash everything. She was the kind of person who would dig and dig. However, when her PI friend produced those pictures, I realized that Nat was a complete liar. Almost comical, really, except that he had the house, the kids and all the money. If Abigail could at least work out a better settlement, then it might be worth it to suffer some more. One thing was for sure, unless there was a huge change in their attitudes, I didn't want to go back to Charleston and raise those kids.

Last night I sent my children emails at camp again. No response. I could see on the server that they had been opened and I assumed delivered. Last week I sent Evan a box of water guns for every boy in his cabin. It was a surprise gift, bought in a moment of thinking I had to win them back. I mean, even though Evan had sided with Nat, he was still my baby.

I called the camp to see if he had received them and they said, oh yes, all the boys were having a wonderful time spraying each other, the weather was very hot. But when I asked the young counselor if I could speak to Evan he hemmed and hawed around and then said they couldn't find him. I knew it was a lie. Evan didn't want to talk to me. Can you imagine how that made me feel?

Sami was worse. I sent her daily emails with no response. I could understand that a young boy didn't answer mail, or maybe he was afraid to because communicating with me might incite Nat. But my only daughter? What was more painful was that I had written her a letter trying to explain that while I didn't understand her animosity toward me, I loved her, I would always be her mother and no one could ever replace her in my heart. I told her about a Christmas I remembered, when she was about six. She had asked Santa for and received her first life-sized baby doll. She was so adorable with it. I would stand in the hall outside her door and listen to her repeat the same words to her doll that I spoke to her. *Please don't cry, baby. You know your momma loves you. There now, that's better* . . . I guess I had hoped she would remember too. But there was no response to my letter. I was numb from that rejection.

I began to paint, and the next thing I knew I found myself trying to paint that same baby doll, undressed, walking toward the viewer and away from something. What was she leaving behind? Or who? I drew in a shadow figure of an old man wearing a hat. The undressed baby and the fully clothed man seemed slightly obscene. What in the world had possessed me to create such a thing? It didn't matter. I had discovered that sometimes painting was like exorcism. It could rid me of demons and bad feelings about almost anything.

My cell phone that never rang rang and I walked over to the table to answer it. It was Abigail.

"Hi! You busy?" she said.

"No, just painting a very strange picture . . ."

"Oh. Well, good, good . . ." She could not have been less interested and began to update me on Nat. "Nat's attorney received the interrogatory, and let me tell you, he is plenty mad too."

"Why?"

"Because of the questions we are asking him to answer. Remember?"

"Well, I'm glad I'm here and not there. Nat would probably be throwing pots and pans at my head."

"The good news is that he has to answer them honestly, because if he lies about anything it could be treated as perjury."

I could hear the excitement in Abigail's voice, but it wasn't like she had anything to be excited about, as far as I could tell. At least not so far.

"You know, Abigail, he's gonna tell his attorney nothing but a bunch of lies. Nat lies to everybody all the time."

"Probably. Why in the world do people act like that?"

"Abigail?" Where and how do you explain somebody like Nat to a normal rational person? I took a deep breath. "For a couple of reasons. One, I guess he knows that he can get away with it. And two, he rearranges the truth so that people will like him and think he's wonderful. Nat thinks it's more important for people to like him than it is for them to think he's smart or anything else. You see, half the time he lies on purpose and the other half of the time he doesn't know the difference."

"Sounds a little pathological to me."

"It made living with him pretty difficult."

"I'm sure."

"I was always apologizing for him. But that same craziness sure made it easy for him to sell a lot of cars."

"I'll bet. Well, I'm gonna play nine holes this afternoon. But I'm on my cell if you need me for anything."

"Why would I have to bother you, hon? You go play and have fun." I thought I sounded kind of upbeat just then and that not only pleased me but I could hear some relief in her voice as well.

"Well, Rebecca, I don't want to alarm you, but the cat is out of the bag, isn't it?"

"Listen, Nat doesn't know I'm here, and anyway, he knows my cell number and have I heard from him in all this time? No. I have not. He's too busy screwing his slut to check on his wife." Then, for the first time since my arrival at Pawleys Island, I really giggled. And Abigail, on the other end of the line (no doubt decked out in black-and-white golf clothes), giggled too. It felt pretty good.

Pretty good until the phone rang again, that is.

It was Huey. He had cracked a crown and had to rush to the dentist. Could I come and cover for him? Of course I would. So much for my painting day.

I changed clothes and hurried over to the gallery, taking another glance at the doll painting. It was beautiful and bizarre all at once. I wondered what Huey would say about it.

"You're an angel!" Huey said on his way out.

"Don't think a thing about it," I said to his back.

The door closed and there I was alone in the gallery for the first time. It seemed very empty and too quiet. Well, I thought, pulling my sketchpad out of my bag, this might be a good time to draw. But as luck would have it, a customer came in, a nice-looking man.

"Hi! If I can help you with anything, let me know," I said.

"Okay, thanks."

Most people just liked to browse, and I wasn't a pushy salesperson anyway. A little while passed, and I noticed him standing in front of a painting of a creek scene.

"That's a beautiful painting, isn't it?"

"Yes, it is," he said. "I'm looking for a gift for my fiancée for her birthday, and I thought she might like something like this. It looks like Shem Creek, and we spend a lot of time there because she has a bakery in this restaurant . . ."

"Wait a minute. Do you mean Mimi's?"

"Yeah, do you know it?"

"Are you kidding? Her pound cake? To die!"

He chuckled a little and said, "Yeah, she's something else. We're getting married next summer. By the way, I'm Jack Taylor."

"Lord! Where are my manners? I'm Rebecca Simms."

He bought the painting and was thrilled about giving it to her. What a nice man, I thought, watching him leave.

Several hours passed and no one called or came in. I began drawing another doll and then Evan's favorite Paddington Bear, and somehow they were personified in a way that was so spooky they gave me goose bumps. All my sorrow was present in those toys. The tourists would never buy them in a million years and neither would any interior decorator I had ever known.

I jumped at the sound of the doorbell. It was Huey. He was holding a handkerchief on his swollen lip and his jaw was very puffy.

"Hi!" I said. "How's your tooth?"

"Uh gawt tho mutch Novocaine tha Uhm dwooling!"

It wasn't funny but I suppressed a laugh with both hands.

"Poor thing! Let me get you an ice pack!" I ran back to his office, where the refrigerator was. It didn't have an ice maker, but regulation plastic ice trays. Huey was on my heels. I popped out some cubes and wrapped them in a kitchen towel.

"Thaks. Uck. I juss hay tha dennis."

"Good thing you have this fridge here. Okay, hold this on your face."

"I haff ta haff a kithen—Uh maigh staave!"

"Yeah, sure."

"Well . . ."

The phone rang and I grabbed it away from him, knowing that if he had spoken, the caller would surely think they had the wrong number.

"Gallery Valentine!" I sang out in as chipper a voice as I had heard myself use in weeks.

"Becca?"

"Nat?"

"I want to talk to you!"

He was screaming so loud that I had to hold the phone away from my head.

"How did you find me?"

145

"What's the difference, Becca? And just who the hell is this *bitch,* Abigail Thurmond? I mean, who do you think you are? You know, my lawyer calls me and tells me you have a new lawyer, this old retired hack, Thurmond."

"What?"

"Yeah, hack. Goddamn it, Becca, you're so pathetically stupid it's almost criminal! You hired a washed-up loser and you don't even know it!"

"Stop it! She's not a washed-up anything, Nat, and I wish you would stop screaming!"

He laughed and said *Whoo yeah!* I could just see him shaking his head the way he always did when he was telling me how wrong I was about anything and everything. I looked at Huey, whose eyes were wide in surprise as he hung on every word. My face got hot and my whole body broke out in a cold sweat, making me shiver.

"You listen to me, Becca. What the hell is this? I mean, *You will please take notice that you are hereby required to answer in writing the following interrogatories, pursuant to Rule 33(b) of the South Carolina Rules of Civil Procedure and Rule 25 of the South Carolina Rules of Family Court . . .* You know what, Becca? I had been sitting here thinking maybe you and I could work things out—you know, go to a marriage counselor or something and try to get back together. But with this bullshit staring me in the face? I don't think so, Becca. No, I don't think I want to be with you anymore because of what you have done. It's obvious you don't trust me and . . ."

Huey was scribbling madly and pushed his note across the desk for me to see.

Tell him to tell his lawyer to call Abigail! Don't let him harass you!

I looked at it and nodded my head. Nat was still raging like a lunatic.

"She wants my income tax returns for the last seven years! She wants all my bank statements! My credit card statements! I don't even know where they are! Do you know how much time it would take to get all this shit together?"

"No," I said.

"Well, let me assure you, it's time I don't have! Just listen to this question! *Have you ever smoked marijuana or used any kind of illegal drugs?* What kind of bullshit is this? Me smoke pot? You must be out of your fucking mind, Becca! And this! *Have you ever been arrested for driving under the influence of alcohol?* Tell your stupid lawyer, Becca, just tell her that if I had, it would be matter of public record and she can go get off her fat ass, go down to the courthouse and look it up!"

At this point, Huey was gesturing wildly for my attention and mouthing, *Hang up! Just hang up!* I shook my head at him. I couldn't hang up because I wanted to hear what he would say next. You see, at the Nat Simms's School of Abusive Behavior, I had mastered the skill of standing still while the firing squad did its job.

"Wait! Listen to this, Becca! *Have you ever viewed or*

purchased pornography on the Internet or shopped at an adult bookstore? I mean, what the fuck is the matter with you? Are you completely fucking crazy now? Is that what's happened to you? You run off to Pawleys Island, and what? Get some job selling clown paintings with big sad eyes? God! You're such a loser!"

"No," I said. "That's not what I'm doing, and I am not a loser, Nat."

"Then what do you want me to think?"

The gallery door opened and Huey left to see who had come in. Huey was thoroughly offended by the language he heard Nat use and by his aggressive tone.

"Nat? You're going to think what you want to think. All I want you to do is answer the questions honestly. That's all. And Nat?"

"What?"

"Please don't call me at work."

"Call you at work? You're goddamn lucky I didn't drive up there and beat the crap out of you . . ."

That was when I put the phone back in its cradle. I just hung up. I was so light-headed that I knew if I didn't sit down I would faint. He had said he was thinking about us getting back together? Did he break up with Charlene? Did he mean it? Was he finally sorry? Was I crazy? I put my head in my hands and considered having a good cry, and then I felt Huey's hand on my shoulder.

"Thoo all ight, honey?"

Well, at least his Novocaine was wearing off. Somewhat. "How could I be?" I looked up at him and I could see that he was worried.

"Nuh, of course thoo aren't." Huey turned his desk chair around and sat opposite me. "Wan to talk abou it?"

"What is there to say?" This was when my eyes started to tear. "He got the interrogatory Abigail sent to his lawyer." I stopped to take a tissue and wipe my eyes. "Huey? He's as mad as he can possibly be. He said I was lucky that he didn't, quote, *come up here and beat the crap out of me.*"

"He threatened you like that? He actually used those words?"

Suddenly, Huey was perfectly articulate.

"Oh, big whoop. He says things like that every five minutes."

"It's not right."

"He doesn't mean it. He's too lazy to do it. Guess what else? He said that Abigail was a washed-up hack. That's not true, is it?"

"Certainly not. She simply doesn't practice law because she doesn't need the money." I looked into his eyes and he added, "She was the finest divorce attorney in South Carolina for years!"

I was quiet for a moment. Maybe Huey was right or maybe he was wrong, but I didn't care about Abigail right then. My stomach was killing me from what Nat had said. The war had begun again, and I wasn't sure I was up for the fight.

Eleven

Rebecca: Bothered by Gnats

Several days passed, and during that time Huey hovered all around me like Nat might jump out from behind the curtains and stab me to death with his Swiss Army knife. He answered the phone on the first ring and kept an eye on the front door. No one would get to me without passing through Huey.

And Abigail? Every time Abigail had a *thought* she called me. She questioned me relentlessly about everything that had to do with the children. When she got tired of asking me about them, she questioned me over and over about Nat and every aspect of our relationship. By the time Friday arrived, she knew more about me and my poorly behaved brood than anyone could possibly want to know.

And on Friday, Nat called again. At work, but on my cell phone.

"Look, Becca, I want to apologize about the other day."

His words were surprising and, believe it or not, sweet. I found myself remembering how much just the sound of Nat's voice had made me blush at one time in my life.

"For what?" I said with as much nonchalance as I could muster.

"For yelling. Look, you have every right to hire

another attorney. And my attorney tells that this thing I'm supposed to answer is normal. So, please accept my apology, okay?"

"Okay."

An apology was unprecedented. Nat could knock over a waiter and his tray in a restaurant—which I had seen him do—and say that the waiter was totally at fault. The water or food could go all over everyone, and Nat would throw his hands in the air and say, *Don't look at me!* I had never heard him apologize for anything in his entire life.

"Maybe if you and I could just get together and discuss this document, it would be good. Anyway, I have some mail from the kids and you might like to read it. Have you had any communication with them?"

I dodged the question, wanting to hear what the letters from the children said.

"Not really," I said. "I sent Evan some water guns and I expect that I'll hear from Sami anytime now."

"Well, tomorrow's supposed to be a nice day, so why don't I drive up there and we can have lunch or something?"

"I have to work tomorrow . . ."

"Yeah, but you have to eat, right?"

"I'll call you back. Okay?"

There was silence for a moment and then he said, "Okay."

Huey was already on his cell with Abigail, and when he saw that I had hung up with Nat, he passed his phone to me.

"Rebecca?"

"Yep. Hey, Abigail."

"Nat called? What did he say?"

"He said he wants to have lunch tomorrow to talk about the interrogatory."

"Ha! No way." Abigail laughed and added, "But, this is typical. He just wants you to remove any questions that might make him look like the skunk he is, that's all. He doesn't want to be convicted of perjury either! Round one, our favor!"

"I'm a little nervous to see him, Abigail."

"You're *not* going to see him," she said.

"He has mail from the kids. I want to see it."

"He does? Hmm. I want to see it too. It could be very interesting for the family court judge. But I don't want you in harm's way. I mean, Rebecca, Nat has a handgun. So, let's be serious about this. And he's volatile. Who knows what he might do?"

"I'm going to call him back and tell him that I'll have lunch with him at Louis's Fish Camp. I'll be fine. Nat's not gonna shoot me. Are you kidding? That would ruin his whole plan!"

Huey, who was standing by, could contain himself no longer.

"I'll be at the next table," he said. "Just let him try to make a scene. I can handle him. I have a black belt, you know."

This was the comic relief we needed. The vision of Huey in an all-white kung fu outfit was pretty funny.

"Well, it's been a while, I'll admit."

"What's he saying?" Abigail said.

Huey took back his phone. If there was one truism about cell phones, it was that everyone seemed to think it was necessary to scream into them. If you were within ten feet of the thing, you could hear everything on both sides of the conversation. Stupid.

"I said, I have a black belt, that I will be at the next table and that if Nat so much as raises his voice above a normal tone for one second, I will stop him."

I could hear Abigail clearly say, *What are you gonna do, Huey? Karate chop his salad?*

Before the day was out, we had a plan. Abigail and Huey would be in the restaurant. I was to say nothing about my knowledge of Charlene, nothing about the private investigator, and nothing about the pictures. I was to listen to Nat, hear him out and tell him that I would talk it over with my attorney and let him know.

"If you don't think you can handle it, Rebecca," Huey said, "I mean, that if you think you're going to be shaky from nerves or something, I can give you a little something."

"Like what?"

"An Ativan."

"Ativan? Oh, Lord! Listen, I took a half of one of those things one time and I slept for twenty-two hours. I'm not good with drugs," I said. "And y'all? I feel a lot better knowing you'll be there. I'll be okay, really. He's not going to get to me. Don't worry."

"I worry about everything," Abigail said.

"So do I," Huey said.

153

Me too, I thought.

I went back to Claudia's condo, thinking I would spend Friday night with take-out food, just painting. Huey wanted Abigail and me, to come for dinner to make a war plan, to role-play it, and go over it until it seemed like nothing to go through a lunch date with the man who had betrayed me and caused me the most unspeakable pain I had ever felt. I thanked Huey and declined.

I called Nat; he didn't pick up his cell, and I left a message to meet me at Louis's at one. I was glad he didn't pick up. The anticipation of seeing him tomorrow had not done a single thing for my appetite or my artistic ambitions.

I decided to continue being miserable by going online and looking at the Web sites of my children's camps. Every day they posted new pictures so parents could follow their children's camping experience. Sure enough, there were pictures of Evan in a canoe with another boy, smiling and waving their paddles and another of him helping a fellow camper blow out the candles on his cake. At Sami's camp, there were pictures of them in some kind of dramatic production and another of her on a tennis court. I sent them both emails, knowing they would go unanswered.

I couldn't make myself feel better, so I decided a hot shower might do the trick. Sometimes it was best to end the day earlier rather than later. I looked in the bathroom mirror and saw someone I barely recognized. I was pale and gaunt, as though I had been in bed for a month, suffering high fever and flu. There were purple splotches under my eyes, the kind I got from lack of sleep. My stringy hair needed to be shaped. It was the middle of the summer and I had no tan. I looked just like the submissive, weak, washed-up housewife he thought I was. I could hear his voice.

There's nothing, do you hear me, nothing you do that I can't hire someone else to do! Your services are no longer required!

I had cried a river when he said that to me and I thought those words would ring in my ears forever. Worse, when he had said them, I had believed him. I was a housekeeper, a driver, a cook, a nag.

That was then. I was not that woman any longer.

I thought more about my appearance while I examined my teeth and gums. I could have called Abigail and asked her to borrow some power clothes, something black that would indicate my new strength. I decided, no, let him think whatever he wants to think. He would find out soon enough that he had taken advantage of me for the last time.

On the other hand, why was I worried about how Nat thought I looked? Was there still some part of me that wanted to be attractive to him? Of course there was. It was only normal. How many songs were written about how the one who fell out of love would regret the good thing they had lost? Hundreds. Did I really want Nat to see me looking this bad? Yes, I did. The other side of me, the victim side, wanted him to see the ravages of his inhumanity. I wanted him to suffer like I had, to doubt himself and to feel guilt and shame and for once in his miserable double dealing existence on this earth, I wanted him to see what a horrible person he was. Would he? Probably not.

Abigail was right. I would be well advised to tell him nothing and just listen to what he had to say. Play the mouse that he thought I was.

I never got into the shower. Instead, I walked out onto Claudia's balcony and listened to the night sounds of the ocean roaring in and pulling away. I wondered if I would have the well of strength I needed when I saw him. I would have to exercise serious self-control. Would I want to throw something at him or slap him and call him a conniving bastard for taking my home and children away from me? For telling me I was a bad mother and making the children believe it? And me! I had believed it too! Or would I want to break down, weep like a pathetic fool and beg him to tell me why he had done these terrible things to me? God knows, another woman was no reason to behave the way he had.

My hair was wet from the spray of the ocean. I didn't care. I didn't want to paint anymore that night. Or eat. I decided to open a bottle of wine and just drink the entire thing myself. Or not.

What was it I wanted besides money? I knew then, right then on Claudia Kelly's balcony, that what I wanted was revenge. It wasn't necessarily custody or the house. It was revenge.

I wanted to humiliate Charlene. I wanted to slap her

as hard as I could. I wanted to bankrupt Nat. I wanted to see him on the corner washing windshields for tips. I wanted my children to hate Nat's guts and love me completely. And I wanted my nice children to replace the aliens who had taken over their minds. How all these things would come to be remained a mystery, but there was no doubt that the thought of them made me hugely satisfied.

I thought I would have had trouble sleeping, but I guess the long drink of salt air had worked its charms. I slept more soundly than I had in weeks. Maybe, I told myself as I brushed my teeth in the morning, it was because a mission had materialized in addition to a plan. Revenge. Instead of dreading lunch, I couldn't wait to get there.

I dressed, wearing a pair of tan cotton pants and a lightweight blue sweater set and brown sandals. The weather report said it was going to be hot and steamy, and I thought, this is news? I blew out my hair and pulled it back in a clamp. I looked all business and not like someone trying to regain the affection of their estranged husband. No cologne. No makeup, except for lip gloss.

I went into the gallery, where Abigail and Huey were drinking Cokes. They were in Huey's office but with his door opened wide, and even from where I was, I knew they were talking about me. Huey was gesturing like a traffic cop at rush hour.

"Morning!" I said. "What are y'all talking about?"

Abigail turned to see me and said, "You, Rebecca!

What else? Please tell Huey to relax."

"Now, Abigail, don't get me started," Huey said, adding, "Good morning, sweetheart. How did you sleep? Probably not at all. Heaven knows, I didn't."

God love Huey. Ever since he had taken me in, his nicknames for me became more familial with each day that passed. At this point I was practically his little sister.

"Actually," I said, "I slept like a bag of stones. I feel like a million dollars today."

"Well, our precious Baby Huey is a Nervous Nellie," Abigail said, smiling. "I think he needs an Ativan worse than he thought you might."

"Nellie indeed," Huey said to Abigail. "Pejorative remarks from you, missy, don't help a thing!" He turned back to me. "Are you really all right? My God, it's like David and Goliath! Have you got your sling-shot?"

I went up to Huey, who was literally wringing his hands, got up on my tiptoes and kissed his cheek.

"Know what? When I first met you, I thought how wonderful it would have been to have someone like you be my uncle or brother. But I think *best friend of my entire life* is accurate and true. You really are, Huey. Honest."

Abigail narrowed her eyes at me. "And? What am I? Chopped li-vah?"

"No! You're a hundred pounds of caviar!"

"Beluga?" Huey said. "God, I crave it! On little hot blinis with crème fraîche . . . what?"

We all laughed and hugged, and the conspiracy of three was official, the musketeer bond of legend was reborn and we realized how much we cared about each other. Victory was possible and more likely so because there was shared conviction, tenacity and enthusiasm. I hoped.

"So, who's watching the store today?" I said. "Can't close for two hours on a Saturday! Gosh! I didn't even think about it . . ."

"Not to worry!" Abigail said. "Miss Olivia and Byron. They should be here any minute."

Within the hour, they arrived and I was just about to receive some advice from Miss Olivia when Abigail launched into a discussion with Byron about getting some help with her house.

"What y'all think, Missis Abigail? Juss cause I be black dat I know all de housekeepers in de whole entire state ob Sout Ca-lina?" Byron did a little soft-shoe and began to sing "Ol' Man River" in his deepest baritone.

"I'll pay you a finder's fee," she said.

"I'd prefer a percentage of the first year's salary," Bryon said without batting an eye.

"Fine. Whatever."

"Done," he said. They shook hands, leaving the details for later. "Give me a week."

I looked at Abigail and we just shook our heads, smiling. Byron was such a character.

"Come with me, dear," Miss Olivia said, taking my arm.

We walked over to the framing area. I didn't know

how much she knew about my story, so I was on guard. She plopped her handbag on the table, perched herself on a stool and straightened herself as tall as she could.

"Now tell me," she said. "You're having lunch with your, your . . ."

"Nat," I said.

"Yes. With Nat?"

"Yes, ma'am."

"And what do you expect to come of it?" Although her blue eyes were faded with age, her ability to zone in on something was not.

"He has some mail from the children he promised to bring."

"Ah ha! Okay! And what does he want from you that Abigail cannot settle with his attorney?"

"Nothing." She had me.

"So then, he wants to see you face-to-face."

"I guess so."

"I see. And you want to see him?"

"Yes, ma'am, I guess I do."

She sighed and put her hand across her chest. "Lord, child, just don't go to meet him expecting much."

"What do you mean?"

"I mean just that. If you don't have big expectations, you can't be disappointed. So expect him to forget to bring the mail, expect him to be less appealing than you thought he would be and expect him to act ugly."

"You're right, of course."

"And Rebecca dear," she said and held up a finger in warning, "don't incite his temper because you don't want to be embarrassed in public. There's just nothing worse."

"You're right. Thank you, Miss Olivia. My own mother could never have given me such thoughtful advice."

I turned to see that Huey and Abigail were gone and Byron was tapping his wristwatch.

"You'd better hustle your bustle, Miss Rebecca, or you're gonna be late."

"Gosh! You're right!"

When I got to the porch of Louis's restaurant, Nat was already at his table. Ordinarily, I loved outdoor meals, but I had a lump in my throat the size of a walnut. I didn't know how I could eat at all.

Huey and Abigail were behind my seat, reading their menus, pretending not to notice me noticing them.

"Hi," I said.

Nat looked up to see me. He didn't stand to say hello. He looked irritated and we hadn't even said two words to each other yet.

"Hello, Becca," he said and managed to squeeze out a halfhearted smile. "Have you lost weight?"

"A little," I said.

"Sit down," he said. "This place looks like it's probably pretty good."

I sat, not waiting for him to have the manners to hold my chair. "It's Louis's. Remember him from Charleston?"

"Oh, yeah," he said, as his dim bulb went on. "That was a great restaurant!"

"Yeah. This is my favorite place."

"Come here with your boyfriend?"

"That is such a stupid thing for you to say, Nat."

He laughed his *heh heh heh* laugh and it made my skin crawl. I glanced over the menu. Things were not off to a good beginning.

The waiter appeared to take our orders.

"I'll have the Vidalia Vichyssoise and the Tuna Nicoise," I said.

"Whaddya fuckin' French now?"

He muttered this loud enough for the waiter to hear and then looked at him to see if he thought he was funny. The waiter did not think Nat was funny. My face got hot.

"I'll have the She-Crab Soup and the BBQ sandwich, but bring me a beer too, okay, pal? Whatever you got on tap is fine."

"Sure thing, *pal*," the waiter said and looked back to me, rolling his eyes. "And a beverage for you, ma'am?"

"Iced tea, please, sweet."

I was mortified.

The waiter brought our drinks and put a breadbasket in between us. Nat dove in, taking a biscuit and slathering it with butter, shoved it in his mouth and continued talking, spitting crumbs at me. I wiped my face and pretended to listen, but for some reason I only heard every few words that he said. I was fixated on his table manners and his lack of polish in general. Did he really think the waiter would like him using the F word? So far, he was acting like a coarse, ill-bred creep who didn't have a care in the world about anyone but himself.

Our soup arrived and I watched in amazement as he slurped and smacked the first few bites. Did he always eat like a pig? No! Well, maybe he did.

"This is not half bad," he said. "So what do you think?"

"About what?"

"Aren't you listening, Becca?"

"Sorry, I was a little distracted, that's all. Tell me again what you said?"

"Jesus!" he hissed. "I said, *some of the questions you want me to answer are messing with my reputation.* Is that plain enough English for you?"

I pushed my soup away and looked at him evenly. "They're just questions, Nat."

"So! You and your lawyer wanna play hardball, huh? Is that it?"

He was hissing, and I could feel Huey's radar on the back of my head.

"No, that's not it. Here's what I want, Nat. I want fairness . . ."

Nat slammed his napkin on the table and leaned forward to me across the table and said, "Look, Becca. I could have you put in *jail* for the things you did to the children. And I might just still do it. You'll never know when, but one day you'll go back that slick little condo your friend loaned you and there will be a knock on your door. It will be a nice policeman ready to take you into custody for child abuse and . . ."

"You wouldn't do that to me and you know it," I said.

"Like hell I wouldn't!"

"Lower your voice, Nat. Please." How did he know where I lived? He was having me followed. Oh, fine. I was very nervous then.

"You take all these questions off the papers and I'll consider your freedom."

"Nat!" I whispered as loudly as I could. "Please! Lower your voice."

"Get rid of the questions, Becca, and we'll talk about fairness."

The waiter removed our soup and put the entrees in front of us. Normally I think he would have asked if there was anything else he could get for us, but apparently he knew we were arguing and wanted to get away. I couldn't eat a bite.

All I knew is that the man opposite me was not the man I had loved. His whole face had changed. His jaw was tighter, his eyes were filled with hate and even his body language was different. He seemed more like an animal waiting to lunge for my throat—some horrible beast that killed without feelings for the victim.

"Did you bring the mail?"

"Don't change the subject, Becca. You always used to do that to try and run the show. It always annoyed me and it still does."

"Well, did you?"

"Will you dump the questions?"

"Nat, so far you have threatened me with jail and baited me with the mail from the children. I don't know which questions you want removed or why. All I want is a fair . . ."

"You stupid bitch! You want to ruin *my* name and my *family's* name? There is no way in hell you're going to get away with it, Becca."

"I'm not trying to get away with anything, Nat. I just want the truth to be known, that's all. In all fairness . . ." I stopped there because I knew I was wasting words.

Nat looked at me, leaned back in his chair and took a deep breath. He was about to change his tactics, because the bullying wasn't as effective as he had hoped it would be.

"You don't *ever* lecture me about what's fair, okay? I already told you that I'll be fair with you. After all, you're entitled to something. I realize that."

"Something? Something?" I was on the verge of hyperventilating. I'll admit that. But now, on top of that, I was getting mad. Or going mad. I realized everyone around us could hear me and I didn't care. "How about you dressed up in your Clemson football jersey?"

I hadn't said it was all he was wearing, who he was with or what he was doing. But he knew exactly what kinky behavior my words implied.

Nat reached across the table and pushed my face, knocking me from my chair. The entire gathering of patrons on the porch of Louis's gasped, as though time was suspended for a brief moment, and seconds later there was insanity all around me. People were saying, *Is she okay? I saw him push her! Let's get the check! Is she hurt? Someone call Louis!*

A waiter helped me to my feet and led me over to the bar.

Huey jumped up and said, "See here! You, you brute!" Huey raised his fists, ready to take Nat on. "If you want to fight, fight with me!"

"Hold on, man!" Nat said, putting his hands in front of himself to keep Huey back. Huey was angry. He was determined to avenge my honor and actually had Nat cornered by the railing when Louis himself appeared.

"Do we have a problem here?" Louis said, with all the calm of a practiced rescue worker.

"Call the police!" someone said.

Louis looked at me for approval and I shook my head. "No police, thank you. Just get him out of here."

"Let's go, mister," Louis said, and took Nat by the elbow. Huey was still scowling and right behind Louis. Abigail was by my side. There was no way for them to avoid passing by me unless I ran inside, and I wasn't about to budge—not from bravery but from the shock of it all, I was rooted to the floor of the porch.

"You'll regret this, Becca," he said.

"I doubt it, Nat."

Abigail said, "No, Mr. Simms, she won't. But you will."

Nat shot Abigail a look and Abigail didn't flinch.

"I'll be right back," Huey said and followed them down the ramp.

As Nat left, I went to the ladies' room with Abigail to wash my face.

"Good grief!" Abigail said. "That was insane! Thank God we were here!"

"Nat seems to have a little thing about pushing my face." I inspected myself in the mirror. "I'm okay."

"Oh, no. You go right to the dentist for x-rays. You may have a cracked jaw, a chipped tooth . . . who knows? We document this, Rebecca. We document everything. I'm going to ask for a restraining order first thing Monday."

"Whatever. Let's get out of here," I said. "I left my handbag at the table."

When I returned, every eye was on me.

"Divorce!" I said, as gaily as I could. "He's a jerk!"

Everyone applauded and laughed a little and finally returned to their meals, giving me back what was left of my dignity.

The bill was on the table.

"He stuck me with the bill!" I said. "Perfect!"

"Oh, no he didn't!" Abigail said. "This goes straight to Harry Albright with a letter!"

"Nope!" Louis said, coming up behind us and snatching it from Abigail's hand. "This is on the house! Darlin'? I don't know you," he said to me, "but anytime you want to talk or have a quiet moment, you come on back here and see me. Now, how about some dessert?"

Huey said, "Thank God you're all right! Did y'all see the chocolate pecan pie?"

"Oh, Huey," Abigail said.

"What?"

She looked at me and then at him. "I adore you! That's all."

TWELVE

ABIGAIL SAYS, TRUTH BE TOLD

I took myself down to Charleston for a number of reasons. One, my golf wardrobe was significantly more up-to-date than my street clothes. Two, I had a ton of papers to pick up from Harry Albright's office, which I could have had shipped or had sent by messenger to Pawleys but didn't because I wanted them in my hot little hands ASAP. And three, I had more business at the courthouse.

Mr. Albright had not been pleased to learn about Nat's outburst at Louis's or that I was filing an order of protection, because that meant we would have to have a hearing. Or that it would be served to Nat at work, Saturday afternoon, his busiest day.

"See here now," he said, "do you *really* think Nat Simms is the kind of man who would hurt someone?"

"For a man who's been practicing law as long as you have, you don't know much about spousal abuse, do you Mr. Albright? You should see my client. Thankfully, her jaw wasn't broken, but she's very bruised. I have pictures and witness statements that I intend to use as evidence if we go to court. I still think the smart thing to do would be to tell your client that he may as well open his wallet and divide by two. There's nothing really spectacular about this divorce. You and I see this kind of thing every day. Just tell Mr. Simms to move out, return custody to my client and give her a fair settlement."

"We may come to some settlement, Ms. Thurmond, but your client is an abusive and negligent mother. No family court judge will ever allow her to do psychological damage to those children again. Or put them in harm's way. No, no. It's clearly in the best interest of the children that custody and possession of the home stands as it is."

"Your case is as thin and as shot full of holes as a piece of Swiss cheese, and you know it. But you want to rack up hours? Be my guest. I'm in no hurry. And the law, Mr. Albright, the *law* is on our side. By the way, we're having the house appraised this week. Thought you might want to inform your client."

I was never so glad of anything more than the fact that I had kept up to date with my CLE hours. Otherwise, they'd never let me in the courtroom. I still hoped it wouldn't come to a trial but if it did, I'd be ready.

It turned out that Harry Albright's office was not actually a sewer, but it certainly was quiet. After all, let's be honest here, Harry's client pool was probably composed of Roman clergy and guys like Nat. Sure enough, his mother was at the reception desk working on a book of *Find the Hidden Word* puzzles. Immediately, my dislike of Harry Albright was transferred to her. It gave me pause to halt this intense intellectual pursuit, knowing that she may have harbored some secret desire for the international crown of *Find the Hidden Word* junkies, but I had a job to do.

"Ahem," I said.

She looked up with all the deliberateness of someone who had been watching me in her peripheral vision from the second I had opened the office door. How dare I have the audacity to interrupt her? Ooh, bad vibes abounded.

"And, you're . . . ?" she said.

I felt like saying, *Listen, you old witch, you're only supposed to work on October 31.* But my inner pro whipped out my new business card and said, "I'm here to pick up the subpoenaed documents in the Simms case."

She gave me a long look, read my business card, rose from her ancient chair, embossed with the crest of a fifth-rate undergraduate school, and picked up a cardboard box, holding it out toward me. "Running your own errands, are we?" She snickered.

This old goat actually snickered at me.

"Thank you," I said, taking the box from her. "And you're working for your son. At least his client got a job from his daddy. Have a nice day."

I didn't close the door behind me. Let the old bitch do it herself, I thought and smiled as wide as the Cooper River.

I threw the box in my trunk and zoomed off to the courthouse on Broad Street. I parked and was racing up the steps when I saw him. Julian Prescott was coming down the steps with someone. But I couldn't see his friend's face. My vision tightened on Julian's eyes like a hawk. He was beautiful. It was almost as though he could feel me there because he took a deep breath long before his face found mine.

"Abigail? Can it be you?"

"Yes. It's me. How are you, Julian?"

He hugged me, I smelled him and, oh, God, he smelled like heaven on this earth. I mean, what was this smell thing anyway? Why did it excite me that the son of a bitch who dumped me smelled good? Well, I'll have none of this again, I thought. I was fine by myself and if I felt the need for a man it surely wouldn't be Julian Prescott.

"Well, I'm fine! I am absolutely delighted to see you."

"You are?"

Every bit of shame and humiliation came rushing back.

"I'll see you tomorrow, Judge."

"Okay, yes, of course!"

Judge? Well, that was some fast-breaking news to me. "Judge?" I said, finding my voice.

"Yeah," he said, "after Lila left me for another lawyer . . ."

"She left you? You're divorced?"

Julian looked across the street trying to think of what he wanted to say. "Yes. I'm divorced. How do you like that? I mean, I could understand leaving me, but for another lawyer?"

I smiled at that. He was the same Julian, witty, handsome . . . single.

"You're right. Who would be crazy enough to choose

two lawyers in one lifetime? Go find a basketball player or some other, uh, what are you looking at?"

"I'm just looking at you, Abigail. How's John?"

"John passed away three years ago. Heart attack during knee surgery."

"Oh! God, I hadn't heard that. I'm so sorry."

I watched his mind move along and remember that he *had* heard about it—first Ashley died, then John, then I dropped out of sight. Surely he remembered. It was the buzz of Columbia for a year or more. But it was such an awful story to even think about and he had trouble of his own at the time. Maybe he was just trying to be polite by feigning ignorance. Glossing things over so that we didn't relive our past right there on the steps of the courthouse. But the troubling point was that he *knew* and preferred not to acknowledge it.

"Hey!" I said, looking at my wristwatch. "I have a few minutes. Do you want to grab a cup of coffee? Catch up a little?"

"Maybe some other time. I've got to be somewhere right now. In fact, I'm already late." He looked at me for a few seconds, during which I remained cool and tried not to let my disappointment show. "But it is great to see you again, Abigail. You look wonderful!" He gave me a peck on my cheek and hurried down the steps, turning back to wave, knowing I was just standing there watching him like a schoolgirl. I was furious.

I listened to the click of my heels of the hard floor of the courthouse. I couldn't stop thinking about Julian

172

and how embarrassed I was that he didn't even want to have coffee with me. I had not seen him in years! He couldn't deny that he was still attracted to me. Why didn't he say, *Give me your phone number* or *Do you have a card* or *Are you practicing law in Charleston now?* No. He just said, see you around, great seeing you, girly girl, gotta go. He didn't ask for my phone number because he didn't want it. He was not interested in my marital status. He was not interested in me. Period. Screw him, I thought; he was probably shacking up with some stupid idiot twenty-year-old who had a daddy thing.

I filed an answer and counterclaim on Rebecca's behalf to request full custody, fifty percent of the assets and alimony and the order of protection, detailing Nat's behavior. Then I went to see the docketing clerk to see if there was a court date available near Labor Day. I wanted this disaster straightened out as soon as possible so that Rebecca could get her children home from camp, back in school and into some counseling, which I knew they desperately needed.

Still upset by my encounter with Julian, I did the only logical thing. I went to Saks to buy some "lawyer clothes." I looked in the mirror and decided I needed some "lawyer armor." This was a case for Armani. One black suit, one navy suit, and three pairs of pumps later, I had a gaping wound in my wallet, but I was ready for battle.

"How short do you want this skirt," the gal from alterations said.

"Shorter," I said. Let's see Judge Julian Prescott drool a river on Broad Street, I thought. In my war chest of depreciating assets, I still had great legs.

"Can you ship this to Pawleys?"

"Sure thing," Rosalie, the clerk, said. "As soon as the alterations are done, and that should be by about next Friday, we'll ship them right out."

"Any chance of getting them before then?"

"Sure! If you need them, I'll put a rush on it."

I gave her my card and said, "Could you call me when they're ready?"

"Sure."

"Listen. I haven't bought clothes in a long time, so if anything comes in that looks like it could do the job in a courtroom, please call me."

"Oh, are you a lawyer?"

"Yes. Yes, I am." I thought about it for a minute. I liked hearing myself say that I was a lawyer. I had missed it.

"What kind of lawyer are you?"

"An undertaker."

We both laughed and she said, "I'll bet you are!"

On the way back to Pawleys, I called Everett Presson.

"Everett? Abigail here. Got a minute?"

"Sure! How's it going?"

"Slow but sure. Listen, what else have you got in your bag of tricks?"

"What do you mean? Like surveillance equipment? New gadgets?"

"Yeah, that and something else."

"Like what?"

"I want Nat Simms's computer. If I include it in the request for production part of discovery, he's just gonna . . ."

"Erase the hard drive?"

"You got it."

"You want me to go get it?"

"Yep."

"Abigail! Are you asking me to actually go in this guy's . . ."

"I don't want to know how you do it. I just want the computer, and I don't want him to know we're coming to get it. Don't get caught!"

"Well, let me see what I can do. Anything else?"

"Yeah, it would be great if you could get an undercover cop to sell him some pot."

"That's a piece of cake. Maybe."

"And Everett? If there's a way for you to track his whereabouts . . ."

"Are you kidding? I have this new GPS deal. All I have to do is stick the button under his car and I can tell you how many times a week this bum goes to church. Hell, I even just bought myself a briefcase with a camera in it, and I can film him having dinner in a restaurant."

"The Gadget King! That might come in handy," I said. "You wouldn't believe his table manners."

Everett had no idea what I was referring to, but he was astute enough to read between the lines. "You really want this guy, don't you?"

"I'm gonna nail his tail to the battery wall, Everett."

"And, I'm gonna help. Jesus, I hate guys like him."

"Me too."

We hung up, and all the way back to Pawleys I fantasized about what I would find in Nat's papers. I walked in the house and dumped the box on the dining room table. The late afternoon light streamed in through the windows, highlighting a haze of millions of particles of dust. Truly, something had to be done about the state of my house before I developed asthma or black lung disease.

I poured myself a glass of diet soda and began looking at the evidence. I don't know why I was so optimistic, because once I started sorting through everything, I saw I was missing months of MasterCard statements, phone bills and so on. But at least I knew what kind of charge cards he had and I would simply subpoena the records from the banks. It would take more time, but I would get the complete puzzle put together eventually. The missing statements were an annoyance because that would delay my readiness to take Nat's and Charlene's depositions. But I still had a few friends at the banks and maybe they could speed things along for me.

It was time somebody explained to Nat Simms that this was not a joke. When there was a request for production, you were legally responsible to comply.

I called Harry Albright's office and spoke to his witch mother.

"Is Mr. Albright there?"

"No, I'm sorry," she snorted, in her officious manner. "He's gone for the weekend."

I left my name and number and hung up, frustrated, knowing my frustration had just begun. That was the thing about practicing matrimonial law—the danger of losing was hidden in the cloak of tedium.

I could already predict the future of this investigation. I would find the name of a cheap motel on his Visa card statement, one carelessly used early in the relationship, before the affair was fully fledged.

I envisioned the whole revolting scene. Old Nat renting a room, desperate in a moment of passion. Charlene, a little sweaty from the humidity and reeking of some cheap cologne from the drugstore and the dry cleaning fluid that stiffened her synthetic clothes, hiking up her skirt and rubbing Nat's pants leg right there in the reception area. The smells of curry and onions wafting all around them, coming from a hot plate in the back room. Pale thin children with wide dark eyes, peering through a flowered curtain made from a bed sheet. A large picture of the Hindu deity Ganesha hung on the wall next to a calendar from a local bank. And the dignified man from Pakistan or India or Nepal who takes the charge card, refusing eye contact with Nat and Charlene, embarrassed by the indignities of his immigration life, hating the fact that his livelihood depended on the continuing immorality of his new countrymen.

I could see the whole sordid business like a movie in my head.

Once I found the first puzzle piece, I would subpoena the records of the hotel and find Nat's name or Charlene's name and the room paid for that time on another credit card, probably from one of the banks in the photographs. I would subpoena the bank of that credit card and discover that the statements were being sent to a post office box. Next, I would subpoena the post office, only to have revealed that the box was rented in a fictitious name. On and on it would go. One carefully hidden and then found piece of information would lead to another and another. I would need every shortcut I would find to move this show down the road. Everything was on my side except time.

That was the sordid reality of divorce in these duplicitous times. My father used to say, *Oh, what a tangled web we weave, when first we practice to deceive.* So did Sir Walter Scott. Neither one of them knew how dead on they were. It was my job to untangle Nat's web of deception and I would do it, one strand, one lie, one nasty little detail at a time.

I was startled by my cell phone. It was Byron.

"Hey, Miss Abigail. Do you have a minute?"

"Sure. What's going on?" I took the handful of envelopes I was holding and threw them back in the box.

"You sound aggravated. You okay?"

Well? It was nice of him to ask, wasn't it? "I'm fine—just doing paperwork."

"Oh, good. Well, I found you somebody to straighten out your house."

"Tell me about her. Or him."

"She's got a college degree in business, but she's got to save money to go to graduate school. She's a neat freak and she's a little hyper, but she's honest and works like a tornado."

"She sounds perfect. Neat freak is good and hyper doesn't bother me. Honesty is essential. Who is she?"

"My little sister, Daphne. She's a ball of fire! Would you like to meet her?"

"Absolutely. Send her over. And Byron?"

"Yes'm?"

"Thanks."

I could feel him smiling through the phone. Byron knew he irked me sometimes, and he was pleased to have me even somewhat in his debt.

Thirty minutes later, I heard a rap on the screen door. I looked up to see a skinny-as-a-stick young girl of about fifteen or sixteen standing there.

"Hello?" I said. "Can I help you?"

"No, ma'am! I'm Daphne and I'm the one who's gonna help *you!* Can I come in?"

"You are?" Gosh! She didn't look old enough to babysit, much less graduate from college! She couldn't have weighed one hundred pounds.

I held the door open, and Daphne walked straight into the middle of the living room. She stood there with her hands on her nonexistent hips and looked around. She ran her finger over the coffee table and an end table, grunting in disgust at the tip of her finger. Then she started talking.

"Byron say you live by yourself and that you are very smart."

"Yes, well, that's nice of him . . ."

"And he also say that you probably ain't much of a housekeeper . . ."

"Well, I have other priorities and . . ."

"Humph." Daphne walked up to me, wiped her hand on her skirt and extended her hand for me to shake it, and I did. "It's nice to meet you."

"It's nice to meet you too." I looked in her face for a glimmer of Byron's features. Her nose was small and narrow. Her cheekbones were high and pronounced. Her smile was wide open with the kind of authenticity that made you like and trust her immediately. In contrast to Byron's height and girth, all this tiny girl Daphne had in the way of family resemblance was attitude. "Do you want to look around?"

"May as well," she said, not waiting for my lead.

I explained to her that I wanted to convert my parents' bedroom to an office, and she agreed that it would be the nicest place to work.

"You can watch the ocean while you figure things out," she said. "Byron said you're a lawyer?"

"Yep, that's right. With one client. But it's a good one."

Although Daphne probably had no earthly idea what I meant, from the condition of my house and having one client to claim, she surmised that I wasn't exactly wealthy.

"You *sure* you can afford me? My work is the best,

but it ain't no bargain."

"I think so," I said and laughed. "I'd sell my jewelry to get help at this point!" She laughed with me, and over the next few minutes the deal was cut.

"Yeah, this is some mess you got here," she said. "I'll see you Monday morning."

I watched her walk away back to her little red car, and I couldn't help but chuckle to myself. She was a little ball of fire all right and probably just what I needed to get my home and my business in order.

THIRTEEN

BURN THIS!

It was about seven o'clock Saturday night when Everett called. I was so deep in thought and focused on preparing subpoenas that the ring of my cell phone scared me half to death.

"Everett?"

"Got it!"

"What? The computer?"

"Yep!"

"You're the best! Okay, so now we have to get it to a technician who can copy the hard drive and tell us what's on it!"

"Already did that!"

"And . . . ?"

"Pay dirt! The mother lode! Porn sites, teen chat

rooms, you name it, we got it!"

"Oh, Everett! You're wonderful!"

"All in the line of duty, Ms. Thurmond. And, I returned his computer. He'll never know, except that I left one wire unhooked. Let him sweat a little, right?"

"Suits me."

"I can bring it to you Monday morning, if you'd like. I'm playing golf at Diamond Back up on the north end of Myrtle Beach, so I'll be in the neighborhood. I loaded all the data on an old computer I had in the gadget museum."

"Your garage?"

"Yup. Wait until you see . . ."

"You know what? I'm so glad you did all this. It's one less thing for me to handle."

"Hey, I know you're flying solo on this mission . . ."

"Well, pretty soon I'm gonna have to make you a partner!"

I thanked Everett again, we said good-bye and I figured it was probably time to call Rebecca. She answered and I didn't like the sound of her voice.

"What's the matter, Rebecca? It's me, Abigail."

"Oh, God, Abigail . . ." Her voice was cracking and she began to sob.

"What's the matter? What is it?"

"I called . . . I called the kids at camp and they told me that Nat had . . . Nat's attorney called them . . . he said I couldn't talk . . ."

"To your own children? What is he? Crazy?"

"And they didn't *want* to talk to me!"

182

"That's even more insane." I listened to Rebecca cry her heart out for a few minutes, and then I said, "I'm coming to pick you up. You gotta get out of that condo. I'll get a pizza and we can talk it all out. Besides, I have a load of stuff to show you."

"Okay."

By the time I got there, I was so mad I wanted to pound Nat Simms and Harry Albright into a bloody pulp. How dare they do such a thing? I knew how. Intimidate the witness. They would do what they wanted and see what they could get away with. I could take care of this with a phone call to Mr. Albright Monday morning and another one to the camp. But in the meantime, Rebecca was stinging from Nat's cruelty and black and blue from his stupidity. She was so uninformed about the law that she probably thought if Harry Albright made that phone call, it was legal to do it. And worse, that she deserved it.

I rang Rebecca's doorbell, and she answered it, looking absolutely dreadful.

"I hate his guts," she said. "And his lawyer's guts too."

"That's the spirit! So do I. Go wash your face," I said, "and let's get out of here."

"Fine."

While I waited, I looked around. There were watercolors in various stages of completion spread all over her table. I stared at them in disbelief. Even though they were drawings and paintings of children's toys, they were startling in a way I had never seen. I was certainly no art critic, but any simpleton could see that these images took Rebecca's work out of the world of commercial decorative art and into another realm.

"Rebecca?"

She came out of her bedroom and down the hall, turning out lights behind her.

"Oh!" she said and began scooping them up to put away from prying eyes like mine. "What do you think?"

"I think they're pretty stunning. You know, we should ask Huey of course, but I think we should show them to someone at the Gibbes, girl."

"Seriously?"

"Yeah, I do. I mean, doesn't South Carolina have a watercolor society?"

"Gosh, I don't even know. Probably."

"Wait! Yes, they do! You should join it. They have shows all over the place and awards that come in the form of cash." We looked at each other, and Rebecca threw her hands in the air as if to say, *Why not?* "Come on. My car is probably reeking of pepperoni."

On the way to my house, I explained to Rebecca that Harry Albright and Nat Simms had no authority whatsoever to stop her from talking to her children.

"First of all, I'm not playing tiddlywinks here with Nat and his Mr. Albright. That Nat was granted temporary custody and the house is a bullshit deal, which will be corrected by the courts. He got his order of protection today, so at least you don't have to worry about Nat bothering you in person for a while. And I think it's time for me to rattle his cage about his answer to our interrogatory."

I told her that I had filed the answer and counterclaim and that we were looking at the week before Labor Day as a court date. Of course, even in a best-case scenario, it could still take a while for it all to be final. She just listened and didn't say much at all. Maybe I was waiting to be thanked? How silly of me.

We pulled up in the yard and got out. Miss Salt Air had almost every single light on. It surprised me how alive and welcoming my house was. It was a monument to my family's history, and while it had always been a vacation home, now it was something else. My permanent residence and a place of refuge. It welcomed Rebecca the same way it did me.

"What a great house," she said, echoing my feelings.

After all, some houses had personalities that bordered on human.

"Thanks," I said. "Been in the family for a jillion years."

We climbed the stairs and went in through the kitchen door. I put the pizza on the counter and set the oven temperature to warm.

"I love funky old houses," she said. "You're on the ocean, right?"

"Yep."

As though she was invisibly summoned, she was already moving toward the front porch. I knew Rebecca was about to fall under the spell of Pawleys Island's wizardry.

I put two slices of pizza on plates, grabbed two diet sodas from the refrigerator and slid the pizza box into the oven. "Wanna eat on the porch?" I called out.

There was no answer, so I went through the living room and opened the screen door. There was Rebecca, leaning over the banister, watching the ocean recede with its musical pattern of swooshing the shore with silver and foam and then whispering good-bye as it pulled away for the night. Inch by inch, the beach widened. There was the beginning of a moonrise. It was going to be a beautiful night.

"Wanna eat out here?"

"Absolutely! This is fabulous!"

She followed me to the kitchen and then back outside. The porch had no table, so we pulled two rockers up to the rails and put our feet up, balancing our plates and drinks the best we could. These minor inconveniences were well worth it, just to have the time to sit in the evening breeze, watch the day slip away as the skies grew dark and listen to the movement of the tide. I thought for a moment that a table would be awfully nice to have out here and made a note to be on the lookout for something suitable. But who would come and sit at it besides me? Rebecca? Huey? God, the population of my world has shrunk to the size of a peanut, I thought.

I took a bite of the pizza and wiped the grease from my mouth with a paper towel.

"Not exactly like dinner with Huey, huh?"

"No, but this is great too," she said.

"Yeah, every summer of my life was spent on this porch."

"Must've been wonderful."

"It was." That was all it took to send me down memory lane. "But things have changed here. When I was a teenager, there was a pavilion where we would all go to dance and listen to music. I'll never forget the summer I learned to shag. We were always sunburned . . ."

"Yeah, you're from the baby oil and iodine generation."

"Go easy now," I said. "And all the girls wore these liberty print shirtwaist dresses made by Ladybug. Or David Ferguson Bermudas with starched shirts all tucked in. We all smelled like Noxzema and Youth Dew."

"What's that?"

"Never mind, you're too young to appreciate the fine details of life before ceramic hair straighteners."

"No, I'm not—I've heard about orange juice cans and Dippity-Do!"

"Yeah, probably in an anthropology class! Come on, you want another slice?"

"No, I'm stuffed, thanks."

I took the plates back to the kitchen, put them in the sink and turned off the oven. I didn't feel like eating either. The whole thing with Nat and Rebecca's kids made my stomach tighten, and the yet-to-be-seen information on his computer's hard drive was another bomb. I had to tell Rebecca about it, and I wasn't looking forward to it.

I put on a pot of decaffeinated coffee and went back outside, turning off the overhead porch lights, leaving the fans turning just enough to stir the air.

"So, Rebecca? We have to talk about something."

"Sure, what?" She sat back in her rocker and put her feet back up on the rail.

As the sun sank behind us, I was quiet for a few moments. The blue dark of night produced the atmosphere of a confessional. It was easier to mount the courage to say the difficult things when you could barely see the other person's face.

"I have a copy of the hard drive of Nat's computer." There. It was said.

"How in the world did you get that?"

"You don't want to know. But let me just tell you . . ."

"No! I *do* want to know! How did you get it?"

"I had someone go in the house and take it, have it copied and replace it to its original spot." I wasn't going to lie. Ever.

"Oh! *That's* nice! Breaking and entering? Stealing? Are you trying to send me to jail or what?"

"Of course not! It's done all the time, Rebecca. Wake up! Normally I would have the wife copy it. But in this case, since you're not living there, I took care of it. Look, if I had tried to subpoena it, he would have erased everything."

Rebecca sighed so hard I could see her chest expand and collapse. "So what's on it? Love letters to his whore?"

"I wish. Unfortunately, Nat's been visiting a lot of

porn sites and posing as a teenage boy in chat rooms."

"*What?*"

"Yep." I babbled on as though I was discussing the weather. "And plenty of trash a family court judge wouldn't like. I say we just sit on it and only use it if we have to, because . . ."

"Wait a minute! Just wait a minute! *What are you saying?*" Rebecca jumped up from her rocker and began pacing the floor. "Porn sites? Teenage chat rooms? Who is this man? This is not the man *I* married! This man stole my house! He turned my children against me and twisted their minds until they were monsters! He's running around with a trashy slut all over town? Porn sites? How sick is he? *Who* is he? That's it! I've had it! Let him keep the house and the kids! They don't want to talk to me? They hate me? Fine! He thinks it's okay to push me off my chair in a restaurant? I quit! I'm staying right here! Screw all of them!"

"Rebecca! Calm down! You couldn't possibly mean what you're saying! Look, you don't want the house? Fine! But the kids? Can't you see what you've got to do here?"

"Yeah! I see fine! They can all go to hell!"

"Rebecca! You're upset and I don't blame you. But believe me, you've got to rescue your children from him! He's sick!"

"No! I am never going to live with anybody who hates me ever again!"

I could hardly believe my ears. I had a very good grasp of what she had been through. But this was beyond my comprehension. What mother would choose to leave her children with someone like Nat?

"Let's not go there just yet. If your children stay with Nat, they will be living in a very unhealthy environment. And, understand this, Rebecca, if we use what I've found as evidence in court, Nat will definitely not be able to retain custody. He'll be lucky to have supervised visitation. So it's a bargaining chit for when we begin to negotiate a settlement. And if you really and truly don't want your children, they could become wards of the state and go into foster care."

"Foster care?"

"Yes, ma'am. That's the law."

"Foster care?"

That pretty much knocked the wind out of Rebecca. She sat down again and even in the darkness I could see her almost dissolve into the slats of the chair. She was very quiet for a few minutes and then began to shake her head back and forth, disagreeing with her own internal argument. She stood and began pacing the floor.

"Look, you don't understand, Abigail."

"Okay, tell me what I don't know." I didn't move. I was going to sit there and listen to her rant like a fool. *Let's just get it all out right now.* And I was becoming very angry.

"Look," she said again, "my own children hate me. Nat hates me. Everybody in Charleston knows about Nat and how he is. Why would I want to go back to that?"

"Um, because another woman, one who is as common a whore that ever walked the docks, will be raising *your* children? She'll be enjoying *your* home, your bed? And if Nat marries her, *your* name? That her surgically improved behind will be in *your* chair at your children's graduations, weddings, baptisms, Christmas dinners and every celebration that happens for the rest of your life? Have you thought about that?"

"No," she said in the meekest voice I had yet to hear her use. "But every time I think about going back to Charleston and confronting them, I feel ill. They're not going to listen to me, no matter what. Too much has happened. It's too late, Abigail. My children will never love me again. They think I'm nothing but a nag."

"I don't doubt that you're not anxious to go back to Charleston, but, Rebecca, think about this. You need to be seriously deprogrammed and so do your children. You know how people who join cults get brainwashed? They hear a thing over and over, and no matter how crazy it is, after a while they believe the craziness is true! Remember Jonestown? That's what's happened here. For whatever reason, Nat has made you and your children believe that they are better off with him, and it's just absolutely not so."

"Well, Nat *sure* did a good job convincing everybody."

"Listen to me. You don't know what it's like to be without your children. You don't want that, Rebecca. And you really don't want to be the one who put them in harm's way. Every night I struggle to sleep. All I can see is my beautiful boy Ashley's face, and I weep for him every single day."

"*How* did you put your son in harm's way? It was an *accident,* wasn't it?"

I took a deep breath and told her the story that even Huey didn't know. "I was driving the car, Rebecca. I had been drinking some wine. I was yelling at him; it was raining and a sixteen-wheeler blew a tire and skidded into us, and I lost control of the car. If I had been completely sober, or if I hadn't been yelling at him, maybe I could have controlled the car . . ."

"Oh, my God, Abigail, I didn't know. But you *can't* blame yourself! It was still an accident!"

"Oh, I blame myself plenty. I sat there in the pouring rain, with his head in my hands, begging him to take a breath, his blood all over me and his eyes vacant . . . He was gone. Just like that. Gone forever." I began to cry. "What will you tell yourself if something happens to your children because Nat is negligent? Will you blame him? No. You will blame yourself, Rebecca. Believe me, you will blame yourself."

At that point tears were streaming down my face and hers. There was terrible gulping and gasping as we cried together in separate rocking chairs. We became quiet, sniffed loudly and looked at each other like survivors of a catastrophic event, stunned by the damage but determined to pick up the pieces and go on.

"How am I going to get through this, Abigail?"

"With me and Huey and the family court right by your side."

"I'm so sorry that I said what I did, Abigail. You must think I'm horrible."

"Forget it, Rebecca."

"You're right. If something ever happened to Sami or Evan I couldn't live with myself."

"Every mother has her moments. Lord knows, parenting children is the hardest thing in the world to do. Especially with a hostile spouse. You've stood enough. But it's long past time for somebody here to be the grown-up and make things right."

"And that's me, right?"

"Yep. That's you. I'm sorry."

Fourteen

Tighten Up

It was eight-thirty Monday morning and I heard noises. How had I slept so late? Then I remembered that I had been up until the wee hours, preparing to do battle with Harry Albright. I threw back the bed sheets and stumbled out to the porch. There was Daphne with a broom, sweeping with a vengeance.

"Good morning!" I said, squinting hard in the blaze of the climbing sun.

"Good morning to you too," she said. "I said to myself, Girl? You're gonna need every speck of daylight the sun throws on us today to get Miss Abigail's

193

house clean. And Lord knows, I was sure right about that! When's the last time these steps got a good sweeping?"

How about never? Sweep the steps? Isn't that what ocean breezes were for? I must have appeared confused. Daphne shook her head.

"Here's your delivery," Daphne said.

"Thanks!" It was the hard drive from Everett.

"Go on and get your coffee," she said. "I got a million questions for you."

"Okay," I said. "Just give me ten minutes."

"Take your time." But I heard her mutter under her breath, "Humph, she bess be drinking *two* cups!"

There was another recognition of Byron's gene pool—his little sister was a wise guy too. Ah well, a dose of dry levity now and then might be good.

I took a fast shower and reemerged with wet hair, shorts, a polo shirt and flip-flops. I hooked up Nat's computer and did a fast check of his favorite places and screen names at AOL. I was shocked. Nat was a very bad customer.

The coffee was brewing and I was cutting half a banana into my shredded wheat, preparing to begin the day with yet another culinary marvel from my repertoire. Daphne stood in the doorway with her hands on her hips.

"Want coffee?" I said.

"No, uh uh, too hot for coffee. I'm gonna just get a glass of ice water, if that's okay."

"There's bottled water in the fridge."

"Humph. That stuff is a waste of money if you ask me."

Waste of money, indeed. She opened the refrigerator and scrutinized the contents. There were two liters of Evian, several cans of Diet Coke, a half gallon container of skim milk and various bottles of salad dressing and condiments of every description whose freshness dates defied my memory. She poured herself a glass of Evian.

"Just to try it," she said. "See if it's different." She took a sip, then a long drink, draining the glass and refilling it.

Evian had gained another convert and I would be the benefactress of her newly acquired habit. Oh, so what.

"Good, huh?"

"Yeah, um," and she continued in a very Caucasian Madison Avenue accent, "actually it has a clean finish and it's light, much like the new Beaujolais." Then she giggled, covering her mouth with her hand.

"You're a stitch," I said. "Just like your crazy brother."

"Humph! That fool? Listen, Miss Abigail, just to let you know, when I was in college? Every Halloween I would dress up in a pleated skirt and a blazer with pearls and speak very correctly. Guess what I was?"

"God help us! A white girl?"

"Worse. A Tri Delt!"

I started laughing, and she started laughing, and then she became suddenly serious.

"What?"

"Okay, I been thinking about this here house all weekend and this is what I came to decide. That bedroom? The front bedroom? If that's gonna be your office, it can't have no bed in it. I'm calling Byron to get his bony behind over here and we're moving it all to the back room. And I'm thinking that you got all kinda things going on and you needed an office last week, so here's what I want you to do." Her emphatic words came flying from her mouth without so much as a breath in between sentences.

"What?"

"Go shopping. Go down to Charleston and buy a desk. And a chair—no, two chairs and a sofa and some bookcases too. If you need to work, you can use the dining room table for today, but if you want people to come here and respect you, you can't take them in the bedroom that belonged to your parents a hundred years ago with that beat-up old bed and them faded-out chairs."

"But, Daphne! I'm not opening a law office here!"

"By and by, we gone see what we see. Meanwhile, either you are a professional woman or you ain't. Now, go do something to fix yourself up and then git! I got a lot of work to do! What color you want this room to be?"

"Color? Shoot! I don't know. Paint it beige. My mother always said, *When in doubt, do something neutral.*"

She rolled her eyes at me for the first of what I knew would be a million rolls.

There had been no discussion, really. She had simply arrived and decided that my life was a sham waiting to be discovered. There was a lot of truth to be said about appearances. I had been arrogantly shabby long enough. That was fine for the house, but not for an office. Feeling something between dread of what she would do and the eager anticipation of a child promised a birthday party, I called Rebecca.

"Listen," I said, "I'm going down to Charleston to deliver a ton of subpoenas and to shop for furniture. Wanna come? We can have lunch at Rue de Jean or something. And we can go over all the stuff that's coming back from my first round of subpoenas. Not to mention all the ugly evidence I found on Nat's computer." I had uncovered lots of evidence there and in the bank statements—some of it expected but one particular item had my attention. I wasn't sure how to tell Rebecca what I suspected.

"Sure, fine. That sounds good. Hey, guess what? You know my friend Claudia? She's coming to Litchfield this week to see me. I can't wait for you to meet her."

"Well, and I can't wait to meet her either!"

On the road to Charleston, Rebecca and I chatted like only two gals off for a day of shopping can do: incessantly. And, thankfully, not too much about Nat beyond the contents of his hard drive, which was disgusting. But, *disgusting* was eclipsed by *need to discuss,* which I decided was healthy for Rebecca, particularly in this case. Anything I could do to strengthen her resolve to take back her children was positive.

"He really said that?" she said.

"Yep! He was talking to some teenage girl from Austin, Texas, and told her she was awesome and he would love to see what she looked like in a bathing suit."

"Nasty!"

"He must have used the word *awesome* a hundred times. And *cool*."

"What's the definition of *cool* anyway?"

I started to laugh. "Interesting question! *Tell me, oh, sage! What is the meaning of cool?* Well, I used to think I *was* and then I was sure I *wasn't* and now I think it's stupid to want to *be* it."

"You can say that again! But how do you explain your overcoordinated style of dress? Isn't that an attempt at cool?"

"Ah! She's thinks she's got me! Look, Yul Brynner once said he wore black all the time because he never had to worry about things matching. I'm cool with Yul."

"Who in the world is Yul Brynner?"

"Never mind."

So, we stayed on course by talking about what a sleaze Nat was, the size of her possible settlement and old movie stars that were decades away from her frame of reference. Which, of course, only reinforced that fact that I was not cool.

We talked about everything except our Saturday night crying jag. I was glad she didn't ask me for any more details of Ashley's death. I was still raw, and Saturday night had made me so miserable that all I did was wind up reliving the whole experience. What possible good did that do? No, feelings were not for me anymore. The few times in my life I had indulged my feelings, disaster struck. So it was a relief to talk about shopping.

Where to start the retail blitz? We decided to go to Morris Sokol in the city and GDC in Mount Pleasant. Both had furniture and accessories for immediate delivery. GDC was our first stop.

"This used to be a grocery store," I said. "I think it was called the Colonial? And Krispy Kreme had a shop down on the end there."

"I wouldn't know," Rebecca said. "It's been GDC since I can remember."

"I should get *ancient and decrepit* tattooed across my forehead."

"Honey, if I look half as good as you do when I'm as old as you are, I'll throw a party!"

"Right. Thanks."

I got out of the car and my momentary thought of an emergency call to Dr. Kevorkian was overwritten by the window displays. I wondered when the last time was that I had actually bought something for my house on Pawleys or my house in Columbia. Ages. I had no intention of changing the porch, the living area or my bedroom and even though I knew that crazy little Daphne was right, changing even one room made me very nervous. But I decided to set up the back bedroom with my parent's belongings and give away the old relics that had furnished it since the Roosevelt era. If I could make it look close to how it had when they occupied it, maybe it would assuage my discomfort.

It took Rebecca and me exactly thirty minutes to choose a partner's desk and a leather wing chair on wheels, two upholstered club chairs and a small sofa, a coffee table, two end tables and a large rug to anchor the whole room. They agreed to deliver it all the very next day. I was thrilled, not by what I had bought but by the efficiency of the venture. I still needed bookcases and some kind of a file drawer. I just wanted to get the job done. And I was ravenous.

Rue de Jean was able to give us a table because we had the good fortune to arrive before the lunch crowd crush.

"I love this place," Rebecca said as we looked over the menus. "Nat would never bring me here."

"Too chic for his blood?"

"Yeah. If they didn't have a television monitor hanging from the ceiling with ball games blasting, he wouldn't go."

"Lovely. Well, you won't miss that part of your former life. By the way, do you know someone at Nat's office who could confirm Charlene's cell phone number?"

"Sure. I can call one of the girls. Why?"

"Well, I've got statements from SunCom for Nat's bills since last February, and there are approximately forty calls every day—incoming and outgoing—from the same number. I'm pretty sure it's Charlene, but this helps us further establish his infidelity."

"It's not like we need all that much help in that department, but I'll make the phone call anyway. Why in the world would they call each other that many times a day? They work together!"

"Yeah, I know. Seems idiotic, but it fits a pattern of compulsive behavior. Most of the phone calls are under a minute during the day, but the ones at night get quite lengthy. And I have MasterCard statements that show almost daily visits to a motel on Highway 17 for a period of almost eighteen months, and the occasional shopping spree at an adult novelty store."

"That is unbelievable." She paused for a moment. "God, he is such a pig."

"No argument there. Anyway, when we have gathered all the information we need I can tell you the chief administrative judge is going to ask us to go to mediation. They hate these things going to court because court is so expensive."

"Do we have a judge for our hearing yet?"

"Nope. I should hear this week. There are four of them. One's a reasonable woman, one stinks—that's Campbell—the other one's okay, I hear, and then there's a new guy. But as soon as I know, you'll know. Getting the right judge is critical."

"Getting fed is more critical right now. I'm having the French onion soup and the croque monsieur."

"Yum! I think I want the roasted chicken."

We ordered and ate and at the end of lunch I gave her the real discovery I had found.

"Okay, I have one more thing to tell you, and this is

just a curiosity at the moment. If we can confirm this, there could be criminal action taken against Nat and Charlene."

Rebecca's face shot up from her plate and she leaned in toward me.

"*What* did you say?"

"Well, according to Nat's tax returns, he earned one hundred and eighty thousand dollars last year."

"Yeah, and he also owns twenty-five percent of the business."

"Which we will have audited. But he spent two hundred and seventy thousand dollars last year."

"What?" Rebecca shook her head for a moment trying to make sense of what I had said. "Two hundred seventy thousand? And on what? Where'd he get the extra money? That's a difference of what?"

"Ninety thousand."

"Holy crow! Where'd he get it?"

"That's the question, Watson. Maybe he took out a loan we don't know about, but I don't think so because there's nothing in his canceled checks to show repayment. I think he's skimming Daddy's business with the help of Charlene. Maybe."

"Oh, my God! His daddy will kick his behind from here to *China!*"

I smiled like a cat. "Acquiring money in this unseemly manner and spending undeclared income is a felony, and if it's true that this is what they were doing, the IRS will be very interested in having a chat with old Nat and Charlene."

"You don't know Tisdale Simms! By the time he's done with Nat there won't be any Nat left for the IRS! How do you think they did it?"

"Do you want dessert?"

"God, yes."

"I think that when people would want to secure a car deal they might have given Nat a check for five hundred dollars or a thousand dollars. The business is called Simms Autoworld, right?"

"Right."

"So, Nat gets a buying customer, they make the deposit check out to Simms without the corporate title and he gives the check to Charlene. Only Charlene deposits it in a special account that pays for hotel rooms, vacations, plastic surgery, et cetera."

Rebecca's eyes sparkled with surprise. "Maybe I'll have pie."

The rest of the meal was littered with comments like, *Do you really think Nat's a crook?* And, *Just what do you think they were doing in an adult novelty store?* And, most important, Rebecca said over and over, *I can't wait to see the look on Nat's face when he sees that everyone knows he's a pathological, narcissistic liar and an abusive son of a bitch.* To that I would reply, *Don't be surprised if he thinks the whole world is wrong.*

At almost five o'clock, after finding lamps and bookcases at Morris Sokol and delivering the subpoenas, we drove back to Pawleys. I dropped Rebecca off at her condo and went home to see what havoc Daphne had created. Byron's car and Huey's car were in my driveway. Had Huey come to play the conductor in Operation Gentrify?

The first thing I noticed was the smell of paint and the sounds of sixties music from Motown. As soon as I came in the back door I felt the tiniest of all urges to dance. I say tiny because, let's be honest, it had been a while since anyone would have called me a rocking kind of gal.

All the doors and windows were open and even from the kitchen I could see furniture piled up the whole way to the front porch. They were having a party without me.

"I'm home!" I sang out, hoping for an answer and navigating my way through the maze.

No answer, just two off-key male voices singing "Under the Boardwalk" with great gusto. I peeked in the bedroom, the former shrine to my parents, and burst out laughing from the sight before me. There were Huey and Byron wearing white painter's jumpsuits and white painter's caps, their faces splattered all over with drips and dabs of paint. Huey was using a roller to paint the walls and Byron was on a ladder painting the ceiling. Daphne was wearing a large shirt over her clothes and on her hands and knees painting trim. Painter's tape edged every angle of the room, and the floor was covered in drop cloths.

"Good grief!" I said. "I wish I had a camera!"

"Thank heavens you decided to take this up on a Monday! Great God! I feel like Tom Sawyer!" Huey said and came to kiss my cheek. I backed up, not wanting to get paint in my hair.

"You're some mess, Huey Valentine. You've got cream-colored measles all over you!"

"I do? Heavens! Byron? Give me a little cloth with some turpentine on it, please. By the way, it's *Rich Cream,* Benjamin Moore."

"Of course it is," I said and shook my head.

"Byron?" Huey said.

Byron looked down from his ladder and said, "You want me to come all the way down this ladder to get a wet cloth for you? You must be kidding. I'm a little busy? Hmm?" He went back to his painting, ignoring Huey.

Byron was right, Huey was acting spoiled. I loved it when Byron called Huey on his nonsense.

"I'll get it, precious," I said and looked around the room for something to do the job.

"It's water-based," Daphne said, getting up to stretch and take a break. "Just wash it off!" she said to Huey and turned to me saying, "So what do you think?"

Huey pursed his lips. "Wash your face! Wash your face! Next you'll tell me to brush my teeth!"

"Oh, Huey!" I said and wiped his face. Then I looked all around the room, which had taken on a completely new personality. It was reborn and fresh. It was clean as a whistle and optimistic. The walls, ceiling and trim were creamy and warm. Even with the absence of furniture, the room was already very pleasing.

"It's going to be beautiful!" I said. "How can I thank y'all?"

Their smiles were wide and satisfied.

"You can feed us," Huey said. "I, for one, am starving!"

I agreed to call Louis's for takeout and changed my clothes to help them. Everyone wanted to finish that night, and although I couldn't see how we would, I didn't argue. By ten o'clock, after a picnic of sorts that included fish and chips, lots of coleslaw and lemon meringue pie, we sat back with steaming mugs of coffee to assess our work.

"Tomorrow we will pull the tape and remove the drop cloths. Then we can touch up after the furniture's in place," Huey said, tapping the tip of his finger here and there, testing for dryness. "I haven't worked this hard in a thousand years."

"Ever?" Byron said and opened his eyes wide in a bold glare.

Huey bristled and made guffing sounds.

"Hush up, you!" Daphne said and rolled hers. "Don't pay him any mind, Mr. V."

I smiled and Huey sighed.

Later, as I tried to sleep, knowing the mountain of disorder that waited for me on the other side of my bedroom door in the morning, I thought about generosity. The day had been a turning point in a lot of ways. The advent of Daphne had brought change, and while I avoided change whenever possible, her determination to make things right and presentable to the outside

206

world had opened up my mind. Maybe that old bedroom would be a home office for one date with the courts or maybe it would find another purpose. It didn't matter at that moment. What counted was that it was the generous spirits of Daphne, Byron and Huey, which had tilted the axis of my world ever so slightly, and that slight tilt was enough to change the way I felt about a lot of things.

FIFTEEN

SHOW AND TELL

Daphne had my credit card and was gone to shopping for curtains. She said, and she was right as usual, that the room looked too institutional.

"Let me just get something light to hang up there until you decide what you really want."

"Fine," I said. Like I had a choice in the matter?

I was home alone realizing how much happier it made me to be organized. In a mere two days, Daphne had lightened the entire complexion of Miss Salt Air by two shades.

I was in excellent spirits for other reasons as well. There were few things more gratifying to a matrimonial attorney that had a client in the right and a defendant who was as dumb as a post. Nat Simms was as dumb as a post.

My nationwide search for bank accounts in Charlene's name or in Nat's name had turned up just what I thought. Or hoped. Turned out that our Bonnie and Clyde had an account in Beaufort, South Carolina. That account sent its statements to a mailbox in Charlene's name in Charleston *and* that sweet little account had seen deposits and withdrawals in excess of two hundred thousand dollars over the last year. Well, what do y'all know? Imagine my surprise.

All these thoughts were swimming around and all this damning evidence was laid out before me in my beautiful, okay, lovely new office, organized that very morning. I had purchased a most useful oversized month-at-a-glance calendar from Staples and notated every phone call, hotel visit, motel visit, vacation, deposit, withdrawal and expenditure Nat had made for as long as the records showed. It was highlighted in other colors to show Rebecca's birthday, Mother's Day, their anniversary, class plays, parent teacher conferences and so on. Without fail Nat had an afternoon of sweaty ooh la la with Charlene and a blizzard of phone calls on all dates corresponding to anything of remote importance to Rebecca.

Just to demonstrate the real depth of the callous depravity of Nat and Charlene, on Rebecca's wedding anniversary Nat had Charlene tucked away in the Ritz-Carlton in Jacksonville, Florida, in the honeymoon suite no less, while she recovered from a trip to Dr. Nip O'Tuck. She had ordered lobster and champagne that night from room service. Rebecca and Nat dined at an

Outback Steakhouse, where Nat was interrupted on three occasions by cell phone calls from Charlene. Nice. Very nice going, Nat.

As the information flooded in, I could've told you almost anything you wanted to know about Nat, Charlene and all their personal habits. No wonder Rebecca had been so fooled by Nat. There were so many transgressions of his marriage vows that I'd been forced to lay it out on a calendar grid like a scorecard just to see who was where when.

But the details were well worth the gathering. Just like a good general knows the time to strike the enemy is when victory is a foregone conclusion, I looked at my telephone and imagined the invisible line between it and Harry Albright's office as a lit fuse that would dissolve its way to Nat and Harry, leaving nothing but ashes in its trail. I was almost giddy as I dialed Albright's number and thoroughly deflated when I learned he was out of the office for the remainder of the day. I left a message with his cantankerous mother that I was waiting for the overdue interrogatory from Nat, and hanging up, I decided to make some phone calls. First I called the family court in Charleston to see if we had been assigned a judge.

A gal named Anice Geddis answered the telephone.

"Ms. Geddis, this is Abigail Thurmond calling, and I am wondering if you can help me with a piece of information."

"I can try," she said.

"I represent Rebecca Simms in the case for divorce

against her husband, Nathaniel Simms." I gave her the case number and the date and hour of our hearing.

"Can you hold for just a moment? Good gracious, the phones are ringing off the hook today!"

She put me on hold; I waited for a while, and finally she came back.

"Judge Prescott has that one."

"Julian Prescott?"

"Yep. We only have one."

"Okay. Thanks."

Oh, swell. This presented a huge ethical problem. I knew I had to ask for another judge and decided to call Julian and see what he wanted to do. Sure enough, his office number was listed with information, and after a short wait, he picked up the line.

"Julian? Hey, it's Abigail."

"I knew that! How are you?"

"Practicing law again. Um, listen, we have a small issue here."

"I heard that about you resuming your practice. Hey, are you irked with me because I didn't go with you to get a cup of coffee that day?"

"No, Julian," I lied. "I couldn't care less about that. The problem is that you're the judge on a case I'm handling."

"Oh. But that, I mean, we, um, that was years ago! Do you *really* think anyone would care?"

Well, he certainly got over *me,* didn't he? I could feel myself turning every primary and secondary color associated with the swelling soufflé of rage and humiliation.

"It doesn't matter, Julian. You know that." My stupid heart was pounding.

"No problem. Give me the details and I'll recuse myself."

"Thanks. I can email it over if it's easier."

"You have email? You?"

"Yeah. So. That would be great. Thanks."

"Okay . . . my email is JPrescott@Prescottlaw.com."

I wrote it down and mumbled, "Okay."

There was an uncomfortable pause and then he said, "Okay, then. You doing all right?"

"Yeah, I'm great. You?"

"Oh, everything's fine. Staying busy, you know . . ."

Somebody had to put a stop to the drivel, so I stepped up. "Okay. Well, you take care, Julian." I pressed the off button of my phone.

I stood there trying to recount the conversation word for word. All I could take away from it was that there was absolutely no desire on his part to engage me in anything more than polite informalities. I felt like I'd been slapped. Worse, I could feel tears burning the sides of my eyes. Surely he realized the price of my relationship with him had cost me more than anyone should have to pay for one mistake. One mistake.

But had it been a mistake to sleep with Julian when I was married to John? Of course it was morally wrong. But the affection and desire I felt for Julian was not a black-and-white situation. It had *nothing whatsoever* to do with John. When I fell in love with Julian, it was as though I had no control over it. It was a riptide, and it never occurred to me that I could resist the undertow. It just happened.

I smelled him before I saw his face in the crowd around the bar. He didn't smell like the men's fragrance counter at Dillard's, okay? He just smelled clean and manly. We were at the old Hyatt in Chicago, and there were twenty or so of us there having drinks at the end of a long day of lectures. I was seated on a bar stool talking to a gal from Minneapolis, and he leaned in behind me trying to attract the bartender. He ordered a glass of Merlot and I remember thinking, *Gosh, red wine sounds good all of a sudden.* So I said, I'll have one too. He said, put it on my tab. I objected and he said something like, *Why can't I buy someone a drink,* and proceeded to buy a drink for a total stranger standing next to him on the other side, a squirrely-looking male, I might add, to prove his point. He said he was feeling generous, that he loved Chicago and who was I?

We began to talk, and for the first time in years, I felt alive. He treated me like I was interesting and smart and he looked at me in a way that no man had ever looked at me before, as though he knew my every thought. He made me feel young and beautiful and, God help me, sexy. Maybe the most important part of my first encounter with him was that he really listened to me. And we laughed, really laughed. That was the beginning of the affair right there over a glass of wine. It didn't matter one whit that we were fully dressed and in the company of many people. He hung on my every word and I hung on his. The air between us sizzled and we never discussed whether or not we would wind up in bed and was it right or wrong. It was like this—if we didn't sleep together, we were going to die. We had a one-way ticket on a freight train to hell.

Yes, he was right to say it had all happened so long ago that no one would probably have cared, but for me, seeing him and hearing his voice made it seem like it was beginning all over again. What a fool I was!

Look, if he had ever made me feel dirty or used, I would have hated him, but for a different set of reasons. But at that moment, I thought it was worse to feel insignificant or ridiculous, and he had just made me feel both in the course of a two-minute conversation. To pile on the misery, I realized that some part of me, some very weak and pathetic part of me, still cared deeply for him.

"Oh! Get out the violins!" I said to the thin air and decided to go for a short walk on the beach.

I kicked off my shoes and walked along the water's edge, letting the cool surf wash over my feet. It didn't take long until I had my emotions under control again. All I had to do was tell myself *get over it* about a billion times. I decided I had too much to do to waste my time fretting over Julian Prescott. Intellectually, I knew it was absurd. Absurd. Yep. That's what it was. Get over it. Get over it. What if I went to my grave as an old lady and I still wasn't over it? That was one of my little issues. I never got over *anything*. I hung on to bones like a mad dog.

Thoroughly annoyed with myself, I walked back to

my house, kicking through the white sand and cut my big toe on a broken shell. I sat on the bottom step of the walkover that bridged my yard with the beach and watched the trickle of blood. Great. I was bleeding. It would probably get infected, I would have to have my toe amputated and never be able to wear thongs again—and, believe me, a thong sandal was the only kind of thong I had in my wardrobe. Julian would never fall in love with me again if I lost a toe. And, and, and . . . it was time for Little Miss Sunshine to buck the hell up! Or at least to get a Band-Aid.

I hobbled back inside, washed my toe and gave it first aid. All I kept thinking was how long it had been since I'd had any kind of minor accident that caused me to bleed, and I realized it had been a very long time. But I could bleed like anyone else, and then a whole new thought popped into my head about, you got it, Julian. Maybe it wasn't that he didn't care about me. Maybe he had just sworn off relationships. Wasn't that what men did? Crawled in a cave to heal wounds? I mean, sure I won the prize for lousy personal life, but maybe he was first runner-up? Who knew?

I was considering it (engraved trophies perhaps?) when my cell phone rang. It was Rebecca.

"Hey! It's me. What are you doing tomorrow?"

"Tomorrow? Well, other than making the world a better place by changing one life at a time through our legal system, nothing."

"Want to drive with me to the Charleston airport to pick up Claudia? I'm taking the day off."

"Sure. Why not? What time do you want to leave?"

"Early. Around eight? I can't wait to see her and I can't wait for you to meet her. She's really and truly a wonderful woman, and God knows she's been a great friend to me."

"Can we stop by Saks? I bought some clothes last week, and if they haven't shipped them yet, I could just pick them up myself."

"Let me guess—something black?"

"Pretty grim, right?"

"Yeah."

After a little giggle, a *thanks a lot* and a *see you in the morning,* we hung up.

I went back into my new office, which I could already see was going to draw me in much in the same way you lift pot lids on someone's stove to see what's cooking. My message light was blinking and, lo and behold! there was a message from Harry Albright. I couldn't dial the slime's number fast enough.

"I'll put you through," Broom Hilda said.

"Ms. Thurmond! I have your interrogatory. Would you like me to FedEx it or do you want to have it picked up?"

"I'll pick it up myself. I actually have to be in Charleston tomorrow, so I can just swing by. Oh, and Mr. Albright, I think we should discuss my client's right to be in contact with the children's camp and her prerogative to speak to them during scheduled calling hours." At least I had the presence of mind to do then what I should have done earlier.

Dead silence from the cockroach, and then, "What seems to be the problem?"

"Under the law, you and Mr. Simms cannot interfere or stop her from speaking to her children. You know that."

"Ms. Thurmond, the judge granted sole custody to Mr. Simms because your client is an unfit . . ."

"Hold it right there, Mr. Albright. She's been convicted of no crime. These children were coerced and I think we both know it. And my client looks like a Mother Superior next to yours and we both know that too."

"You're referring to that alleged unfortunate incident at Louis's Fish . . ."

"*Alleged,* my big, fat foot. There were a hundred witnesses. Look, Harry, and yes, I'm calling you Harry and you can call me Abigail if you'd like, if there's one thing you and I have both seen enough of, it's kids getting used as tools in divorce, so let's back off, okay?"

"We use what we have, Ms. Thurmond. But I will call the children's camp today."

Fine, don't call me Abigail! "Thank you very much." I hung up the phone and said, "Asshole!" The nomenclature was tailor made.

We drove to Charleston the next day, going over and over what I was uncovering in discovery, and with each revelation Rebecca became more and more annoyed.

"You can call your children anytime," I said.

"Great. Now let's see if they want to talk to me."

By the time we got to the airport she was coming to

the same conclusions I had known for years—divorce is a battlefield. The only thing that made going through it tolerable was the knowledge that a solid game plan and intense preparation could—not definitely *would*—but *could* bring some justice and a sense of closure.

We were sitting outside of the baggage claim in my car, waiting for Claudia to appear, when Rebecca said the words I longed to hear. "What in the world would I do without you, Abigail? Thank you for this, for everything."

"Jeff Mahoney," I said and rolled my eyes.

"Boy, you can say that again."

People began coming out the automatic doors, and Rebecca got out of the car to look for her friend. I clicked open the trunk and felt the car bounce as one of them threw in Claudia's suitcase. I didn't know it then, but in just moments I was about to meet my secret weapon.

We laughed and talked our way into Charleston, picked up the envelope with Nat's response, which I did not open and did not tell Rebecca what it was and swung by Saks, where they watched the car while I ran in and picked up my black clothes from alterations.

I was thinking two things. I couldn't wait to be alone and read the papers from Nat and Harry. If they were honest responses, Rebecca was going to be plenty upset. There was no reason to put her through that in a car along with her friend who had just arrived, so my plan was to read them in private and discuss them later with Rebecca and then with Harry Albright. So, unfortunately, they would have to wait until I had some privacy.

Second, I was thinking about Claudia. She seemed awfully nice, and she was everything Rebecca had said she was—very pretty, flawless skin, warm personality, great sense of humor and smart like Harvard. It wasn't until later, when we had updated Claudia on Rebecca's trouble and while we were drinking iced tea on Claudia's balcony that we tripped over an excellent addition to our bag of tricks. Claudia said, in all innocence, "Can I see the pictures of Charlene? I've never seen a picture of a home-wrecking whore."

"Of course," Rebecca said. "You won't believe how ugly she is."

We drove over to my house to get them from my files.

"Great house," Claudia said. "Classic Pawleys."

"Thanks. It's a work in progress."

Daphne was in my office, finishing hanging the new curtains. They were just plain cotton voile sheers, but they greatly softened the room and filtered the direct sunlight.

"The curtains look great, Daphne! Y'all, this is Byron's sister. She's helping me get my life organized."

"That's a full-time job for ten women, 'eah?" Daphne said and smiled at them.

"Very funny," I said. "This is Rebecca, my client, and this is Claudia, her friend from Atlanta."

When she realized I had my one and only client with me, she became all business. "It's nice to meet y'all. Can I get y'all something to drink?"

218

"Tea, anyone? Coffee?"

They said no thanks, that they were just going to stay for a few minutes.

Daphne excused herself, and I handed Claudia the pictures of Charlene's before and after, not the ones that would mortify Rebecca.

"Whew!" she said, looking at photograph after photograph.

I was standing there thinking, *You betcha, whew!*

"Is she ugly or what?" I said.

"Homely as a mud fence," Claudia said. "What in the world is he thinking?"

"He's a pig, right?" Rebecca said.

"Oh, he's a whole barnyard of pigs!" Claudia said, and then paused, adding, "You say he paid for her to fix her ears, chin, nose, breasts, eyes and backside?"

"And her teeth. And probably implants for her cheekbones too," Rebecca said. "But I'm not positive about that."

"I've got just a few of Nat's canceled checks to various doctors, but not everything," I said. I had little to no idea about the costs of cosmetic surgery, but I asked her anyway. "If you had done all this surgery, Claudia, what would you have charged?"

"Who me? Honey, I charge as much as I think I can, within reason, of course. This stuff's pretty competitive these days. But it's not cheap. The big money seems to be in microdermabrasion. Those patients pay the mortgage. And nose jobs. Nose jobs bought my condo."

"Just give us a ballpark number," I said.

Claudia looked hard at the photographs.

"Fifty thousand, maybe more. It depends on a lot of factors—OR time, whether or not she had a local or she needed an anesthesiologist—I have a sterile clinic in my office, but sometimes I have to use the hospital—it all depends on the patient and the procedure."

"Would you be willing to give expert testimony in court?"

"Of course! Rebecca's my oldest friend! I can't believe what he's done to her! Y'all! I just can't believe this!"

"It's pretty unbelievable," I said and started to giggle.

"What are you thinking, Abigail?" Rebecca said. "You've got that she-devil look on your face."

"That fifty thousand is one *very nice* chunk of change. And remember, it's also a marital asset. Hoo! Boy! I'll bet y'all this. Nat Simms isn't going to be happy that we know about it. Probably—no, not probably—for *sure* he has never revealed this information to Harry Albright. And we can all be doubly sure the *judge* isn't gonna like it one little bit!"

Rebecca was looking out the window at the water and Claudia was still looking over the pictures.

"Add on ten thousand," Claudia said. "Her teeth are definitely resurfaced."

"That's even better," I said.

"Well?" Claudia said. "Rebecca? You ready to go do some shopping?"

"Sure."

"What are you doing for dinner, Abigail? Want to join

us for something fried in a basket?"

"Let's go to Huey's for drinks," I said. "Watch the sunset?"

"Who's Huey?" Claudia said.

"My best friend," I said. "Better brace yourself."

They left, so I called Huey and invited us over. He was delighted to have a new face in our little crowd.

"See you at seven?" I said.

As soon as we hung up, I sat at my new desk, opened the envelope and began to read.

Have you ever had sex with another woman during the time you have been married? Nat took the Fifth. *Visited a hotel?* Nat took the Fifth. *Smoked pot?* Nat took the Fifth. *Abused alcohol or prescription medication? Physically abused your wife? No. No. No.*

On and on it went—one lie after another. I got so mad I thought I would scream, but I called Albright's office instead. He picked up the phone almost immediately.

"What can I do for you, Ms. Thurmond?"

"You know, Mr. Albright, this procedure is not a joke."

"Do you hear me laughing, Ms. Thurmond?"

"This interrogatory is packed with lies and denials. Do you want to go to court?"

"Ms. Thurmond? You'll have to prove that they are lies. And you might like to know, the judge just signed the paper today for us to begin a discovery process of our own."

"What took you so long? We go to court in three weeks."

"Oh, don't worry, we'll be ready."

I didn't like the tone of his voice. It sounded like he had something on Rebecca.

"Well, just to let you know, I intend to deposition Nat and Charlene."

Big silence.

"To what end?"

"Mr. Albright? I think we would like to try and settle this in mediation. Save our clients a lot of money."

"I don't think my client's ready to settle."

"Really? Oh! One other thing . . . we are beginning a valuation audit of the family business. If there's anything funny in the books, it wouldn't bode well with the IRS for your client."

This friendly tango continued until I proved myself to be more equipped to clobber him and to be just as stubborn as he was.

"Tell your client to settle, Mr. Albright. At the end of the day, this battle won't be worth it for him in terms of money or his reputation."

"Okay. What do you want?"

"The house, custody, child support, a fair settlement of assets and alimony for life."

"Gee, is that all? You must be kidding, Ms. Thurmond."

"I've never been more serious in my life."

"Then get ready to go to court, Ms. Thurmond, and get ready to lose."

I hung up the phone and looked at it.

"You son of a bitch," I said. "We'll see about that."

Daphne, who had been standing in the doorway probably taking notes, said, "Ooh! We better open a window quick!"

"How come?"

"Get the bad cunja outta 'eah on the next breeze!"

When all the windows were finally opened wide and the sheers billowed out and up in the gusts of cool air, she turned and faced me.

"That nice lady's in trouble?"

"Yeah, well, no. Divorce. Her husband's a dirtball and his lawyer is an animal, that's all. They don't scare me."

"That's good! Good! Good for you!" She swung her fist through the air, socking the jaw of an invisible opponent. "Go get 'em!"

I had to laugh with Daphne. She was such a little wiry ball of energy—not really understanding what was going on but wanting to be supportive. How did that character Byron have such a fabulous little sister? Maybe Byron was fabulous too?

Later, when I arrived at Huey's and while we waited for Rebecca and Claudia to arrive, I took Byron aside and said, "I am totally in love with your little sister, Byron. She is *exactly* what I needed!" I handed him a check with his finder's fee.

He arched his eyebrows and said, "She's my momma's true pride. Someday my little sister is going to rule the world. Thanks."

"You might just be right!"

Rebecca and Claudia finally came through the door, and Rebecca looked flustered. Huey took Claudia's arm to take her to Miss Olivia for the introduction and the inquisition that was sure to follow. I turned to Rebecca.

"What's up? You look a little discombobulated."

"Nat called. He broke up with Charlene. He wants me to call off the dogs. He wants us to sit down without lawyers and divide everything down the middle. He said, *You know I'll be fair with you, Rebecca. Haven't I always been fair?*"

"What did you tell him?"

"I told him that I didn't think he knew the meaning of the *word*."

Sixteen

Rising Tide

Over the next days, some things improved and others did not. Huey, Rebecca and I were at the gallery talking about the September show. It looked like Tom Blagden, the award-winning photographer from Charleston, was going to open the season, and Huey was out of his mind with excitement.

"Do you understand what this will mean for us? It's huge! Huge!"

"You'll have to cater that one, Huey."

"You're right! And press! We'll have press everywhere! Goodness! We'll need the right invitation! I mean, after all, the right invitation makes all the differ-ence!"

"Huey! Don't worry about it!" Rebecca said. "I'll take care of the invitations for you! There's a new sta-tionery store right . . ."

Life was moving all around me. Huey was planning his season. Claudia was coming by before she flew back to Atlanta. Rebecca was becoming more entrenched in life at Pawleys. And I was the one with the shovel, digging Rebecca out of her hole that she found rather cozy. Everyone seemed to be making for-ward motion except me. I had stepped back into my past. Maybe it would redeem Rebecca; maybe I would learn something. I didn't know then—only that we were too far down the road to turn back.

Seeing Claudia had done Rebecca a world of good. There was simply no substitute for an old friend and all those years of shared history. She praised Rebecca's watercolors, and naturally, Rebecca framed one for her as a gift.

"You can't give me this!" Claudia said when Rebecca gave it to her.

"I think it's the very least I can do," Rebecca said.

Claudia was thrilled.

"Gosh, y'all, this has been the best vacation! But I guess it's time to go home and lypo some fannies!"

"What a way to make a living," I said.

"You said it. But then, after I do a hundred chins and noses for vanity's sake, along comes a kid with a cleft palate and I'm glad I hung in there."

"Claudia goes with a bunch of doctors to Costa Rica every year and does free plastic surgery for kids who need it."

"Yeah, me and thirty men. You'd think I would've found a husband by now. I've got doctors coming out of my ears all the time."

"You'd never marry a doctor," Rebecca said.

"Why not?" I said.

"Humph! They all think they're God!"

"So do lawyers," I said. "And I should know."

"Yeah, but you're one of the good guys," Rebecca said.

I shook my head, hoping Rebecca was right.

Claudia gathered her things and said, "I gotta catch the shuttle. Rebecca, you ready to go?"

"Sure."

"Hey, listen, if y'all get a date for court, I'll come back for sure, and if you need me to testify, Abigail, just try to give me some notice."

I felt reasonably sure that we would never go to court. At that point I had enough incriminating information on Nat Simms to put him behind bars if it ever became public. Even if Nat wasn't smart enough to realize it, surely Harry Albright was, but so far Harry hadn't budged. I thought that they were still counting on Rebecca's former weaknesses of character to carry the day, that ultimately she wouldn't fight back.

If dealing with Nat and Harry Albright wasn't annoying enough, there was the weather to talk about.

The storms brewing in the southern Atlantic Ocean

were a national obsession and a regional migraine. A tropical depression, to which I was paying some degree of attention, had become Tropical Storm Alex and then Hurricane Alex with a category three rating and winds of one hundred twenty miles an hour. Behind Alex was Bonnie and Charlie, and before I knew what was happening there were so many sightings of the Gray Man that I imagined he was grinding trenches on the shores of Pawleys Island. Too bad he couldn't charge overtime. He would've been the wealthiest specter beyond the veil.

Ah, hurricane season! August was to be a month of hurricanes, disappointments and surprises.

We had our hearing over Rebecca's order of protection. All four of us were there. The judge asked me to define the terms of it, and while I could have used the opportunity to bring up other issues, I stuck to only those things relevant to Rebecca's safety. I had taken Nat's temper and Jeff Mahoney's warning of it very seriously. We said that we wanted Nat to stay away from Rebecca, that he was not to come within five hundred feet of her and that if he had any business in the Pawleys Island area he was to give me forty-eight hours' notice. The judge looked at Nat Simms in disgust, signed the papers and whacked the desk with his gavel.

Deposing Nat was an exercise in frustration. Before a deposition, my obligation was to inform the opposing attorney of everything I had found during discovery, which of course I did by putting it in the hands of the

U.S. Postal Service the night before, knowing Harry Albright wouldn't receive it on time and that he would be forced to attend the deposition, as I was always fond to say, naked. Shucks. I should've used FedEx, but golly, counselor, I wasn't thinking! So sorry.

Albright reluctantly agreed that I could depose Nat in his office, and naturally, I took Rebecca with me. I told Rebecca to dress very conservatively, which she did. She was not allowed to say a word while I interrogated Nat, but I encouraged her to glare. Albright sat quietly by Nat while a court reporter recorded everything. Like the interrogatory, Nat's answers to my questions were sworn testimony and perjury would be punishable under the law.

Nat lied like a cheap rug almost every time he opened his mouth. It went like this.

"Mr. Simms, have you ever rented a hotel room with Charlene Johnson?"

"No, I have not."

I sighed deeply and taking my time asked, "Then how do you explain two hundred receipts for motel and hotel rooms on your charge card statements over the last eighteen months?"

"Ms. Johnson suffers from terrible headaches. She commutes to our place of business from Orangeburg. Sometimes it's necessary for her to rest during the day. We would rent the room for her and deduct it from her salary. It's just too far to drive back to Orangeburg, and apparently a nap makes her feel much better."

I looked at him and at Albright and wondered if they

thought anyone in their right mind would believe his utter horse manure. Nat and Albright simply smiled the smiles of the foolhardy.

"And did you ever visit her during these episodes of *ill health?*"

Nat glanced at his attorney and then answered. "On occasion, I would stop by to check on her."

"That seems like an extraordinary measure for an employer to take for an employee who earns slightly more than minimum wage."

"We value our employees. Ms. Johnson has been on the team for almost seven years."

"I see. Have you ever had sexual intercourse with Charlene Johnson?"

Nat stopped cold. It was time to play hardball. He looked at Albright for advice and Albright spoke.

"On counsel of attorney, my client would like to exercise his right under the Fifth Amendment."

"Have you ever smoked marijuana with Charlene Johnson?"

"I would like to exercise my right . . ."

Well, well. Wasn't Nat a quick study?

"Have you ever hit your wife, Rebecca Simms?"

"Never."

"Been violent with her in any way?"

"Never."

"What about last spring at a family cookout where you smashed her face with a hot hamburger right off the grill?"

"That was an accident."

"And more recently at Louis's Fish Camp, a restaurant in Pawleys Island, where you pushed her off her chair?"

"She must have been sitting crooked on her chair. I don't know why she threw herself on the floor. Ask her."

Once again, very smug. Not amusing.

"Have you ever taken a check that was given for a deposit on a car at your family's place of business and deposited it in your own account?"

The tone of Nat's skin went from rosy Caucasian to chalk-white albino, and he turned to Albright, who asked for a recess of five minutes. Normally, I would have objected to a recess, but I had accomplished my mission, which was to let them know we knew exactly what Nat had been doing.

When they returned, Nat exercised his Fifth Amendment right one more time, and then another and another. It was clear that Nat Simms was all done answering questions for the day. Any half-witted attorney would have immediately called and asked for mediation to try and reach a settlement. My phone was silent for the remainder of the day.

The only fun I had was meeting Charlene face-to-face. Once again, Rebecca came with me, dressed like someone from the Ladies Altar Society and Charlene showed up looking, well, very inappropriate. Rebecca had fought me about attending this meeting, but I argued her into submission.

"Look, Rebecca, I've been through this a hundred

times, and I can tell you that it will give you the strength you need to fight Nat and win if you can look her in the eye and not flinch. She stole your husband, for God's sake! Don't you want to make her squirm?"

"Making people squirm isn't my thing."

It was true—that wasn't Rebecca's nature. That was a litigator's trait. Like me.

"Okay, then let me put this to you another way. She sees you. You're classy; she's cheap. At least she can go home and feel guilty!"

"I think people like her use any excuse they can dream up to justify the things they do. She might feel guilty about snapping at her manicurist for cutting her cuticles too close, but she'll never suffer a moment's remorse about tearing a hole right through my life and the lives of my children."

"Still, if you look her in the eye with daggers, it might unnerve her and she may possibly give us something to use."

"Oh, fine. I'll come."

During Charlene's deposition, Charlene claimed her Fifth Amendment rights about a thousand times, which essentially means, *Yes, I did the thing, used the drug, made the phone call you are asking me about.*

But she wasn't very clever about it. When I said, "Have you ever had sexual intercourse with Nat Simms?" She replied, "Yes." But when I asked her, "Have you ever had sex with Nat Simms in his marital bed at his home on Tradd Street?" she said, "I'd like to exercise my right to take the Fifth."

Rebecca's face turned so red I thought she might lunge across the table and choke Charlene. I put my hand on Rebecca's arm and finally got the reaction from her I sought. Rebecca began shooting Charlene hate rays.

It went on.

"Have you ever been drunk with Nat Simms?"

"No."

"Have you ever smoked marijuana with Nat Simms?"

"I'd like to exercise my right . . ." And she giggled while refusing to incriminate herself.

In fact, the hyena giggled and snickered so much that her attorney, also retained by and paid for by Nat, had to reprimand her. Nat was clearly lying about the termination of their affair. It was as hot and nasty as it had probably ever been. Okay, I didn't describe her ensemble and I can hear you saying, *Hey! What was she* . . . She was wearing one of those stretch tank tops at half-staff with a built-in bra, from which her synthetic orbs were well on display. Her jacket sleeves were too long and her skirt was too short, and I don't care where you're from, you don't wear rhinestone-trimmed three-inch heels during the day if you ever want to be invited to join the Charleston Yacht Club. And most especially not with fishnet stockings.

The night after Nat and Albright's mockery of the law, Huey, Rebecca and I had dinner at my house. Miss Olivia was feeling a little under the weather and stayed at home to rest. The weather was getting worse, and low pressure sometimes affected older people, making them sluggish.

Byron and Daphne had offered to cook for us, but the truth was that Byron had it in his mind to teach Daphne to cook and serve with a little panache. She was highly insulted that he thought he knew more than she did. All afternoon they had been in the kitchen fussing all around, bickering over garnishes and *to doily or not to doily*.

We went out on the porch with our drinks to eyeball Mother Nature and to try to predict the impact of her next rage.

The eastern sky looked angry. Low dark rolling clouds the color of coal crossed the horizon in warning of what was to come. The ocean was swollen, its rollers five times their normal size and banging the shore, fuming.

"This Hurricane Charlie has me worried," Rebecca said. "It seems like there are so many more storms this year than last year—one after another. What does this mean?"

"Nothing, Rebecca dear," Huey said. "It just means that we are finally having a normal hurricane season. We've just been getting off lightly these past years."

Daphne was passing a tray of broiled scallops wrapped in bacon. They were placed on the paper-doilyed bamboo tray in a semicircle with a small bowl of dipping sauce in the center.

"This looks delicious, Daphne," I said.

"I hope so! That crazy brother of mine made me

arrange them five times!"

I took one, and she turned to Huey, who debated the plump juicy merits of each one before choosing.

"So how goes the battle?" Huey asked, popping a scallop in his mouth. "Anything new? I'll have another," he said to Daphne.

"Now that Rebecca has been deposed, pretrial is Friday," I said.

"How did that go?" Huey asked.

"Fine. It infuriated Albright because he couldn't get anything of value from Rebecca," I said.

"Oh, Lord! Do I have to go to pretrial?" Rebecca said in a weary voice.

"No, no. Just me and good old Harry. Should be a blast."

"And for the great unwashed like myself who've never experienced the joys of the courtroom, what happens in pretrial?"

"It's basically just a conference with the lawyers and the chief administrative judge to go over the details of the trial like how many witnesses do we intend to call, is discovery complete—that kind of thing. What they are really trying to do is figure out how much court time you need and to make sure the lawyers are prepared to go to trial."

"Ah! Well, that makes sense to me," Huey said. "Save the taxpayers' money and all that?"

"Exactly!" I said.

"Rebecca, dear?" Huey said. "How are you holding up?"

"Very well. I finally got to talk to my children in camp."

"Mother McCree! When were you going to tell us this?" Huey said, his eyes expanding like a flounder's.

"Gosh, it only happened an hour ago, and I'm still trying to remember everything they said."

"Well, first of all," I said, "how was the tone of it?"

"I called Sami first," Rebecca said. "She came on the line and I just said, *Sami, what's happening between Daddy and I has nothing to do with how I feel about you. I love you and I just want to know that you're all right. Has camp been good?*"

"What did she say?" I said.

"I could hear in her voice that she was becoming emotional. I think she thought it would be a big battle, but I decided that I would just tell her I loved her and see where it went from there."

"Boy, that was smart! And so?" Huey said. "*She* said?"

"She said camp was okay, that she was nervous about coming home and nervous about starting school. But that she was excited that her daddy was going to buy her a car."

"A car?" I said. "Well, that's the first I've heard about that!"

"Yep! Apparently, he's buying her a Mini Cooper and she's been watching the manufacturing progress online all summer. Hers has its own ID number and so on."

"Heavens! I've never heard of such a thing!" Huey was shocked.

"That's worse than Cabbage Patch dolls," I said.

"What's a Cabbage . . . ?" Rebecca started to ask but I cut her off.

"Just forget it—an old craze that had mothers giving each other black eyes at Toys 'R' Us stores all over America about twenty Christmases ago."

"Oh. Well, anyway, she just talked about a play she was in and the Garden Party Dance and what she wore. The hostility in her voice began to melt a little. I mean, she wasn't saying anything like, *Mom, I'm so sorry about what I did to you,* or anything like that. I didn't bring up the messy things and neither did she. But she did tell me that she missed me and that she was sorry she hadn't written to me. I just said, Sami? *I think it's more important that you just enjoy yourself at camp—the school year's hard enough.*"

"She must've been relieved," I said.

"She was. Before we hung up she asked me when she was going to see me, and I said, *Well, we'll have to work that out with your daddy but I'd like to take you back-to-school shopping and all that,* unless she preferred to go with him. Then she giggled saying something like, *Can you see Daddy at Citadel Mall?* It was a good conversation, I mean, as good as it could have been."

"When I called the camp, I had a wonderful chat with the director. I gave her the short version of what was going on, and she assured me that she would have Sami in the right state of mind when you called. I'll tell you some of these camps are amazing, aren't they? She must have had quite the heart-to-heart with Sami. Or not! I'm just glad it went well, Rebecca. What about Evan?"

"Same thing, more or less. He got on the phone and said thanks for the water guns and that he couldn't wait to come home. He said he missed me and told me he loved me when I told him that I loved him. Boys are a lot easier to communicate with, I think."

"Well, it's a good first step," I said. "When *do* they come home?"

"This Saturday. They start school next week. I'm sure Nat knows that and I'm sure he's got their schedule all organized."

"Oh, I can see Nat now!" Huey said. "He's got a dry erase board attached to the kitchen wall and all their schedules are neatly blocked out! Right! Their rooms are all neat and tidy and he's got car pool all arranged!"

"Oh, my God," I said. "Y'all! I've been so hyperfocused on winning this case I didn't even think about how Nat's gonna handle the children! Do *you* think he can do it, Rebecca?"

"He ain't got a snowball's chance in hell," she said with a droll little smile. "In fact, he's already called me asking if I would pick them up at the airport."

"What? What did you tell him?"

"Why, I told him I couldn't! That I had to work! He said so did he and I just said, *Nat! The children have been gone for almost four weeks! Surely you've prepared a homecoming for them! And as to a ride from the airport, you told me there was nothing I did that you couldn't hire someone to do, so hire someone!* There was a big silence on his end of the line. And then he said something like, *Fine, Becca, be that way!*"

"Be that way? Be *what* way?" Huey said, and we all began to laugh.

Daphne reappeared with another tray of hors d'oeuvres—this time baby radishes filled with a smoked salmon spread, topped with dill sprigs.

We descended on them like locusts, and Daphne said, "Humph! Somebody's hungry! Good thing dinner's almost ready."

Rebecca looked askance at me, and I just said, "She's Byron's sister. Remember?"

We shook our heads and smiled as Daphne slipped back through the door.

Dinner was outstanding. Daphne and Byron had prepared small cups of she-crab soup, fried whole flounders with a homemade tartar sauce and bundles of string beans on the side. Dessert was a citrus crème brulée. All through dinner we talked about Claudia and the upcoming trial and how excited Rebecca was knowing her children would be home safe and sound, even if they were going to be living with Satan for the moment.

And while I had prepared for Friday's pretrial hearing, there was no way I could have prepared for the weather. It was to be Friday the thirteenth in every sense of the word. That morning I woke up to howling wind and torrential rain. Driving to Charleston was not going to be a picnic.

It wasn't.

I literally crept down Highway 17, never going more than forty miles per hour. At one moment it seemed like I might blow right off the road into the trees, and in the next I struggled to see through the driving rain that pelted my windshield without mercy. In the rare moments the rain relented, I wished for one of those giant SUVs that normally frighten me. I was never so relieved to see Mount Pleasant come into view, and I wondered how I was going to drive over the Cooper River Bridge. But the hand of God was in the morning, because by the time I got to the foot of the bridge the rain had all but ceased and the wind still gusted but less so. Off to my right was one of those emergency signs run on a generator that flashed *Speed Limit—25 MPH!* Good idea, I thought as I took the old bridge's first span, driving like I had a trunk filled with eggs.

The rain started again. I parked on Queen Street, and with my hat pulled down, my collar turned up and my sturdiest umbrella running defense at an angle of forty-five degrees, I made it into the courthouse without getting completely drenched. People were huddled in the entrance, obviously trying to decide whether to break for it or wait.

"Don't go out there unless you have to," I said to a group of them.

"Hurricane Charlie," someone said. "Bad tourist!"

"What a mess!" someone else said.

I looked back. Broad Street had taken on the Lake Effect. Fronds from the palmetto trees littered the sidewalks and road. Rainwater in the flooded gutters raced in currents to the choking drains, and masses of paper from an overturned corner waste bin swirled through the air. Airborne coffee cups and pages of the *Post and Courier* slapped against oncoming traffic. Crumpled brown bags with discarded chunks of muffins and bagels dissolving in puddles—it was a helluva mess, all right.

The pretrial went along as expected until the judge brought up the sixty-four-thousand-dollar question: Had we been to mediation? Albright, in all his wisdom, spoke up.

"My client is not of the mediation mind-set," he said.

"Excuse me?" the judge said.

I suppressed a snicker, and the judge looked over to me as if to say, *Is this guy for real?*

Albright shrugged his shoulders and put his hands in the air sending the *So whaddya want from me?* signal.

"We will have mediation one week from today. I'm recommending you use . . ."

Harry was nonplussed by the order, but for once in his miserable life he offered his office as a site without being asked. It probably wasn't the first time Harry Albright was put in his place by the authorities.

We were leaving the building and the rain continued to pour down. It had grown dark and foreboding like a January late afternoon.

"Looks like ark weather," Harry said.

"Boy, no kidding," I said.

"You driving back to Pawleys in this?" he said.

240

"I guess," I said.

"Why don't you check yourself into a hotel? I mean, I wouldn't want my wife driving in this. It's too crazy."

Hellooooo? Was this Harry Albright speaking to me, concerned for my safety?

"You're probably right," I said. "Thanks."

"Hey, if you get yourself killed, you'll ruin my whole party."

Now *that* was the Harry Albright I knew.

But he was right. For Harry Albright to make that remark, I knew I shouldn't be so nonchalant.

I got to my car and drove around to the Charleston Place Hotel, giving my keys to the poor fellow on duty at the outdoor valet desk.

"Checking in?" he said.

"If I can?"

"Any luggage?"

"Nope. Not even a toothbrush."

Fortunately, they had one room left, and even more fortunate for me, the hotel was attached to a shopping mall. I picked up a nightgown at Laura Ashley and some toiletries from the concierge and went up to my room on the third floor. It wasn't the imperial suite reserved in case Pat Conroy showed up, but it was dry, and that was what mattered. The room had a queen-sized bed, a small sofa, a desk and a chair and an armchair with a footstool. There was a closet, a nice bathroom and a television. Over the bed was some Audubon print of cranes standing around in a marsh, framed in dark wood. What more could a girl want? Suddenly, I was very hungry and I contemplated room service, deciding then to eat in the dining room and check the most recent scuttlebutt on the storm.

The doors were open, even though it was midafternoon, because people were streaming in, milling around, looking for a dry spot and something to drink.

The captain came out from the swinging doors of the kitchen and called everyone's attention.

"May I just say that we are not normally open at this hour, but because of the storm we're bringing in a television for everyone to watch the weather as it unfolds.

"The chef and his staff are preparing platters of sandwiches and warming up huge pots of minestrone and seafood chowder. The price for this ad hoc buffet will be a flat fifteen dollars per person—not including alcoholic beverages, of course—but it does include hot or iced tea and coffee and some cookies or cake or whatever they can rustle up. We would also encourage you to share tables with each other, as we are sure to be short of seating. Thank you, and the bar is now open!"

Needless to say, the bartender was doing a brisk business as people began throwing back cocktails with no intention of going anywhere. I was glued to Hurricane Charlie's progress as he moved from Florida toward the coast of South Carolina.

I helped myself to the buffet and sat alone at a table for two. The seafood chowder was delicious and just what I wanted. It was filled with pieces of rich tomatoes and onions and every spoonful held a shrimp or a morsel of whitefish. I had a turkey sandwich in front of me, and I dialed Huey's gallery on my cell. Luckily, the call went through and Rebecca answered.

"Are you okay? We're closing up in a minute—this weather! How'd the hearing go?"

"Fine! I'm fine and I'm in the Charleston Place Hotel, where I'm spending the night."

"Good idea!"

"Anyway, pretrial went fine—we go to mediation next Friday. I'll call you tomorrow, okay? Y'all okay?"

"Oh, we're fine! I'm getting everything off the floor in case we flood. Huey's outside with Byron, boarding up the windows! The wind is fierce!"

"Okay, well, give him my love and tell him to be careful! And you too!"

I disconnected and smiled to myself at the image of Huey and Byron in the wind trying to nail huge sheets of plywood to the windows. Just as I took a huge bite of my sandwich, I heard the velvet voice say, "Excuse me, ma'am? Is this seat taken?"

Mouth stuffed with turkey, lettuce and tomato, I looked up into Julian's face. I struggled to swallow and indicated to him to sit in the seat opposite me.

"Well, hello, Judge. What's a nice guy like you doing in a place like this?"

He smiled, put his food down and pulled the chair out to seat himself. Even though he was merely pulling a chair away from a table, he did it with all the style of James Bond, played by Pierce Brosnan, of course.

"Any port in a storm, little lady, any port in a storm."

"I see." Jesus! Could the conversation be any more

243

banal? God! Get interesting, Abigail! "Are you staying here? I thought you lived in the city."

"Nope. Sold it. I'm building a house on Wadmalaw and meanwhile staying at Kiawah. It's too far to go in this storm. I'm wait-listed for a room. How about you?"

"Got the last one."

"Really?"

"Well, that's what they told me, but you know they always have a few rooms to spare."

"Well, I hope so."

He was lying and I knew it. He was practically leering at me. Or maybe he had a natural leer. Well, maybe he did but the spark between us was still very much alive. He was hoping that I would invite him to stay with me. I could tell. Well, hell would freeze first.

Time ticked by, one minute of witty repartee to the next, during which I restrained myself from asking him why he had dumped me, but it was always on the tip of my tongue. His eyes never left my face and mine never left his.

The next thing I knew, they were serving dinner. Julian was nearly at the bottom of the bottle of wine he had ordered. For the first time in years, I had a glass of wine too. I had forgotten how relaxing it was. Just one glass and I felt warm all over. Julian ordered another bottle, and I said, Oh, don't order it for me, and he said something like, I'll share it with our neighbors.

Well, don't you know I had another glass, and don't you know the hotel's electricity went out? The hotel's generator kicked in, providing us with very minimal lighting for the hall outside the dining room and only two small lights behind the bar. But there were plenty of candles, and let's be honest, all girls north of forty look better in candlelight.

"I'd better go see if they got my room," he said. "This is not a good sign."

For my part, at that moment I couldn't imagine anything more wonderful than being caught in a storm, with no electricity and with Julian. I prayed to God that they didn't have a room for him.

The good Lord heard my prayers.

"No luck," he said. "Now what?"

"Tell me you think I'm fabulous," I said.

"You're fabulous," he said, retaking his seat. "Why?"

"Tell me you adore me," I said, leaning across the table.

He smiled. "I adore you. You know that."

"Okay. I do?"

"Abigail? What's going on here?"

"It's like this, Judge. You can either spend the night on the couch in my room or you can take your chances elsewhere. There are plenty of nice-looking people in this room. See that salesman over there? He's from Peoria. He'd probably love a roommate!" Inside, I was dying of laughter. I had been emboldened by the grape.

He took a deep breath and cleared his throat.

"Abigail, listen to me. I think you are the most incredible woman I have ever known. I have the greatest respect for you. You know that. If you will allow me to bunk down for the night on your sofa, you may depend on me to remain a gentleman. I take a solemn oath." He held his hand over his heart and then gave the Boy Scout salute.

"Okay," I said. "Cross your heart, hope to die, take a needle in your eye?"

"Let's hope it doesn't come to that."

The bartender swiped Julian's credit card and said, "I'll put this through as soon as the power's back on."

"No problem," Julian said and led me by the elbow, with the corked remains of some elixir from Napa in his other hand, toward the elevators to paradise.

The elevators were operating, but not so well. We could hear the calling voices of some people over us, obviously stuck in between floors.

"I'm just on three," I said. "Let's take the stairs."

The emergency lighting was on in the stairwells, but it was still hard to see. I tripped a few times and Julian was always right there to catch my fall.

"Graceful thing, aren't you?"

"Yeah, gosh, I'm a regular ballerina!" I said and laughed.

We rambled around the third floor trying to find the right room number and finally found it. The key had been getting warm in my hand from the moment he asked for the check, and I opened the door as quickly as I could. It wasn't that I didn't want anyone to see me, recognize me and know that I was going into a hotel room with a judge. Because, number one, it was so dark you wouldn't have recognized Arnold Schwarzenegger if he had been breathing right in your face, and two, I just wanted him in the room with me. I was so happy that I didn't care if the whole world knew.

I pulled back the curtains, letting the ambient light fill the darkened room.

"The air-conditioning's off," I said. "Think we should crack the window?"

"No, but I think we should open it."

"Wise guy."

"Step aside, madam, let a man do this for you."

He put the bottle on the desk and tugged at the window, opening it just enough to let the fresh air in. It was still raining, and the wind was even more powerful than it had been in the afternoon.

"Good grief!" I said, "Do you think this is the end of the world?"

"Not for us," he said, "but this is some wild storm. Do you want a little wine?"

"Sure," I said, thinking, why the hell not? "There are glasses in the bathroom."

I found a candle in the drawer next to the Bible and lit it. I dripped some wax into the soap dish and stuck the candle bottom in it, holding it until it held firm. Julian was standing next to the window, looking out at the sky. I put the candle on the coffee table.

"Sit," I said, "and tell me what's really been going on with you."

Julian sat next to me and began to talk and talk. He said he was sorry that we had not stayed in touch, but that he knew contact would mean continuing our affair.

We both agreed that having an affair was a cheap and tawdry business and we both preferred to think of ourselves as above that kind of behavior. He said I deserved more. I said I thought he did too. We were both lying our respective asses off.

When I asked him if he had been seeing anyone, he said, "No one of any real significance. What about you?"

"Me? No. I've just been putting myself back together again—losing Ashley and then John was a lot to go through. That's why I packed it all in and moved to Pawleys."

"And are you doing okay now?"

"I think so. Yes, I'm as healed as I guess I'll ever be."

It was very late and the lone candle was almost melted away. We had begun our conversation with Julian in the armchair and me on the sofa and ended it with both of us, shoes off, facing each other on opposite ends of the couch. It was time to lie down and sleep, and we kept avoiding the topic, wondering how in the world to work it out without feeling weird about it.

Finally, he said, "Well, ma'am, you'd better get off my bed unless you want to stay up all night."

I stood up and looked down at him. "I have a proposal."

"What?"

"How about we sleep on the bed, on top of the bedspread and use the extra blanket in the closet to cover up? No hanky-panky, just sleep?"

"Deal."

"Thank God! I'm sleeping already!"

We crawled on the bed; I shook out the blanket and covered us up. Despite the month, the room was chilly from all the rain and wind. I curled up next to him with my head on his shoulder, and soon I heard little panda noises coming from him. Julian was asleep and I was in his arms.

In the morning I woke up fully dressed and realized Julian had kept his word. I slept like I hadn't slept in years. He was in the bathroom. The day had dawned, and despite the continuing storm, sometime during the night the power had been restored to the hotel. The air-conditioning hummed, and I was pleasantly comfortable.

"Julian?"

He poked his head around the corner with a mouth filled with toothpaste.

"Yes, darling?"

"Are you using my toothbrush?" He called me *darling!*

"Guilty! Sorry!"

"Oh, who cares?" Later, I'd dip it in bronze and keep it in my jewelry box.

A few minutes later he sat on the bed next to me.

"Abigail?" He took my hands into his.

"Yes, Julian?"

"Will you have dinner with me tonight?"

"Of course I will!"

"Are you going back to Pawleys this morning?"

"Yes, I have to check my house. Do you want to drive up?"

"I'd like that. Yes. I'll try to get there before dark. And Abigail?"

"Yes?"

"I'm staying the night."

"Okay." I got up and opened my purse, found a card with my phone number and address and gave it to him. "Do you still promise to conduct yourself as a gentleman?"

Wasn't I coy?

"That was last night, Abigail. Tonight could be very different."

"Maybe. Maybe not," I said, lying through my teeth, smirking like Alice's cat.

I walked him to the door and I couldn't tell you now if I was breathing or not. He opened the door, turned back to me, kissed me on the cheek and walked away. I closed the door and leaned back against it. *Yes! Thank you, God! Yes!* And then I had a horrible thought! Sleeping with him was one thing, but did he expect me to *cook?*

SEVENTEEN

STORMY WEATHER

Thank heavens I had the presence of mind to stop at Whole Foods in Mount Pleasant on the way back to Pawleys. Let's be honest, Pawleys might have been the center of the universe, but the food shopping options were slim. I picked up sourdough baguettes, three kinds of cheese, lots of fresh fruit, vegetables, fresh-squeezed orange juice, olive oil in an ornate handblown bottle from some teensy town in Italy that cost four times what it should have but if seen on my kitchen counter might make me look like I knew what I was doing, homemade sausages and chicken. When in doubt, cook chicken. I almost forgot wine. I didn't have a drop of anything in my house! Julian drank red. Merlot. They had about fifty kinds of Merlot. Oh, swell. Okay, I told myself, use your head. Buy the most expensive one and it can't be too bad. I found something from California for twenty dollars and bought two bottles. Done.

It was still raining and windy and little did I know but Hurricane Charlie was headed for Myrtle Beach, Pawleys and Litchfield. I kept thinking that Julian would call and cancel, and if he didn't that maybe he should. But he was a big boy and if he really wanted to be with me, a little rain and wind shouldn't stop him.

That little bit of rain was falling at the rate of an inch

an hour and the old windbag was blowing at around seventy miles an hour by the time I passed Georgetown. The closer I got to Pawleys, the worse the weather became. There was no way Julian was coming unless he didn't have a radio or a television. I prayed that he didn't.

The other pressing issue on my mind was Rebecca's children flying in from Maine. Rebecca probably wasn't even worried, but I had a knot in my chest, thinking about them stuck in the Charlotte airport, or Newark, without a dime to their names to even call anyone. What if they got separated? What if they were hungry?

By the time I got home at about three, finished bringing in all the groceries and dripping water all over Daphne's clean floor, that mystery was solved. Rebecca called.

"Hey, Abigail! Are you busy?"

"Hey, yourself! Is the gallery open today?"

"Sort of, but only because Huey wanted to make sure all the paintings were safe. I'm going home in about an hour. Listen! I have to tell you something that's gonna crack you up."

"Go ahead! Crack me up!"

"Sami just called me . . ."

"They got in okay?"

"Oh, yeah, they're fine. Late, but everything's fine. So, who do you think Nat sent to the airport to pick them up?"

"No way! Charlene?"

"Yep. So Sami calls me and says, *Mom, who's Char-lene?* And I said, *Daddy's whore.* I said it just like that, really sweet and all, just like I was saying she was Nat's sister. And she said, *Is Daddy gonna marry her?* And I said, *Gosh, I don't know; you'll have to ask him.* Then she said, *Mom! I don't want to live with her! She's a pain in the behind!* And I said, *Well, Sami, that's what you said about me too, isn't it?* Then she got real quiet, and after a few seconds I said, *Are you there, Sami?* Finally she said, *Mom, this just isn't gonna work. I mean, she's embarrassing!* And I said, *Well, Sugar, I'm sure you and your dad can work this all out. After all, it was your decision to live with him, wasn't it? Now tell me, how was camp?*"

"You didn't say that!"

"Yes, I did too! And, Lord, Abigail! She went on a rampage, whispering so that Charlene wouldn't hear. She was still in the house, probably reading the hall-marks on the silver. She said she couldn't stand Char-lene's accent, that she's a low-class redneck, that she's stupid, that she dressed like a teenager but all her clothes were at least one size too small, that she curses in front of them, that Evan couldn't stand her either and on and on! I was dying to burst out laughing, but poor Sami was so upset at the prospect of Charlene in her life that I couldn't!"

"Unbelievable. Unbelievable. I still can't get over the fact that he sent her to the airport in the first place! *That's* the incredible thing!"

"She said that Evan gave her some lip and Charlene

said, *I'm gonna tell yewr diddy!* You don't know my Evan. He's got a mouth! Oh, my God! Nat has his hands full now!"

"Isn't it interesting that Sami called you to tell you this? I mean, another child might have kept it under wraps longer. But this is a good sign."

"Why?"

"Because it will certainly be easier to persuade the courts to return custody to you."

"Listen, let's not rush the custody thing, okay?"

"Rebecca! You can't leave your children with Nat and now with Charlene too!"

"Abigail, let's think about it for a minute. Charlene might be gross and disgusting, but I doubt that she's going to place the kids in some physical danger. All she's going to do is embarrass the living hell out of them."

"Rebecca! Wait! Your kids are still impressionable! If she's around them all the time the next thing you know, they'll be, they'll be *hillbillies!* And Nat and Charlene carrying on right in front of their eyes? It's immoral, for heaven's sake!"

"And so is two-thirds of what's on television! Abigail! Listen to yourself! You sound like an old prude! You don't think Sami can handle herself? She's practically driving her new Mini!"

"Rebecca!"

"And Evan? He knows how to get around the block too!"

"Rebecca!"

"What? Abigail, my kids are very slick, and a week around Charlene will make me look very appealing. I'll be getting the children back either in mediation or in court. If they can fly from Maine to South Carolina by themselves, they'll be just fine for a while. I say let them go scratch their mad place for a few days. It won't kill them!"

"Scratch their mad place?" I started to laugh. I could hardly believe my ears! Rebecca wanted to teach her children a lesson, and it sure seemed like they needed it.

"I gotta get out of here before my car floats away! I'll call you later. What are you doing tonight?"

"Tonight? Oh! Uh . . . I have a friend coming for dinner, at least I think so, but with this crazy storm and all, who knows?"

There was a pause, and I knew Rebecca was suspicious.

"Abigail? Are you having dinner with a man?"

"You're awfully nosy, Miss Rebecca, you know that?"

"Ha! I knew it! Well! Good luck!"

"Thanks."

Go scratch their mad place? I loved it!

The phone didn't ring and the phone didn't ring and after I shaved everything, moisturized everything and got dressed in five different black outfits, I began to get nervous. Julian was probably coming. Maybe I should change the sheets? Was the guest room made up? Where should I tell him to put his things if and when he did come through the door? If I told him to put his stuff in the guest room, would he be insulted? I decided to set the table and then decided, no, better to check the guest room.

Daphne and Byron had done a good job of making the old room look pretty good. My parents' old bed was made up in all white linens and covered with their old quilt that I hadn't seen in ages. She must've found it and washed it along with the ruffle-edged cottage curtains that actually looked new. It was amazing what a little soap and water could do.

I turned on the bedside lamp and the room seemed comfortable enough. I put a bottle of Evian (which was now being purchased and consumed by the case, it seemed) and a glass next to the bed and a few blooms from my centerpiece in a bud vase. I thought, well, that should just about do it. The bathroom was clean as a whistle and I simply loaded the towel rack with fresh towels and put a new bar of soap next to the sink and in the shower. For a final touch, I hung a terrycloth bathrobe on the hook of the bathroom door and pronounced the room ready.

Daphne had thrown out all the old magazines and catalogs that were stacked up all over the house, and as if by magic every room seemed larger. Yep, Miss Salt Air was looking very good for her age. I hoped Julian thought the same of me.

It was six o'clock and time to set the table. It was curiously funny how for three years I hadn't cared if the plates were chipped, if the silver was polished or if the napkins were pressed. Along comes Daphne, she snaps her fingers in every nook and cranny, and the next thing you know, I'm fussy! I'd like to say that I was calm about the whole night, but if there was a hurricane blowing outside, there was at least a wind advisory buzzing around between my ears. I set the table with the best china I had and lots of candles. After all, there was still the possibility of losing the electricity. By the time I had the flowers and glasses all in place, it looked, well, not too bad.

It was six-forty-five and no sign of Julian. Stupid! I hadn't taken his cell phone number! But if I had, I probably would have called him a thousand times and made a fool of myself. Damn it! I hated feeling so out of control! I decided to start cooking. If I waited for him to walk in before I started cooking, it would still take another hour to cook the chicken. And who knew? If the lights went out, we'd have no dinner at all, so it was definitely better to start cooking. Besides, hopefully we had better things to do than to stand around my prehistoric kitchen and wait for the chicken to surrender.

I looked in the mirror one more time. I had mascara under my eyes. I'd have to remember to check that from time to time. And my lipstick was already gone. I reapplied it and put it in my pocket. But it made a bulge! I couldn't have that! So I stuck my lipstick in the kitchen drawer and tried to remember to periodically check my lips out in the reflection of my toaster.

I preheated the oven to four hundred degrees and told myself to snap out of it. I put the chicken pieces in a big

Pyrex dish and drizzled them with olive oil and squirted them with lemon juice. Next I added fresh rosemary and a ton of salt and pepper. Then I laid the sausages in between them and sliced an onion over the whole pan, said a little prayer (Dear Lord, please make this taste good. Thank you, Lord. Amen.) and shoved it in the oven.

Seven-fifteen. No Julian. I started slicing the mozzarella and tomatoes and opened a bag of salad. Lettuce on the plate, tomato, mozzarella, tomato, mozzarella, tomato, mozzarella and chopped basil over the whole thing, olives down the sides, sliced roasted red pepper here and there, marinated artichoke bottoms to the left and right, and voilà! A side dish!

Seven-thirty. No Julian. Should I call the police? No. Wash the string beans. Get a grip. What if he didn't show up at all? What if he got in a wreck? What if? What if? What if? *BREATHE!* Okay. It's all good, I told myself. If he doesn't show up, I'll have chicken and salad and so what? So what? *So what?* I would fall apart and weep, *that's* so what. And then, I told myself, life will go on. I took the string beans, nipped their bottoms and threw them in a pot, covering them with water, tossing in some salt.

I walked out to my back porch to see if there were any headlights roaming around. Nothing. Nada. Zilch. It was as dark and depressing as it could be. My yard was filled with little ponds, and I would have frogs croaking for a thousand years. Maybe malaria. Typhoid fever. Maybe I needed to brighten up my attitude? But where was Julian? Many people had left the island because of the storm, but I didn't think it was life-threatening, and besides, I had a date. *Really? Where was he?* I asked myself for the hundredth time.

Ten minutes to eight. I could smell the chicken and opened the oven to give it a look. It was browning and probably needed another fifteen minutes. I sliced the baguette and put the pieces in a Ziploc to keep them fresh. I opened the wine, thought about having a glass and then realized Julian wasn't coming.

Who was I fooling? I turned off the oven and went into my bathroom. I was washing my hands, staring at my face in the mirror and giving myself the devil. *Did you really think he would come? He's a good-looking successful man who can have any woman he wants at any age! He doesn't need an old hag like you! You must be delusional!* The tears began creeping over my lids and I got so mad at Julian Prescott and at myself that I started to scream. *Damn! Damn! Damn! What's the matter with you? And damn you, Julian! Why do you hurt me like this? What's the matter with me? Why do I leave myself open like this? Shit! Shit! Shit! I'm such a fool!*

I was so angry with myself. I, who had sworn off relationships and emotional anything, had succumbed to pheromones and carnal desire and vanity in the space of minutes. All it took was a chance meeting with him on the courthouse steps and one sexless night in a hotel room. I knew better and was acting like a smitten teenage girl anyway. Why hadn't he tried to rip my clothes off last night? Because he didn't want to, that's why. I got madder and madder, and the fact that I had been such a fool made me even more angry. *Damnit!* I said as loud as I could. *Oooh, just wait till I see you again, Julian Prescott! I am NEVER speaking to you again!*

The phone rang. I splashed water on my face, grabbed a towel and ran for the phone. It was Rebecca. Crap.

"You busy?"

"Oh! No. No, not at all. What's up?"

"Sami called me again. Listen to this . . ."

I listened and didn't hear a word she said except that it had something to do with some transgression the children had committed that caused Nat to fly into a rage and threaten the kids that if they weren't nice to Charlene there would be huge repercussions for them.

"Sami was upset and I just said, *Well, Sami? You'd better learn to live with them because this is what you wanted* . . . is that a riot or what?"

"Justice is sweet."

"What's wrong, Abigail? You don't sound good."

"Oh, nothing. My friend hasn't shown up or called or anything and it's getting late—that's all. I'm okay. Just a little concerned."

"Oh! Well then, don't let me keep you! He might be trying to call and here I am running on! I'll talk to you later."

"Okay."

We hung up and I looked at my watch. Eight-thirty. Shit. I walked around my house screaming at myself.

God, I was such an idiot! *He didn't try to screw you last night because he didn't WANT to screw you last night! Why can't you get that through your thick head?* I was seriously embarrassed and feeling very low.

Nine o'clock. Nine-ten. Then I saw headlights! Wonderful, beautiful headlights, blasting like the sun through my kitchen door, filling my house with glorious light, changing everything, and then I said to myself, Girlfriend? You ain't got a stitch of cool in you. Jeesch! Calm down.

I could hear his footsteps. Music! Oh, get over it.

He knocked and I checked my face in the mirror—not too bad—and went to answer.

"Hello! Anybody home?"

"Well, look what washed up in the storm!"

Julian stepped inside and proceeded to drip everywhere. He got out of his soaking-wet jacket and looked around for a place to put it.

"You wouldn't believe what the roads are like! Trees are down, limbs everywhere! I left Charleston at five o'clock!"

"Here. Give me that." I slipped into the guest bathroom and hung it up in the shower. "Don't think a thing about it! I've just been cooking away and then the phone rang . . ."

"You're telling me? I *tried* to call you so many times but I didn't have service and . . . am I too late for dinner?"

"Nope! You are right on time!"

"Well, do you have a smooch for this old codger?"

"You know it!"

I kissed him lightly and pulled away. He stopped me and looked at me with the most peculiar expression.

"Abigail? Have you been crying?"

"No! I mean, yes! Oh, Lord, I was watching this old movie on the Lifetime channel, and what can I say? Sappy movies make me cry like a baby. Dumb, right?"

"No, it's charming. Why don't you go wash your face and I'll pour us a glass of this lovely wine—oh, I brought some wine too! And chocolate! And flowers! They're all on the back porch with my things."

"Be right back," I said and smiled at him. God, my heart was pounding like a trip hammer. I was so happy he was there and so happy I had a moment to escape to compose myself. I closed the door and inspected myself in the mirror. Good grief! I didn't have a drop of makeup left. Very quickly I applied whatever I could grab, spritzed again with cologne, ran my hand through my hair and checked my teeth. Then with measured steps I left my bathroom, clicked on the CD changer and the sounds of Nat King Cole filled the room. The seduction trap was set.

Julian was in the kitchen, peeking in the oven and the pots.

"I turned the oven back on to warm up the chicken. It smells delicious! And you look beautiful, Abigail."

"Well, thanks Julian," I said and took the glass he offered me. "Here's to seeing you again. Oh! The flowers are so pretty!"

"You're welcome. Here's to seeing you too."

We clinked, we sipped and I turned on the heat under the string beans.

If you were expecting us to dive on the floor and make crazy love, you've got the wrong two people. No, one of the joys of middle age was the dance, the mating ritual, the innuendo and all the teasing that led to the eventual act itself. Shoot, I knew we were going to sleep together. So did he. Setting up the guest room was a joke, and he didn't drive through a hurricane for a plate of chicken, did he? I intended to hold out for at least as long as it took to load the dishwasher. I could do the pots in the morning.

After some cheese and crackers and a second glass of wine, dinner was ready. Julian lit the candles and I plated our food.

"This looks wonderful," he said. "Thank you for having me."

Having you is the operative term, I thought and didn't say. I just said, "Oh, Julian, I can't believe you drove through this awful storm to get here! We could've had dinner next week! But I'm glad you did."

I don't have to tell you how the rest of the night went. But I will. Julian ate four pieces of chicken, two pieces of sausage, some salad and string beans. That boy was licking his fingers! The second bottle was opened and I built the chocolates into a little tower on a plate and put them in front of him. The warm glow of the candles, a satisfied appetite, wine and chocolate before us and the promise of romance—damn! How could it get any better? It did.

He said, "I've got a wild idea."

"Let's hear," I said.

"Let's see what's up with this storm. You got a jacket?"

Was he insane?

"Sure," I said, "I'll go get it. I hung yours up in the shower in that bathroom." I pointed him in the general direction and went to my bedroom closet. His duffle bag was on the floor next to my bed and I thought, *Okay, bubba, you presume a lot, you know*. My intention was to give him a little grief about it, but that's not exactly what happened.

Julian was on the front porch with the lights turned off. His hair and jacket were blowing like mad and he was getting sprayed from the rain. Men didn't care about that sort of thing, and to tell you the truth, neither did I. There was nothing sexier than salt spray and moonlight thrown together on a night like that. I stood beside him and he pulled me around in front of him, both of us watching the Atlantic. He put his arms around me and put his lips on the back of my neck, and I mean, honey? That man could have my neck for as long as he wanted. I was already so weak and stupid, my caution had blown by Cape Romain and was headed for Massachusetts! Whew! What would have happened if I'd served red meat?

"Abigail?"

"Yes?"

"Abigail?"

"Yes, Julian?"

"What a great name."

"Thanks. Julian's pretty groovy too."

"We have to talk about this for just a minute or two."

"Okay. Want to go inside?"

"No, I love it out here. I'll just get our glasses."

He was gone, and I thought, now what the hell? What's bothering him about all this? It was perfect! Perfect! What could be the matter?

He was back, and even in the dim light I could see that he was serious. I took the glass and leaned against the railing.

"So what's bothering you, Julian?"

"Oooh! Okay. Abigail, it's like this. I'm not a young man, you know."

"What are you talking about? You're in your prime!"

"Well," he chuckled a little and then said, "not so. But that's okay. Life's good and all that. It's just that in certain areas, things have changed."

"You mean . . . like what?" Did he mean Bob Dole Disease? Ah, come on!

"Well, it's okay, really, because I can just take . . ."

I put my fingers over his lips. *A pill.*

"Don't say another word, baby. I'll meet you in headquarters in half an hour!"

Did I have to say HEADquarters? But it didn't bother Julian. No, Julian threw his arms around me, his head back, and had the biggest belly laugh I had ever heard come from him.

"Abigail? You know what, sweetheart?"

"What?"

"You just might, just *might* be the perfect woman after all!"

EIGHTEEN

MEDIATE

The following week was one of frustrations. The remnants of Hurricane Charlie were a problem to be dealt with, and every day we watched the Weather Channel to chart the progress of two new hurricanes, Danielle and Earl. Thankfully they proved to be mediocre challengers.

Rebecca kept us up-to-date on the news about her children. Sami was calling her a minimum of four times a day, giving us reruns of *Charlene Ruins Your Life— The Reality Show from Hell.* Apparently Charlene, in an effort to help Nat get the kids organized for school, offered to take them back-to-school shopping at a retail establishment of considerably less cachet than their normal haunts. Sami pitched a fit and called Rebecca.

"She carried on like I don't know what and I just said to her, *Well, darlin'? Your daddy has to support me, you, Evan and his whore too. I guess money's a little tight. Maybe you should babysit or you could ask your grandfather for some money?* Well, you know old Tisdale ain't giving nobody a nickel. Then I said, *So tell me, how's school? Do you like your new teachers?*"

You couldn't help but giggle. Rebecca had gone from

the cookie-making, pillow-plumping mother of the year to tossing aside the kid gloves from her iron fists and giving her very spoiled children a hard lesson in their new and chosen reality. At first I couldn't understand why she hadn't rushed to Charleston and zoomed her children off to the Gap or wherever they normally shopped, but then she did have limited funds and probably didn't want a face-to-face encounter with Nat or Charlene. Yes, on consideration, an excursion like that had land mines at every turn.

The more I thought about it, I realized what strength it took Rebecca *not* to give in to Sami's whining demands. If she could just hold out until she regained custody, she could lay down some new ground rules and put her children back on the right track. Meanwhile, she did seem to possess a teensy sadistic streak because she certainly was enjoying the banter with her daughter. But what mother had not been so exasperated with her children that she wanted to make her children face themselves instead of always making everything right in their world? It wasn't in a child's best interest, especially a teenage girl, for a mother to constantly give in. It was like giving the dog steak from your dinner plate so he would stop begging. It was clear that indulgence had been the pattern in her relationship with Sami.

The noise from Evan's quarter was not as vitriolic as Sami's. Boys were more reasonable. I suspected that Evan was internalizing his bitterness and/or frustrations and Sami was probably telling him that calling their mother was useless. But one thing was certain: both children weren't happy about Charlene and probably wished they were living with their mother and not Nat. That had taken only three days of Charlene and her twang. Worse than everything else, it certainly appeared that Charlene was residing on Tradd Street. Like they say, there goes the neighborhood.

Julian called for a few minutes every day. We planned to spend the following weekend at Pawleys, and I was looking forward to it. Being with Julian was just *right*. He was an ideal companion. Wild understatement. The man was *fabulous*.

We decided that first night at Pawleys that we wouldn't talk about Lila or John—at least not about the period in time when we were married to them and discovered. There was no point. I mean, there would always be some feelings of guilt, but only because we got caught. If we hadn't been caught, it would've been the most deliriously euphoric romance of all recorded history. If that sounds wrong, then you have never been caught in a moral or ethical conundrum; your soul is without sin? I doubt it.

Here's how it goes. You are married for a thousand years to someone no longer well suited to your moods, someone who has lost interest in you and in life in general, someone who no longer wants to learn and discuss the world, and in fact they look at you funny when you want to discuss an op-ed piece on the Middle East. *For what? Who cares?* You want to visit Vietnam or Bhutan just to see a place that seems mysterious and exotic.

Their most far-fetched idea of exotic is a pineapple and ham pizza while watching a movie with subtitles. You're married to someone who figures he might need two more cars in his lifetime, who thinks aerobics are a waste of time, that getting drunk is an entitlement that comes with advancing years, and he hasn't had on a bathing suit in ten years. You look at this guy and say to yourself that you don't feel old, you don't act old, you're not like him, but you hang in there because you said you would years ago when you were so young that you can barely recognize yourself in the wedding pictures. You realize that this *till death do us part* thing is a lot longer than anticipated. You realize you made a serious mistake—you married the right person for the girl you once were but not for the woman you have become. You're stuck.

You don't fret about it too much because that will only make your state of mind worse. You don't talk about it to anyone because it's undignified. You don't get divorced because you get along well enough and you look at the poor thing snoring in his armchair and you feel perfectly horrible to have had any of those thoughts. But what about sex? What's sex? That perfunctory business that follows and precedes a shower? Oh, my. Oh, well. You decide that your best bet is to forget your own sexuality, stay busy with your work, go to museums and concerts and travel with girlfriends and life will inch toward the grave. Maybe it won't have been the most satisfying of lives, but you'll have done a lot of the things you wanted to do.

Don't count on it.

At the first sniff of that kind of laziness, the universe throws you a fastball, a curve ball and then a spitball. If you're lucky. Or unlucky. It depends on your point of view.

Love finds you. You float on the wings of romance, you are horrified by the depth of feelings you suddenly have for another person, you are knocked off your feet and ultimately flat on your back, dreaming about having your legs in the air!

That's what happened to Julian and me. Neither of us were the kind of people who ever set out to just screw around. We never had before and we never did again. But I have to say that in the time we had been apart, Julian had obviously done a better job of keeping me off his mind than I had. But that was how it was with men. When they made up their minds, that was it. They want to quit smoking? They quit. They want to lose ten pounds? It's gone. They break up with you? They do it and are able to stay away forever, if need be. But, when faced with you again, they lose their composure and resolve just like you do.

Like a lot of men, Julian was the kind of guy who really didn't want to be single. He was a fully domesticated cat, who liked home cooking and who also played golf and tennis. I think love of simple food and sports contributed to the ease with which he sort of slid back into my life. We decided, what the heck, Lila was gone, John wasn't coming back, why not give our relationship a slow start and see where it went? Well, maybe it wasn't exactly slow. I hated to admit this, being the dedicated and sworn, shriveled up, card-carrying old crone that I was swiftly becoming, but having Julian around made me feel awfully good. It just did. And if somebody objects to the fact that I became happier because I had a M.A.N. at the moment, tough nuggies. Excuse me, but an intimate relationship with an intellectual peer of like interests and similar background was a very pleasant way to pass some time. Especially, ahem, the intimate part. And, if it ever stopped raining, I planned to get him out on the golf course and show him where the bear went in the buckwheat. I wasn't getting married tomorrow, you know.

Friday rolled around before I knew it, and it was mediation day. I knew this would be a disaster, but, if for no other reason than enlightening our clients, it would be worth the effort. Nat needed to be made familiar with what his legal responsibilities were and what going to court would do to his reputation. Rebecca needed to understand exactly where she stood in terms of Nat's willingness to give her that to which she was entitled under the law and to gauge the size of the fight that was sure to be.

I drove down to Charleston with Rebecca, planning to drive back with Julian, stopping along the way for weekend supplies.

Every time I went to Rebecca's condo, I scanned the parking lot for an Everett Presson type, crouched in a basic sedan behind a newspaper, watching Rebecca's door, waiting for a parade of men and, hence, incriminating evidence. Not only were there no men, but I never saw a PI either. I didn't know if Nat had just made that up, but I suspected that he had. Bullies were often liars and Nat had proven himself to be both. Somebody had probably heard that Rebecca was in Litchfield and told him.

We arrived at Harry Albright's office a little early, and his miserable mother showed us to the conference room. The walls were painted taupe. The large rectangular table was glass topped, deliberately so, so that opposing clients and their attorneys couldn't give signals under the table. It was surrounded by eight green leather armchairs. No windows. No artwork. No sideboard with a pitcher of water and glasses on a tray with fake flowers. It could not possibly have been a more boring room.

We waited for the mediator, Harry and Nat to arrive. The mediator was the first to show. Her name was Mary Ann O'Brien.

"Good morning," I said. "I'm Abigail Thurmond, counsel for Rebecca Simms."

"Good morning," she said. "Nice meeting y'all. Are the others here?"

"Not yet," I said.

"Figures. Is your client familiar with mediation procedure?"

"Basically."

I looked at Rebecca and I could see that she was nervous.

"Well, there's no mystery to this. What we're going to

do is: you'll tell me what you want. Then I will go to, I assume, the other office here and talk to your husband and his attorney and see what they are willing to give. We go back and forth like this until we can reach an agreement. When it works, this process saves the courts a lot of time and money. Besides, it's always better if you can work things out without the world watching, right?"

Ms. O'Brien smiled. She seemed like a very level-headed and nice person. She was tall and slender with the most massive head of thick glossy black hair I had ever seen. I imagined she had done this a thousand times, and as soon as we got under way I knew that I was right.

Nat and Albright were in Albright's office, and Ms. O'Brien was in the conference room with us, going through the documents.

"You're asking for custody of the children and the house, the house contents and half of all your assets. You're seeking alimony in the amount of three thousand dollars a month and child support for the children in the amount of five hundred dollars a month for each child. Tuition through college, health care . . . looks pretty normal to me. How many years have you been married, Mrs. Simms?"

"Seventeen."

She nodded her head.

"Ms. O'Brien," I said, "I don't think we are asking for anything that unusual. However, if we go to court, we have enough damaging evidence on Nat Simms to send him to prison."

"Such as?"

"Skimming the family business, fraud, adultery, lewd behavior, recreational use of illegal substances."

"And you can prove all this?"

"You betcha."

She glanced at Rebecca, who was mortified. Mary Ann O'Brien knew at once that Rebecca, like a lot of women, was the victim of her husband's midlife reality check. What was absolutely stupefying to Rebecca was everyday news to Ms. O'Brien.

She excused herself with a sigh. "Well, let's see what they say."

Time passed. We could hear raised voices through the walls, but we couldn't make out what they were saying. An hour went by and Ms. O'Brien returned.

"Well?" I said. "How goes the fray?"

"Not good. We're about as far apart as you could be in terms of a settlement. Your husband insists that you have nothing on him he can't refute and that he can prove you have been a negligent mother. His attorney is prepared to subpoena their guidance counselors and a few of their teachers. Apparently the mother of one of your daughter's friends is willing to testify against you. He categorically insists on keeping the house because he believes it's important to keep the children's routine the same. That's for openers."

"I can hardly wait to hear what else . . ." I said.

"As far as alimony, he says no. He wants child support from you—three hundred dollars a month, more as a good-faith gesture for the sake of the children's psyche than real support. He says he will give you a cash settlement of fifty thousand dollars, medical coverage for six months, whatever is in the house that was a gift to you, your personal belongings and that's it."

"You must be kidding," I said.

"He can't do this to me!" Rebecca started to cry.

"Rebecca! Don't get upset. This is normal. Let's work up a counteroffer."

It went on like this all through the morning. We called out for sandwiches and worked straight through the afternoon until four o'clock. We dug in, sent them a fifth offer and here's what we got back.

"Okay," Ms. O'Brien said, in a very tired voice. "It doesn't appear that we're making much headway. Their current offer is this: your husband has custody of the children and the house and you pay child support of four hundred dollars a month. He gives you a lump-sum payment of one hundred and fifty thousand dollars. That's it."

"What?"

Rebecca wasn't handling this well at all. Neither was I.

"Listen, Ms. O'Brien. Their residence on Tradd Street was appraised at *one point two million dollars.*" I slid the appraisal toward her for the third time that afternoon. "Nat's share of his family business is valued at *four million dollars.*" I pushed the valuation across the table again. "He's an *abusive,* pot-smoking, adulterous *felon* who doesn't know the truth from a hole in the wall. I suggest you take Harry Albright outside and tell him that if we go to court, I'm gonna humiliate him and send his client to the cooler unless Nat Simms gets real. *NOW!* This *entire day* has been an insult to our intelligence." I was furious, but then I added in a cool voice, "But of course, it's *your* call."

She tapped her pencil on the glass-topped table a dozen times or so and then said, "Fine. I'll be back."

Thirty more minutes passed until Ms. O'Brien returned.

"No go," she said. "I'm sorry, Mrs. Simms. Your husband is a very stubborn man."

"Seventeen years of marriage? Raise two children? Run a house, be faithful and loving? And this is it? I don't think so." At this point I knew we would be so much better off in the courtroom, for Rebecca's sake. She was devastated to see how unfair her husband wanted to be with her. Who wouldn't be? Rebecca had tears streaming down her face as she had off and on all day long.

Ms. O'Brien apparently agreed with me, because she said, "I think you'll find the family court judges more amenable than your husband and his attorney, Mrs. Simms. There's more precedent for divorce law than any other law on the books. I'm sorry I couldn't be of more help. I really am."

We shook hands and Ms. O'Brien left.

"Come on," I said. "Let's get out of here."

"Okay," she said. "God, he is such a bastard."

"You'll get no argument from me."

276

We stepped out into the afternoon air, and I looked at my watch. Four-thirty. I was supposed to meet Julian, but I had no intention of letting Rebecca drive herself the whole way back to Litchfield alone. She was too upset—not good for driving.

"I have to make a phone call," I said and walked about five feet away from her.

I reached Julian and told him what had happened and he said, *No, absolutely drive her back. We should've thought of this in the first place, but no bother! I'll meet you there before eight, okay? Drive safely!*

"Oh, Abigail!"

I wasn't about to listen to her wail in the middle of the street.

"Oh, Abigail *what?* You listen to me. Your husband is a fool. Harry Albright is billing him for more hours than Elizabeth Taylor ever paid for all her marriages combined, and guess what? You and I are going to court to have ourselves a triumphant victory!"

"Oh, Abigail. What am I going to do?"

"We are going to do the thing that always makes us feel better, that's what."

"Which is?"

"We're calling Huey to see if he'll have all of us for dinner. I'm too tired to cook."

"Me too."

Huey was thrilled. I had already told him all about Julian. He couldn't wait to meet him.

Julian was on time, which was a good thing, as my nerves had been heavily tried last week. Besides, I was exhausted from the day. But as these things are wont to go, I became mysteriously energized when I saw him coming through my kitchen door.

"Hey! You look so handsome!"

I gave him a kiss and stood back, taking in the full length of him, deciding he had gone to considerable lengths to put himself together for the evening. He was wearing an ivory linen sport coat over a navy silk polo shirt and navy linen pants. Woven loafers, no socks. Pretty cool for a guy who probably hid his AARP card deep in his wallet behind his membership card to a fitness club.

"And you're looking pretty smart yourself! So what are we doing about dinner?"

"Ah! Men and their stomachs! Don't they ever think about anything else?"

"Yep. Money. Golf. Sex."

"In that order?"

"Not always."

"Well, tonight I have a special treat for you."

"I was hoping you would . . ."

I blushed and, as per normal for me, as normal established itself anew in my southern climes, felt a flutter. Flutters would have to restrain themselves until later.

"I'm taking you to my best friend's house for supper."

"Oh. That fellow Huey?"

"Yep." I rushed around turning off lights.

"Nice house?"

I stopped dead in my tracks and looked him in the

face. "Well, it's not as grand as this house, but it's not a slum."

"On the ocean?"

"Let's go. You'll see. It's on the Waccamaw."

We drove over to Huey's, and I gave him the update on Rebecca's case in the car.

"Well, mediation doesn't always work. Who's your judge?"

"Shelby."

Julian burst out laughing. "Perfect! Perfect!"

"Why? What's so funny?"

"Adrian Shelby is the toughest, no-nonsense judge we've got. She's gonna take Nat and Harry Albright apart! Whew! What a blessing! You couldn't ask for a better pick. She *hates* arrogance, I mean hates it! You should go to church this Sunday and thank the Big Guy upstairs."

"Well, hallelujah! Here, make the right, right here."

He swung into the side road and said, "Good thing you're with me. I never would have found this."

We went along the road until the big house came into view.

"Keep to the left," I said.

"Holy smokes! This is some spread."

We parked and got out, and Julian whistled low and long.

"How many acres do they have?"

"Enough. Come on."

Julian charmed Miss Olivia all night and everyone else too. Over dinner of cold watercress soup, baked flounder, scalloped potatoes and sliced tomatoes, Julian told stories about his practice and reassured Rebecca.

There was some conversation about Rebecca's upcoming trial. Miss Olivia was listening intently.

"What does one wear into a court of law?"

"Why, Mother?"

"Whatever you would wear out to dinner or to any place of business," I said, not thinking about it.

"Well, if all y'all young people think that I am going to miss this, y'all are all out of y'all's blooming minds! I think we should all be there, don't you?"

"Absolu-mont!" Huey exclaimed. "We'll all stay at the Governor's House."

Rebecca covered her mouth with her hands and managed to squeak out, "Oh!"

Julian said, "You have some very nice friends, Rebecca."

"Yes, I certainly do."

"I thought the governor lived in Columbia," Miss Olivia said. "Did he move?"

"No, Mother, it's Edward Rutledge's old place downtown."

"You say that like I remember the day that upstart signed the Declaration of Independence! Like I made cookies for Jefferson and the whole bunch of them!"

Everyone had a good laugh and Julian took the floor again. He went on to compliment Miss Olivia on her eternal youth and Huey on his home and told him he looked forward to visiting the gallery. He asked Miss Olivia about the history of the plantation and the provenance of the antiques, bringing Huey back into the conversation as he dickered politely with his mother on the origins of the clock in the living room and the sideboard in the dining room. If there had been a headline for this picturesque gathering, it would have said, *How Gentry Conduct Themselves at Dinner*. When the meal was ended, Miss Olivia took us back one hundred years.

"I declare!" Miss Olivia said. "I believe I would be so pleased to have this gentleman escort me to the living room for a little cognac."

"It would be my honor," Julian said and winked at me.

You could almost hear the rustle of her hoop skirts as she sashayed from the room.

"He's *fabulous,* Abigail!" Huey mouthed with no sound.

Rebecca bobbed her head in agreement. Byron, who was clearing the table, said nothing.

"Well?" I said to him.

"Well, since you asked . . . I say that's a mighty fine gentleman you brought here tonight."

We stood to follow them to the other room, and Huey said, "Abigail! You know what? Your complexion is absolutely radiant! What are you doing different?"

Rebecca and Byron broke out in a fit of giggles and I blushed for the second time that night.

"Oh! Abigail! I'm so sorry!"

"Well, I'm not. Let's just say it's nice to know I'm not dead quite yet."

Nineteen

All Rise

The day of justice had almost arrived, and we were as well prepared as we could be. I still could not believe that Harry Albright would allow Nat Simms to go to court. Why didn't he come up with a settlement offer? Amazing. Unless something incredible happened, this was going to be disastrous for Nat because I intended to use every single piece of evidence I had. Every single one.

So did Harry. As it turned out, I discovered that Rebecca had been ordering psychotropic pharmaceuticals on the Internet and that while she lived with Nat she had developed the unfortunate habit of immodest alcohol consumption before dark. But if I lived with Nat Simms, my liver would've looked like Plymouth Rock. However, I was furious with her for not telling me this and told her so.

"Rebecca? Do you understand that they intend to use this against you in their custody argument?"

"Yes, I do. But I don't take those pills anymore. Look, I was depressed, okay?"

"Rebecca, if anyone here understands depression, it's me. Too well. But you get meds from a licensed psychiatrist, not from a Web site! And what about this alcohol abuse?"

"I didn't think of it as a problem. It never was. Sometimes the mother of one of Sami's friends would come over in the afternoon for a glass of wine and to organize car pool or something, and when any committee met at my house I served wine. But I was never a fall-down drunk! That's absurd!"

"Are you sure?"

"Yes, Abigail, I am positive."

"Okay, then I'll take care of it."

The night before the trial, we all checked into the Governor's House Inn on Meeting Street, within walking distance of the courthouse. Huey arranged all the lodging and orchestrated our accommodations. He and Byron had the Kitchen House. Byron was to stay upstairs in one suite and Huey would be downstairs in the other. It had two fireplaces from 1760 and very generous living and sleeping spaces on both floors.

"I'm taking the whole kit and caboodle," he said. "Byron can organize cocktails on the porch and we can discuss the day in private."

Miss Olivia was ensconced in the Wagener Room on the first floor for ease of mobility. Rebecca was registered in the Laurens Room, and I was in the Middleton Suite. Our rooms had lush canopied beds, fireplaces and generous outdoor sitting areas. The Rutledge Suite was reserved for Claudia. You would have thought we were having a wedding instead of a divorce.

"I am so glad I got here!" Claudia said when she opened her door for Rebecca and me.

"I'm so glad you *came!*" Rebecca said, hugging her friend.

"Well, if I have to be subpoenaed, this is the way to suffer through it!"

"Gosh," I said, walking in and looking around, "one room is as beautiful as the other! Did y'all see the living room and parlor?"

"Charming," Claudia said. "Absolutely charming."

"Yes, it truly is." Rebecca said.

That night we, including Byron, had dinner at McCrady's, and Julian joined us. We talked and ate but even the delicious dinners of baked Chilean sea bass, beef Wellingtons and wild salmon could not diminish the morning's business, which weighed heavily on our minds. We all decided to turn in early. We walked the short distance back to our inn and said good night.

"Try and get some rest," I said to Rebecca.

"Listen, Abigail. No matter what happens tomorrow, I just want you to know how much I appreciate all you've done and are trying to do for me. You've opened my eyes to a lot of things, you know."

"And you've opened mine too."

Even though I balked, Julian decided to drive back to Kiawah Island.

"It's too late, Julian! The road's dark and . . ."

"Shhh! Save your objections for tomorrow. I want to see you bright-eyed and bushy-tailed in that courtroom!"

"Are you coming too?"

"Are you kidding? Wouldn't miss it!"

We were the first case on the docket and arrived there thirty minutes early, going through security screening, giving a moment's thought to what the world has come to that we need metal detectors everywhere. I had three boxes of papers with me—bank statements, tax returns, credit card statements, printed dialogue from Nat's ventures into teenage chat rooms, receipts from adult novelty stores and the whole gamut of damning detail, including photographs of important occasions in the children's lives where Nat is either missing or, if he's photographed, obviously disgruntled. In addition, I had a historic amount of cards and letters written to Rebecca from Nat and the children over the years, demonstrating their affection for her.

It had always been my habit to arrive early to give my client the opportunity to calm him or herself and get used to the idea of being in a courtroom, which can be extremely intimidating for anyone.

We had subpoenaed Jeff Mahoney, Charlene Johnson, Claudia Kelly, our accountant and our valuator. The population of the courtroom was sparse. There were a few folks of unknown allegiance sitting in the back rows who gave us no notice as we filed in, except one. Tisdale Simms himself. I would have known him anywhere.

I spotted Claudia reading a newspaper. Huey, Byron and Miss Olivia were seated to her right. I dropped the boxes on our table and went back to say hello.

"Early bird gets the worm," Claudia said. "Good luck!"

"Thanks," I said, hoping chance was not my best weapon.

"You go get 'em, Abigail darling!" Huey said and blew me a kiss.

"Abigail!" Miss Olivia said and curled her finger for me to come to her side. I shimmied down the row and put my ear close to her mouth. "Mash that son of a b-i-t-c-h like a grape, you hear me?"

"Yes, ma'am, I'll do my best."

A man touched my arm. "You're Abigail Thurmond?"

"Yes."

"I'm Jeff Mahoney," he said.

"Ah ha!" I said and shook his hand. "Thank you for being here."

"No problem. Glad to help."

Buoyed by their support, I made my way back to the defendant's table with Rebecca. Julian was nowhere in sight, but I guessed he would probably slip in and out. I was sure he had his own agenda for the day.

Nat and Harry Albright arrived, took their places and the games began.

"All rise!"

Judge Adrian Shelby came through the door, and I was relieved to see that her judge's robes had feminine detail. This would bode well for her opinion of Rebecca, who was dressed like the consummate Junior Leaguer. Judge Shelby wore a lace scarf at her throat to which she had attached a beautiful cameo. Julian had told me all about her. This judge was a lady, reputed for her genteel manner and her steel spine. She did not suffer fools, arrogance in counsel or witnesses, or any of the games played to sway her opinion. Her under-graduate degree was from the University of Virginia and she earned her JD at Harvard Law School. If you screwed with Judge Shelby, you rued the day you did. I could feel Nat and Harry squirming without even looking.

"Thank you for your respect to the court," she said. "Please be seated. Just as a reminder, all cell phones are to be turned off—not that you'd get great reception anyway. All right then. Is the plaintiff ready?"

"Yes, your honor, we are," Albright said.

"And the defendant?"

"Yes, your honor, we are."

"Are there any preliminary matters to bring to the court's attention before we begin?"

"No, your honor," Albright said.

I looked around to see if Charlene was there, and she was not. "Uh, excuse me your honor, one of my witnesses seems to be absent."

"The name of the witness please?"

"Charlene Johnson."

Judge Shelby went through the list of subpoenaed witnesses and found her name. There was documentation that Charlene had been served and was supposed to be there. Judge Shelby sighed and arched her eyebrow.

"Do you know where Miss Johnson might be found at this hour of the day?"

"At her place of business. Perhaps."

"Which is?"

"Simms Autoworld out on Highway 17 South."

She flipped through the papers a little more. "She is employed by your client, Mr. Albright?"

"Yes, she is," Albright said.

"She is the paramour of Mr. Simms," I said.

Judge Shelby shot me a look, which at first seemed like rockets from hell would rain down all over me, and then her face softened. She turned to the deputy sheriff standing in the area of the bench.

"Well, let's just see if one of Charleston's finest can bring her in. I just hate it when we invite someone to a party and they don't show up. Let's go get her. Now."

The deputy nodded and spoke into his two-way radio. Another officer appeared, took Charlene's name and address from the judge and left. Charlene was about to have a bad day. The story of her being arrested and taken away in handcuffs would do very little to elevate her social status among her new neighbors on Tradd Street.

Judge Shelby spoke again. "Can we get this underway until Ms. Johnson joins us?"

Harry Albright stood and gave a brief opening statement that was so foul it made me wonder how he could live with himself.

"Your honor, my client Nathaniel Simms, a leader in this community, is a fine man. As everyone knows, Simm's Autoworld has spearheaded more charitable events than any other privately owned corporation in Charleston. His generosity is renowned. He is loved and respected throughout the community by people from all walks of life. And yet sadly, there is no joy to be found in his own home. The atmosphere has deteriorated to one of walking on eggshells to avoid the rage of his wife. His wife is cold and withholds affection. In addition she has become a drunk, a drug addict and a harpy. Their relationship has become so intolerable and eroded to such a point that he feels compelled to seek divorce, permanent custody of their two children and seeks to repair the children's self-esteem and general mental health by keeping them in their own home. Thank you." Harry Albright sighed dramatically, shot me a look and took his seat.

I stood and positioned myself in front of the judge, made eye contact with her and then turned back to Harry and Nat.

"Your honor? I think it was Big Daddy in *Cat on a Hot Tin Roof* who, through the genius of Tennessee Williams, coined the phrase *bull and mendacity*. If you lived to be one hundred and twenty-seven years old, you would never meet a finer lady than Rebecca Simms. She is neither a drunk nor a drug addict. She is no more a harpy than the average mother who tries to get her children to perform normal, age-appropriate household chores. No, your honor, my colleague's description of Rebecca Simms is bull and mendacity, which we can easily prove." I turned back to Judge Shelby. "It is her husband, Nat Simms, who is the scoundrel here. He is an adulterer. He is verbally and physically abusive. He is intimidating and threatening, but perhaps the most heinous in his long list of sinful acts is the way he has misused his God-given talent for selling by manipulating the affections of their children to turn them against their own mother. My client wants this divorce as much or more than Nathaniel Simms does, but she deserves custody of her children, her home and a fair settlement. Thank you."

I gave Harry Albright a cold stare and took my seat.

Albright called his first witness. Nat. The judge swore Nat in and he took the stand. They went through the preliminary business of Nat identifying himself, his residence and so on, and then Harry's horns popped into view. Beelzebub had arrived.

"Mr. Simms, can you please explain to the court why you are suing your wife, Rebecca Simms, for divorce? And why you are seeking custody of the children on the grounds of *habitual* drunkenness including the use of *narcotics?*"

"Oh, my God, it's just so sad," Nat said. "Rebecca was ruining the lives of our children as she ruint her own self. Every day I would come home from work and find her lying on the couch, passed out while the children were running wild, eating peanut butter and jelly sandwiches for dinner. Dishes was piled up in the sink and the whole house was a pigsty. Then I come to find out that she's taking these pills . . ."

"I'd like to enter this pill bottle into evidence," Harry Albright said.

The clerk took the bottle, filed and marked it.

"Let the record show that this bottle of one hundred and twenty dosages of twenty-milligram strength Prozac was prescribed to Rebecca Simms from an online pharmaceutical company out of Miami, Florida."

The court reporter clicked away, entering Harry Albright's description into the transcript. Big deal, I thought. Half the women in this country take something so they don't go postal with assholes like you.

"Now, Mr. Simms, tell the court. How was your wife's relationship with your children?"

"It was just terrible! She was always nagging them to do this and that! Those poor kids couldn't ever just be kids, you know what I mean?"

"No, please explain."

"She had them on these schedules that were so booked up that they couldn't ever play with the neighborhood kids. First off, they had school, then they had soccer and piano, basketball and ballet, gymnastics and Mandarin . . ."

"Mandarin? Do you mean they were learning the Mandarin dialect of Chinese?"

"Yeah, she was always trying to stuff their heads with all kinds of foolishness. And nag, nag, nag. Make up your beds! Put your dishes in the dishwasher! Do your homework! Take a shower! Brush your teeth! Where are you going? Nag, nag, nag. They just couldn't take it no more. We were all just miserable with all the haranguing and carrying on. Just miserable."

"And so, tell us, Mr. Simms, how did you come to gain temporary custody of your children?"

"They begged me to let them stay with me and to get rid of their mother."

"And how were their feelings documented?"

"They went to see their guidance counselor who helped them write letters to the family court seeking relief from her. I had already told them that I was going to divorce their mother so as they could have a happy home. Oh, God . . ." At this point Nat choked up and began to cry, shoulders shaking and the whole nine yards.

Albright handed him a tissue and said, "No further questions at this time. Your witness."

Albright had written, directed and together with Nat delivered one of the most practiced, phony dramatic scenes of sentimental crud I had been forced to endure in many a moon. I stood and approached the witness stand with the stone face of a sphinx.

"Mr. Simms? Are you able to continue?"

"Yes." *Sniff!*

"Would you like a moment to compose yourself?"

"No. I'm okay."

"Okay, then. Mr. Simms? How would you describe the first ten years of your marriage? Were they happy ones?"

"Yes. Very happy. I mean, we fought and all, like most people do, but overall they were good years." Nat blew his nose loudly and took another tissue from the box nearby.

"The first fifteen?"

"Um, that's hard to remember exactly . . ."

"Please answer the question to the best of your recollection."

"Pretty good, I guess."

"You were in love with each other?"

"Yes. We were."

"Good. So these drug and alcohol problems really just surfaced in the last two years?"

"Yeah, I guess so."

"Did you ever try to get help for your wife? I mean, get her into a substance abuse program? Seek some psychiatric medical help for the problems that led her to use Prozac in the first place?"

"Um, no," Nat said, in a mumble.

"Could you speak up so that the reporter can correctly transcribe your reply, Mr. Simms?"

"I said, no, I did not."

"I don't understand, Mr. Simms. You say you were happily married for fifteen years, that you were in love with your wife, and when she seemed to be having some kind of trouble, for the very first time in your marriage *she's troubled,* and you took no action to help her. Is that correct?"

The courtroom was so quiet that when someone cleared their throat, it was very distracting. Nat looked at Albright hoping for a signal. I glanced at Albright who was reading his notes, unaware that Nat wanted coaching. Nat shifted in his chair and gave a calloused response.

"Look, Rebecca was living *The Life of Riley*. What kind of problems could she have that are real problems? It was all a bunch of bull."

"I see. Well, maybe she had a problem with your

adulterous behavior."

"Objection!" Albright said.

"Sustained," Judge Shelby said. "Counsel will avoid conjecture."

"It's not conjecture, your honor. I'd like to enter into evidence the following: over two hundred fifty receipts from various motels in the Highway 17 locale, twenty-five hundred dollars of SunCom cell phone bills for calls made between Nat Simm's cell phone and Charlene Johnson's cell phone and receipts from various adult novelty stores, including the purchases of edible panties and flavored massage oil."

The clerk, a lovely lady who probably ironed altar linens for the bishop of Charleston, took a deep breath and accepted the first box.

Nat smirked, and unfortunately for him, at that moment the judge was fixated on his face. His smirk ratcheted her ire up about ten notches. Harry Albright stared at the ceiling in dismay.

"Mr. Simms?" the judge said. "Would you like to give us an explanation for these expenditures?"

"Uh, uh . . . well, you see, your honor, Charlene Johnson has been working for my family's business for many years. And she gets these headaches. Real bad headaches. Just terrible for her."

"Yes?" the judge said as though she were waiting for the first drop of ketchup to leave the newly opened bottle.

"Yes, well, we, um, that is, I would send her off to a nearby motel to rest because she lives all the way up the road in Orangeburg and . . ."

Judge Shelby rested the side of her face on the heel of her hand and stared at Nat.

"Do you realize that you are under oath, Mr. Simms?" she said.

"Yes. Yes, I do."

"And do you know what it means to testify under oath, Mr. Simms?"

"Yes."

"Just so there will be no confusion, Mr. Simms, it means you have to tell the truth or you will be found in contempt of court, fined and sent to jail. Now, would counsel like to repeat the question? What was the question anyway?"

"Uh, Judge, actually you were asking the questions. But I guess I could pick it up with another," I said and turned back to face Nat. "Mr. Simms, are you now or were you ever engaged in an extramarital affair with Charlene Johnson?"

"Uh, uh, not really. I mean, we spent some time together. We were friends and I could talk to her about anything. When Rebecca started going all crazy she would listen to me and try to help me figure out what to do. I never meant for Charlene to think there was anything more to it than that. You know how women always want more than you want to give, right?"

Judge Shelby and I exchanged the incredulous kind of look that only two women can when confronted with a low-down lying dog of a chauvinist.

I took a breath, crossed my arms and looked at Nat

Simms in the eye. "All I'm looking for here is a yes or no answer. We will get to the details later. So is it a yes or a no, Mr. Simms?"

"I would have to say it's a no. Yes, it's a no."

"Excuse me," Judge Shelby said, "was that a no?"

"That is correct, your honor," I said.

Judge Shelby made a note for herself, probably noting Nat's lie, and looked up for us to continue.

"Mr. Simms, how do you account for the purchase of the edible panties and the flavored massage oil?"

Judge Shelby closed her eyes for a brief moment and shook her head.

"Oh, that? Those were gag gifts for a buddy of mine. He was getting married and we gave him a bachelor party."

The judge made another note for herself.

I said, "All right then. Your honor? I'd like to enter the following into evidence: these are charges and receipts for a number of plastic surgery procedures—breast augmentation, collagen implants for the chin and cheeks, abdominoplasty, which is a tummy tuck, gluteoplasty, a surgical lifting of the buttocks, rhinoplasty, which is a nose job, a series of twenty-eight sessions of microdermabrasion to remove sun damage from the face, neck and décolleté"—I paused for a breath and continued—"a series of ten sessions of Botox injections, otoplasty, which is the surgical procedure of pinning back of protruding ears, and a bill for dental resurfacing of the teeth. All of these procedures were performed on Charlene Johnson and paid for by Nat Simms."

"Great heavens!" the judge said in a gasp. "Is this true, Mr. Simms?"

"Look, Judge, I can explain . . ."

"Please do!"

Well, Nat went on with some new cock-and-bull story about how Charlene had never had good dental care. Her family lived out in the country and didn't have access to a good dentist. And her ears had always bugged her, and her nose too. Once she got those things fixed she got it in her mind that she wanted to start appearing in the television ads for the business with him, since the old man said he didn't want to do them anymore, that he was getting too damn old to have his face up there on the television set while decent people were trying to eat their supper. She thought better bosoms might give her some star quality.

Nat said he didn't have the heart to tell her that she would probably never make a TV ad with him, but he helped her, he said, because he felt sorry for her and that was all there was to it. Yep, that was all there was to it.

Nat continued his prattle and the entire courtroom listened, jaws dropped and eyes wide. Just when the growing collective of minds gathered thought we had heard the headlines of tomorrow's *National Enquirer*, the courtroom door swung open and there was Charlene Johnson. She was handcuffed and nearly hyperventilating in resentment and the language of her new improved body spoke volumes—she was as proud of herself as a Las Vegas showgirl and as angry a woman as I had ever seen. A rumble of commentary broke out and Judge Shelby slammed her gavel for order.

I couldn't wait to get Charlene on the witness stand.

TWENTY

THE DETAILS

There was a little chaos, and then the courtroom settled down. Charlene was brought before the judge. As she made her way toward the bench, head tossed back in defiance, there was a pronounced pump to the swing in her backyard. Every eye was on her bright pink clinging jersey dress, which left little to the imagination. Her black patent leather pumps had three-inch heels and tied around the ankle. The surgeon had taken her gravity-defying breasts to awe-inspiring dimensions and had given new definition to the term *booty*. I imagined the rear landscaping was intended for balance as much as anything else. Lord knows, if she hadn't been anchored into those shoes and toting ballast in the northeast quadrant to equal the southwest, friends and family would've made another career picking her up off the floor.

Good taste had taken a holiday.

Once again, as the snickering and whispering reached a new crescendo, Judge Shelby found it necessary to restore order with a whack of her gavel. Try as she did to maintain a straight face, the smile of judgmental self-righteousness crept into the corners of her mouth. Even Sandra Day O'Connor would've tossed the court a perceptible sign of amusement.

Nat was still on the witness stand and I told him he could step down for the moment.

"Are you Charlene Johnson?" Judge Shelby said.

"Yeah, and I don't understand why you all had to drag me into this. I ain't . . ."

"You were subpoenaed, Ms. Johnson, *obviously* as a hostile witness . . ."

"I ain't gonna get in the middle of his shit . . ."

"You will refrain from the use of foul language in the courtroom . . ."

"Well, that's all this is, you know . . ."

"And you will not interrupt the judge."

Charlene became silent and turned to face Nat, seething with anger.

Charlene, who had great difficulty with the whole concept of speaking only when spoken to said, "You wanna know what's going on here? I'll tell you plain and simple. This man is a bas—"

The judge held up her hand as a sign for Charlene to stop talking, then sighed with the war-weary face of a judge who has done battle with all manner of wronged women and who held particular disdain for those who lacked reasonable decorum.

"Counselor? Shall we swear in your witness?"

"By all means," I said.

This wasn't the order in which I intended to take the testimony of my witnesses, but several factors came into play. Charlene was looking like a flight risk. Before she caught the next plane to Hawaii, I wanted her on the record. Second, Charlene was obviously furious with Nat and ready to napalm his credibility. It was best to capture her point of view while the napalm was still fresh and frothy. And last, I didn't want her found in contempt of court, hustled off to a holding cell, building a temper tantrum the size of the Sears Tower and then refusing to testify. *That* would've been a disaster. Besides, Judge Shelby was smart enough to put all the pieces together without me following my prearranged menu.

"Do you swear to tell the truth, the whole truth . . ."

"Yew ken betcha yer bottom dollar on *that!*"

"Please answer *I do.*"

"*I do.*"

As I gathered my thoughts to begin interrogating Charlene, I thought to myself, *Oh, my God in heaven, this is a first. I've got a certifiable nut bag on the stand and there's no predicting and very little controlling what will happen!* But I took comfort in the fact that Shelby was a cool head and if things started getting crazy, she'd call a halt to it. I approached the bench.

I went through the normal beginning questions for the benefit of the transcript and the folks in the peanut gallery and looked back to see Julian slip through the door and stand against the back wall. He was going to love this, I thought.

"So, Ms. Johnson, can you describe the nature of your relationship with Nat Simms?"

"Right here in front of all these uptight people?"

Charlene smiled from ear to ear and the air thickened with rumbles of guffaws and snickers. A slam of the gavel quieted things down.

An unsmiling Judge Shelby turned to Charlene. "The witness will kindly answer the question without trying to entertain the courtroom."

Charlene closed her eyes and shrugged her shoulders. "I worked for him."

I cleared my throat and began again. "And the length of your employ?"

"Over seven years. I came to work for him right out of high school. First I was answering phones in the service department, and then I got myself promoted up to the receptionist in the sales department. Now I organize contracts, titles, leases and everything else that has to do with buying a car after the salesman has cut the deal."

I decided to start out with a bomb and let old Charlene know that she was near the edge of the cliff.

"Okay, let me understand this a little more fully, Ms. Johnson. If someone comes into Simms Autoworld and buys a car, you're the person who gives him the contract to sign . . ."

"Right, right, right, and I try to sell him extended warranty if it's a used car and all that stuff."

"And how successful are you at selling extended warranties? I mean, don't people generally resist those?"

"Objection! The question is irrelevant!"

"Where are we going here, Ms. Thurmond?"

"I am trying to establish the character of the witness, the level of her responsibility and her value to the business. We know she has longevity with the company, but I gotta tell you, your honor, if you'll just indulge me for a few minutes, the reason for this line of questioning will become clear."

"Overruled."

"Thank you," I said and turned back to Charlene. I had to look away again because her eye makeup was applied with such gusto it was off-putting. I couldn't imagine how a woman could even get *that* much mascara on normal lashes. They looked like awnings. Ridiculous.

"Does that mean I should answer the question?"

"Please. Just tell the court how successful you were in selling extended warranties."

"Well, before I got my new titties, I wasn't too good at it at all." Gasping and laughter filled the air. Then, in a moment of unbridled horror for the genteel, she actually cupped her synthetic mammaries.

The gavel slammed once more, and Judge Shelby said, "Ms. Johnson, this is the last time I am going to remind you not to use coarse and vulgar language or to behave in a coarse and vulgar manner in my courtroom. The next time you say something so crass or make a motion so crass, you will be fined in contempt of court and sit in county jail for thirty days. Is that clear?" She shook her head and looked at me. "Proceed."

"I'm sure your breast augmentation helped your confidence and, therefore, your sales. But before we discuss your various plastic surgery procedures, I'm wondering about something else. Did you ever have the occasion to receive a deposit check from a customer simply made out to Nat Simms and not Simms Autoworld?"

"Of course, it happened all the time." Charlene's face was blood red. Maybe it was sinking in that this wasn't a joke or a show.

"And what did you do with those checks?"

"Objection!"

I felt like saying, *Oh, put a sock in it, Harry,* but I looked to the judge, who understood exactly where I was going, and she said, "Overruled."

Charlene sat there wondering if answering the question would implicate her in a crime.

"Please answer the question, Ms. Johnson."

"Nope. I ain't got a lawyer, and if I tell the truth I might get myself in trouble, so I ain't answering that question."

Harry and Nat were whispering to each other.

"You have to answer the question, Ms. Johnson," I said.

"Objection! Let the witness be informed that she can take protection from self-incrimination under the Fifth Amendment."

Charlene looked confused at first and then remembered what she had done during her deposition. In addition, I guessed she had watched *Judge Judy* or *LA Law* often enough to recall that she didn't have to testify against herself. She looked over at Nat and Harry, with their self-satisfied faces, because they had saved Nat by reminding Charlene of her rights. Charlene might have been a screaming redneck, but she wasn't totally stupid. And she was furious with Nat for her own reasons.

She said, "Look, I'll tell y'all whatever y'all want to know, but I want to be impuned, okay?"

"You mean you want witness protection? Immunity?"

"Yep. That's it."

Harry Albright almost burst his carotid artery with his objections, and finally after five minutes in Judge Shelby's chambers it was settled. The judge ruled that Charlene Johnson had complete immunity.

"This is a divorce hearing, not the Enron fiasco. I want to hear what Ms. Johnson has to say. End of story."

When we reentered the courtroom, the public seating area was filled. I suspected that while cell phones weren't ringing, people were text-messaging each other in a fury to come watch the spectacle.

The hearing resumed.

"I had asked you, Ms. Johnson, what you did in the case of a check simply made out to Nat Simms instead of Simms Autoworld?"

"I deposited them."

"In the company's account?"

"Sometimes."

"And where did they go at other times?"

"In other accounts that me and Nat set up for our own selves."

Nat put his head in his hands and Albright shook his head.

I entered the accounts into evidence from four different banks, and Judge Shelby was smoldering. As a general rule, judges and the laws of the land don't take kindly to embezzlement and tax evasion. But Shelby said nothing then. She simply listened.

"And what did you and Mr. Simms do with that money?"

"Well, all sorts of things. Mostly we had fun with it."

"I see. Did it pay for your hotel rooms?"

"Yes, it did."

"And dinners in nice restaurants?"

"Yes."

"Are you involved in a romantic relationship with Mr. Simms?"

"I was, but we broke up. It was the biggest mistake of my life."

"What was? Breaking up with him or getting involved with him in the first place?"

"Getting involved with him. Look, at first he just wanted to flirt. I could understand that. That's how men are. They like to flatter you and then you flatter them back and then they think they're hot sh—, you know what I mean? I didn't say the word but you know what I meant, right?"

Judge Shelby looked over her reading glasses down at Charlene and said, "The court thanks you for your restraint, Ms. Johnson. Please continue."

"Well, Nat started telling me that I'd be so pretty if

my ears got fixed, and I said, well, you know I can't afford to do that! Shoot, he only paid me seven dollars and sixty cents an hour. So he said, look, I can pay for it, so I said okay. Then it was my nose and my teeth. By that time we were very hot and heavy and he said he wanted to marry me. But then he seemed to be losing interest, so that's when I went and got my chest fixed. And doncha know it, he came sniffing around again like a hungry dog just looking for a place to bury his nose. And I guess I fell in love with the son of a . . . gun. Son of a gun's okay, right?"

I couldn't believe it, but I was almost feeling sorry for Charlene. But not for too long.

"Didn't you know he was married and had children?"

"Of course I knew that! Everybody knew that! But he lived in this beautiful house in downtown Charleston and he had two beautiful children that he said we could raise together. A nice house and a family was all I ever wanted in this whole world, and I knew *I'd* never get it. Not unless a miracle happened. Bagging Nat Simms seemed like a miracle to a girl like me. I didn't care if he wanted to have sex three times a day or how he wanted to do it either. All I wanted was to be in that house fixing his dinners and reading story books to little innocent children, making them all happy."

I paused for a moment thinking of the thousands of women like Charlene who could so easily justify the wreckage they caused. Was it in the name of love or loneliness or greed?

"But I gather things didn't work out?"

"First of all, it wasn't very nice. I mean, I know that his wife is as homely as a hog, I'm sorry to say it . . ."

Rebecca gasped and I knew she was probably on the verge of crying, just listening to Charlene. What woman wouldn't be upset?

"And she doesn't nurture Nat like he needs, but after I spent a few days with those children, I didn't want no part of it. Nope, I quit."

"I see. Could you explain to the court what caused this change in your feelings?"

"Look, I can't have my own kids, but that don't make it right to steal another woman's family. It was bad enough to be taking her husband, but he didn't love her anymore, and I figured they would wind up divorced anyway. So that wasn't such a big deal. The real killer was that Nat just didn't want to give her anything after all those years she put up with them. No, no. Once I got in that house I saw a very different side of Nat Simms and I didn't like it at all."

"So, you say he didn't want to give his wife what you considered to be a fair settlement and you had some guilt over taking her children away from her? And these things upset you. Is that correct?"

"Yeah, that's right. And they all bossed me around like I was the maid! Nat never said a word about the sassing and all to his kids. He just smiled and said, well, if they want to go to the mall, take them! I didn't get into this whole mess to be somebody's chauffeur! He was supposed to love me and respect me, and he didn't. Then we all started fighting, and finally I just said to hell with it. It wasn't worth it just to live in a big house."

Charlene shot the judge a look, and Judge Shelby was so entranced by the story she was hearing that she blew off Charlene's careless use of the word *hell*. Maybe she agreed with her.

"So, we may assume that the relationship is over now?" I said.

"You may assume that for sure, but there's something else to say that you didn't ask me about."

"Which is?"

"That house spooked me. Everywhere I looked was his wife's something or other. I would say, oh, aren't these towels pretty? His daughter would say, my mom embroidered them. Or I would say, oh, this is such a beautiful afghan, and his son would say, my mom made it. There was so much stuff in that house of hers that it would never be mine. Even these beautiful murals of birds and the marsh that she painted on their dining room walls. Besides, that house was hers and the whole plan Nat had was just greedy and nasty. He's a terrible man."

The courtroom was silent as everyone took it all in. It was the first time I had ever had a hostile witness who actually wound up testifying for my client.

"Thank you, Ms. Johnson. We may have to call you again, so please stay in town."

"Oh, I ain't going no place! I wouldn't miss this for nothing."

I nodded my head.

"Your witness," I said to Albright.

"Your honor, we have no questions at this time."

"Then you may step down, Ms. Johnson. The defense would like to call Dr. Claudia Kelly."

Nat and Albright looked around to see who Dr. Claudia Kelly was and in minutes it was all revealed.

Claudia took the stand, and after the requisite questions she explained in her most professional manner that the sum total of all of Charlene Johnson's surgical procedures could well have exceeded fifty to sixty thousand dollars. I entered the receipts I had found into evidence and made the remark that these were marital assets of which my client was entitled to half.

Poor Charlene. She had been a good girl for as long as she could. Charlene jumped from her seat and began screaming as loud as she could.

"If you think you're getting these back, you can *forget it!* These boobs are *mine* and these *teeth* are mine and this *fanny* is all mine! Go get your *own* because there ain't *no way* . . ."

Whack! Whack! Whack!

Judge Unamused Adrian spoke. "Ms. Johnson! Sit down and be quiet! Let me tell you something, your plastic surgery bills are the most offensive use of marital assets I have ever seen in the entirety of my professional career. Normally, in so much as the definition of *normal* applies here, your *improvements* would be evaluated and fifty percent of the cost of the surgeries would be awarded to the wife. But if I hear one peep from you, one *peep,* I will order half of them *literally* removed! This court is in recess for lunch. We reconvene at two o'clock."

TWENTY-ONE

. . . AND I'M THE LAWN MOWER

H uey and Byron were taking Miss Olivia back to
the hotel for a quiet lunch, and the rest of us
planned to walk to a nearby restaurant. It was
unusual that the judge had ordered such a long lunch
break, but that was probably due to her need for
recovery time from the overall vulgarity of the
morning's session. God knows, I needed a break.

Claudia, Rebecca and I were leaving the courthouse
when I saw Julian coming toward us.

"Abigail! I knew you were good, girl, but I didn't
know how brilliant you were!" He gave me a big kiss
on the cheek. "My God! What a show! Shelby must be
ready to throw Albright right out the window!"

"Albright's an idiot," I said. "They should've settled."

"Like the young people say," Claudia said, "no
freaking duh!"

We took two more steps, and suddenly Tisdale Simms
took Rebecca's arm to stop her and speak to her.

"Becca. Forgive me. I had no idea about Nat and his
. . . his running around and all of this horrible business.
I'm an old man. He's my only son. I *believed* in him."

Rebecca burst into tears and blurted, "But I was married to him for all these years and you never even called me! You never even called me *once!* I took care of your wife all through her illness until the day she died. I gave you two grandchildren. I did everything I could . . ." Rebecca's voice, filled with pain she had never spoken of, tapered off into whisper, and then she said, "Oh, what's the use?"

She pulled her arm away and he grabbed it again.

"Listen, please! You're right. I should've realized there were two sides to every story. I'm asking you to *forgive me,* Becca. When this whole thing is settled those children are going to need a man in their lives. Nat's not going to be any use to you after today. Or me either. That lying sack of shit in there is not the nice boy his mother and I raised. I don't know how in the world he became so deceitful to you, to me, to everyone. I can help you. I want to help you. You and the children are all I've got now. Please don't turn your back on me."

I was standing right next to her and listening to everything they said to each other. I could feel Rebecca's frustration and disappointment in her father-in-law. It was so typical of families and how they divided their allegiances during a divorce. I looked at Tisdale's face, deeply lined from years of living, his teeth worn down from age and his red-rimmed eyes mirroring the sincerity of his plea.

"You're their grandfather and nothing will ever change that. I forgive you. Of course I forgive you. I probably would've done the same thing if I were in your shoes." She didn't hug him. She just stepped away. "When this is over, we'll talk, okay?"

He nodded his head, "Okay, then. Thanks."

When he was out of hearing I said to Rebecca, "That was the noble thing to do, Rebecca. Makes me proud to know you."

A small grin of satisfaction crossed her face. But it was a grin born of pain. It made me think again of the well of disappointments and slights Rebecca must have felt in the absence of Tisdale's loyalty. And the loyalty of her friends and acquaintances. She had done as much charity work as any woman I had ever known and there had been no calls from them, wondering what they could do to help. But you're only as good as your last dinner dance, and perhaps she had fallen out of that circuit. It was summer after all, and she had moved to Pawleys. Yes, that was probably why.

"So where should we go?" I said. "I feel like a big hunk of raw meat for lunch."

Claudia giggled, and at that same moment a man tapped her on the shoulder.

"Excuse me! I'm Frank Del Mastro from the *Post and Courier*. Dr. Kelly, would you like to comment on the judge's remark regarding Charlene Johnson being in possession of Rebecca Simms's assets?"

"We don't talk to the press, Claudia," I said.

"Hey, I'm a whole big girl, Abigail," she said with a tone that surprised me, but then, has anyone ever been able to tell a doctor how to behave? "Listen, Frank, you can go tell the world that I said if Judge Shelby wants to repossess fifty percent of Charlene Johnson's improvements, I'll do the procedures on the house!"

The reporter scampered away, taking notes and very pleased with himself. Claudia burst out laughing, and then Rebecca got tickled. I stood there in Mother Superior mode for a moment, and then I realized how funny the thought of it was. Over lunch at Slightly North of Broad (SNOBs to the foodie cognoscenti), needless to say, we were reduced to giggling ninth graders, describing Charlene missing half of everything.

"Can you see it? She goes to sit down and needs a pillow to even things out!"

"Wait! Visualize this! She's trying to sell a warranty package to some poor man and has to put a canteloupe down one side of her shirt first!"

We thought we were pretty darn clever until we got back to the courthouse. On the front steps was a film crew from every local network affiliate, newspaper and radio station.

"I guess it's a slow news day," I said. "Don't talk to them."

We were bombarded with questions, microphones and clicking cameras. With Claudia on one side of Rebecca and me on the other, we took the steps as quickly as we could. They were on our heels like bloodhounds.

"Do you think the judge will really make Charlene give back a breast implant?"

"And half her buttocks?"

"How much of a settlement are you expecting?"

No comment! No comment! No comment!

They followed us right in to the courtroom, where the public seats were completely filled and the overflow lined the walls. I knew that when Judge Shelby entered the courtroom, she was not going to be pleased. I was right.

Everyone stood, and she scanned the room carefully, putting everyone present on notice that this was a serious proceeding. Her expression was inscrutable, but I knew enough about her from the morning's session to know she wasn't about to allow her courtroom to become a circus.

"Thank you for your respect to the court. Please be seated." She folded her arms across her desk and looked across the sea of faces, faces anticipating an afternoon of entertainment, making mockery of the broken lives of Rebecca and Nat, the takeaway value being raunchy gossip about Charlene's transformation and how pathetic Rebecca had become. Shelby reached up, removed her reading glasses from her head, folded them, placed them on her desk and leaned back. The room was absolutely silent as she scanned it once more. "All right then," she said, "I can see we have a lot of newcomers to today's hearing, and I also see that a lot of you are from the press. I'm going to lay down some guidelines, which, if not followed precisely, will result in your immediate expulsion from the courtroom. No cell phones, no talking among yourselves and no pictures are to be taken, which includes the videotaping of this session. Any and all conversations with the defendant, the plaintiff or the witnesses in this case are to be conducted outside this building. Do I make myself clear?"

There was some rumbling and movement and the sounds of cell phones being powered down. Throats were cleared, cameras were put back in their cases and the courtroom became quiet. Judge Shelby motioned to Albright to get the party started.

"I'd like to call Dr. Karen Tedesco to take the stand."

Dr. Tedesco came forward, was sworn in and took her place in the witness chair. She was the quintessential image of a fifties high school guidance counselor. Imperious and smug. Brittle-mannered and buttoned up. Unmanicured but tidy, not that tidy was bothersome, but her tidiness probably extended to excruciatingly clean hairbrushes and refrigerator hydrator drawers compulsively scrubbed with disinfecting agents in the belief the efforts helped to ward off head colds or neuralgia. Her shoe rack probably held ten pairs of round-toed sensible shoes and a row of blouses covered in tiny prints. She probably hadn't had great sex in thirty years if ever and *never* with someone of another social class. Okay, okay, you know the type.

Her identity and profession noted for the record, Albright began his questioning.

"Dr. Tedesco, how long have you known the Simms children?"

"For five years."

"And would you call them troubled children?"

315

"No, not at all. They were good children. Never in any trouble."

"Good. Now, can you please tell the court how you came to know the children had problems?"

"It began last winter when I found them waiting in the rain for their mother to pick them up from school. It was getting dark and I saw them outside on the front lawn of the campus. They were getting drenched, poor things. So I went up to them and said, *Is someone coming to pick you up?* Sami, the older one, said something like, *Mom's late again.* So I just sort of put that in the back of my head and waited another twenty minutes until she arrived. Mrs. Simms said there was an accident on the Cooper River Bridge and she was stuck. Then it happened several more times and I started making notes about it. I mean, how many accidents are there on the bridge? Not that many." At that point Dr. Tedesco straightened herself and pursed her lips in Rebecca's direction. "Let's be honest. It's not safe for a child to be left like that what with all you read in the papers these days."

"So, the children's safety was compromised because they were frequently left unattended after school, sometimes in the dark and sometimes in inclement weather."

"In my professional opinion, yes, it was. And their health as well."

"What other kinds of things got your attention about the Simms children?"

"Well, in the early years, Mrs. Simms was always around the school. She served as class mother many times and was very active in the parents' organization. Suddenly, I didn't see her at all! She didn't attend the science fair and other activities the school had for the children to show what they were doing in class. I actually called her to see if everything was all right in the home and she didn't sound right to me."

"What do you mean she didn't sound right?"

"Well, if you want my honest opinion, she sounded a little whoopee."

"Can you define whoopee for the court?"

"Of course, you know what that is—either alcohol or drugs."

"Do you recall what time of day or night you made that phone call?"

"Yes, it was around five o'clock. I remember that distinctly because I was about to go home. My colleagues leave as fast as they can, but I like to stay and do paperwork when the school finally gets quiet." She looked up at Shelby as though the judge would put in a good word for her with the board of education. Shelby all but sniffed at her.

"Okay, just one more question, Dr. Tedesco. How did you come to be the one to help the children write letters to Judge Shelby asking to live with their father instead of their mother?"

"One day I saw Sami crying in the hallway. Her locker was jammed and she couldn't open it. That happens from time to time. Anyway, she was obviously very frustrated, and so I asked her if she wanted to come into my office and talk for a moment. She said that she would. Well, then the poor girl started pouring out her heart to me. She said her mother had turned into a monster and that she fought with the whole family all the time. She seemed to know that her father intended to file for divorce and she didn't want to live with her mother."

"Can you qualify *monster?* I mean, were there specific incidences of cruel behavior on the part of the mother?"

"No, not exactly *cruel.* I would say that Sami felt that she couldn't make her mother happy no matter what she did. She was a very unhappy young lady. As was her brother. She begged me to help them."

"I see. No further questions."

I stood to have my moment with Dr. Tedesco.

"Dr. Tedesco. How common is it for teenage girls to be unhappy?"

"Oh!" she said, smiling. "Teenagers? They're never happy! They love to find things to complain about, but that's also a natural part of the maturation process—you know, that the adults have to be wrong or out of style so that they can justify breaking away and trying things on their own."

"Yes." I paused. "Well, that's always been my thought too. It's a very volatile time in their lives, hormones kicking in, worrying about popularity, getting into college and all those things . . . am I right?"

"Oh, my yes! Just look at the national suicide statistics. Shocking!"

"Yes, and heartbreaking too. I guess what has me

bothered about your testimony so far is that there's no abuse, no serious neglect, nothing beyond Sami's normal fluctuating teenage emotions over a ride home from school, which—correct me if I'm wrong—is ten blocks from their home, and that in her teenage judgment she thinks that she and her brother would fare better in the custody of their father. Did she tell you why she thought that was the case?"

"Well, I know that their father spent a lot of time with them, especially on the weekends, taking them to Clemson games all over the southeast. Sami wants to go to Clemson and become a cheerleader. I guess they have more fun with him."

"More fun? Fun?" I stopped and looked at the judge. "Well, fun *does* have its place in a parent-child relationship. Not as important as raising children with good morals, values and good personal habits."

"Objection!"

"Sustained. Ms. Thurmond? You know better."

I arched an eyebrow at Shelby and she arched one back in agreement. Fun Dad. Party Dad. Good-time Dad. No, the message was clear to all present and Tedesco was not happy about her testimony being trivialized.

"All right, her mother was late picking them up some of the time. Do you recall when that began?"

"Yes, it was last winter, because it started getting dark earlier."

"And this implication that Mrs. Simms sounded like she had been using drugs or alcohol when you spoke to her on the phone. When was that?"

"That was sometime after Easter. And before school ended for the year."

"And you said earlier while being questioned by Mr. Albright that you began to document how frequently Rebecca Simms was late to pick up her children. Can you tell the court how many times that was?"

"Twice, after that first time I spoke to Sami and Evan about it. But as you know, Sami said there had been other times."

"Twice? That many! Wow. I see. Since you were building a file against Mrs. Simms, did you bother to ask her why she was late? A dental appointment? Maybe a flat tire?"

"No, I did not."

"So basically, you wrote letters with the children to this court to support a claim that it would be in the best interest of the children to live with their father based on *three* late pickups that you witnessed, the *whining* of a teenage girl and the supposition that paternal custody would be more *fun* for the children?"

No answer.

"Please answer the question."

Dr. Tedesco began to bluster. "Well, it sounds very . . . I mean, the way *you* put it . . ."

"Yes or no?"

"Yes." It was a yes with the sound and size of a mite.

"All right, Dr. Tedesco, you may step down. I'd like to call Jeff Mahoney, your honor."

Mahoney took the stand and hammered Nat Simms's

reputation as a man, a husband and as a father.

"How would you describe Nat Simms as a man?"

"If I answer that question, I'm afraid I wouldn't have very many flattering things to say, Ms. Thurmond. He's not my favorite neighbor."

"Well, then, try to describe his character in a factual manner, based on incidents you have actually witnessed."

"You mean like last Christmas at the Joneses' holiday party? I was standing there next to Nat and two other gentlemen in their dining room next to the buffet. The room was very crowded. We couldn't help but overhear John Smiley's wife going on and on about the great job Rebecca had done putting together the nativity pageant at church. Then she went on about Rebecca's watercolors—she's an artist, you know."

I just nodded my head so he would keep talking.

"Jim Hardy leaned into Nat and said something like, *You must be awful proud of her*. Nat said, and I'll remember these words till the day I die, *She makes me sick*. Then he took his glass of wine and threw it on the back of her dress. Rebecca jumps, Smiley's wife shrieks and Nat says something like, *Oh! I'm so sorry! I tripped!* He wasn't sorry. It was deliberate. I saw it with my own eyes."

"I see. And are there any other incidents you can recall?"

"Yes. A lot of them. Virtually every time I ran into him when he was with his wife, something snide would come out of his mouth."

"Do you mean a snide remark about his wife?"

"Yes. And when he was with the men, like a Super Bowl party or something, it was always a game of one-upmanship. He's just generally obnoxious. Almost intolerable."

"Okay. And how would you describe him as a father?"

Jeff Mahoney looked down and chuckled, shaking his head.

"Pathetic. Look, my daughter is in Sami's class. How about this? She told me that Nat promised his daughter breast implants when she goes to college to help her chances of becoming a cheerleader, if and only if she would make a strong argument that she wanted to live with him. Is that good parenting? Isn't that a little sick?"

"Thank you, Mr. Mahoney." I turned to Albright. "Your witness."

"No questions."

Things were progressing nicely, even better than I expected. Dr. Tedesco's testimony had been proven insignificant and Mahoney told the tale we needed. It was time to put Nat back in the spotlight.

"Your Honor, I would like to recall Mr. Nat Simms," I said.

"You're still under oath, Mr. Simms," Shelby said.

Nat sat in the witness chair and looked at me with his *so what* face. Any other man would have been sheepish or furious from the implications of his loathsome behavior. But not Nat. He could not have cared less what anyone thought of him.

"Mr. Simms, do you use the Internet?"

"Sure. Everyone does."

"Have you ever visited a chat room?"

"Sure. All the time. It's fun."

"Have you ever posed as a teenager in a teenage chat room? Or visited a porn site?"

"No. Why in the world would I do that?"

"Your Honor, I'd like to enter into evidence the hard drive of Nat Simms's computer that has hundreds of records showing visits to teenage chat rooms and pornographic Web sites."

Nat started laughing as the clerk took the evidence.

"Would the witness like to tell the court what's funny about this?"

"I have a son, you know. You don't think boys go to porn sites? He's a red-blooded American boy with a healthy interest in women! And the teenage chat rooms? You know . . ."

I gave him sufficient rope from which he could hang and dangle his sorry ass.

"I have a teenage girl! So what's the big deal?"

Nat looked all around the courtroom with his hands extended as if to say, *Right? Right?*

"The big deal, Mr. Simms, is that the computer tower is located in your bedroom and almost all of these site visits happened after two o'clock in the morning and on weeknights. Are you saying that your children sneaked into your room at that hour and used *your* computer? When they have their own laptops?"

Little beads of sweat formed on the witness's forehead and he stuttered, "Uh, uh . . ."

"Probably not in the best interest of the children to live with a parent who frequents porn sites."

"Objection!" I looked at Albright. I'm happy to report that my colleague did not look well. Had Albright truly thought I wouldn't use it? It was in the interrogatory and the deposition. Just because Nat lied then it didn't mean I couldn't use the evidence.

Shelby ignored Albright and looked at me. She was getting disgusted and it was all over her face.

"Mr. Simms, is it true that you actually promised your daughter surgery as a reward for her lobbying efforts to help you win custody?"

"No."

"Did you ever discuss plastic surgery with your daughter?"

"No."

What? The liar! "Not ever?"

"That's right. Not ever."

"Did you make promises to her of any kind if she would help you in this custody argument?"

"No."

"Does your daughter know Charlene Johnson?"

"Yes."

"What does she think about her?"

" 'Bout the same thing we all do."

"Which is?"

"That she ain't nothing but a liar and a social climber. I couldn't get rid of her. That woman was driving me *crazy!*"

Charlene was on her feet that instant, trying to get from her seat to the witness box.

"WHAT?" Charlene screamed. *"YOU SON OF A BITCH!"*

Whack! Whack! Whack!

"I wasn't gonna marry her. I mean *look at her!* She's a freak!"

Just as Charlene almost got to Nat and was in midair diving for his throat, the burly deputy grabbed her, stabilized her and held her arms behind her back.

"YOU BASTARD!" Charlene spit and washed Nat's ugly face.

"That's it. Charlene Johnson? You're in contempt of court!" Shelby turned to the deputy and said, "Get her out of here!"

"I HOPE SHE GETS YOUR LAST PENNY!"

Whack! Whack! Whack!

"This court is adjourned for the day! I want to see counsel and their clients in my chambers! *Now!"*

If anger was tangible matter and Judge Shelby had possessed the power to paint the air with it, all of us would have succumbed to fits of spasm from its electrical shock beginning at the doorway to the places where we stood around her desk. Shelby was beyond furious.

"This case is a disgrace," she said, "and never should've seen a courtroom. *Never!* This is an appalling waste of my time and the taxpayers' money. Mr. Albright? You knew the nature of your client's behavior, his lies, and yet you allowed this display?

Shame on you! I'm going to file a recommendation with the South Carolina Bar Association that you be censured! And you! Mr. Simms? Running around? Porn sites? And even skimming the family business? That's a matter for another court, but you may be sure that I will inform the IRS of your criminal behavior. I have heard enough nonsense from both of you! Mr. Simms? You can't stop trumping up charges against your wife? You can't settle? Fine! Then I'm going to settle it for you. I'm going to make this decision tonight and read it in the morning and, by golly, you'll comply, Mr. Simms or you'll find yourself behind bars. Do either of you need any clarification? We reconvene at ten. Good day!"

Harry Albright and Nat Simms slithered out of her chambers like the snakes they were. We watched him go, listened to the solid clunk of the door behind them and then turned to each other.

"Thank you, Judge Shelby," I said. "Would you like us to leave as well?"

"Of course you can go, but I thought you might like a moment to let them disappear and let the media disperse. Whew! This has been *some* day."

"It was horrible," Rebecca said. "I never even got a chance to tell my side."

It was true. All the filthy garbage was rolling down the streets in a windstorm of gossip's delight and Rebecca felt tainted by it.

"Rebecca? Listen, I trust Judge Shelby to adjudicate this fairly. I really do. If I trust her, you should too."

"It's going to be all right, Mrs. Simms. Go get a good night's sleep."

The courtroom was empty as Rebecca and I passed through it. I imagined that Claudia, Huey and the others had probably gone back to the hotel. I hadn't seen Julian since the morning. He was probably lost in the crowd. I couldn't wait to tell him what had gone on and to hear what he had to say.

From the lobby we could see there was a commotion on the courthouse steps. A crowd was gathered and the police were trying to restore order.

"Maybe we should take another exit," I said.

"Wait! Oh, my God! It's Jeff! Abigail! Hurry!"

"Mahoney? What in the world? You wait here! There's press everywhere."

I pushed open the doors just in time to see the arresting officer slap handcuffs on Nat Simms and Jeff Mahoney.

"Okay!" the police officer said. "Show's over! Everybody go home!"

Albright was picking up his briefcase and his papers that were scattered everywhere. I don't know why, but I went over to help him. I guess I felt a little sorry for him.

"What happened?"

He looked at me in utter disgust and said, "Nat didn't appreciate Mahoney's testimony and suggested they settle their differences in manly tradition."

"Good grief! And Mahoney took him up on it?"

"He didn't have much of a choice. Self-defense.

Guess we had better go bail them out?"

"I'm gonna take Rebecca back to the hotel and then I'll meet you down at the pokey."

"Let me go see if I can get the police to let them go. They're probably still here because they'd have to get their patrol cars out of the parking garage and all."

"Thanks, Albright, I owe you one."

"Help me find some decent clients and we'll call it a day."

I couldn't believe it, but when Harry Albright smiled, he didn't look like the scum of the earth. Like we say in the Lowcountry, if you lived long enough, you'd see everything.

TWENTY-TWO

PEANUT GALLERY

Rebecca and I walked the short distance back to the Governor's House Inn. Huey was waiting in the lobby.

"Oh! Rebecca! Abigail! What a day! What a day!" Huey was very excited. "We're all meeting on the porch of the Kitchen House. If I had known divorce could be so invigorating, I might have dabbled in the law myself! My goodness, y'all must be exhausted!"

My cell phone rang. It was Harry Albright. "Don't worry about Nat and Mahoney. I was able to get all the charges dropped."

"That's great news. Thanks, Harry."

"Yeah, well, I'm gonna go have a stiff scotch. Maybe two. See you tomorrow."

I looked at my cell phone and thought, well, if I'd realized before today that he was a mammal, I would have told him to go get toasted and send me the receipts.

"Who was that?" Huey said.

"Harry Albright. Nat and Jeff Mahoney got into a scuffle on the courthouse steps and Albright got them off the hook. I think I might like a glass of wine."

"Did I miss something?" Huey said. "The courthouse steps? My dear, Rebecca, you are *so* much better off!"

"I know," Rebecca said.

She seemed a little down, and while I understood why, I wished she would cheer up. The day had been a decisive victory, and now it was all over except for the actual reading of the will. My patience was hovering around empty.

We passed the reception desk and the manager stopped us. He was a small, hairless man, and despite the fact that he was no doubt at the top of his class in hotel and hospitality training, he was very overexcited and stuttering a little.

"Mrs. Sim—uh, Simms?"

Rebecca said, "Yes?"

"Mrs. Simms, there have been a number, I mean, quite a few phone calls for—for—fuh you—Diane Sawyer from *G-g-g-good Morning America*, Katie Couric from the *Ta-ta-Taday Show* and Paula Za-Za-

Zahn from CNN. Kim Hubu-bu-bard Hubbard called from *People* magazine. Bruce Smith from the Associated Press. Oh, my! Is there something the hotel can do to help you?"

Rebecca took the messages from him and looked at me.

"Maybe," I said. "We'll let you know. Thanks. Thanks a lot."

Huey, who had walked ahead of us and was waiting at the door to the garden, hotfooted it right back to our sides.

"What in the world?" Rebecca said. She looked bewildered.

"Wire services. It's the miracle of technology. You'd better brace yourself."

"What's happened, Abigail?" Huey said.

"Rebecca is about to have her fifteen minutes of fame."

"No, I'm not," Rebecca said, and during the short walk to Huey's rooms she said over and over, "I'm not calling these people back. I just want to be left alone."

Miss Olivia and Claudia were waiting for us on Huey's porch. When we told them about the calls from the networks and magazines, the conversation changed gears from courtroom drama to media drama. I looked up to see Julian crossing the courtyard.

"Good evening!" I was so happy to see him, and from the corner of my eye, I saw Miss Olivia perk up. She was sweet on Julian. He kissed my cheek and shook everyone's hand, and Byron poured him a glass of red wine. "Congratulations on today, Abigail. And, Rebecca. Now why all the long faces? What are we all so serious about?"

When we told him what had happened, all he said was, *You're pulling my leg, right?*

"These reporters are just gonna dog Rebecca until they get their story," Claudia said.

"Claudia's probably right," I said.

Byron was passing peeled shrimp that were so sweet they must've been swimming that morning.

"These shrimp are incredible, Byron."

"I drove over to Simmon's this afternoon. Right off the boat."

"Have you spoken to your sister, Daphne?"

"No, do you need me to call her?"

"Well, if you're talking to her, maybe you could ask her to tape the news for me."

"No problem."

"She's wonderful, you know."

"She's a rascal."

Byron smiled, and I thought to myself that he must love being here and included in everything. And why not? He was practically family, except for the obvious.

"Oh! Wait!" Huey said to Rebecca. "I'll call Frances DuBose from London Hair! She'll come for me if I beg her, and she can do your makeup too. She's fab-u-lous!"

"Hold on, everybody," Rebecca said. "I don't want all this, this intrusion. Wasn't today bad enough?"

Miss Olivia, who until then had been very quiet,

spoke up. "Now you listen to me, Rebecca. I've got something to say . . ."

"Can I get you something, Mother?" Huey said.

"Yes, you can give me two minutes of your attention, that's what." Everyone got quiet. "But a little more sherry might be nice." She held her glass in Huey's general direction, but her eyes were honed on Rebecca's face. "Sometimes notoriety comes to us whether we like it or not. And that's what has happened to you today. You have uninvited attention. I can understand why you wish it would all go away—that's testament to your refined nature. You're too young to remember the Watergate trials, but I can assure you that Sam Ervin no more wanted to be in front of all those television cameras than Judge Shelby wanted all that nonsense in her courtroom today. Notoriety doesn't make you any less dignified, young lady. It all depends on how gracefully you manage to handle it." Huey handed her glass of sherry to her. She looked up at him sweetly. "Thank you, son."

Once again, Miss Olivia had put things in perspective.

"You know, Rebecca," I said, "you really do have an opportunity here. Think about it. Just a couple of hours ago, you were disappointed that you didn't get to tell your side of things. Now, suddenly, without warning, you could have two hundred million people listening to whatever your little heart wants to say. So if they're gonna torment you until they get their story, what's the story you'd like to tell?"

"It surely sounds worthy of consideration, Rebecca," Julian said.

I could see the wheels in Rebecca's mind start to turn as she stood and walked to the porch railing. She picked a sprig of confederate jasmine and twirled it between her fingers.

It was true enough that the trial had been a distasteful experience, and there was no doubt that in the least case the story would be carried in the local media. At last there was something for them to talk about besides the weather. True, there was another tropical depression stirring around in the Caribbean, but it wouldn't make landfall for another week. And this was Rebecca's window of opportunity to talk about morality, if she chose to do so, or about the perils of plastic surgery. What would she choose?

"Whatcha thinking?" Claudia said to her.

"I'm thinking that maybe if I had paid closer attention to Nat's antics when they began, that maybe I could've pulled him back into the marriage."

"I don't think that's so for a minute!" Huey said. "What are you going to wear tomorrow? Does anyone know what time Saks closes? You can't go in there tomorrow looking like, I don't know, like a teacher!"

"Yes, I can, Huey, and I will! What's the matter with looking like a teacher? This is how I dress!"

"We're getting off topic here, my friends," I said. I wanted to pinch Huey until he was black and blue and he knew it. "So, you think if you'd acted earlier on, insisted on counseling or something, things may have played out differently?"

"Maybe. But I didn't because I *couldn't*. I mean, look, y'all, if there's one thing I've learned through all of this it's that having friends like all of you saved me. That's what was always wrong in my life with Nat. I had no other family around to support me."

"Well," Miss Olivia said, "there's your message! You get on those cameras and tell American women just that!"

"She's right, Rebecca!" Claudia said. "Isolation is a dangerous thing!"

"No man is an island!" Huey said and pointed his finger to the porch ceiling.

Everyone looked around and gave Huey a little heat. "Oh, puhleeze!"

"What? It's true! Isn't it?"

"Listen," I said. "They're right. We all need someone in our lives, impartial observers as well as friends who demand and deserve some accountability. Let's figure out what you're going to say and let's return these phone calls."

"Abigail?" Rebecca said. "What if the judge doesn't rule in our favor? What if I don't get my children back? Or my house? Won't I look like a fool?"

"You can't be serious, Rebecca," I said, taking a spring roll from Byron, dipping it and getting the sticky sauce all over my arm. Rebecca handed me a wet wipe from her purse. "Judge Shelby tore them to bits in her chambers and then *kicked* them out! So the question is not whether or not you win—you've already won—the question is how large is your settlement going to be."

"I can't say with authority," Julian said, "but I can tell you that I've known Judge Shelby for a long time and she's not going to reward Nat's shenanigans. No, sir."

Everyone agreed with Julian and me. The cell phones came out, the phone calls were made and Rebecca would grant interviews after the judge read the decision.

Later on in the evening after a dinner of continuous hors d'oeuvres from Byron and a huge platter of cheese, fruit and bread, which arrived as a gift from the hotel's management just in case we might be somebody important, Julian and I sat on the porch with Huey. We listened to the lessening drone of traffic and felt the approach of midnight.

"Frances DuBose said she'd be here at seven-thirty. She's a wizard. Rebecca's going to look like Holly Hunter in the flesh—all that translucent complexion is so wasted. If I had skin like Rebecca and Ms. Hunter I'd . . ."

"You'd what? Be a movie star? Come on, darling," I said to Julian, "time for all the old coots to call it a day."

We told Huey good night and went to sleep thinking we were well prepared for what the morning would bring.

My hotel phone rang at six o'clock. It was Huey.

"Get up and come quickly, Abigail. I've already ordered coffee for all of us. It's the morning papers— and not just the local ones—listen to this! *An Eye for an*

Eye, Okay. But a Breast for a Breast? This is some trash, sugar."

"Give me ten minutes."

"Who was that?" Julian said, half asleep.

"You sleep, sweetheart, I'll be right back." I washed my face, deciding I could apply some makeup later. Maybe Frances DuBose would take pity on me. Maybe she could spackle my wrinkles. I showered, dressed for court and slipped out, leaving Julian a note, telling him where to find me.

By the time I arrived, Huey's suite was abuzz. Everyone had a copy of the newspapers. The headline that Huey read to me was in various font sizes in every single edition.

"What am I going to do?" Rebecca said. She was dressed, but her wet hair was in a towel.

"You're going to get your hair blown out," Huey said, "and remain dignified."

"Well, this is some fine mess we've got here, Ollie," I said to no one in particular. "Laurel and Hardy," I said to Rebecca's puzzled expression.

"*I* knew that," Huey said. "More coffee?"

"I know you knew that. We're almost as old as Methuselah, Huey baby, and yes, I'll have some coffee."

"I think it's pretty funny," Claudia said. "I mean, come on, who's going to take this seriously?"

"Taking it seriously is going to be Rebecca's gig," I said. "She's the one who has to talk to these jokers after the judge passes her ruling. What time is it?"

336

"Seven-thirty," Huey said. "I'd better go wake up Mother."

We watched him go and I turned to Rebecca. "Well? Have you thought about what you're going to say to the press?"

"Yep. Don't worry about it. I'm going to have my say. I decided to make it a press conference and then I can get it all over with in one fell swoop."

"Great idea. Did you arrange it?"

"All done. That precious little bald man from yesterday was thrilled out of his mind to make the phone calls and set it all up. And Claudia?"

"Yeah, hon?"

"No quips, okay? If they happen to ask you anything, please be serious."

"Good Lord, Rebecca! I will! I was just *kidding* yesterday and *so* was Judge Shelby! There's *not going to be* any reverse surgery! Come on! I think all of this press coverage speaks to the depths of *Nat Simms's* depravity! Don't you? Come on! This isn't about you!"

Claudia was right. Except for this. The spotlight was on Rebecca, not Nat. Howard Stern could glamorize Nat's Svengali number that he did on Charlene, but the real players wanted to know how a nice gal like Rebecca felt about it.

Frances DuBose knocked on the open door, coming in on Huey's arm, showing her the headlines, and introduced her to Rebecca. "Gracious!" she said and shook her head. "Don't you worry, Rebecca. I'll have your hair looking beautiful in no time. Is there a spot where I can plug in my straightener? And blow dryer?"

"Right here. Can I get you some coffee?" Byron said.

"Oh, thank you. That would be great."

"Now, let's see about your face," she said to Rebecca. "I brought just the right . . ."

"Wait a minute! I don't want too much makeup. I sure don't want to wind up looking like Charlene, okay?"

"Right," Ms. DuBose said. "But we have to bring out those eyes of yours!"

"Listen to Frances, Rebecca. Where's Miss Olivia?"

"Performing her morning toilette," Huey said. "She's going to meet us at nine."

The morning was under way and rolling. It seemed like when I thought five minutes had passed, I would check my watch to see that thirty minutes had gone by. Before I knew it, we were back in the courtroom. Nat and Albright were at their table; it was standing room only and the media was there in full force.

Judge Shelby was somber. She repeated her warning from yesterday's hearing. She opened her folder and put on her reading glasses. Then she stopped, removed them and looked across the crowd, sighing. Shelby looked tired.

"I have given this much thought," she said. "I have read the financial declarations, the appraisals of personal property and the valuation of Mr. Simms's percentage in his family's business. I have reviewed and considered all the testimony and evidence. I am clear on all aspects of this proceeding except one. I would like to swear in Rebecca Simms and ask her a few questions myself."

Well, that was a surprise, but what could Rebecca do except take the stand and swear to tell the truth—not that anyone needed a Bible to encourage Rebecca to be honest.

Shelby smiled at Rebecca as she took the oath, and when she was finished she said, "Please be seated."

From the quizzical expression on Shelby's face, I knew she was looking for the right words to use to get the answers that she wanted from Rebecca.

"Mrs. Simms, your husband is suing you for divorce on the grounds of habitual drunkenness including the use of narcotics. It was mentioned in Mr. Albright's opening statement and alluded to by the children's high school counselor. We've never heard from you on these accusations. So I want to ask you to explain them."

Rebecca was very nervous. Everyone could see her hands shaking. But she was not to be underestimated in her courage to let the truth be known.

"Judge Shelby, thank you. Thank you for this opportunity to tell a little bit about my side of things. May I have a glass of water please?"

I poured it and brought it to her. "The truth will set you free," I whispered.

Shelby heard me and smiled.

"My family was so happy until about a year and a half ago. I knew something was wrong with Nat. It was obvious that he wanted me out of our home, and I may have suspected that he had another woman—in fact, I did suspect it but I never had any evidence of it. I couldn't prove it. But his whole attitude toward me changed, and he worked very hard to change the feelings of our children toward me as well. It got very ugly around our house. The uglier it became, the more depressed I got. Every time I would go online on the computer and I kept getting these pop-up ads to buy medicine online, so I thought I would. I would try taking something to see if it would help my depression. I thought that maybe my own sadness was sort of feeding his discontent. If I could get happy again . . . well, you understand, right? If a pill could improve my relationship with him, I was willing to give it a try."

"And how long did you take them?"

"For about a week. They made me very out of it in the head and very forgetful."

"Like remembering to pick up the children from school?"

"That only happened once during that time, but after that I just quit taking them. Actually, they made things worse because I was so ditzy that Nat screamed at me even louder and more often."

"I see. And what about the alcohol?"

"Judge Shelby, you can ask anyone. I'm not a big drinker. I might have two or three glasses of wine at a party, and that's only a couple of times a year. No one would ever accuse me of being drunk all the time. That's just, well, it's ridiculous."

"Fine, Mrs. Simms. I have what I need. You may step down."

Rebecca returned to her seat beside me. She was trembling. I squeezed her hand and said, "Good job."

Shelby cleared her throat.

"All right then. This court awards full custody of the children and the house to Rebecca Simms, with the proviso that they begin family counseling immediately for a period of one year, the frequency of those visits to be determined by the family counselor. As to visitation, that is to be worked out between Mr. and Mrs. Simms to something that is reasonable rights of visitation—such as every other weekend, one month to Mr. Simms each summer, rotating annual holidays, etc.

"Mr. Simms has forty-eight hours to vacate the family home. He is to take with him only his personal possessions—clothes, toilet articles—and further division of household property will take place in thirty days to allow a time period for the children to adjust to the changes.

"Now, about money . . ."

Judge Shelby awarded alimony and child support to Rebecca and one half of the interest in Nat's business. Nat would also have the pleasure of the legal expenses. At the end of it all, Rebecca came away with almost sixty percent of their assets, which well covered the costs of Charlene's Medical Mystery Tour. It was a generous settlement and we were thrilled.

When Shelby was finished reading her decision, she stood to leave the courtroom, reminding everyone that interviews were to be conducted outside the building and to kindly vacate the room as there was another case on the docket in thirty minutes. People began filing out. It was hard to believe it was all over.

I looked over at Nat and Albright. Nat was slouched in his chair, but Albright was on his feet packing his briefcase. I caught his eye and he came over to shake my hand.

"Congratulations," he said.

His face was so sincere that I worked to disguise the pleasure I felt in the win.

"Thanks."

Nat stood and came to Albright's side. He looked down at Rebecca and snarled.

"Well, I hope you're *happy*, Rebecca. You've all but wrecked my life."

"I didn't wreck your life, Nat. You wrecked it yourself."

Nat made a guttural sound of disgust and they walked away. I turned to her.

"You okay?"

"Yeah. I just want to call Sami and Evan and tell them what happened."

"I can help you with that if you'd like."

"No, I'll be okay. They are my children, after all. I just have to make them mine again. Hey, Abigail, thanks for everything. I could never see my way through this, but you did."

"You are entirely welcome. It's nice when things work out every now and then."

Huey, Claudia and Jeff Mahoney were waiting for us, smiling and anxious to congratulate us. I assumed

Byron had taken Miss Olivia back to the hotel.

"What a grand day this is!" Huey said. "Your hair looks fierce, Rebecca."

"Oh, Huey!"

"Let's get out of here," I said.

Mahoney took Rebecca's arm, and Claudia and I took Huey's.

The steps were mobbed with television cameras and reporters. We worked our way through them as politely as we could, declining comments. The press conference was next.

The hotel had cleared the furniture from the parlor and set up a table and chairs at the far end. By the time we arrived, the room was full. Rebecca told me that she had prepared a statement and when I asked her if she wanted me to go over it with her, she said, "No, I'm not sure I'm even going to use it. But thank you, Abigail."

Rebecca was shaky as she made her way to the microphone. I sat beside her at the table and waited for her to begin. Rebecca put her notes in front of her and took a long drink of water.

"Should I just start?"

"I guess so," I said. "Whenever you're ready."

"This is a little sick to me, you know."

"Don't throw away your chance, Rebecca."

Rebecca cleared her throat, turned her notes over and said, "Good morning. You have to wonder what the world has come to when something like this becomes national news. It's a little bit bizarre to me, anyway."

She paused and I looked around at the crowd of camera crews and reporters nodding their heads in agreement. But we all knew that they were just doing their jobs, churning the water so that Rebecca could ride the wave.

"I know everyone has come here to talk about what I think about my ex-husband's girlfriend and do I wish the judge had ordered half of her plastic surgery reversed. My life, her life and in fact, *your* life is not a reality show for the amusement of others. Think about it. What Charlene Johnson did was just another demonstration of what extraordinary things women do in the name of love. And that's what we had in common—we loved the same man. And we can both do better than to settle for the kind of manipulation and embarrassment we have endured. Do I feel vindicated? No, I do not. I feel sad. I'm not opposed to plastic surgery, but I don't believe any responsible doctor should dramatically change someone's appearance unless their patient requests it because *they* want it—not because their boyfriend wishes they had a bigger bra size or their husband wishes they had a fuller backside. This whole country has gone a little crazy desperately seeking youth and beauty because eventually we *all grow old. That's life.* And let me tell you something, I'd rather spend the rest of my life alone than *one* night with a man who thought that changing *me* would make *him* happy."

Rebecca reached in her purse and pulled out a foil-wrapped wet wipe. She choked up as she opened it, and sobbing, she began to scrub her face, removing every trace of makeup. There was a heavy silence as the cameras flashed.

"Look," she said. "This is me. This is who I am. Not the makeup. It's inner makeup that matters."

Rebecca, her emotions now gone completely out of control, got up and ran from the room.

It's inner makeup that matters!

Not bad, Rebecca, I thought as I picked up her purse.

"You're her attorney, aren't you?"

I began digging through the contents. "Yes, I'm Abigail Thurmond."

"Do you have any comment?"

"Yes, I'd like to know if she has another wet wipe."

I found one, opened it and used it on my face as well. Cameras flashed, I got up, mustering my sense of humor and my pride and left the room to find Rebecca. Huey caught my arm at the back of the room.

"That was bloody brilliant, Abigail. Bloody brilliant. I'll never use my bronzer again."

"Oh, God, Huey! You're priceless!"

I rapped my knuckles on Rebecca's door and Byron opened it. Julian was there with Claudia and Miss Olivia. Rebecca was sitting on her bed against her pillows with her knees up to her chest, tissue box at her side, still weeping and intermittently blowing her nose.

"I'm such a *fool!* Did y'all see what I *did?* I *completely* lost my cool in front of a zillion people! I had this chance to talk about a million things—anything!

And what did *I* do? I washed my damn *face!* What's the *matter* with me?"

"It was *phenomenal,* Rebecca! You did *great!*" Claudia said.

"No, I *didn't!* I looked like an *idiot!* The entire country is going to be making fun of me for the *rest of my life!* I'm going to be that stupid woman who took *off* her makeup on national television!"

"So what? You sent a message to women *everywhere,* Rebecca!" Huey said.

Miss Olivia was sitting across the room in an upholstered armchair that was so big it made her appear tiny and withered. But her attention to the conversation was as sprightly focused as ever.

"What do you think, Abigail?"

"I took off my makeup too."

Everyone, including Rebecca looked at me and said, "Oh, my God! You did! You really *did!*"

And then we started to laugh and laugh.

"Well, at least I'm not the only national idiot!" Rebecca said.

"Nobody's a national idiot," Julian said.

The phone rang and Claudia answered it. It was Nat.

"He wants to talk to you," she said, handing the phone to Rebecca.

"Hello?"

"I don't need forty-eight hours to get out of here. I'm leaving now. You can pick up the kids from school and have at it, Rebecca. I'll come back and get the rest of my clothes this weekend. I'll be staying with Char-

346

lene in Orangeburg. I made her bail and we made up."

"Fine."

"Fine? Is that all you have to say? Fine? How about thank you, Nat? Do you think you could choke out a simple thank you?"

"Hey, Nat? How's this? Thank you for getting out of *my house?*" She dropped the phone back in its cradle and looked at us. "I hung up on him."

"Well, that's better than *being* hung up on him," I said, thinking how clever I was. "Let's get some lunch. I'm starving!"

"I'll come along," Julian said, "but only if you girls put on some lipstick."

The great white shark that lives in the hearts of all women was poised to strike on dry land, and Claudia, Rebecca and I shot him straight lines of death rays.

"It was only a joke! Jeesch! You're all so sensitive!"

With plenty of groans, the consensus comment was, "Very funny, Judge."

"Okay, I'll buy lunch for everyone. Are we okay now?"

"It's a start," I said. "It's a start."

TWENTY-THREE

HOME FIRES BURNING

After lunch, Claudia and I went back to Rebecca's house with her. She hadn't stepped foot in it since the day she walked out, and she had no idea what she would find.

Where she lived on Tradd Street, on the tip of the peninsula, is the most historic and unique section of Charleston. Every few steps you passed a window box with flowers tumbling over its edges followed by a wrought-iron gate a few feet away. You peeked through the gate and behind it was a magical garden of clipped and shaped boxwood topiaries, azalea and camellia hand-pruned shrubs and specimen plantings of ornamental grass borders. Pyracantha and ivy climbed ancient walls of tiny handmade bricks and lead decorative pots overflowed with brightly colored geraniums and begonias. The whole area was so bewitching that you would find yourself longing to trespass just to dip your hot feet in a stranger's fountain waters. Rebecca's home was one of those, but her garden was hardly a nominee for "yard of the month."

We pushed open the heavy gate and Rebecca gasped. The flowers in her planters were dried up and gone to another incarnation. The grassy areas had not been mowed in several weeks. Her roses were spindly and filled with black spot. Forgotten bicycles and skateboards had been dropped and left, and the out-door table was littered with fast-food cups and bags. The courtyard fountain sputtered and the water lilies were thick clumps of strangling overgrowth.

"Oh, Lord!" she said. "My fountain is full of green gunk! And look at this yard! It's a mess!"

"These are all fixable things," I said. "Don't you have a gardener?"

"Well, we *did!* Looks like he's on vacation!"

"Just call him," Claudia said. "Nat probably told him to take a hike."

We climbed the steps and Rebecca stopped. Running shoes caked with mud were piled on the porch near the door.

"What?" I said.

"I don't have keys!"

"Let's just try the door and see."

Sure enough, Nat had left the front door unlocked, and we walked right in to her center hall, as any robber could. On our right was her living room, and the dining room was on the left. I assumed the kitchen was behind the dining room and that a study or a guest room was behind the living room. There was a delicately curved flight of stairs to the second and third floor and a powder room tucked under the stairwell on the first floor. Rebecca went from room to room and disappeared into the kitchen.

It was a classic Charleston row house, beautifully detailed, but to say it was filthy was charitable. Her house was desperately in need of dust cloth, vacuum cleaner and Windex action, followed by some big bowls of flowers and the smell of something good, like chocolate chip cookies coming from the kitchen. Rebecca's children were going to be shocked enough as it was to find her there. It was obvious that we all needed to help her pull the house together.

Claudia and I were trying to figure out what to do when Rebecca came bounding down the steps.

"The dishwasher is full, the dryer is full of clothes, every bed is unmade and heaven only knows when the last time was they changed the sheets! There's nothing in the refrigerator to eat, everything's covered in an inch of dust, the bathrooms are gross . . ."

"Rebecca! Get a grip, honeychile! I'm a full-service attorney and Claudia's a full-service friend. We already got this nailed! She's gonna fold the laundry and change the beds . . ."

"I am?"

"Yes, you are!"

"I guess I am."

"And I'm commandeering the vacuum cleaner and the dusting. You tackle the kitchen and the bathrooms, and in the end we'll divide up the work again, okay? Feel better? Gee niminy! I should've brought Daphne!" That gave me an idea. I dialed Huey on my cell phone and he picked up right away. "Huey? How much do you love me?"

Huey, thank all the saints in heaven, loved me a lot. He was bringing dinner, doing a general grocery shop for the house and picking up fresh flowers.

"What's the children's favorite dinner and dessert?" he said.

"I don't know. Hang on." I found Rebecca in the kitchen, rummaging around the storage closet, pulling out all the cleaning supplies. "Hey! What do your kids like for dinner?"

"Spaghetti, garlic bread, salad and chocolate cake. There's no milk in this house or bread or anything!"

"Stop whining! Get to work!" I went back to my phone. "Huey?"

"I heard it all. Boy, she really has her bloomers all twisted in a knot, doesn't she?"

"Yep. So would you. You should see this place." I walked back out to the hall where Rebecca couldn't hear me. "Don't worry, I'm billing Nat for our hours on this one too!"

"Well, psychologically it will be very good for those kids to come home to a clean house. Am I right?"

"Well, Claudia and I think so, or else we wouldn't be rolling up our sleeves!"

The business of restoring order got under way. You couldn't hear yourself think with the noise of the vacuum cleaner, the slamming of doors as Rebecca took bag after bag of garbage, magazines, catalogs and old newspapers outside. The flushing of toilets, and running water were the backup music for the old Motown music I had blaring from 102.5 on Rebecca's sound system. Claudia and I were singing along at the top of our lungs, and even Rebecca joined in. We still knew all the words to "Stop! In the Name of Love!" and

"My Boyfriend's Back." We sounded so terrible that I half expected all the neighborhood dogs to start howling.

Claudia must have passed me fifty times with armloads of sheets and towels, the children's laundry, and Nat's as well. She stopped as she was carrying a laundry basket of Nat's clean clothes upstairs.

"This irritates the crap out of me," she said.

"What does? Did you say crap? Is that how doctors talk in Atlanta?" I giggled. I liked Claudia. She understood the value of well-used slang and she didn't care what anyone thought about it either.

"Yeah. Crap. All doctors in Atlanta say it. It's required. Listen, I'm folding Nat's panties like the son of a bitch is my husband and we're going to Europe or something. Shouldn't I just throw them in a suitcase and help get him out of here?"

"Actually, that's not a bad idea. Ask Rebecca where they keep the luggage."

"Third-floor attic closet. Already saw it."

"What?" Rebecca said, coming in the room.

We told her and she said, "Why should I give him the luggage? I'll never see it again!" She sailed out of the room bound for the kitchen and I looked at Claudia.

"My goodness, Doctor Kelly. You have the oddest expression! What are you thinking?"

"I'm thinking I should do something extra special for my girlfriend, that's all."

I went back to my vacuuming and about fifteen minutes later, Huey walked in with six bags of groceries, dumping them on the floor in the hallway.

"There's more in the car," he said. "Come help me before I drop dead. Whoo! So much pressure!"

Claudia came outside and took the flowers from the front seat. She was laughing so hard I thought she was going to start having convulsions.

"Claudia! What ever on this earth could be so funny?" I said.

"My dee-ah! Do you need a chaise to recline until this hysteria passes?"

"*Y'all!* Y'all are *not* gonna believe what I did!"

"What?" I turned to Huey and said, "She's been doing Nat's laundry, and she's not too thrilled about it."

"Oh! *Now* I am! In fact, I'm so happy I got to wash and fold Nat Simms's cheap U-Trow and socks that I could dance!"

"Clau-dee-ah!" Huey said. "*What* did you do to them?"

"Yeah, fess up, Dr. Mengele. What did you do?"

"Promise not to tell?" We crossed our hearts and she said, "Well, I left the attic door open, and when I went back to the third floor I noticed they had fiberglass insulation in the walls . . ."

"No! You *didn't!*" I knew immediately what she had done.

"Yes! I did! Every last pair!"

"What am I missing here?" Huey said.

"Wake up, baby, and smell the chai!" Claudia said. "The fiberglass was dusty, and all I had with me was Nat's clean laundry. I merely turned his socks and underpants inside out and dusted the fiberglass insulation. Then I turned them back on the right side, folded them and put them back in his drawers. That's all. No biggie." She smiled, turned away and then back to us. "And if y'all tell Rebecca," she said with a south Georgia drawl, "I'll jess haveta kill all y'all till yewr choked dead."

Huey was astonished. His jaw was hanging open so wide I could count his caps.

"What a *woman!*" he said. "Wait until I tell Miss Olivia! She will *love* this story!"

"She's a little dangerous. Come on, let's get inside and finish up. Her children get out of school in less than an hour."

Forty-five minutes later there were roses in place on the dining room table, a bud vase of gerber daisies on an end table in the living room and another in the kitchen window. The whole house smelled like lemon wax, the chocolate brownies that were baking in the oven and the spaghetti sauce that simmered on the stove. The living room pillows were in their correct positions, the beds were all made with fresh linens, the bathrooms sparkled and clean towels waited on the racks. Nat and all his bad aura had been scoured, dusted, Windexed and swept right out the door.

Rebecca said, "Now this house looks like it's supposed to! Everything looks so pretty and clean! How can I ever thank you?"

"I might need an organ donor some day," I said.

"I'll go pack your stuff at the hotel, check you out and

bring it back over here," Claudia said.

"Why don't you spend the night here with me and fly out of Charleston tomorrow?" Rebecca said.

"You nervous?" Claudia said.

"Yeah."

Claudia looked at us for an opinion. I think we all felt that Rebecca's first night back in her house and with her children should be hers alone. But we also understood why Rebecca was feeling as she was. If those were my kids, I'd have a good case of the jitters too.

"Tell you what," Claudia said. "I'll stay for dinner. How's that?"

"That's just great! That's fine. Thanks."

"Huey? I think I'm gonna miss work tomorrow," Rebecca said.

"And the next. But don't worry, honey. My door is always open to you. I'll find a framer. But you just keep painting. You hear me?"

Rebecca and Huey hugged like they would never see each other again. "I'll come up Saturday," Rebecca said. "I have to empty Claudia's condo. Get all my stuff."

"Bring the children!" I said. "I'll take them to the beach."

I gave Rebecca a hug, and we sighed hard, looking at each other like trench buddies.

"We won," she said.

"We won big-time," I said.

Huey and I said good-bye to Claudia, and she promised to call us after dinner to give us the latest, and then Huey followed me back to the hotel.

Walking through the parking lot with me, he said, "God Almighty! I feel like I just married off a daughter!"

"Yeah, but boy, am I glad things turned out the way they did!"

"I could use a bourbon," he said. "You know, a little celebratory shooter to mark the occasion? Hmmm?"

"Pass. I'd rather have a glass of wine on my porch at Pawleys."

"I'll see you at seven," he said. "And I'll bring dinner. Byron can help. We'll tuck Mother in for the night with a sandwich and a sherry."

I started to protest, thinking I would just steam a big bowl of shrimp, and then I realized how tired I was.

"Deal," I said.

I began the drive up Highway 17, listening to Walter Edgar on NPR, and called Julian on my cell.

"Hey, babe! Thanks for lunch. Wanna come up to Pawleys for dinner?"

"It's been a long time since someone called me *babe*. I have to be in court so early in the morning. Can I take a rain check for the weekend?"

"Sure. No problem. So guess what Claudia did?" I told him about Claudia, the fiberglass insulation and Nat's underwear, and he had a hoot!

"Oh, Lord! You women are so crazy, wonderful, terrible! You make me feel like a college student! I couldn't think of a nicer guy for that to happen to! Fabulous!"

We talked for a while about the settlement and about all sorts of other things and then about us.

"I'm becoming quite fond of you, Abigail, but you know that."

"Yeah. Me too. It's pretty incredible, isn't it?"

"Yeah. You make me wish I was building a house on Pawleys instead of Wadmalaw."

"Well, you don't have to build on Pawleys. There's no room to build anyway. But I can always find you a place to stay, as long as you behave."

I could see him smiling through the phone. What we had was so easy, so good and so natural. And finally, the timing was right.

We hung up and I drove a while longer, realizing I had passed the place where Ashley died, and for the first time I had not even noticed. *I had not even noticed!* Maybe it was Ashley or some piece of him telling me to move on with my life, that he had forgiven me. Perhaps he had seen the courtroom, what had transpired, and maybe it was because I had gone back to Rebecca's house to help her even further—maybe all those things combined had earned me some reprieve. Maybe it was Ashley and John together. My heart ached for them then as it did every day, but somehow, from somewhere outside of me, I was feeling better. Not a lot better, but even to feel the slightest increase in ease of mind was monumental. Healing seemed to come in tiny increments of peace. Still, I couldn't help but wonder if coming to the aid of Rebecca had been cosmically instrumental in lifting the cloud of my own despair.

I thought again about Rebecca and me removing our makeup on national television, and I had to laugh to myself about it. I had always been so prissy and buttoned up tight, worrying that the black thing I was wearing matched another black thing I was wearing. How ridiculous! My priorities had certainly changed. The networks probably wouldn't even run the tape. It didn't matter. By that simple act of defying the entire beauty empire and castigating its worth, some chain of bondage was broken. In a peculiar way, I was empowered by it. Maybe I'd go buy a red sweater.

When I arrived home, Daphne's car was in the yard and she was at the top of my steps with her hands on her bony little hips.

"Where have you been? This phone's been ringing off the hook! I was worried sick! I called your cell phone about a thousand times! Congratulations!"

"Thanks. You finished?"

"Finished what? Cleaning this house? This house is as clean as a whistle. You know it! Clean as a whistle. Here, give me that bag! You shouldn't be carrying all this stuff at one time, 'specially when I'm standing right here, waiting to help you!"

"Huey's coming for dinner." I handed her my hanging bag. "Who called?"

"Half the world! You got calls from all kinds of people from newspapers and radio stations—all the names and numbers are on your desk. What's going on? Did Ms. Simms shoot her husband in the head?"

"Nope, he shot himself in the foot. We kicked his butt

in court, he lost every piece of dignity he ever had and over fifty percent of everything else to boot, and guess what? I feel pretty darn good about the whole thing!"

"Well, all right then. I'm glad to know that Ms. Simms got her justice 'cause that is one very bad-to-the-bone man! Yes, ma'am! He is bad to the bone! But he ain't done with his foolishness yet. Somebody needs to start reading Psalm Fifty-four and pray that man dead."

"What are you saying, Daphne?"

"Humph. You don't know about Psalm Fifty-four? David said, *Let their death surprise them; let them go down alive to the netherworld.* Shoot, my momma had a friend and her husband ran around like an old alley cat. Then he spent up all the money and beat her and the children till they all had to go to the hospital. She and my momma said that psalm every day for a month, and don't you know that man dropped dead? Forty-one and he dropped dead on the floor."

"What?"

"Yes, ma'am! It's a fact. Ask Byron. Poor Ms. Simms. Her husband buying his trashy girlfriend all those body parts! What's the matter with men these days? Hmm? Tell me that if you can, but you can't, 'cause if you knew the answer to that, you'd rule the whole world!"

Wait a minute, I thought. I had never discussed Rebecca's case with her.

"How do you know all this about Mr. Simms?"

"How do you *think?* Byron, of course! Shoot, he's

worse than an old washwoman at the clothing line! Besides, nowadays we all got clothes dryers, so who's he gonna tell? And who am I gonna tell? Nobody but you, 'cause you're the only one I know who even cares!"

She had followed me to the bedroom, and the first thing I noticed was that the furniture was rearranged.

"I moved it like this for very good reasons," she said.

It looked a thousand times better, I had to admit, but *still!*

"Let's hear," I said.

"Well, the headboard was between those windows. Winter's coming, and if you have a draft—and you do in every single window in this place—you can get sick. And with the headboard on the back wall, the room looks better from the porch. Before, it was all chopped up. Besides, you can get in bed and watch the ocean roll in and the sun rise too. That's the best part. What time is Mr. Huey coming?"

"Seven. He's bringing Byron to help."

"Maybe I'll stick around and help my brother. I haven't seen him in a while."

She was right about it all. I'd had many a stiff neck in January. The room looked so much larger with the bed away from the middle of the room. This arrangement made the bed look important, and if there was anything I wanted, it was for Julian to think my bed was just that.

"Yeah, hang around. You're right about the room, Daphne. Thank you. But how did you move all this heavy furniture by yourself?"

"An inch at a time. That's how. An inch at a time."

What a proverbial statement, I thought. How many things happened in our lives one inch at a time? Certainly weight loss, spiritual growth and the arrival of a repairman of any kind. And healing from the death of your loved ones.

As nervous as Rebecca was to take the helm, it was probably a good thing that Nat had not given her too much time to think about it. As an added bonus, Nat's decision had not given him any extra time to poison the children's minds about how Bad Mommy had wasted him in court.

I hung up my clothes, looked through the mail and the phone messages and was tempted maybe, hmm, a thousand times to call Rebecca. I couldn't shake the thought of her. How had it played out? Did the children run into her arms, crying, saying how sorry they were and how glad they were that she was home? Probably not. Were they angry to see her and discover she had regained custody? No, they were probably just on guard. Were they strange and distant? Probably a little. Did they notice there were no more potato chips in their beds and that their bathrooms were clean? Definitely not.

I couldn't wait for Claudia to call, and I kept checking the reception on my cell phone to see if she'd have a problem getting through. The signal was strong. She would have no problem. I clipped the phone to my belt because this was one call I didn't want to miss.

Just as the sun was slipping away for the day, Huey and Byron arrived with a picnic basket.

"What fabulous things have you brought, Mr. Wonderful?" I said and pecked his cheek.

"A meal from the gods to toast the victorious!"

"Meat loaf and mashed potatoes?"

"Silly girl. Caviar and blinis—three hundred and twenty-five delicious grams of it, pâté de foie gras with toast points and petit cornichon, and two bottles of Veuve Clicquot champagne to wash it away!"

"Veuve Clicquot *Reserve!*" Byron said.

"Holy Moly! Fabulous!" I said.

"I'll set up the table on the porch," Daphne said. "Come on Byron. You can help me."

"You get the dishes and I'll bring the basket."

"Um, I don't have a table on the porch," I said.

"You do now," she said. "The judge had it delivered yesterday."

I followed her outside, and there it was. A small square glass-top table on a black wrought-iron frame and two wrought-iron chairs. It made the rest of my rocking chairs look decrepit, but I knew I could solve that with a paintbrush. There was a card in an envelope taped to the top.

"I didn't read it," Daphne said.

"Then how'd you know he sent it?"

"Um, um . . ."

"Don't ever lie to your attorney," I said and smiled at her. There was probably not one thing about me she didn't already know.

"She's a nosy thing," Byron said. "Don't waste your energy on privacy, Miss Abigail!"

I opened the envelope. It had a pencil drawing of St. Phillip's church on the front, and inside he had written, *For a million shared sunsets and sunrises! Love, Julian.*

Well, the old boy was having a Hallmark moment, wasn't he? Then I quickly calculated how many years a million days was and thought, was this a marriage proposal? Nah, no way. He was just trying to be romantic.

Time crawled along as Huey and I rehashed the whole court case, stuffing our mouths with the delicious treats he had brought. We laughed about Charlene's appearance but then finally concluded that she was the hero of the day. It was her assessment of Nat's character that had really shown the entire courtroom what kind of despicable person he was.

"Some people are just like that, Abigail. If it's good for them, then it's good. If it's bad for them, then it's bad. They rearrange morality to suit their ambitions. Nat simply thought he could do what he wanted and never suffer any consequences."

"You are absolutely right. But you know what? I understand a little of what Nat felt. When I met Julian years ago, the feelings I had were so euphoric and all-consuming that part of me couldn't understand why I shouldn't have this happiness. I mean, how could something so good be so wrong?"

"Honey, it's just lust. And you know lust ain't nothing but the devil dressed up to be beautiful. The Bible doesn't say he's a trickster and a liar for nothing, you know."

"I prefer to remember it as bad timing."

"Tell yourself whatever you want. Lust is lust. The difference is that you and Julian had the strength to walk away from each other. That stupid Nat blew up his whole family and acted like a disgrace."

"Well, Huey, the truth is that my family eventually blew up too."

"Yes, but that wasn't because you had a brief dalliance with Julian! Good grief, Abigail! Are you still feeling guilty? Put it aside, girl! There ain't anything you can do anyway!"

"Dalliance? Oh, Huey! I love that. It makes my scandal sound courtly. You know what, Huey? It was a chain of unbearable pain that began with Julian. First, I met him and fell for him. Then John and Julian's wife, Lila, found out about us. Lila left Julian and he left me. John became depressed and started drinking. Then I drank with him because I felt guilty and I missed Julian. He never called.

"John and I fought like all hell. He gained an enormous amount of weight, all the while withdrawing from me. I had been drinking when I got in the accident with Ashley. John blamed me for his death and for everything wrong with his life. His knees went bad from the weight gain, but he just kept piling on the pounds. He goes in for knee replacement surgery and his heart stops. You think I don't feel guilty?"

"Yes, but Abigail, my dear Abigail, you didn't skim the business and speak ill of John to everyone you knew. Nat committed the worst kind of sins here. Look what he tried to do with Rebecca's relationship with her own children! The odious, heinous skunk!"

"Well, I broke John's faith and trust in me. I broke his heart, Huey."

"Let me tell you this, Abigail Thurmond, and you remember this too. Maybe you were weak, but when you realized you could walk away from Julian, you did. If John never forgave you, that's on his Christian soul, not yours. You were sorry; he couldn't forgive. Isn't pride a sin too?"

I hadn't considered John's unforgiving heart. I reached over and covered Huey's hand with mine. "You are such a dear man, Huey Valentine, and I love you so much."

"Well, I love you too," he said. "You're the best woman friend I've ever had. And you do so many good things. I can't stand it for you to torture yourself over the past. Besides, if the good Lord hadn't wanted you to be with our friend, the judge, He wouldn't have brought Julian back into your life. So, go think about *that* for a while!"

"Well, Huey darling? It's one of those things that I'm never going to know for sure, isn't it?"

"It doesn't matter, Abigail. Really, it doesn't matter. The important thing is that you and Julian found each other again and you had one helluva day in court today! I am so happy for Rebecca, I just can't tell you. And I am so proud of you."

"Thanks, sweetheart. Oh, Lord! I wish Claudia would call us! What time is it?"

Finally, the quiet exploded with the ring of my telephone. It was Claudia. I put her on speakerphone so Huey and I could listen together.

"Claudia! We're pacing the floor like expectant grandparents! Tell us what happened!"

"No," said Huey. "We're bingeing on some of the best caviar and pâté I've ever had! Not to mention swilling down some very excellent champagne! But do hurry, Claudia! Tell us!"

"Listen," she said, "what's the biggest tearjerker movie you ever saw?"

"*An Affair to Remember*," I said. "Or maybe *Imitation of Life*."

"*Beaches*," Huey said. "Or maybe *Bambi*. I cried all through grammar school after that one."

"He's shitting me, right?" Claudia said.

"Probably not. Come on! Tell us!"

"Okay, I went back to the hotel and by the time I packed up all her stuff, my stuff, got it all in the car, checked out and got back to her house, the kids were there. It was intense. First they were around the kitchen table crying, all of them sobbing. I put a box of Kleenex in the middle of them and went upstairs to put Rebecca's stuff away. When I got back downstairs, they were drinking milk and eating brownies."

"Were they still crying?"

"Evan wasn't, but Sami was still very upset. I have to give Rebecca a lot of credit. She said, *Look, I'm not going to say ugly things about your daddy. Not today and not ever. He's your father, you love him and you should. But your father had some very peculiar ideas about how people can behave and the judge didn't agree with him. Neither did I, neither did your grandfather and neither does society in general. Now we have to start acting like a family again.* Then Sami threw a little fit."

"What did she say?" I said.

"She said something like, *Well, Daddy promised me certain things and I'm going to get them and you can't tell me what to do either!* Rebecca said, *Sami? From this moment forward, we're going to speak to each other in a loving and respectful way. I'm not sure what your father promised you, but we can talk about it. If it's reasonable and appropriate for you.* You should've seen the look on Sami's face. Sami knew Rebecca was fully informed about the promised breast augmentation just by the way Sami cowered. It was priceless."

"So little Sami isn't going to get big breasts quite yet?" I said.

"You got it," Claudia said. "Anyway, Rebecca was great. She went on to say, *We're going to take care of each other and we are going to work everything out, one issue at a time.* Then she told them about the therapist that the court had ordered and they talked about Nat's visitation and so forth. Oh! And did I tell you about the flowers?"

"What flowers? The ones we bought?"

"No. The ones that arrived from Jeff Mahoney with a note saying congratulations and welcome home."

"Whoo hoo!" Huey said. "I knew that man had his

eye on Rebecca! I liked him. Did y'all like him?"

"Sure, he's okay," I said, "but no rocket scientist. But a sweet guy."

"Yeah, he's a nice man. A very nice man. But then the doorbell rings and guess who's there?"

"Charlene with an apology?" I said.

"Jeff Mahoney in a raincoat?" Huey said and laughed.

"No, you pervert! It was the old man, Tisdale, with an armload of probably a hundred pink lilies for Rebecca and cell phones for the kids with his number programmed in. I swear to God, y'all, I almost started crying."

I looked around to see Huey dabbing the corners of his eyes. I pulled a tissue from my pocket and passed it to him.

"That's pretty powerful," I said.

"It was. So I slipped out of there. They didn't need an audience."

"You did the right thing, Claudia," I said.

"Well, it seemed like the thing to do. The days ahead of them are going to be pretty bumpy. Have you had the television on?"

"No, why?"

"You'd better check out CNN. After they tried to terrorize the entire southeast over the next hurricane—this one's Gaston, just for the record—they ran the footage of Rebecca and you taking off y'all's makeup. Oh, and they included your infamous quotes of the day. *I'm looking to see if she has another wet wipe!*

God, Abigail, you crack me up!"

"Oh, my God," I said in disbelief.

"Wait! So then, Paula Zahn whips out a cosmetic wet wipe and tells Aaron Brown that the wet wipe she's holding is a weapon of mass destruction. *This,* she says, *is a weapon of mass destruction!* So she removes her mascara on only one eye, pretty messy actually, and she poses this question. *What would happen if all the women in America took off their makeup for a day? Would the floozies go out of business? If they did it for a week or a month, would the stock market drop? I say bravo to Rebecca Simms and Abigail Thurmond!*"

"What?" I was so startled that I had to sit down.

"Oh, Abigail!" Huey said. "You're famous! Oh! And I knew her when . . ."

"Abigail? You should know that Aaron Brown thought it was a pretty cool thing y'all did too. Anyway, you know that Sami's and Evan's friends will be blabbing all over school tomorrow. It's going to be pretty embarrassing for them. I mean, the headlines from this morning will be all over every dinner table in Charleston tonight."

"Oh, my!" Huey said, "I hadn't even thought about that!"

I hadn't either. But I knew that people were vicious and that although Rebecca had won the battle to regain her home and children, she may have lost her family's good name because of Nat and Charlene. As much as I wanted to, I decided not to call her that night. She needed the time alone.

After everyone left and I had thanked them for all their support, I walked out to my porch to look at the ocean. It was a beautiful night and so hard to believe that another hurricane was on its way. I sat at my new table and thought of Julian. How thoughtful to buy a table with just two chairs for us! I wondered how long we would last and I realized that the relationship we had, just as we were, was really all I wanted. I was in no hurry to live with him or get married. But I adored him. That much was certain.

I wondered about my career. Was I retired? Was it over? When Judge Shelby read her decision, I felt such a rush of adrenaline. Did I really want to walk away from that? I said to myself, *Look at the change in Rebecca's life because you got involved. A mother was reunited with her children!* Well, to be honest, it wasn't perfect without a loving father in the home, but then there was no such thing as happily ever after, was there? I hoped Rebecca would fall back in love with her children and I hoped they would love her again too. But even if none of them did ever really hit family stride again, putting Rebecca back in the home and moving Nat out was absolutely in the best interest of the children. At least the children would have the benefit of a kind and levelheaded mother who, underneath it all, loved them very much.

Maybe I would put the word out that if there was another case like Rebecca's I might be interested in handling it. If I took one or two cases a year it would keep my intellectual life interesting and maybe I could do someone some good.

I looked all around the empty beach. No Gray Man. No storm on the horizon. Just the graceful water washing the shore and a sky filled with stars. I thought about Ashley and John, and for the very first time since their deaths I could feel their love around me. *Be happy,* they seemed to be saying. *Everything's going to be all right.*

Twenty-four

Rebecca and Gaston Would Like to Chat

The next morning I got up early. I wanted to make a big breakfast for the children and get them off to school feeling like somebody loved them. I purposely did not turn on the news or open the newspaper because I was afraid of what I might see or hear. Sami and Evan had been traumatized enough. I went to wake them, first to Sami's room and then to Evan's, and before I shook their shoulders I stopped to look at them, still asleep. You could not find a trace of worry or stress on their faces. It was my responsibility to prepare them well so that the rest of their day would go smoothly. But I couldn't control what saucy chatter their friends had heard from their parents.

Over pancakes and sausage, juice and milk, I began the morning's conversation.

"How's breakfast, Sami?"

"Good, thanks, Mom."

She was cutting her pancakes carefully and making a point of her excellent table manners with each bite. Evan, on the other hand, was eating like a starving animal. I thought I might have to hold his ears back out of the plate.

"Yeah," Evan said, "we haven't had anything but cereal and Pop-Tarts since we got back from camp. This is real good."

I knew that, of course, by the number and variety of boxes in the pantry—if it was coated in sugar, we had a box of it.

"Thanks, son. Listen, I need to talk to y'all about something and I'm not quite sure how to begin." They looked up at me, sitting in my old spot. It was a curious feeling to resume my authority at the breakfast table. I put my coffee mug down and said, "Look, I'm just going to spill it, okay? I can't send you off to school not knowing what was in the papers and on the news last night."

"What? Is Dad okay?" Evan said.

"Oh! I'm sure he's just fine. No, this is about Charlene. Remember her?"

"God! Do we ever! She was disgusting!" Sami said and rolled her eyes. "So what happened? Did her boobs burst?"

Peals of laughter filled the air and my concerns evaporated. I even chuckled with them.

"No, her boobs didn't burst, as you so delicately put

it, but they almost got repossessed." I thought, let that sink in her precocious mind and see what comes back.

"Repossessed? What do you mean? That means taken back!" Evan said.

"No, duh, dumb-ass!"

"Sami! Please don't use that kind of language, and your brother's not a dumb-a-s-s."

"Whatever," she said. "So what happened?"

I was about to take away their childhoods. I didn't want to tell them. But I didn't want them to hear it from a bunch of kids and have the truth made to be more grotesque than it was, if that was possible.

"Look," I said, "Daddy didn't always use his best judgment in certain cases. And in the case of Charlene, he bought those big bosoms for Charlene and paid for them too. And several other surgical procedures as well. All cosmetic. All intended to make Charlene more attractive to him and to make Charlene happier about her appearance."

"That's awful! Daddy made her get operated on?" Sami said. "I don't believe it! You're lying!"

"Wait a second, young lady. I never said Daddy made her do anything. I am saying that she wanted it done, Daddy supported it and, in fact, he paid for it. There's a huge difference."

"So what do we care about that?" Sami had a very bad attitude with me.

"Do you remember last night that I said we were all going to speak to each other in a loving way?"

"Yeah, I guess."

"Okay, then let's not make me the bad guy here. Let me finish telling you the facts and then you can draw your own conclusions, although the judge did that yesterday."

"What did the judge say?" Evan asked and drained his orange juice. "More?"

"Sure, sweetheart." I poured out another glass for him from the container. "The judge said that the money Daddy spent on Charlene was an extraordinary amount and that fifty percent of it should be returned to me. You see, what they do in family court is add up everything a couple has and divide it in half. The wife gets half and if there are children, she gets a little more to help support them."

"So what else is new?" Sami said sarcastically. I shot her a look and she said, "Sorry, I just meant that even I know that."

"What's new is that the newspapers picked it up and made a big deal out of it. I got interviewed by the media and said some things that you might hear about today. I just didn't want you to walk into school and get blindsided. I thought you should know that the media has made a fuss about it."

"Why did they do that?" Evan said.

"Because the amount of money Daddy spent on Charlene was so much. That's why. I mean, it was a *lot*."

They quietly stared at my face, looking for clues of what it all meant.

After a few minutes, Sami said, "You're ashamed of what Daddy did, aren't you?"

"It's pretty embarrassing," I said. "But what can I do?"

"If my husband did that, I'd kill him," Sami said.

"The thought crossed my mind, but look, we're not here to bash Daddy over the breakfast table. I just didn't want y'all to hear about what Daddy and Charlene did from someone else. And if someone gives you a hard time, you just say, look, *I didn't have anything to do with it, okay?* Try not to get sucked into some long conversation about it. Come on, you're gonna be late. Y'all got lunch money?"

That was how the day started. I made breakfast for them as I always had. I drove them to school. I told them I loved them and I hoped for the best.

When I got home the phone was ringing.

"Hello?"

"Rebecca Simms?"

"Yes?"

"Please hold for Katie Couric of the *Today Show*."

Maybe it was a joke. There was a short pause, and then Katie Couric, or someone who sounded just like her, came on the line. Before I could panic and hang up, she started talking.

"Rebecca?"

"Yes?" I recognized her voice. It was *her!* Holy shit.

"Rebecca? This is Katie Couric calling."

"Yes?" *Quit saying yes! Say something reasonably intelligent.* "Is this being taped?"

"What? Oh, no! Goodness, no! But I would like to

have you on the show tomorrow morning. Would you like to do that?"

"No. I mean, no, thank you."

"Why not? Listen, you don't have to fly to New York. Our folks down there can come to you and we can do a remote interview. You've seen those, right?"

"Yeah, sure. It's just that I don't want any more publicity, that's all. But I appreciate the offer."

"Wait a minute! Haven't you had your television on? You got every single female anchor across this country to wash off their makeup this morning in support of you! Even the nitwits on the Weather Channel! *Even me!* And, lemme tell you, Matt almost fainted when he saw me without makeup! He and Al were doing Halloween screams and the whole thing—it was crazy!"

"I don't know, Ms. Couric, I just . . ."

"Hang on, girlfriend. If I can get a colonoscopy on television, you can do this, right? Come on! Say yes!"

She had a very good point. Oh, what the hell, I thought. Why not? But it seemed so ridiculous.

"Can I have my lawyer with me?"

"Abigail Thurmond? You bet! I was gonna call her next. You South Carolina girls are something else! Listen, thanks. I know it's an intrusion, but I promise to make it as dignified and fun as we can."

She said the producer would call and set up a time. After that, I couldn't tell you what she said, I was so nervous. I called Abigail and told her.

"I saw it! Did you see Paula Zahn last night? It was wild! And Rebecca, how did last night go?"

Abigail listened as I recounted the night, telling her about Tisdale showing up and how sweet he was. The only real news of the night was that Tisdale told me privately he was throwing Nat out of the business. He said he couldn't stand the sight of him after the shame he had brought his to his name.

"Of course, I said to him, *Well, how do you think I feel? And the children?*"

"And how are the children? Were they good to you?"

"They were okay—Evan was easier than Sami. Evan's a boy, you know? They're easier to deal with all around. Mainly, they aren't sure how their life has changed yet. I'm not expecting any apologies for their lousy behavior in the past and not to mention their lack of loyalty to me. I'm just encouraging them to change their behavior as of *now*. Their loyalty can be regained as we go through each day."

"Well, that's smart. Did they say anything about the house being all clean and about dinner and all the things you did—um, we did?"

"Not one word. But I don't think they didn't notice. I just think they decided to go along and see what happens. But I told them about the newspapers and all, just so they would be aware in case the other kids teased them. So what are we doing about Katie Couric and that whole thing?"

"I'm coming to Charleston and I'm sleeping in your guest room. We can figure it out tonight. And you can tell me about Jeff Mahoney! Don't you know that you're supposed to tell me everything?"

"Oh, right! Yeah, he sent flowers. Look, I think they were guilt flowers, don't you? I mean, he sure did make scrambled eggs out of my life and then you came along . . ."

"That may be, but I think that man has plans for you."

"Really?"

After we said good-bye, I went upstairs to shower and dress and took a long look at myself naked in the mirrored sliding glass door of my dressing room. I didn't look like Jennifer Aniston but I wasn't completely drooping yet either. I didn't have the slightest interest in Jeff Mahoney, but now that I thought he might have been interested in me, I felt this surge of, well, maybe it was desire? I grappled with the notion of being pursued and stood up straight, holding in my stomach. My thighs needed work. They were flabby. Whose weren't? Maybe I would join a gym. But first, I needed to work in my yard.

How stupid of me! I was going to shower and dress and *then* work in the yard? *Hello!* Okay. Here's the part where you discover that I'm a little bit neurotic. I threw on clean underwear because I couldn't stand to wear the ones I had worn yesterday, even though I was going to get dirty and sweaty in the garden. I don't think that's strange, because if I passed out in the yard and someone walking by saw me and called EMS, the forensics department at the hospital would know that my underwear was recently changed. I mean, let's get our priorities straight.

It was one o'clock before I felt like I had made

enough progress to stop working in the yard for the day. I had accomplished the basic things. I threw some chlorine in the pool skimmers. I gave all the pots a good soaking and thought to myself that I would just wait to see what revived itself. Sometimes plants did that. Resurrected themselves, as I intended to do. I cleaned up all the garbage, put away the children's bikes and so forth, deadheaded the roses and sprayed them, picked up all the twigs and turned up the mulch that had been flattened by all the rain. Then I did the big nasty—I cleaned out the fountain, happy at the end to see the clean water spouting from the mouths of the three big fish in its center. If the garden didn't appear to be thriving, at least it was presentable. And best of all, I had figured out how to handle all the insanity of the media attention and its probable impact on the children.

I went inside to make a salad and flipped on CNN. A spokesperson from Johnson & Johnson was talking about anticipated sales of wet wipes and the reporter, all smiles and mirth, was suggesting that Abigail and I become the faces for the products. I turned the television off. It was too much. Didn't we have a war in Iraq to talk about?

By the time I was showered and dressed and had fed myself a little leftover spaghetti—let's face it, in times of nervous anxiety, some carbos can do you good—it was time to go for the children.

I went slowly through the car line and saw them. Their faces were angry and upset. They got in, slammed the doors and said nothing.

"Well? How was your day?"

"I *hate* Daddy! This has been the *worst* day of my life!" Sami said.

Evan said, "Jamie Olden is a dick."

Dick? I pulled the car over to the curb and turned to Evan in the backseat. "You may be right, Evan—in fact, another one comes to mind—but we will not use that kind of language." I sighed. "So Sami, want to wait until we get home to give me the download, or shall we just hear it all now?"

The expected backlash had slammed her so hard that she was almost speechless. But not quite. She didn't say anything during the ride home and when she went through the back door, she stormed right up to her room and slammed the door. I knew enough about Sami, and about young girls in general, to know the thing to do was give her time to cool off but not enough time to build a fresh case against me.

"You want a brownie and some milk?" I said to Evan.

"Sure," he said and threw his backpack on the floor. "But Jamie Olden is still a dick."

I let it slide. "What did he say to you?"

"That my dad's girlfriend is a freak of nature."

"You should have corrected him—she's a freak of surgery. I'm going to go get your sister and we're gonna have a family meeting."

I took a large portion of the pink lilies Tisdale brought last night, put them in a vase for her and climbed the steps to her room with it balanced on my hip. I knocked on her door.

"What?"

We were having some issues getting that *talk to each other like people who love each other* agreement to kick in.

"Want to cut school tomorrow?"

That got her attention. She opened the door; I went in and placed the vase on her dresser.

"Are you serious?"

"Yep, come downstairs and talk to me and Evan. I have a plan."

Reluctantly and with a moderate amount of teeth sucking, she followed me to the kitchen. I poured her a glass of milk, refilled Evan's glass and looked at them.

"Okay, I just want you to hear me out and then you can say anything you want. Deal?"

"Okay," Evan said and stuffed a whole brownie in his precious pudgy little mouth.

Snnnck! Sami sucked her teeth and looked at the ceiling. "Whatever. It doesn't matter. My whole life is ruined anyway."

"No, it's not."

"Yes, it is," Sami insisted. "Do you know there wasn't one person in school today who didn't make some crack about you taking Charlene Johnson's fake boobs from her?"

"It doesn't surprise me. Y'all ever hear the old worn-out cliché about making lemonade out of lemons?"

Sami groaned and Evan said, "Yeah, so?"

"Here are the lemons—Charlene Johnson and all her plastic surgery, this divorce, Daddy taking money out of Granddaddy's business that he wasn't supposed to take and all the lies that Daddy told. The very worst thing that Daddy did was to make you believe that I wasn't a good mother and that you weren't important to me. As a result of that, we had some terrible words with each other and didn't feel good about each other at all."

At this point, Sami was staring at the table and Evan was uneasy, shifting in his seat.

"So then Daddy sues me for custody, the house and child support. He doesn't even want to give me enough money to live. I call my friend Claudia in Atlanta, she gives me her condo, I get a job in a gallery in Pawleys Island, start selling my watercolors . . ."

I went down the order of events as they happened, the courtroom story of what Judge Shelby had said about taking back Charlene's bosoms and other body parts and how Claudia had offered to do the reversal surgery for free. We finally arrived at the press conference.

"The press conference was very uncomfortable for me. I made this big statement about how plastic surgery was for train-wreck victims and that I would rather be alone for the rest of my life than live with a man who wanted me to have an operation to change my face and make him happy. The room was so quiet that I got unnerved and started to cry. I reached in my bag for a tissue but all I had was a wet wipe. I used it to wipe mascara from under my eyes and then worried that my whole face had mascara on it and I just kept wiping. Then I made this statement that it was inner makeup that mattered, not cosmetic makeup. Abigail Thurmond, my lawyer did the same thing.

"Last night, Paula Zahn from CNN took off her makeup on TV and saluted Abigail and me. Today, every single broadcast reporter across the country did the same thing and talked about how image-crazy women had become and how devalued we were when we got older and how values and integrity matter more than appearances . . . Oh, did I mention that Katie Couric called and I'm being interviewed on the *Today Show* tomorrow?"

"*WHAT?*"

Now I had their full attention.

"That's why I thought you might like to cut school. You know, hang out and meet a bunch of people from NBC? It doesn't happen every day of the week . . ."

"Cool," said Evan. "I'm in!"

"Oh! My! God!" Sami was completely stunned. "Mom! This is awesome!"

"Yeah, it's a good thing I cleaned the house yesterday, right? More milk?"

"Mom! This is unbelievable! Does Dad know?"

"No, I don't imagine that he does."

"Is he gonna get mad when he finds out?" Sami said.

I looked at her square in her face and said, "Sami? After all your father has put me through and put my children through, all in the name of giving himself the legal right to run off with another woman, do you think *I* care what *he* thinks?" I started to laugh and as I laughed I saw her face change. The bitterness fell away and she began to enjoy my victory. After all, my victory could be hers too, if she wanted it to be.

"We are all in this together, Sami, Evan. We may as well make the best of it."

For the rest of the afternoon, the phone rang and rang. It was the local NBC producer. Could he come to the house and scope out the best spot to do the interview? Sure, I said, come on over. Tisdale called, asking if I had seen Nat, who had not come to clean out his desk as he had promised to do. I said I would probably be the last person he would call unless he had to and I thanked him again for the flowers and cell phones for the children. Huey called to wish me luck. Claudia called and we rehashed everything.

Chinese takeout was spread all over the kitchen counter by the time Abigail arrived. Abigail was charmed by Evan and Sami, who asked her so many questions about my life in Pawleys Island, our friends there and my painting that I thought she would ask them to give her a moment to breathe, but she didn't. Abigail, with her endless supply of poise and wisdom, made them see another truth: mine. And hers. She was so great with my kids. She must've been a great mother.

I knew the children were on the fence about what Nat had done. No child really wanted to hate their parents. And I didn't want them to hate him; I finally honestly didn't want that. I just wanted them to understand that when you make bad choices, there are going to be consequences. While they thought their dad had made some very selfish decisions, they weren't old enough to understand that he had used them in the process to get what he wanted.

They weren't old enough to comprehend a lot of what had gone on between their father and me, but I wanted them to see that families have obligations to each other that sometimes supercede personal ambitions. It was a lot for them to grasp, but I figured that while they were at the ages they were, trying to figure out who they were, they may as well try and figure out who they want to become. I wanted them to understand that marriage vows, parental obligations and mutual respect in families were just a few of the things left in this cockeyed world that were truly sacred and worth fighting for. Abigail and I walked them through a lot of those ideas. They took it all in for the duration of that evening and I hoped that it would stay with them. But for children, and even adults, the kind of learning that stays with you comes by example, not a conversation around plastic containers of lo mein, sweet-and-sour pork and fried rice.

The dishwasher was humming, everyone was in their rooms and I was getting ready for bed. I heard a little knock on my door and opened it. It was Sami.

"Can I sleep in your bed?"

"You bet! Hop in!"

There were no sweeter words to my ears, and all through the short night I slept with my little girl at my side. I wanted to cry, I had so many feelings of relief and sorrow combined. But I didn't want to wake her, and besides, I wasn't sure I had any tears left. At one point during the night, I got up and checked Evan. His covers were kicked off, his pajama bottoms were twisted and his round little tummy was exposed, rising and falling with his breath.

"Turn over, baby," I whispered. I straightened out his pajamas, covered him up, smoothed his shaggy hair away from his eyes and kissed him on the top of his head. I left his door ajar, just in case. But I knew he would sleep—the bed may have looked like downtown Baghdad, but Evan's mind was off somewhere, bliss-fully dreaming about pizza and soccer.

That night my mind shifted from the surprising joy of having my children with me again, and the worry that I had ever let myself believe I would not want to be with them anymore. That must have been some self-defense mechanism I used because I was sure at the time they didn't want *me*. My mother's abandonment had made me question my worth all my life. Whether or not it would be pleasant to live together and be their mother didn't matter then. I didn't expect that anyway. If nothing else, I would use every power I had to make them psychologically stronger than I had been. That was something I could give them that had real value.

When the alarm went off at six, I felt like I had only been asleep for an hour or less. I stared at myself in the bathroom mirror. Did I really have the nerve to go on national television with that face? Yep, after I soaked my eyes with cucumber slices for a bit, I sure would.

As soon as I opened my front door, the bustle began. Tech crew swarmed my living room and dining room while the rest of us huddled in the kitchen, pouring coffee and flipping eggs. Abigail looked fine, like she had been to a spa. I felt like an old rag.

"I can't believe what I look like this morning!"

"You look like Miss America." She threw a handful of ice cubes in a baggie and handed them to me. "Get in the shower, wash your hair and, while it's in a towel, ice your eyes. Ice is a miracle drug." I looked at the clock. We were supposed to go on the air in an hour. I had time to make an attempt to look presentable.

I stepped out of the shower, wrapped myself in that sexy terrycloth robe Nat gave me and made a mental note to burn it, and as I stepped into the dressing room, there were Abigail and Sami, pushing the hangers in my closet. Possible outfits were laid on my bed.

"Mom, have you thought about what you're gonna wear?"

"Nope—probably a nice cotton sweater and a pair of slacks. I have a lime green sweater set somewhere around here."

"Lime green? Mom! You wanna look like Kermit? No, no! Something in navy? What about that navy linen tunic?"

"Too messy on camera," Abigail said. "Where are your sweaters?"

They finally settled on a royal blue cotton boatneck sweater and capri pants with tiny red and white checks.

"Don't you think it's a little patriotic? And summer's almost over."

"Rebecca. It *is* Labor Day weekend. Patriotic is

exactly the message we want to send."

"Okay! Whatever you think . . ."

They filed out with the clothes, saying they would press them, and I was to put the ice bag on my swollen eyes.

This whole rigmarole of the day before me was beyond absurd. What the hell was I doing going on the *Today Show*? I hadn't cured cancer. I didn't fly to Mars. I wasn't a big-deal *anything*. It seemed more ridiculous at that moment than ever. But I figured, let Katie Couric sweat it. She made the big bucks. Not me. Then I started thinking about all the truly stupid topics that made their way to network programming and felt a little better.

After ten minutes, I got up to dry my hair and inspected my eyes. They did look better—a lot, in fact. Well, if hair is half your looks, I knew I had a fifty per-cent chance of presenting myself as reasonably attrac-tive. It came out great for once in its stringy life. I brushed my eyebrows and plucked the strays and iced my eye area again. Then I moisturized the daylights out of my face and neck. I put some Vaseline on my lips and stood back giving myself a critical review.

"Not horrible," I said, to no one.

Sami came rushing in with my clothes. "Hurry! They want you downstairs!"

"Okay. Hey, thanks for your help, sweetheart."

"No big deal. Hey, Mom?"

"What, baby?"

"Do you think I could sit on the couch next to you?"

I looked over to see that Sami had also washed her hair and put on her favorite royal blue sweater and jeans. On camera, we would look like bookends. I thought about it for a moment.

"Sami? It's not up to me, you know. But why would you want to do that anyway? We don't exactly share the same politics in this department."

"So, you *did* know, didn't you?"

"Well, in general, mothers do eventually hear it all."

"I changed my mind. I thought about all the stuff you and Abigail said last night and I realize it's pretty sick to get fake boobs just to be a cheerleader. In fact, cheerleading might be pretty stupid too."

"I don't know—it's athletic and would keep you in good shape. Not all cheerleaders are dimwits."

"Look, Mom. If my stupid classmates see me on the *Today Show* sticking up for families and whatever you talk about, it might help me be able to walk in there tomorrow and not be . . . you know what I mean, right?"

"Not be humiliated by the fifty thousand dollars of surgery your daddy paid for his whore to have when he wouldn't spend a dime on a marriage counselor for us? Hmm, let's see?"

"He wouldn't pay for a marriage counselor? He never told me that! Jesus, what an ass!"

"We're not going to call your daddy an ass, okay? *We* know he's an ass, but we're not going to say it." Sami giggled and I gave her a hug. "Okay! Let's see if there's a spot on the couch!"

There was. We watched the monitor showing the outdoor plaza at Rockefeller Center and there were dozens of women waving up wet wipes and signs that said things like *Go Rebecca! Go Abigail! Southern Women Rock! The World Needs a Mental Extreme Makeover!*

The support was stunning.

Katie Couric was surprised to have an additional guest, and after asking Abigail and me a lot of questions, she got around to saying something about Sami. "And who's this, Rebecca?"

"This is my daughter, Sami, and I think she has something to say as well."

"Sami? What do you think about all this attention your mom's getting?"

"Well, I think it's très cool, Katie," Sami said like she'd been giving interviews for years. Even Katie giggled at her confidence. But Sami's face was a sober as Judge Shelby's. "Look at my mom. She's beautiful! She's beautiful inside too, and she's right, that's what really matters. Inside makeup."

"Inside makeup. I love it. Boy, I hope my daughters grow up to think like you do, honey. Okay, Ms. Simms? Ms. Thurmond? And you too, Sami! Thanks for being with us and we wish you lots of good luck!"

It was over.

"You were great, Sami!" I gave her a big hug.

"Yes, you were fabulous!" Abigail said and hugged her too.

"I didn't get to do *anything!*" Evan whined.

"Oh, shut up, Evan," Sami said. "It was a woman thing."

A woman thing! Priceless.

Inside of an hour, all I needed was to run the vacuum cleaner to erase every trace of NBC. All the cables, the generators, the trucks and the army of people were all gone.

"Boy, am I glad that's over," I said.

"I wish they'd come back," Sami said. "It ended too quick."

"Yeah, it was quick but now it's time to go back to normal life, don't you think?" Abigail said.

"Normal life sucks," Sami said.

"Well, you could go live with Charlene and Daddy in her trailer in O-burg . . . just a thought," I said.

Sami's jaw locked and her face darkened. She made a hellish noise that rose from somewhere deep inside the cage of her adolescent frustration.

I realized I was in for years of mood swings until my little imp had imps of her own. There was nothing like having children to teach yourself how to behave.

Abigail and I exchanged knowing looks. She knew what I was in for and missed that turmoil more than anything. I was uncertain of what lay ahead and realized how important her friendship was. I needed her advice, and if she could figure out how to give me some of her strength, it would be okay too.

Abigail said, "Well, thanks for letting me stay over last night. Are y'all still coming up this weekend? Julian's driving up this afternoon. I don't think that storm is going to be much."

Sami and Evan were standing there and jumped on

the chance to go anywhere near Myrtle Beach.

"Oh, please let's go! Mom, *please?* Come on! It's Labor Day!"

I looked at them and back to Abigail.

"Well, we're not going to have great weather, but so what? Why not? Go pack!"

TWENTY-FIVE

PARADISE AND PAWLEYS

I called Tisdale to tell him we were driving up to Pawleys for the holiday weekend.

"If you'd like to join us, we'll probably have a barbecue on Sunday or Monday."

"Well, we'll see. There's supposed to be another storm. This is a pretty busy weekend for car sales. Next year's models are almost out, so we cut prices on all the 2004 models. But I just might do it."

"Oh, and Tisdale? If you hear from Nat, tell him he can go in the house and get his clothes, and if it's not too uncomfortable for you, remind him that he's not supposed to take anything else yet, just for the sake of the children's comfort level."

"I'd have no problem telling him that. In fact, if you want, I can go with him to make sure he doesn't run off with the silver."

"Oh, I wouldn't worry about that. I think his tail is pretty well situated between his legs, don't you?"

"I wouldn't trust that sumbitch with a nickel, and he's my only son. He's my only son. Good Lord. This is the first time I've been glad that his mother's dead because this would break her heart. It really would."

"Well, a lot of hearts are surely damaged if not broken. He'll come around someday. You know, the prodigal son and all that."

"I hope I live to see it."

"I hope so too! Try and come to Pawleys, Tisdale. It would be so good for the kids, and you'd love Miss Olivia's plantation. It's really gorgeous."

He was just glad to be invited. Poor thing. He had worked so hard all his life and had built a fortune, but money didn't guarantee happiness. It helped, but it didn't guarantee it.

We were just outside of Mount Pleasant, passing Awendaw, talking about the *Today Show* experience. Some of Evan's friends had called to say they had seen Sami and me on television, and how come he wasn't on too? He complained again and again that it wasn't fair.

"Look, Evan, life's not fair, okay? It just isn't."

"Mom's right."

"I mean, let's just start with our happy little family. What happened? You think that was fair?"

"Boy, Mom," Evan said, "you sure have gotten *cold*."

I knew I didn't sound like the old mom they had kicked around because I wasn't the old mom and would never be that person again.

"Son, I love you to pieces, but your feeling of being

slighted is a dinky little potato. It should be the worst thing that ever happens to you. And I'm not cold at all. What happened this summer changed me. It changed all of us."

"She's not cold, butt-breath, she's stronger."

"Mom! Sami called me . . ."

"Sami!"

"What? Sooooor-ry, Evan."

I could see her grinning in my peripheral vision. Things were normal then. Sami insulting her little brother on the heel of a compliment was worth the teensy reprimand to her and a message to me that all was well. Well, an appearance on a national television program should boost anybody's spirit. At least for a day or two. Her moods had a short shelf life.

"So, Sami? Did any of your friends call you?"

"No!"

"Well, they're probably jealous."

"Mom, teenage girls are horrible. They can't stand it for anybody to get anything."

"You mean like notoriety?"

"Yeah, that's the word. I mean, they make fun of the smart kids and call them nerds and losers."

"I know. It's always been like that. And when the smart kids get accepted to Yale or something, they say, yeah, well, all he does is study and he's got no life. Right? P.S. Ten years later they're begging the nerd for a job, saying they were best friends in high school."

"I doubt it," Sami said and added, "Well, maybe."

I could feel the gears turning in her head and in Evan's head. They were thinking about what I said. That may seem like a small thing but it wasn't. For the last year they had been brainwashed by Nat to discount every word that came out of my mouth. Now, all of sudden, their daddy had been made a public laughingstock and people like Katie Couric and Paula Zahn were calling their mother and telling her what a great gal she was. Not exactly what Nat predicted.

They were not completely won over, and I wasn't honestly expecting that yet. But I knew as long as I provided a loving home, kept them fed and was diligent about their general well-being that their outward signs of affection would grow. When they were very little, I couldn't have found two sweeter children on the planet. Those little precious hearts were still in them somewhere. I had to coax them out.

"Are y'all hungry? Wanna do drive-through? Or do you wanna go someplace nice?"

"I'm starving!" Evan said.

"He's always starving! You pick it, Mom. I don't know what they've got around here."

We were almost at Pawleys and I decided to take us to the Hammock Shops.

"I know a fun place," I said and pulled into the parking lot.

"Cool," Evan said.

Cool was what Evan said to describe all things pleasing to him.

The Hammock Shops was home to more than twenty

little businesses, including the Hammock Shop itself, where we could watch a demonstration of how they are still made today. I decided we would get sandwiches and eat outside, and then walk around a little, giving them a chance to catch the tempo of the area, which was a little slower and a whole lot more relaxed than downtown Charleston.

"Mom! This is so cute! Look at this Christmas shop!"

Sami's and Evan's faces were plastered to the windows, and their eyes grew large and they darted from one ornament to another.

"Look, Mom! Here's a shrimp wearing a Christmas wreath!"

"There's a Santa lying in a hammock! Can we buy it, Mom?"

Christmas was a million miles away as far as I was concerned. I didn't dwell on the thought of last year when Nat bought me a suitcase and a hanging bag for my gift and told me to use it. God, I thought I had totally buried that memory, but I guess I had not. My mind skipped back to Christmas years ago. Barbie dolls and Transformers. Legos and princess costumes. Cookies for Santa. Paper chains made by the children on the tree, reading stories about snowmen and trains that could.

"Mom! Did you hear me?"

"No, baby, what did you say?"

"I said, I want to go in and look around. Okay?"

"Maybe after lunch, honey. Let's eat first and then we can go in all the shops if you want to."

I got fried chicken for us from Louis's takeout with big biscuits, coleslaw and iced tea. We found an empty picnic table and opened everything up to share it with each other. The chicken was right out of the fryer, and on tasting it all of us said *Mmm!* at the same time.

"Know what?" I said and took a sip of my tea.

"What?" Sami said.

"This is the kind of chicken that makes you dream about chicken."

I don't know why, but Sami and Evan thought that was the funniest thing they had ever heard.

"You dream about chickens, Mom? Come on!"

"All right, my little wisenheimers, here's the plan. After lunch, you can both choose one ornament for the tree, and then we're going over to Litchfield to drop off our stuff. Then I'm going to take y'all to the gallery to say hello to Huey. After that, we'll see. Maybe we'll go buy some groceries."

After the bones were licked clean, everything was thrown away and hands were washed, we got away with one shrimp holding a sign that said *Merry Christmas, Y'all!* and a sea turtle wearing a Santa cap. They were adorable.

When we got to the condo, there was a note on my front door.

Rebecca, Darling!
Welcome back! Byron and Daphne
cleaned up and made the beds for
the children. I can't wait to meet them!

*Dinner is at my place at eight. Mother is
making her string beans!*
Love, Huey
P.S. The painting over the sofa is sold!

"Well, here we are!" I said and opened the door.

Sami went right to the sliding glass door and looked out at the ocean.

"Awesome!" she said. "And look! Evan, come here! There's a pool too!"

"Wow!"

I almost fainted for two reasons. The painting over the sofa was my doll painting and the price tag was twenty-five hundred dollars. Sami turned and saw me and then stood by me and stared at the painting. Of course she saw the price tag and my signature in the lower right hand corner.

"Mom? Did you paint this?"

"Yeah."

"Seriously?"

"Yeah."

At this point all three of us were gawking at my painting.

"I thought Daddy said your paintings were stupid," Evan said.

"Twenty-five hundred dollars isn't stupid, you moron," Sami said.

"Your daddy said a lot of things."

I felt their little arms slip around my waist, and I put mine around their shoulders.

It wasn't necessary to say anything then. The proof was right in front of them and it was just one more nail in Nat's coffin.

"Well, let's unpack," I said. "Evan, you take the bedroom across from mine, and Sami, you take the other one."

"Okay," they said and left to see what their rooms were like.

I saw that the refrigerator was filled with all the things necessary to make breakfast and that Byron and Daphne had made a trip to Blockbuster. There were a dozen DVDs sitting on top of the entertainment center in front of the row of pictures of Sami and Evan. A pile of new beach towels waited on the dining room table, with a bottle of sunscreen and two new visors that said *PI*, for Pawleys Island. I almost choked up and then took an oath to never cry again. But I was so moved that all the critical friends I knew at Pawleys took a hand in welcoming me back. Even darling Miss Olivia was making her string bean salad.

The sky had become dark and huge raindrops began to fall, pelting the windows. I looked out through the balcony doors. The wind was picking up and the palmetto trees rustled in the wind. Well, I thought, we sure aren't having dinner on Huey's terrace. Hurricane Gaston. A French hurricane?

I called out to Sami and Evan.

"Turns out it's not a beach day, kids. So what do you want to do?"

We watched movies and ate microwave popcorn until

seven, got dressed and drove over to Huey's.

Huey was waiting at the door. I didn't know if he was watching the storm or waiting for us. In any case, his eyes became lit with excitement when he saw my children.

"Come in! Come in! Get these precious children out of this detestable weather!"

"Thanks, Huey!" I handed him our umbrella, which was soaked and dripping. "Sami? Evan? This is Mr. Valentine, my boss and, well, my best friend too."

Huey looked from Sami to Evan and said, "Well, now, we'll have none of that mister business! Call me Uncle Huey! And Sami? From this moment on, you have become Samantha! Why Samantha is a grand name! A glorious name! A name that should be in lights, don't you think?" He took her arm to lead her to the living room, where everyone else was gathered. "Come meet my mother, Miss Olivia! She's the grande dame of the entire plantation and can tell you stories you would not believe!"

Evan, still standing in the hall with me, yanked my sleeve.

"Is that man crazy?" he whispered behind his hand.

"Yes. And everyone should be crazy like Huey Valentine."

TWENTY-SIX

ABIGAIL'S CLOSING STATEMENT

Rebecca's children were the stars of Friday night, and Huey was beside himself with the sheer delight of their company. I knew he was very fond of Rebecca, and her children were the welcome dividends of his affection for her. Huey had no siblings, no nieces or nephews. He was such a wild-boy personality and more colorful than any rain-forest bird, you could understand why he had never been hauled off to a church to act as godparent. But he was reasonably settled now. In his tiny world that revolved around his mother, business and plantation, there was no place for children, until that moment. Instantly, he became Uncle Huey.

Needless to say, Rebecca's children had never met anyone like Huey in their lives. There was some eye rolling and snickering from the children, to which Huey returned each eye roll and snicker with amplification. A mutual fascination society was born.

He brought Sami to Miss Olivia's side and she sat in the spot that Miss Olivia patted. Even the inquisitive Miss Olivia was rejuvenated by Samantha's youth and wanted to know every little thing on her mind. She had seen her on the *Today Show* and complimented her on her natural poise. Sami, who had no grandmother, was on her best behavior and giggled when Miss Olivia asked her at what age she intended to marry.

"Get married?" she said. "I guess when my white knight shows up with a big diamond."

"Yes, young lady, you are absolutely correct to wait for a big diamond," Miss Olivia said. "For all the fool nonsense you'll have to endure being a wife and mother, you should have a big piece of bling to show for it."

"Bling, Mother?" Huey said.

"I watch television, you know! I know what the young people call things!" *Cough! Cough!* "Huey? I am so parched . . ."

"Let me refill your glass, Mother."

"He's a dear son," she said to Sami. "Now tell me about your plans for your husband. Will he be older or younger? A doctor or a professor? Or maybe a television network executive?"

When Huey saw that Sami was falling under the spell of Miss Olivia's charm, he went back to Evan.

"Dear fellow!" he said. "Would you like to see what's going on in the kitchen? All these old people are so boring, don't you think?"

I knew perfectly well that Huey was going to turn on the kitchen television and let Evan watch whatever he wanted to watch. Byron would give him cookies and chocolate milk. Between them, they would conspire to spoil Evan rotten. But who could resist a young boy with a freckled nose and a little tummy, and who had perfect manners? Not any of us, that was for sure.

All evening, the adults focused on Sami and Evan. And the children reveled in the attention. Rebecca's heart was swollen with pride.

On the way home I said to Julian, "Isn't it remarkable how Huey and Miss Olivia just came to life because of Rebecca's kids?"

"It was like watching dry sponges soak up the Waccamaw. Those kids need someone like Huey and Miss Olivia to love. And vice versa."

"Everybody needs somebody to love."

Julian reached over and squeezed my knee.

Julian and I promised to take Sami and Evan on a tour of the big house on Saturday, and because Huey had keys, we could go in after hours. But Hurricane Gaston was becoming more than a nuisance. It never stopped raining Friday night and by Saturday afternoon it was still pouring. The Weather Channel said we could get up to ten inches, and that amount of water would flood roads everywhere.

Julian and I were at my house, watching the ocean. The tide was abnormally high, and I was concerned about the causeway getting washed out. The whole thing about hurricanes was that other variables came into play—the tide, erosion, the temperature of the water, the direction of the wind and so on.

Over time, meteorologists had distorted our perception of danger, because no one worried anymore about a storm unless it had winds in excess of one hundred fifty miles an hour. But you can take this to the bank— if you don't think it's frightening to drive even a heavy

SUV in driving rain and wind of fifty miles an hour, try it sometime. Category one? Category two? It wasn't the number that mattered. By the time they stuck a name on the storm, it was time to plan for another place to sleep in higher elevations. Or make sure you had plenty of nerve, batteries and water.

Julian opened the door to the front porch.

"Julian! Don't go out there!"

"I just want to watch for a minute. The ocean's almost up to the dunes in some places."

"I'll put on a pot of coffee," I said and decided not to watch him be skewered by a flying palmetto frond and die a miserable death on my front steps.

The phone rang. It was Huey.

"Abigail? I know you just ate here last night, but I need you to come for dinner again tonight for two reasons. One, I have a hundred quail in my freezer, and if we lose power, I don't want to lose them. And two, the storm's going to make landfall somewhere between here and McClellanville. They said we're supposed to get terrible amounts of rain, and I don't have the nervous system to worry about you all night stranded on a sandbar. Please pack your things and come. Rebecca's already here with the children. So, stop . . ."

"Okay."

"What? Did you say *okay?* Why! I can't believe it! I'll tell Byron to make a cake!"

"Julian loves quail stew, and so do I. See you soon."

I poured two mugs of coffee and turned as I heard Julian's footsteps.

"What's wrong?" I said when I saw the look on his face.

"Abigail? I think I just saw a goddamn ghost!"

"Male?"

"Yes."

"Wearing gray?"

"Yes! How did you know?"

"Did he look at you? Or the house?"

"Both."

"Okay. It's safe to go to Huey's. Honey? You just saw the Gray Man and the house is going to be fine. Screw Gaston. Let's pack."

"Nonsense . . . it was probably just some damn fool . . . maybe not."

"When we get to Huey's, I'll tell you all about it."

"Don't you want to batten the hatches first?"

"What's to batten? The only thing here that I couldn't live without is you!"

But that wasn't entirely true. I wanted my pictures of Ashley and John and my mother's Bible. I had a box of things—my passport, car title, insurance papers, etc.— all put together in case of evacuation.

We drove slowly, leaving the island. The drive across the causeway was frightening as the marsh water was already sloshing over the road. Businesses were closed, windows were boarded over and the Lowcountry was hunkered down for its fifth major storm of the season. There was a huge live oak fallen over Highway 17, and what little traffic there was had to drive around it. The gas station on our left had lost its canopy. It had collapsed on the pumps. Branches were down everywhere and the wind tested the endurance of everything around us, blowing from every direction at once. Lights were out, and I knew that if we lost power in one place, we were likely to lose it all over.

"Gaston is not the French ambassador," Julian said.

"You can say that again," I said. "Here's our turn."

"Once again, I'm sure glad you're with me, because I'd sure never find it in *this* weather."

"Yeah, well, I'm glad I'm with you too."

We drove cautiously down the road and the avenue of oaks. Fallen branches and deep puddles were everywhere. There wasn't a dog or a bird in sight, and most of the houses were dark. Thankfully, there was light at the end of the road. Huey, only by the hand of Providence, still had electricity.

Huey met us at the door. We were soaked to the skin, just from the trip from the car. He had spread beach towels in the foyer for us to step on.

"Good gracious! Give me your shoes and whatever else you can shed with any decorum."

We took off our yellow slickers and sneakers. I was wearing black slacks and a black cotton sweater with a white golf shirt. I could have rung out my slacks over a sink and provided enough irrigation for all his houseplants. Julian and I stood there in our own little pools of water.

"It's raining," Julian said, deadpan.

"Yeah. We got wet."

"Heavens! I told you two not to play in the puddles!

Now, there are terrycloth robes in the guest room closet. Go get them on before you catch a cold."

Miss Olivia was seated in her chair by the fireplace, telling Evan and Rebecca a story. She spotted us and said, "Mercy me! You both look like something from Davy Jones's locker!"

"Hey, Miss Olivia! I know it! How are y'all doing today with all this crazy weather?"

"Fine! Fine! Hurry along, dear! I want you to help me tell these lovely children about the Hot and Hot Fish Club!"

"What's the Hot and Hot Fish Club?" Julian said, peeling off his wet khakis.

"Ah! It was a venerable institution founded here a couple of hundred years ago, started by men, run by men and enjoyed by men. Exclusively." I looked at myself in the bathroom mirror. My wet hair hung in a hopeless mass of ringlets.

"And the purpose was?"

"The usual—hunt, fish, eat, drink, swap stories and have fun."

"Sounds civilized."

"I think it's a good idea for men to have their own clubs, as long as they are strictly social, that is." I pulled dry clothes from our duffle bags and shook them out. "Do you think lipstick would help?"

"Um, sure. Or not."

That wasn't exactly the reply I was hoping for. *You look perfect! You don't need it!* It sure would be nice to get sick of platitudes, I thought. Julian was his own

407

man, though. He didn't have much use for insecurities and false vanity or women who went fishing for a compliment. And although I was guilty on all counts, usually I fought hard to keep my flaws hidden.

"Come on," I said. "Let's join the others."

We were all in the living room, telling stories of hurricanes we remembered. When Julian told the story of his Gray Man sighting, he directed his attention to Miss Olivia and Rebecca, which naturally brought on lots of questions from the children. Miss Olivia told the children more about the Gray Man and Alice Flagg than even I had ever heard. Their mouths dropped.

"Bull," Evan said.

"No way," Sami said.

"I don't know," Julian said. "I believe only what I see with my own eyes, and I would take an oath that I saw the Gray Man today. There wasn't much to it, really. It was just a man walking the beach. But there he was."

The smells coming from the kitchen were mouthwatering. But outside the wind howled like a freight train, rattling the windows. You could hear branches crack and fall, and then it would be quiet for a few minutes until the wind picked up again.

"Did you hear that, Mom?" Sami said to Rebecca.

"It's just the storm, baby."

And that's when the lights went out.

"Mercy!" Miss Olivia said. "I can't even see my glass!"

I was ready to take odds that it was empty.

"Everyone! Don't move!" Huey said. "Let me light candles."

"I'll help you," I said.

Within minutes, we were in candlelight. If there was one thing Huey had, it was candles. On the floor of his hall closet was a case of fat columns and votives that could burn for hours.

"I went a little overboard with after-Christmas sales last year," he said. "But I don't mind smelling cranberry in August, do you?"

"Nope, or bayberry. Gosh, I wonder how Byron is doing?"

"He's got Daphne in there helping him so he's okay. Besides, he can finish the stew on the cooktop. It's propane."

"A blessing, to be sure."

"Smells like Christmas," Miss Olivia said as we gathered around the table and Julian held her chair. "Thank you, Julian."

Huey put six large candles on a platter in the center of the table and little votives in front of each plate. The light was very low but sufficient to see the plates. Byron appeared with Daphne. Byron carried the large tureen of stew, and Daphne had another one of rice. They began to serve. It wasn't lost on me that we were having an eighteenth-century moment—on a plantation, dining in candlelight, being served by African Americans. And although Daphne was only working to save money for graduate school, did Byron intend to be Huey's manservant for the rest of his life? Probably not, but I decided to discuss it with Huey later on.

"Shall we offer thanks?" Miss Olivia said.

Now, this was not a particularly religious household, so saying grace was unusual. But since Mother Nature was threatening to take us all to the Pearly Gates at any moment, petitioning the Lord seemed like an excellent idea.

"Let's bow our heads. Dear Father, thank you for this wonderful meal and this truly excellent company. Please protect us from Hurricane Gaston, and should you have occasion to speak to Chalmers—that's my husband, y'all—would you please tell him I love him?"

The children giggled and elbowed each other. Miss Olivia continued.

"And Lord? Please bless and keep Rebecca, Sami and Evan safe from harm and fill their lives with the joys of love. Amen. Shall we begin?" Miss Olivia picked up her fork and the rest of us followed.

I looked over and saw one tiny tear slip from the corner of Sami's eye. She sniffed and began to eat, choking up and bursting into tears.

"Sweetheart! What ever can be the matter?" Rebecca said.

"Samantha! Dear girl!" Huey said.

"I'm sorry!" she said in a wail.

"Excuse us, y'all," Rebecca said. "We'll be right back."

She took Sami to the powder room, and without the noise of the exhaust fan we could hear every word they said. In a nutshell, it was this.

410

"Mom! Did you hear what she said? She *prayed* for us! To fill our lives with joy and love? To keep us safe? Mom, when's the last time someone ever did something so nice for us?"

"I know, baby. It's true. Come on now, our dinner will be cold."

They rejoined us at the table, and for the duration of the meal, Sami campaigned to move to Pawleys or Litchfield, or that even Georgetown would be better than downtown Charleston. It might have seemed incredible to some people that the small-town living of that area was preferable to the vast opportunities of Charleston, but to Sami it was. She was looking for a place to be a child again, to restore some peace of mind, one last blast of childhood before she had to face the rigors of college. She was starved for affection and approval, and here was a place where both seemed to flow like the river.

When asked what he thought, Evan shrugged his shoulders and said it didn't matter much what he thought, but he would like to see the Gray Man for himself and catch a fish in the Waccamaw.

"I can take you fishing anytime you want to go," Huey said, smiling.

"You can? Really?"

"Of course! I was quite the sportsman not too many years ago. And I used to fish with my father all the time! Maybe we can build a club house on one of the little islands and start our own Hot and Hot Fish Club!"

I pictured Huey and Evan, fishing from opposite ends

411

of a little boat, coming home at the end of a long afternoon of drinking Cokes in bottles, Evan's ears frayed around the edges from hours of listening to Huey's stories about the glories of his family's history and with a string of fish to feed us all.

I looked around the table. Julian had Rebecca's attention, telling her stories about family court and the crazy things people do to each other. Miss Olivia was listening intently to Sami as she talked about teenage girls and how mean they are. Miss Olivia, of course, was nodding her head in agreement. Evan would interrupt Sami every other minute and Miss Olivia would pat his hand saying, *Just a minute, Evan. Let's hear what your sister has to say, and then I can listen to you!*

Sami wanted to move into this world of rivers and wildlife and generations living all together? Well, why not? This was the place I had come to put my life back together, and so had Rebecca. It had worked out beautifully for us. Sometimes people needed a change of venue to sharpen their focus.

Dinner was over, and we were debating what to do next. I thought we should all go to bed because in the morning the storm would surely be gone. The wind continued to wail and shake the house. Somewhere outside a shutter was flapping furiously.

"I'll go see about it," Huey said.

"Need a hand?" Julian said.

Evan stood up to go with them.

Rebecca said, "Where do you think you're going?"

"This is man's work, Mom."

Rebecca looked to me and then Huey.

"Be careful," she said.

Just those words and Evan grew a foot taller.

There wasn't anything so unusually fantastic about the night, with the exception of the storm. But if I had to push a pin in the map of our lives to mark the point of a small leap forward, it would have been that night.

The young hearts of Evan and Sami were on the mend. Rebecca entrusted Evan to Huey and Julian, letting Evan know she had faith in his ability to maneuver the weather. You wouldn't have taken a million dollars to miss the expression of masculine pride on Evan's face when she let him go out in the night with the men. *Be careful*.

Miss Olivia was enthralled with every speck of them, but Samantha most especially. Maybe she viewed them as surrogate grandchildren. Rebecca, the daughter she never had. I didn't know. But in the years I had known Miss Olivia, I had never seen her so satisfied. I heard her say that in the spring she would take them to see the hundreds of egrets and great blue herons that made their nests on the property, that one day she would show Sami the diaries of her Revolutionary War ancestors and that if she was very good, she'd teach her how to make her string bean salad.

I wondered what Rebecca would decide. Would she sell her house and move to Litchfield? Would she fall in love with Jeff Mahoney? Would she grow a respectable reputation as an artist? I couldn't say with any certainty, but I had a strong feeling that we would be neighbors very soon.

And, Julian and me? Well, we were in step with each other and a little bit in love. Okay, maybe more. I just wanted time to pass and see where events took us. If our love was meant to be forever, then it would be. There was no need to rush to anything.

Later, when everyone was tucked in for the night, I listened to Julian's gentle snoring and waited for sleep to come. The wind and rain seemed to be lessening.

What a night! Another hurricane! Huey had done everything he could to see about our safety, our comfort and our well-being. I loved that he cared enough about us to want us all under his roof. We were important to him and he was very important to me. I loved him better than any brother I could have known. And his mother too. I wished Miss Olivia would live forever, but death was already creeping in her shadows.

I was a lucky woman. Tragedy upon tragedy, and now I found myself but a few years later counting my blessings for all the love I felt and all the love I felt I had to give. But in the end, didn't the most important and precious things we gave each other come from our hearts? So far, all hearts were open for business and doing fine. Yes, we were doing just fine.

I t was late October and the damp chill of fall was all around us. Rebecca had not sold her house in Charleston; she had merely closed it up.

"The gossip at school is killing the kids, Abigail. They come home every day crying."

"Kids can be so cruel."

"Claudia said that I could use her condo, even *buy* it if I wanted to, because she never gets here as much as she would like to. She said, *Just pay the utilities and it's yours*. What do you think?"

"I think, pay the utilities and put the kids in school here. They can go to Waccamaw."

"Can you help me arrange it?"

"Are you kidding? In a snap! I can't wait to tell Huey! He'll be thrilled!"

At the first mention of Rebecca's return, Huey immediately started shopping for a boat with the intention of teaching Evan to fish. Thank God Julian stepped in, was available and willing, because Huey finally admitted to me that the closest thing he had done related to fishing or water sports of any kind in over twenty years was to order Dover sole in a restaurant. So Julian brought his Boston Whaler up to Pawleys and parked it in my yard.

"Very attractive," I said.

"What? I think it looks good!"

I put my hand on my hip and looked at him.

"Be glad I didn't bring my big boat!"

I put my hand on my other hip and said, "Julian?"

"Okay! Okay! I'll find a dock for it."

"Oh, shoot, I don't care. Anyway, the important thing is to get young Evan out on the water and teach him to fish."

"Abigail? Right from the very beginning, I never said anything when Huey was going on and on about his fishing expertise. I could tell he didn't know bait from tackle. I'll get them both out in the boat this weekend and make fishermen out of them. Don't you worry."

"You, sir, are my hero!" I gave him a noisy smooch on his cheek.

Rebecca had transferred her children to the Waccamaw school system and moved back into Claudia's. Thankfully, the children loved the new school and found the move to be easier than they had thought it would be. The plan was to finish out the school year and then decide whether or not to make it a permanent move. It made good sense to me.

Tisdale made frequent visits, and of course we took him for dinner at Huey's and introduced him to Miss Olivia. I had believed Tisdale's age to be somewhere in the zone of seventy. Apparently, he was older. But the fact that he was younger than Miss Olivia didn't matter to her at all, as she batted her eyes at him like a young debutante. He was delighted by it. They remembered many of the same songs and movies or restaurants that had been out of business for years. All that reminiscing gave them hours and hours of happy conversations.

And for as much as Tisdale enjoyed Miss Olivia's company, they doted on Rebecca's children together. Sami and Evan reveled in all the attention. Any onlooker would have assumed that they were the grandparents.

It was a gorgeous Saturday afternoon. The marsh grass was turning from bright green to its winter colors of russet and gold and the sunsets were richer shades of crimson and amethyst. That time of year was powerful as my attention drifted from outdoor activities to planning for other things, like which books I would read over the winter. I thought about walking the beach with Julian, bundled up against the icy breezes and damp weather. We would build fires together and talk about life. And about us.

For the first time in so many years, I could plan for holidays with someone I loved. Our little gang spoke of an elegant Thanksgiving dinner at Huey's, and the next night Julian and I would host a casual oyster roast on the beach at my house. Claudia was coming for Thanksgiving too, and along with Rebecca, Sami and Evan they were all determined to feed us on Saturday night.

"We'll have a barbecue!" Rebecca had said last week, and everyone agreed.

But that Saturday, in mid-October, the boys were out on the boat and Rebecca and Sami were at my house on Pawleys to have lunch and stroll the shore. After a finger-licking feast of salami sandwiches with baked potato chips and diet sodas—hold the pickles, please; the girls don't want the salt—we were putting the dishes in the dishwasher and talking about the absurdities of life.

During the last month, offers flowed in from all over the country for Rebecca to endorse various health-related products and programs. She declined them all, saying it was ridiculous to capitalize on her divorce by singing the praises of fried eel chips that were supposed to be rich in essential oils, make you lose weight, take ten years off your face and prevent every disease on the planet. Inner makeup, indeed.

"Are you kidding me? I'd rather get *sick!*" Rebecca said, showing me the letter she received. "I couldn't put an eel chip in my mouth for a million dollars."

"I would," Sami said.

"I hate eel! Despise it! Loathe it! Eel's the nastiest thing in the whole blooming ocean!"

"Tell us how you really feel, Mom," Sami said.

"Yeah, well, you can't hardly kill the nasty buggers. My daddy's fishing buddy caught one once and cut it up in chunks. Two days later it was still pulsing. You think that's not gross?"

"That's gross," I said.

I had just turned on the dishwasher when the phone rang. It was Byron.

"Miss Abigail, oh, my God, I can't get Huey on his cell phone!"

"Byron? What's happened?"

"It's Miss Olivia! I went out to the terrace to take her a tray of lunch and she was in her chair sleeping. 'Cept she wasn't sleeping, Miss Abigail . . ." He began to cry so hard, like he was a baby. I wished I could've reached through the phone and put my arms around him. My whole body went limp and I dropped into a kitchen chair. I already knew the terrible news he was struggling to tell me.

"I'll be right there, Byron. Just hang on."

I hung up the phone and looked at the earnest dread in Rebecca's and Samantha's faces.

"She's gone," I said. "Oh, dear God."

Sami turned in to Rebecca's arms and whimpered.

"I have to go over there right away. Please, stay here, okay?" I scribbled Julian's and Huey's cell phone numbers on a piece of paper and handed it to Rebecca. "Keep calling them until you get them, okay?"

I grabbed my bag and drove over to Huey's as fast as I possibly could. When I got there, I didn't even remember the drive. All I could do was think about how devastated Huey was going to be, and he would be *completely* devastated.

Byron was standing in the driveway, and I jumped out of my car. He was almost hysterical. I went right up to him and hugged him as hard as I could.

"It's okay, Byron. It's okay. Go call Daphne and tell her I need her help."

"I didn't know what to do, Miss Abigail! I knew she was dead, but I couldn't tell EMS to come get her and let Huey find his momma in a morgue! That ain't right! And it wouldn't do no good to call the doctor! She's already dead!"

"Where is she?"

"On the terrace. Right where I found her! Oh, Lord!"

"Get Daphne over here as fast as you can."

I ran to the place where Miss Olivia was gently slumped in her chair. A little breeze swirled crisp leaves around her feet, as though her spirit was riding on the little currents of air, swirling here and there, having a look at everything. Her eyes were closed and you could believe that she was just napping, except for the absence of her breath. Only her left hand was hanging from her side. I placed her arm across her lap. It was cold. I pulled a chair up to her side and decided to just wait with her body until Daphne arrived.

"She'll be here in two minutes," Byron said as he came toward me from the house.

"Did she have a local physician?"

"Doctor? Oh, Lord! Mostly she went down to Charleston, but she did get some medicine for bronchitis last year."

"Go see if the medicine bottle is still in her bathroom cabinet and call the doctor on the label. Or call Huey's doctor. Tell them it's a matter of life and death and to hurry."

"What if they tell me to go to the emergency room?"

"No, wait." I took a deep breath and felt my eyes burning. "Tell them Miss Olivia Valentine of Evergreen Plantation has passed away and it would not be possible . . . Oh, Byron, if that happens, call me to the phone."

I tried to figure out what had happened to Miss Olivia. She was sitting on her terrace, reading a magazine, watching the Waccamaw, which was the place she loved most in all the world. I picked up the magazine from the ground and saw she had folded its pages back to the horoscopes. God bless her, Miss Olivia had gone to the heaven reading *Town & Country*.

I heard the crunch on the gravel and knew Daphne had arrived. Her car door slammed, and in a matter of seconds she was at my side.

"Oh, no! What a terrible shock! When Byron called me I didn't know what to do first so I just came straight here! Oh, Lord! I said, oh, Lord, not Miss Olivia! It's gonna kill Mr. Huey! So many other bad people to take before her! Lord knows, dead people scare me, but not Miss Olivia. No, not her. But why her? Why now?"

I put my arm around her skinny shoulder and said, "I guess God wanted to take her home, Daphne. Listen, I don't want Huey to come home and find her like this, so I want you and Byron to help me move her to her bed. We can prop her up under the covers and wait for the doctor and Huey to arrive."

"Yeah, it would be terrible for Huey to see her like this. I'll go get him," she said.

It was a bit of a struggle, but they managed to carry Miss Olivia to her own bed. Daphne turned down the covers and I removed her shoes. All together, we slipped her tiny body between the sheets. She couldn't have weighed more than one hundred pounds.

"Did you get the doctor, Byron?"

"I spoke to the nurse. He's calling us back."

We straightened her out and pulled the covers up over her waist, folding her hands over her stomach. She looked peaceful and beautiful in the rose-hued after-noon light that streamed through her windows, washing her bed in a warm glow. I felt so incredibly sad. The world had lost a great woman when Miss Olivia closed her eyes.

It was two o'clock then, and another hour passed before the doctor called to say he was on his way.

And finally, Rebecca called.

"Julian just called and I told him, Abigail. I hope it was all right to do that. He's almost back at the dock anyway. Do you need me to get anything? I'm leaving to come over right now."

"No, thanks. I'm going outside to wait for Huey. I'll see you soon." I hung up and looked over to Byron. "Maybe we should make a pot of coffee or something. Do you have any cookies or a coffee cake? There will be people coming and going for a while."

"I'll take care of it," he said. "Don't worry."

Byron had moved from near hysterics to a somber mood. I knew he was feeling like I was—sorry to lose someone as wonderful as Miss Olivia, somewhat afraid of shouldering Huey's pain and trying to think through the logistics of wake and funeral and how life would stop until they were over. And that when they were over, there would be a huge gaping hole in all of our hearts for a long time to come. Huey would feel it for the rest of his days.

I went outside and down to the river, and sure enough, I could just make out Julian's boat in the distance. When they finally docked, I took Evan's hand and helped him off the boat. They were quiet. I could see that Evan and Huey had been crying and that Julian was upset as well. He had not known Miss Olivia long but he loved her like we all did.

I hugged Huey hard and said, "Oh, Huey, I'm so sorry."

Huey said, "Thanks. Me too."

Byron came outside and ran to Huey. Huey threw himself into Byron's arms and began to bawl. Huey's racking sobs unnerved Byron; then Byron lost it and just wailed along with him.

I saw the doctor walking across the lawn at the same time Julian did. Rebecca and Sami were right behind him. Daphne was leaving.

"I'll go greet him," Julian said.

"Miss Olivia is in her bedroom," I said. "Let me say good-bye to Daphne."

Evan ran for Rebecca and Sami and I was left with the inconsolable Huey and Byron.

"I'll be right back," I said. "Daphne! Wait!" I caught up with her and said, "Listen, thanks for coming and helping me today. I realize that it was above and beyond the call of duty. And to be honest, I didn't have anyone else to call."

"No big deal. I'm glad I could help." She looked all around at the vast property, and then she said, "This is some gorgeous place, isn't it? My stupid brother sure stepped in it, didn't he?"

"Uh, well, it isn't so bad to work in an oceanfront house on Pawleys, is it?" I was just teasing her.

She shook her head and looked at the ground. Then she looked up at me with the strangest expression that I couldn't read.

"Well, this has been some day, huh? What a shock!"

"Ain't over yet," she said and turned to walk away. "See you tomorrow!"

"No, you're right. It's going to be a long afternoon and night. See you tomorrow!" I wondered what she had meant and decided it meant nothing. "Thanks again!" I said and went back toward Huey and Byron.

Byron had his hand on Huey's shoulder, consoling him. Poor Huey, I thought. His heart's broken.

"I have to go in there," he said and broke down again.

Huey wanted to see his mother and he wanted to be alone when he did. Finally, he went in her house and to her bedroom.

"I'll be right outside the door, Huey," I said.

"Thanks," he said.

Julian and Byron waited with me. We didn't know what to say to each other. What could anyone say? That she was elderly and had enjoyed a good, long and happy life? Or that at least she wasn't sick and had to suffer a long illness? All those things were obvious and useless to those people she had left without so much as a good-bye. Finally Byron spoke.

"I'm going to go start dinner," he said. "We have to eat, don't we?"

There were some issues about how we would put Miss Olivia to rest. First, she had long ago dropped a formal religious affiliation with any congregation. She said she didn't need a minister to help her talk to God. She had said on many occasions that she talked to God all the time and that she felt very good about her Christian soul. But it seemed wrong not to have some kind of a religious service for her, because we needed it even if she had felt she would not.

The children, uncomfortable with the notion of Miss Olivia's dead body in the next room and very sad they had lost someone they had only recently attached themselves to, sat together on the sofa in the living room with Rebecca for a while. Miss Olivia's death had shocked them, and they cried.

Huey finally came out of the room. The doctor, a kind fellow whose name I think was Dr. Harper, called the funeral home, and they were on the way to collect Miss Olivia's body. He waited until the funeral home arrived and left, and then he shook hands with everyone, offered his condolences and said, "If I can do anything, just call me. I'll be at home tonight."

"Thank you very much," Huey said. "This is a very, very sad day for me. I appreciate you coming. I know you only treated Mother a few times. It was very kind of you."

"Mr. Valentine, you probably don't remember me, but many years ago your mother took me, my wife and my children all around the Flagg house. She told us stories of her grandmother and great-grandmother hiding from the Yankees. And how they hid their silver and jewelry in barrels and buried them near the riverbanks. She brought the entire Civil War to life for them. My children were enthralled with every word she spoke. My son went on to become a history professor—he teaches at the College of Charleston—and anyway, it all began with your mother. She was quite a lady. I know you'll miss her." Dr. Harper removed his glasses and wiped them with his handkerchief. He put them back on and said, "This may sound a little strange, but I am honored to be with you today."

You could almost see Huey's plumage rise and spread like a peacock's. I saw then that Huey needed to hear stories about his mother, about good things she had done, and those words would get him through the coming weeks.

Walking back to the house, I said to him, "You know, Huey. I can't stand to think of you out here all alone with just Byron. I mean, it won't be good for you. Would you like to come and stay with me on Pawleys for a few days?"

"All alone? Whatever do you mean? Are *you* all alone on Pawleys with *just Julian?* Let's have cocktails, shall we?"

Did Huey mean what I thought he meant?

He went to the kitchen and when he came back out he said, "Byron will bring drinks right away. I think Mother would want to be toasted, don't you?"

"Absolutely!" Julian said. "Why don't I bring in glasses and open a bottle of wine? You know, make myself useful?"

"Normally, I would say let Byron do it, but I think we should get going here. I don't know about you, but I can't remember a single occasion when I have had a higher need for a bourbon. So yes, thank you, Julian."

"I'll help too," Evan said and followed Julian.

"Me too," Sami said. "I'd like a Coke in a bottle."

"That's my girl!" Huey said and turned to me and Rebecca. "Mother's instructions were very explicit. She did not want a wake or a funeral. She wanted to be cremated and have her ashes spread on this land, in particular around the terrace area, so she wouldn't miss sunset cocktails. She wanted a party."

"Well then, let's give a party in her honor," I said. "Do you want to have some religious or spiritual segment in there? I mean, just someone to lead the group in a prayer for her?"

"I don't know," Huey said. "It would seem terribly odd to everyone if we didn't, wouldn't it?"

"I think so," Rebecca said. "I mean, it wouldn't have to be maudlin or orthodox either."

Julian came in with four wineglasses and an open bottle of red wine. Byron was behind him with a tumbler of bourbon, a small bowl of ice and a plate of cheese and crackers.

"We're talking about Miss Olivia's celebration of life party she wanted," I said, adding, "Thanks, sweetheart." I took the glass from Julian.

I turned to see that Byron made no movement from the room. He was having a drink. He was no longer dressed in his service jacket. He was wearing a nice shirt. This was unusual.

Huey raised his glass.

"To mother! Miss Olivia Valentine! Mother? Wherever you are, I hope you can hear me and know that I think you are the finest woman I have ever had the privilege to know. I hope you are with Daddy and that you know we all love you and will miss you for the rest of our lives!"

"To Miss Olivia!" Byron said, and we all touched the edges of our glasses.

Everyone began talking at the same time.

"She was absolutely wonderful," I said.

"Yes," Rebecca said. "Extraordinary."

"I'm going to get dinner on the table," Byron said.

"I want to be like Miss Olivia when I get old," Sami said.

"We should all try and be like her starting this very minute!" Rebecca said.

"Dinner is ready!" Byron called.

Huey took Rebecca's arm to lead her to the dining room, saying, "How in the world will I—I mean how will the world be without Miss Olivia?"

We gathered in the dining room around the table, which was set for seven people. We were just six. I didn't have the heart to correct Byron or to point it out to Huey. It was a good thing I had the sense to keep my tongue in my head because it was Byron whom Huey seated in his mother's place. Finally, the obvious dawned on me. Huey was not alone. His discretion had probably, no most definitely, been for his mother's sake.

I hid the fact that I was slightly aghast and then chastised myself for being aghast when I saw how seriously Byron took the occasion. He knew it was a serious statement and was not the least bit flippant that evening or ever again. It was Huey who provided the stand-up routine from that moment forward. Byron was all propriety.

Julian and I went back to our house, thanking Byron for another excellent meal and offering Huey our shoulder or our heart if the mood struck at any hour.

In the car I said to Julian, "Did you know that Huey and Byron were a couple?"

"Sure, I did."

"Well, I surely did not! I never even considered it!"

"Does it bother you?"

"No, of course not. But the deception does. I mean, I've been everywhere with Huey and never saw an inkling of anything between them!"

We pulled in my driveway and got out.

"People see what they want, Abigail. Come on, let's get us a glass of wine and go look at the stars. Maybe we can see Miss Olivia shooting across the sky. By the way, I met a fellow down in Charleston who's looking for a good lawyer. His wife ran off with his best friend and . . ."

"Shhh! We can talk about that tomorrow."

The moon, almost full, hung over the Atlantic, causing it to sparkle like millions of crystals, glittering, floating on the water, all there for anyone to behold. You could almost scoop them by the handful, put them in your pocket, string them tomorrow, make a necklace or a bracelet with mystical powers that made you invincible.

"Where do you think she is, Julian? Miss Olivia, I mean."

"Right here in our hearts, sweetheart. Just like you've always been since I met you years ago. Love never dies. People do, but love doesn't."

Hearing those words and being there with Julian was enough for me. Pawleys had transformed me, like it did for most people who went there.

This island was a place where you figured things out, made sense of your life and learned to live with yourself, forgive yourself, all the while humbled by its astonishing power and beauty. You didn't need jewelry with mystical powers to have that. You just needed some time on Pawleys to find the truth of your own heart and to be grateful again for life.

Center Point Publishing
600 Brooks Road ● PO Box 1
Thorndike ME 04986-0001 USA

(207) 568-3717

US & Canada:
1 800 929-9108